I0761045

A Fearful Thing

The Fifth Book in the Rebecca Series

A FEARFUL THING

WALKER BUCKALEW

Fideli Publishing Inc.

WWW.FIDELIPUBLISHING.COM

Library of Congress Control Number: 2021914325

ISBN: 978-1-955622-85-1 (soft cover)
ISBN: 978-1-955622-84-4 (hardcover)

Copyediting by FRANCES ARCHER
Cover art, design and photo by REEL VIDEO AND STILLS

Published by Fideli Publishing, Inc., Martinsville, IN 46151

www.WalkerBuckalew.com

Author's Note

This book may be read separately from previous books in the Rebecca series, but new readers may wish to know that it is a sequel to these titles:

- *The Face of the Enemy*
- *By Many or By Few*
- *Such Thy Mercies*
- *Choose You This Day*

The first four novels in the series take place one (fictional) year apart, starting in the late 1970s and continuing into the early 1980s. This novel, *A Fearful Thing*, takes place four years after *Choose You This Day*, and thus is situated in summer of 1985.

That being the case, the Cold War between the then-Soviet Union and the United States is depicted as being in full swing. Desktop computers are found commonly in business and academic settings, and in some households. No handheld communication devices are in widespread use, and the internet as a popular means of communication is still on the horizon.

Regular readers of the Rebecca stories are aware that, except where a setting *must* be fictional (e.g., the Mangusons' Lodge near Birmingham, England), real sites, presented fictionally, are used whenever feasible: for example, St. David's Cathedral in Wales in the first novel; Navy-Marine Corps Stadium in Annapolis, Maryland, in the second; the Italian coastal village of Amalfi in the third; Israel's Yad Vashem and Tel Megiddo in the fourth; and New York City in all five novels, including this one.

In the years between the writing and publication of *Choose You This Day* and this novel, I completed two stories for young adults: *The Visioners: Into the Wilderness,* and *Visioners2: Into the City.* Both young-adult novels feature Rebecca's twins, Joanna and Samuel, who, in fictional time, have grown from infancy in *Choose You This Day* to early adolescence in the two *Visioners* stories.

In this novel, *A Fearful Thing,* Joanna and Samuel are four years old. The main characters are in their early mid-30s.

Walker Buckalew
Greer, SC

CHAPTER ONE

REBECCA MANGUSON CLARK GLANCED UNOBTRUSIVELY AT THE digital runner's watch on her left wrist. She saw that it read 1152 hours, eight minutes until noon in London.

"Girls," she said softly to her rapt audience of seven four-year-olds, "we will start the story right there when I see you again in the fall."

"Ohhhh no-o-o," came the piping chorus. "Please, Mrs. Clark. …"

Rebecca smiled as she rose from her knees. "I'm just as keen to see what happens next as you. I won't forget, young ladies. And neither will you."

The children looked at each other and decided to agree with their revered teacher, if for no reason other than not to leave her disappointed at the end of their school year. They nodded resignedly and rose to their feet.

Fifteen minutes later, Rebecca busily helped her four-year-old twins into the new 1985 Volvo sedan she used daily for the short trip back and forth to the Anglican preschool where she taught each morning. She regretted the fact that the children were gender-separated in this preschool, simply because it meant that she spent the morning in the same classroom with Joanna, but not with Samuel. She missed him during those hours, and found herself sometimes surprised, both at what he had learned and at what he had not, when she conducted her own "home school" every afternoon. *Are boys and girls always this different in what and how they learn?* she mused often to herself. *Were Luke and I this different when we were four?* she mused just as often, thinking of her beloved twin brother.

Now the school year was over, and she looked forward to having both of her children with her all day. She would continue her informal, but nonetheless systematic, investigation into the differences in her twins' interests and behaviors. The prospect excited her.

As she turned her right-hand-drive Volvo onto the main thoroughfare that linked their church and school with her little family's undistinguished flat, her liquid gray eyes focused on the black Mercedes sedan trailing five car lengths behind, one lane nearer the curb. Wishing briefly that she had taken time to test the new vehicle for its hard-cornering ability, she switched on the right-turn signal, wheeled right, fast, across two lanes of approaching traffic, and accelerated hard. The car responded beautifully.

Seconds later, her eyes grew wide at the sight of the Mercedes materializing in the mirror, cornering just as hard and successfully as she had, despite its having had to cross the same two lanes of approaching traffic, and having started in the extreme left-hand lane of the main thoroughfare, all in mere seconds, obviously in order to pursue her and her precious cargo. She pushed the Volvo's accelerator to the floor.

Rebecca knew the neighborhood well, having lived in this same lower-middle-class London district for nearly a decade now. Without using the turn signal, she braked sharply and whipped the big sedan to the right into an even more constricted alleyway, then right again into a driveway that, she knew, connected with the thoroughfare she had abandoned 20 seconds earlier. Finally, barely slowing, rubber screaming, she arrowed hard left onto the thoroughfare that would take her back toward the school.

Prepared for further evasive maneuvers, she accelerated again and studied her rear-view and side-view mirrors as she moved one block … now two … now three … in the direction opposite her home. Convinced she finally had lost the pursuers, she responded to her children's now-incessant queries.

"Yes, dears," she said patiently. "I know Mum has been driving too fast. And I know we've turned away from home. We're going to your Uncle Luke's office."

Luke Manguson came out the side door of the building that housed the international consulting firm in which he, his wife, Kory, and Rebecca's husband, Matt, had worked for two years. Kory and Matt had driven that morning, separately, to the Cambridge area on business, but Luke, thankfully, was in the building.

He exited at a run.

Rebecca, not wanting to leave the twins alone even for a moment, and not wanting to take the time to get them into the building, had simply stopped at the curb until she saw two of her brother's colleagues leaving to walk to lunch. She asked one of them to retrieve Luke quickly, and the young woman, seeing something in Rebecca's eyes that communicated urgency, had wheeled immediately to comply.

Rebecca motioned for Luke to join her in the car, and he slipped athletically into the left-hand passenger seat. Seated, he turned immediately to pay his smiling respects to Joanna and Samuel, then turned to look quizzically at his sister.

This full turn to his right had brought the left side of his face and neck into full view of his sister, and she had studied for the 100th time the pattern of pockmarks that marred his otherwise handsome countenance. She had been driving another right-hand-drive automobile on the occasion of that wounding, racing in desperate flight from their pursuers along the Amalfi coast of Italy, five years ago almost to the day. The high-performance vehicle driven by their enemy had finally overtaken them, and, as the two cars were momentarily side-by-side, a gunman had emptied both barrels of his shotgun into Luke's face and neck.

Now she forced herself back to the present. "We were followed," she said to him quickly.

"What d'you mean, Mum?" asked Samuel from the back seat.

Rebecca, never one to hide real problems from her own children, responded to her son's question. "There was a car following us, dear. I didn't like that. And that's why we've come to see Luke."

"But …" began Samuel.

Rebecca turned to the child again. "You'll need to be quiet now, so that your uncle and I can talk. You may listen, and then after we've finished talking you may ask." And she raised her eyebrows at the youngster, seeking understanding and agreement.

He nodded.

Rebecca then turned to Joanna, asking her the same question with raised eyebrows and a small smile.

Her daughter nodded as well.

Luke studied his twin during this exchange, her face turned fully to her own left in order to look at each child. This brought the right side of Rebecca's face into full view. And he looked hard at the familiar V-shaped scar that ran from her mouth all the way to her right ear. He had seen this cruel cut as it was made in a Brooklyn warehouse, six years previous. On that occasion a 12-inch screwdriver had been driven into his sister's face until she had twisted away from her captors long enough for him to unleash a stream of automatic rifle fire just over the two thugs' heads, driving them into panicked flight, but leaving Rebecca with the dramatic facial scar.

The children now silent and attentive, Rebecca and Luke looked at each other intently.

"A black Mercedes sedan," she said, "following one lane over, about five car lengths. I turned right, across traffic, so quickly that, in order to follow, the driver would have to take near-emergency action to get that turn done. And he did. I lost them quickly and came straight here."

Luke nodded.

And now brother and sister faced forward, each thinking hard. Each knew the other would speak, but only when there was something pertinent to say. Neither of them had the gift of small talk. Neither wished to have it.

"It's been four years," he said finally.

"Or five," she replied, "depending on whether the Nazi plot was a separate event entirely, or connected to the previous emergencies."

"I preferred to think of it as separate."

"So did I. If it was separate, then we took off the head of the original snake on the Amalfi coast."

"And in San Francisco," Luke added.

More silence followed, the small twins mirroring the adult twins' intense concentration, but now lost in their own childish thoughts, those thoughts having mostly to do with lunch.

"Either way," he said finally, "it's time to move, Rebecca."

The two couples —Rebecca Manguson Clark and Matt Clark, and Kory van Dijk Manguson and Luke Manguson —arrived at the Birmingham Lodge in a four-auto sequence: Rebecca and her brother via the M40 and the M42 from London, Kory and Matt via the A14 and M6 from Cambridge. They had rendezvoused 5 miles from the Lodge and circled the rendezvous point sufficiently to confirm to their satisfaction that they had not been followed. The guard passed them through the Lodge guardhouse gates at 0207 hours, according to Rebecca's digital watch, which was always set to military time for efficiency's sake. As her former-Royal-Navy brother and her former-U.S.-Navy husband repeated to her *ad infinitum,* no need for useless appendages like a.m. or p.m.

They all knew that the use of their emergency action plan could perhaps be unwarranted. But they also knew that, if they were to wait to assemble more evidence, they would be placing themselves and the children at risk. So, with no evidence whatsoever other than the presence of the black Mercedes trailing Rebecca as she drove home from the preschool, the two couples had placed the long-rehearsed plan into immediate effect.

This meant that none of the four had returned to their homes the day of the escape. Among them, they owned four automobiles. All four automobile trunks were always packed for emergency escape from London or from wherever else they might be working on a given day: clothing for the adults and the children; basic foodstuffs; and defensive combat equipment of the sort that the two families' common Christian perspectives allowed them. That included Luke's all-purpose shoulder holster, its compartments crammed with the variety of implements and weapons —none of them firearms —that he required to keep safe those who depended upon him for protection against those who would prefer them captured or dead.

Both they and their parents —Elisabeth and Jason Manguson, Martha and Paul Clark, and even the group's latecomers, Amelia and Andruw van Dijk —had found themselves mildly surprised three years earlier when June had arrived with, for the first time in five years, no crisis. That month had come and gone with no overt threat to the Christian church worldwide, nationally or locally. None, at least, that was made plain to any of them.

In the absence of crisis, there had been no visions. Neither Rebecca, nor her parents, nor Rebecca's mother-in-law Martha had experienced the overpowering supernatural visitations that had warned them and guided them and enlightened them during each of the previous four summers, and, in the case of the senior Mangusons and of Martha Clark, long before that. During the first of these crisis-free June months, the group remained on edge and unsettled for much of the summer, doubting their own senses. But fall had come, and then winter and spring, and finally another quiescent June. And then another.

But now this.

They had agreed even during that first drama-free summer that there could be no reason to think that they would never again be called upon to engage the enemy in these extraordinary ways. They had accordingly formulated a handful of interlocking emergency plans, and they had kept themselves both alert and current on all components of each plan and of each plan's subsets.

It was all very military, but then, as they frequently acknowledged to each other, this was an ongoing war that had never been truly won. They had won many battles, but this enemy was, they remained confident, always regrouping and reconstituting itself for the next attack. They referenced often the passage in the 12th chapter of the Third Gospel: *This very night your life will be demanded of you.* They intended to be ready every day. And they were.

On the night of their arrival at the Lodge, Rebecca and her mother had succeeded in getting Joanna and Samuel to their small guest beds by 2:30 in the early morning, and 15 minutes later the adults had assembled in a meeting room down the hallway from the children.

The Lodge was a renovated and modified 19th-century country mansion on what was now the outskirts of Birmingham. Elisabeth and Jason Manguson had purchased the property decades earlier, when Rebecca and Luke were children, and their reconstruction had included conversion of the mansion's original World War II bomb shelter into a true underground living space, replete with meeting room, chapel, and two dormitory rooms, always ready for use in crisis.

Setting up operations in the underground complex was foremost among the topics for discussion during the hastily called meeting. Related discussion included consideration of the question of whether or not to empty the Lodge of its guests as soon as that morning's breakfast had been served, and whether or not to summon Martha and Paul Clark from their home in Oakham, and then Kory's parents from their home in London. Complicating the discussion was the fact that neither Rebecca nor Martha Clark nor the elder Mangusons, the four recipients over the years of divine messages —actually *visions,* in plain terms —had yet been so visited in this emergency. Absent this critical ingredient, and with only the single, fleeting incident on the streets of London as evidence, they could not as yet be certain that a new crisis was upon them.

So it was that they resolved, albeit tentatively and uncertainly, to await further information, whether from human sources or … preferably … not.

An hour after the meeting's close, Rebecca looked in on the twins one last time, softly closed the door, then just as quietly opened the door across the hallway from the children. She saw that her husband appeared to be sleeping, as she had expected.

She smiled at him across the semi-darkness of the room, moonlight filtering softly through the gauzy curtains. Matt Clark had been brought to her doorstep, quite literally, by the first of their modern-day crises. He had been fresh from his five years' service as a U.S. Navy officer, and, she remembered as if it were yesterday, had been smitten with her from the moment she had opened the rusting gate in the Lodge's perimeter wall and had exchanged his first awkward words with her.

The two of them had fought together in those June days against the incomprehensibly evil personality that had confronted them, a personality that had filled Matt's left shoulder with automatic-weapon rounds as he had desperately and successfully attempted to shield Rebecca with his own body. He had saved her life, and she had returned the favor immediately, carrying his bleeding, unconscious, 6-foot-4-inch, 215-pound body on her shoulders for more than a mile through the storm-laced darkness of Wales' Pembrokeshire Coast Path.

Then had come his graduate studies in New York and long-distance communication between the two of them for an entire school year, followed by another June of danger and violence, a proposal of marriage, and, not long after, a wedding in which the maturely Christian daughter and the newly Christian son of lifelong Christian friends —Elisabeth Manguson and Martha Clark —had been joined in holy matrimony. The third and fourth summers of their lives together had extended the June crisis-pattern and had pulled them ever closer together: husband and wife and new parents and Christian warriors who had fought and fought and fought … and survived.

With the arrival of the twins, and with Rebecca's decision not to work outside the home for several years, Matt, needing to increase his income substantially, had joined his brother-in-law and his wife in a career change from classroom teaching to that of consulting for an international geopolitical think tank. The London-based firm, International Perspectives LLC, favored young men and women who had both military and teaching experience, finding them often to possess the requisite characteristics of analytical and communication skills of a high order coupled with the ability to operate independently for extended periods.

Now, he slept peacefully, unaware of his wife's loving gaze.

"Matt?" she whispered softly from the doorway.

Seeing that he did not stir, and hearing the faint sound of his sleep-breathing, she carefully closed his door and walked to the nearest stairway leading down to the Lodge's ground floor. The Lodge was sleeping.

She padded softly down the steps with her characteristic feline grace, turned into the main floor's west reading room and seated herself near the window. She lifted one of the Lodge's ubiquitous King James Bibles from the lamp stand, placed it in her lap, and, holding it unopened in both hands, began to concentrate.

She began by considering her life and that of her immediate family with the goal of focusing her bedtime prayers on what, she knew, could materialize at any day, at any hour, into a new set of divine demands upon them all. She was determined to wrap them all in a protective blanket of prayer.

Bible still unopened in her lap, she closed her eyes.

Rebecca was now 33 years old. The passage of time itself, her marriage, and motherhood had altered her appearance little since she retired from the international women's tennis circuit in her early 20s. She knew she could no longer run a six-minute mile without strain, could no longer sprint 200 meters in under 25 seconds, could no longer pound her powerful serve into an opponent's court at more than 115 miles per hour.

But she remained superbly conditioned for a "civilian." Her abdomen was as flat as before her pregnancy; the long muscles of her legs and arms were as powerful, sculptured and sinewy —yet still feminine —as ever; and her long fingers and strong hands were still readily able to grasp, clasp, and manipulate objects as disparate as the steering wheel and gear-shift lever of a high-performance vehicle, on the one hand, or one of her brother's 12-inch throwing knives, on the other.

And she was as beautiful as ever: high cheek bones setting off her spectacular, penetrating gray eyes; ramrod posture accentuating her 6 feet of willowy feminine height; and thick, glistening black hair that fell straight down her back, halfway to her waist. The clearly visible V-shaped scar on her right cheek did nothing to diminish her beauty; if anything, it seemed to accentuate the magnetism of her countenance.

The word "elegant" came to others' minds as soon as they saw her, especially if they saw her moving. Whether walking, jogging, climbing or descending stairs, bending or stooping to hang her family's wash on the clotheslines … all movements were regal.

Men still noticed her immediately. So did women. But Rebecca was as unaffected by this attention as she had learned to be as a teen, first developing physically and emotionally into a woman. Her mother, herself a regal beauty in her youth —and, for that matter, still beautiful in the manner of late-50s women —had counseled her teen-aged daughter to adopt the perspective that her Christianity did not require her to pretend that she was plain when, in fact, she was beautiful. Rather, her Christianity required her not to accentuate her beauty artificially, not to manipulate others by playing on their reactions to her beauty, not to credit herself for the glory of her appearance: a God-given and absolutely unmerited appearance.

And Rebecca had learned those lessons well. She had become comfortable with herself —who she was and how she looked —long before the age of 20, an unpretentious and unselfconscious woman who concentrated on a near-continuous prayer life and a near-continuous commitment to service to others. She understood to a remarkable degree for a woman of her age what she and her family considered to be the blueprint of the universe: *my life for yours.* And she understood that this applied universally, from the cosmic level of Jesus Christ's sacrifice for all people in all times and in all places, down to the smallest courtesies of daily life. Holding the door open for another person; acknowledging the humanity of the homeless person on the sidewalk; responding to her husband with the same loving attentiveness she had given him during their courtship … all of life: *my life for yours.*

Now, eyes closed, she began to focus her prayer on her family and on the crisis that, they all assumed, was likely at hand. Her prayer was not lengthy, but it was intensely focused on what appeared to be immediately before them.

And so, in the quiet of the sleeping house, she prayed silently for God's hand … for God's guidance … for God's help … in what she expected them all to face in the next few days. She prayed for wisdom, strength, and courage. She was certain that all three would be needed.

And she prayed for God's help in loving both friend and foe.

"Jason? *Belton* here!"

The call had come in on the Lodge's MI6-installed secure line just after breakfast had been served to the Lodge's guests. Jason Manguson picked up the receiver on the wall-mounted red phone in the Lodge's underground emergency quarters, where he had been checking the camera feeds from the Lodge's 360-degree exterior wall.

New York City private detective Sidney Belton wasted no time. "Ya got anything goin' on over there?"

"Perhaps, Detective."

"What's that mean?"

"It means that Rebecca was followed yesterday on her way home from school with the twins. She got rid of the pursuer, but there can be no doubt that it was pursuit."

"That it?"

"Yes. What do you have, Detective?"

"I got a young Episcopal minister in D.C. —a guy we've worked with before on international cases —tellin' us that he's got intel that th' Soviet KGB has gotten interested in *Rebekka Yahalomin.*"

"What!?"

"Yeah. Not kiddin' ya."

There was a pause while Jason turned over in his mind the Hebrew term, *Yahalomin,* that referenced Mossad's communication teams. In this instance, the expanded phrase, Rebekka Yahalomin, had come to be commonly used by the allied secret services —Mossad, CIA, MI6 —to reference Rebecca and her family's mysterious "special messages."

But the *Soviet* secret service? The KGB? How? Why? And an Episcopal priest?

"How would an Episcopal priest possibly know such a thing, detective?" asked Jason. "And, aside from that, why would the Soviet Union's intelligence agency care anything at all about Rebekka Yahalomin? Neither thing makes sense."

"Well," said Belton after a moment, "ya know we found out four years ago that Mossad, CIA, an' MI6 had all gotten interested in Rebecca, in her 'special messages,' in th' kinds of things she learned about in those 'special visits,' an' th' plain fact that she knew stuff the agencies didn't. An' if those three agencies got that far an' got that interested, I figure th' KGB can do it, too, Jason. An' fer th' same kinds of reasons.

"Know what I mean, Jason? Hmm? Know what I mean?"

There was another pause.

"Yes, Detective, I suppose. But what about my first question?"

"Well, this minister is a kinda big deal in Washington, even though he's pretty young, maybe 35. He's got a lot of senators, congressmen an' congresswomen, Pentagon types, CIA people, an' people from half th' embassies in D.C. —maybe even th' Soviet Embassy —in his congregation. They tell 'im stuff. They trust 'im. An' sometimes he helps us figure things out."

"Wait, Mr. Belton," said Jason incredulously. "This priest might have individuals from the *Soviet* Embassy in his congregation? You're serious, detective?

An atheistic nation would place *Christians* in its U.S. embassy? I would have thought an individual's Christian beliefs would disqualify him or her from any such assignment."

"Well, yeah … but, ya know, these intel agencies will use anybody they can, t' set up whatever networks they need. An' they're not gonna care if ya actually *believe* what yer church says yer supposed t' believe."

Jason shook his head in wonderment at the notion. Then, after a moment, he resumed. "This pastor is a person you've come to rely on, Detective?"

"He was involved a few years ago," said Belton, "when Rebecca an' Luke an' Matt, with a little help from th' rest of us, finally took down that outfit run by th' Jamieson woman and her brother … th' one that had corrupted a million good people on th' planet without 'em even knowin' they'd been had. Ya remember?"

"The Phoenix Trust. Helene Jamieson. Of course."

"Right," said Belton, "th' Phoenix Trust."

There was yet another pause. Belton waited.

"And one or more of this minister's parishioners," continued Jason at length, "has reported a KGB interest in 'the Rebecca special communications unit,' as I believe the Hebrew Rebekka Yahalomin has been translated for us?"

"Yeah. An' I got in th' car an' drove t' th' office t' call ya on th' CIA-MI6 line as soon as he got t' us with that little piece of info. Not 30 minutes ago."

"Thirty minutes ago? That's what, 4 a.m. there in New York?"

"Right."

"So, he woke you with this intelligence, Detective? He actually phoned you at four in the morning?"

"He rides AMTRAK —that's th' passenger railroad system over here, ya know —from D.C. t' New York an' back, couple times a month. Touches base with his clergy contacts and, I'm sure, his political contacts, in Manhattan.

"An' he didn't phone me, Jason. He knocked on th' door. Eleanor is a light sleeper. She woke me up. I went to th' door with my .45 in one hand an' my walkin' cane in th' other. That walkin' cane has a 4-inch spring-loaded knife in its base, ya might remember."

"I do remember. So, the two of you had a conversation in your apartment at 4 o'clock this morning, you're telling me. This very morning?"

"Yeah."

Another pause ensued. Belton waited with uncharacteristic patience.

At length came the final question. "And I suppose you trust this pastor of yours fully, Mr. Belton?"

The answer was unhesitating. "I don't trust *anybody* when we're talkin' about yer daughter, Jason. I don't trust a single person on th' whole planet. Never have. Never will. Not when we're talkin' about Rebecca Manguson Clark.

"Not even sure I trust *you* when we're talkin' about Rebecca. Know what I mean? Hmm? Know what I mean?"

At this, Jason laughed his hearty British laugh and clicked off.

CHAPTER TWO

FATHER JACK MCGRIFF GLANCED UP AT THE AMTRAK DATA BOARD showing the ever-shifting departure schedule from New York City's Penn Station. He saw that his train to Washington was now expected to be 55 minutes late, rather than the mere 15 minutes late the board had shown previously. That would give him time to sit down at one of the small restaurants housed within the station itself. Time at least to have a sandwich for his lunch, maybe even something more substantial.

McGriff liked to eat. Now approaching his 35th birthday, his waist size had increased steadily during his late 20s and early 30s, a period during which he had declined to adjust his eating habits in consideration of the knee and hip issues that had forced him to reduce and then end his daily jogging regimen. He had tried to learn to use low-impact or no-impact equipment, such as treadmills or stationary bikes, to no avail. Just too boring.

That did not, however, mean that he had become physically unimposing. A non-scholarship football lineman at his small Tennessee undergraduate college, he retained much of his early-adult musculature even now, 15 years later. He had simply added about 20 pounds of … well … it could only be fat. Still, at 6 feet, 2 inches tall and 225 pounds, he was an impressive physical specimen.

And, aside from his size and apparent strength, he was what most would call handsome. He had a strong chin, a slightly crooked nose suggestive of his football lineman days, a high forehead, sandy hair cut close, and light blue eyes. In his black clerical suit and priestly collar, he was quickly noticed and easily remembered.

He selected the first restaurant he came to as he circled the waiting area. The hostess smiled at him and gestured to a small round table to her left. He returned the smile and took a seat as she handed him the oversized, single-sheet menu. A waitress was at his elbow immediately, and he asked for the BLT and iced tea.

He adjusted his clerical collar by running his index finger around its circumference, and was dismayed to realize that, despite this usually effective maneuver, it still felt too tight. So, this was apparently to be another consequence of his creeping weight gain: he was going to need to increase the neck size on his collars, not just the waist size on his trousers.

He shook his head. He had once prided himself on how trim he managed to look as he progressed from college athlete into his mid-20s. But no longer. Well, maybe he should give those exercise bikes another crack. Get back down to 200 pounds.

Or maybe not.

Maybe the problem was less the boredom attendant to the use of cardiovascular equipment and more the fact of trying to squeeze two full-time jobs, each filled with its own kind of excitement, mystery and intrigue, into one 100-hour week. Maybe it was time to face the fact squarely that if he were to continue to be an effective counselor- minister to his church's Washington, D.C., flock, and if he were to continue to perform satisfactorily in his clandestine role as an operative paid regularly in cash bundles by the U.S. Central Intelligence Agency, he would need to monitor and reduce his caloric intake. This was a mortifying thought to one who, due to the frenetic pace of his life and to his fast-paced metabolism, had never had to think about denying himself whatever he wanted to eat or drink.

The BLT and tea arrived. He looked at the enormous sandwich. Then he looked at the large glass of tea. The sandwich suddenly looked like a caloric bomb. And the tea was sweetened. He ate three potato chips, wrapped the sandwich neatly in a paper napkin, placed a large bill on the table —one selected from the cash roll representing his most recent CIA payment —got up and walked out of the restaurant.

He walked 10 steps and handed the sandwich to an obviously homeless woman pushing a shopping cart containing her worldly possessions, and continued on. He would spend the remaining time before his train's arrival walking and thinking, not sitting and eating. He smiled to himself with satisfaction. This was a good decision.

Maybe if he made that same decision every day, he *could* drop his weight to 200 pounds again. Maybe.

As he started his stroll around and through the maze that was Penn Station, his mind turned to thoughts of his early morning exchange with Sidney Belton and Dr. Eleanor Chapel. His only absolutely necessary reason for making this particular trip from Washington to New York had been to deliver the urgent KGB-focused message to Belton, quietly and in person. Although McGriff had a CIA-MI6-installed secure line in his church office —an installation that had needed church approval all the way up to the Archbishop of Canterbury in England —he knew that Belton did not have such an installation in his and Chapel's apartment. He also knew that, while Belton's detective agency in lower Manhattan had the secure line set up in the agency's office building, neither Belton nor his agency partner went to the office on a daily basis.

This was not the kind of message that could wait.

McGriff had chosen to visit the Belton-Chapel couple well before sunup that morning. The pre-sunrise approach allowed him to make the contact without use of the telephone or any other means of distance-communication. Much more secure, though less convenient. He did not, after all, enjoy arising from his Manhattan hotel bed at three in the morning, any more than Belton enjoyed being awakened a little after 4 a.m.

McGriff had been both surprised and gratified by the sleepy, rumpled detective's startled, instant-alarm reaction to his message. He had watched, fascinated, while the normally phlegmatic detective changed instantaneously from a caricature of groggy somnolence into a model of fatherly or big-brotherly fury.

As a parish minister, McGriff had experienced the full range of human responses to his privately delivered messages, whether a priestly remonstrance to a parishioner for some publicly known or unknown transgression, or a reluctant-but-necessary communication of a loved one's death. He was rarely surprised by the recipient's response. But Belton's reaction, he was forced to acknowledge to himself, had been utterly unexpected.

He had been confident that his message would get Belton's attention —and, no doubt, that of his wife, Dr. Chapel, the famed Old Testament professor —but he had not expected to encounter raw emotion boiling out uncontrolled. After all, Belton was as experienced as McGriff himself in delivering unwelcome messages to others.

"What!" Belton had shouted, far louder, no doubt, than he had meant to speak in that predawn hour in a weathered Manhattan apartment with paper-thin walls.

"What! Those miserable *dirtbags!* Those contemptible *baseball bats!* Those spineless, cowardly …"

"Sidney Belton!" Dr. Chapel had suddenly exclaimed as she trotted barefoot down the hallway, her usually tightly bound gray hair falling down the back of her hastily donned robe. "What in heaven's name do you mean?"

"Rebecca!" had been her husband's sharp, impatient, interruptive one-word response to his wife.

That single word had stopped Dr. Chapel in her tracks, her hands still working to close the flimsy robe, her pixie-cute face frozen, her startling blue-green eyes suddenly ablaze with her own kind of outrage.

McGriff recalled, as he strolled casually through the Penn Station bustle, that both of them had then turned back to him and, facing him squarely, demanded with their eyes more of him than the single sentence he had spoken less than 60 seconds before. And he had then repeated that sentence for Dr. Chapel's benefit.

"My sources tell me, Dr. Chapel, that the Soviet Union's intelligence agency wants to gain access to Rebekka Yahalomin."

Seeing no change in the couple's unspoken but forceful demand for more, he had then continued. "As you know," he had said carefully, looking from one to the other, "some of the members of my church are Americans who are employed at the Soviet Embassy in Washington. And a few of my parishioners are actually Soviet citizens who take advantage of being in the U.S. to practice the Christianity that has been unofficially discontinued in their homeland.

"They were Russian Orthodox there; they are Episcopalians here, even though there are two Russian Orthodox congregations they could choose if they wished. They want to be as American as they can while they live here.

"An American who serves as one of the appointment counselors at the embassy, and one other source I regard as fully reliable, both reported to me, and independently of each other, that they had heard the same rumor … that the KGB has learned of the longstanding CIA, MI6, and Mossad interest in Rebekka Yahalomin, and that they now want their own access … for their own reasons, of course."

There had been a short silence in the small anteroom while the couple processed the staggering piece of information.

Finally, Belton had spoken. "What would those reasons be?" he had said in his guttural rumble, barely able to restrain himself. "Are they just nuts? They actually think Rebecca an' her family are in th' habit of passin' out 'special messages' t' th' world's intelligence agencies?

"An' even …" he continued, his anger still near the boiling point, "even if that was true —and it ain't —they think th' family is gonna sign up with th' Marxists all of a sudden? Are they just *nuts?*"

At this, Dr. Chapel had glided swiftly to her husband's side. She, all of 4 feet, 10 inches tall and 85 pounds, and looking even smaller barefoot and in her night clothes, had placed both hands around Belton's undamaged left bicep as he leaned heavily to that side, dependent upon his polished wooden cane for support, his right arm frozen permanently at the elbow. She had nuzzled him sweetly and without embarrassment in front of the visitor as she sought to restore his equanimity in ways that only she could.

"Dear," she had said softly, her trace-Southern dialect lengthening the vowels, "if the rumor is true —and it is just a rumor, you know —then I'm sure Father McGriff will speak with his … acquaintances … at the Soviet Embassy. I'm sure he will dissolve the rumor and make clear to the Soviets that the Rebecca Special Communications Unit —that awful label for all of us —has not been tapped for any sort of 'special communications' for four years now, and, even if we had, we would have no interest in sharing such information with the intelligence agency of the Soviet Union. He will just make that quite clear, and that will be that.

"Correct, Father?"

McGriff recalled shifting uncomfortably under Dr. Chapel's gaze. "Well, Dr. Chapel," he had managed after a pause, "actually, I'd imagine the KGB already knows all of that and simply doesn't care. I'd imagine they think they can successfully access your special messages in ways that the other agencies cannot. I'd imagine they think you can be bought, or, if not, intimidated, or, if not, blackmailed into cooperating with them. I know it sounds strange to say that some intelligence agencies have less … ah … scruples than others, but it's so, wouldn't you agree, Mr. Belton?"

At this, Belton had slowly nodded his head, then had stopped, looking down thoughtfully at his bedroom slippers. Then he had shaken his head in the negative and had mumbled the words, "Maybe … maybe … I dunno."

Then he had looked up. "Th' intel agencies pretty much have th' same M.O., I'd say, Father. I prefer ours, an' th' U.K.'s, an' Israel's, not because I think their intel agencies themselves are much more … umm … moral … but because those three *countries* are more, well, more somethin' good … not sure how t' say it … yeah … more *somethin'* good … than th' USSR as a *country.*"

He had looked down again. "But yeah … th' KGB is worse … yeah … maybe th' very worst of 'em all."

Another silence ensued. After this exchange, McGriff found that he was not at all certain how he should proceed. Finally, he forged on as best he could.

"Dr. Chapel," he had said finally, "the reason I got on the train and came up here last night, as soon as a second source had confirmed the American woman's report, was that you two are seen as being just as much a part of Rebekka Yahalomin as Rebecca and her family over in England, as you yourself implied just now when you used that phrase, 'all of us.' The KGB is just as likely to start with you as with them … maybe more so, since you two don't have Rebecca's brother around to guard and protect you, and you are both … you are both so … well."

"Old?" Belton had said helpfully.

"Well, yes," McGriff had found himself replying, smiling. "Just a little."

"And so, more easily kidnapped, let's say?" asked Dr. Chapel.

"More easily kidnapped than Luke Manguson or Rebecca Clark? Oh, my goodness, yes, Dr. Chapel. But then," McGriff had added, again smiling, "so are we all."

After 15 minutes of steady walking around and through the train station, McGriff had tired of the aimlessness of his meander and had used his business class ticket stub to gain access to a waiting area that actually provided almost-comfortable seating for passengers. Once seated there, he allowed his mind to move in a different direction. He began to think of the American woman who had reported the Rebekka Yahalomin rumor to him in the first place.

"Marie Campbell." McGriff murmured her name aloud, enjoying the easy way these particular consonants and vowels slipped over his tongue. She was an attractive widow of about his age or a little younger, one whose husband had been killed a decade earlier in an accident on his U.S. Navy warship in only their third year of still-childless marriage. McGriff had sensed from the start of their acquaintance almost two years previous that she was a woman he would like to know socially. Yet he had done nothing to get that to happen. And he knew why.

It was his years of practice in wearing a certain demeanor around women. A demeanor suitable for a pastor. For one who stands in a pulpit. For one who counsels others, some of whom are attractive women —and most of those, attractive *married* women. He had experienced countless private sessions in which women spoke to him about their thoughts, feelings, and behaviors.

And he, in private, their counselor of choice, always attended thoughtfully to them, expressing his sympathy for their often-difficult familial situations. Gently suggesting what they might do to strengthen those relationships. Praying with them. Praying for them. Available to them as their spiritual advisor.

He had always found it a tricky business.

And so it was that he wore a kind of studied, formal demeanor around most women, including Marie Campbell. The more attractive he found a given woman, the more studied and formal his manner. This helped to keep him a safe emotional distance from them. And, as well, a safe physical distance from them. He never hugged them. He shook hands.

Always.

Most of them immediately saw this, sensed this, and seemed to respect and even appreciate the obvious caution in his behavior. But this habitual caution around women, especially attractive women, carried over sometimes to situations in which his caution did not fit his intentions. A social relationship with Marie had been, so far, a casualty of this built-in caution. But he could change that, he thought.

Or could he?

Well … maybe not.

He needed, he knew, to acknowledge to himself the fact that these highly self-analytical —and, truth be told, self-flattering —thoughts did not get to the root issue. And that issue could be simply put: he was, almost always, uncomfortable in unstructured social situations.

Yes, he was a poised and self-assured public speaker, especially from the pulpit. And confident and empathetic in counseling settings. But socially? He needed to face the fact that, if he planned to approach Marie, he would need to initiate this thing he thought of as courtship without reverting to some pubescent, eyes-down shell of his public self.

He took a moment to picture her. About 5 feet, 5 inches, he would guess. Slender, with small features highlighted by large, sad, brown eyes. She herself was bright and sunny, but her eyes remained sad, even when she laughed, as she did often when in his office for one of her counseling sessions.

Not many people laughed during their counseling sessions with McGriff. This woman did. Marie made him happy.

Her hair was brown and shoulder-length, and she was dressed always in skirt-and-blouse or skirt-and-sweater when he saw her. Usually a suit jacket over her blouse or sweater, especially at counseling sessions, when she had just come to his church office from hers at the embassy. And since he had never seen her other than at church, for worship or for a counseling session, he realized he did not actually know how she dressed on other occasions. If he were to take her to dinner or to a play or to the symphony or on a picnic, what would she wear?

But would she even be interested in going out with him? She liked him, he knew, and liked being with him, he was certain, but that was always in the structured environment of counseling sessions or during the *pro forma* exchange of pleasantries on the front steps of the church after services. She was a self-confident person, yet she was self-contained at the same time. Yes, she liked him, but she never seemed particularly concerned about whether or not he liked her in return.

And she was an employee of the Soviet Embassy, of all things. That embassy, like most in Washington, employed a limited number of Americans as appointment counselors, custodians, receptionists, and the like. Marie was an appointment counselor, one of the women whose job it was to take appointments by telephone with American VIPs in various categories, both business and government. Then, when a particular VIP, one whose appointment she had personally arranged, arrived at the embassy, her job was to meet him —usually a "him" —in person, entertain him briefly, and deliver him to the Soviet staff person with whom the appointment had been made.

The Soviets wanted their appointment counselors to be attractive women in their middle years: women who were native speakers of English, who were personable, and who were skilled in helping their sometimes-uneasy guests to relax, prior to their appointments. Marie was a natural in the role, and had quickly become a valued and trusted member of the staff. And "trusted" meant that at times the embassy's support staff —other women who served as assistants to men who worked in various management and staff positions —would confide in her during their breaks.

Marie's habitual lack of inquisitiveness helped to create an aura of trust that seemed to pull confidential information from those assistants without her having wished in the least that they would do so. She came eventually to know a great deal.

She had sought him out professionally almost 24 months earlier, asking him for advice and counsel not so much on personal matters, but on the interior emotional conflict she experienced as an American Christian employed by the United States' Cold War adversary and potential hot war enemy. As together, meeting twice monthly in his church office, they had worked through these conflicts and as he had seen her become more comfortable in her role at the embassy, there had come to be less and less need for the sessions to continue.

But they had subtly resisted drawing the regular appointments to a close, until last week's meeting, when they had both managed to acknowledge that there was no professional justification for the sessions' continuance. If he had just been quicker on his feet, he might have arranged dinner with her then and there. But the cautionary voice in his head, urging him in social settings to take time to think through every possible consequence, stopped him.

Then had come the alarm —the report of KGB interest in Rebekka Yahalomin —that had prompted her unscheduled drop-by just the previous noon. She had materialized suddenly in the anteroom of his office as he was leaving for a luncheon appointment, and she had asked him with some urgency if she might speak to him for five minutes. Since the staff assistant was not yet back from her lunch —the two of them normally took staggered lunch breaks — he simply stepped around her, closed the door to the hallway, and said, "I really must run, Marie …"

"I know, Father," she had said quickly, avoiding the use of his first name, though he encouraged his parishioners to do so. "But I desperately need you to tell me what to do with the information I unwillingly was given this morning. Please."

Seeing her emotional distress, he had gestured toward the single upholstered chair in the anteroom, and then had rolled the assistant's swivel chair to a position in front of and to one side of her. They had sat thus, quite close to each other, and he had nodded his readiness to hear.

"I and one of the other part-time appointment counselors," she began, "an American, were taking our morning break with several of the clerical assistants — three young Soviet women —when two of them reported the strangest thing, Father. They both said that their bosses —mid-level consulate men —had dictated memos yesterday reporting KGB interest in an Englishwoman and her family.

"They referred to her as a 'messenger.' They said she and her family had a long record of receiving … well … messages … messages they believed were sent —perhaps in dreams —from God. No one seemed to think this was too strange to take seriously. They said these messages sometimes contained forecasts of threats, usually threats to Christianity or to Christians or to churches or to schools or to children.

"I was stunned, Father. I didn't want to ask questions, because I think that's how people get in trouble at the embassy, and so I just listened. The two assistants each said the same thing, that the KGB had learned that at least one other intelligence agency had made use of this woman and her family in the past, and they —the KGB —wanted to obtain their own access. These women didn't know on what terms or exactly for what purpose.

"They even reported that the group had been given a name —they think by Israel's Mossad —a Hebrew term, something like '*Rebecca Yalamene.*'"

"Rebekka Yahalomin," he had said, correcting her.

Marie's jaw had sagged, her sad brown eyes suddenly wide. "You *know* about this woman? This group?"

He had nodded. "I know," he had said, "of the woman and of her family, Marie. She and sometimes others in her small … following … appear to have been selected to receive 'special messages' from time to time. These messages appear to be authentic. These people have known things that no one else knew, and often long before such things could possibly have been known by any means other than … well … I must use the term, 'revelation.' They themselves use the word *data* to reference the messages.

"It's all very Biblical, you know, when you think about it, Marie. It just happens, in this case, to be contemporary.

"When I first learned of all this," he had continued, "some years ago now, I thought immediately of First Samuel 3:1: 'The word of the Lord was rare in those days; visions were not widespread.'

"These people are not some kind of cult, Marie," he had explained further, "and they are not part of some kind of movement. They're just regular people —with a tradition of working in education, in fact —and view themselves as perfectly ordinary Christians, Anglican churchgoers living … most of them … in or near London. There's nothing crazy about any of this. I've never met them, but would like to, someday."

She shook her head, brown eyes still wide. "But why does the world not know of them … of her … of this Rebecca? Why is this not in the newspapers and on television? How is it secret, and yet you have this information?"

Her voice trailed off.

"Well," he had said, "I need to say, first, that I did *not* know anything about what you just told me, the things your co-workers at the embassy reported this morning. *That* is news to me, and disturbing news indeed.

"As for the general fact of Mrs. Clark's 'special messages' —her name is Rebecca Manguson Clark, Marie —you'll understand that intelligence agencies are the least forthcoming organizations in the world. The only things that news agencies ever know about the CIA or MI6 or Mossad or KGB are things that the intelligence agencies want them to know. Those agencies —the allied ones — have never wanted information about Rebekka Yahalomin to become common knowledge.

"I happen to know a little about Mrs. Clark mainly because our congregation here includes people from many embassies, from many departments of the U.S. government, and, not unimportantly, those individuals' spouses as well.

"People tell their ministers things," he had concluded, "whether their ministers want to hear those things or not. Sounds to me as though the same thing sometimes happens with you when you're at work at the embassy."

A silence had fallen upon them then, each of them thinking about what the other had said. At length Marie had broken the silence.

"Father," she had said hopefully, "is there anything we can do? This woman is a Christian, you've said. And surely if the KGB is 'interested' in her, this will mean that she and her family are in danger, yes?"

"Possibly yes, Marie," he had replied. "But possibly no. Sometimes these agencies just play games with each other. This may just be part of the game. Your two friends may have heard something simply because their bosses decided to create a rumor.

"But I know whom to contact about this. I'll check on the veracity of the report, and, if there is anything to it, we'll get a warning to Mrs. Clark within 24 hours. You may have saved her life, Marie. But whether or not, let me run with the ball. You've done exactly what you should have. I'll get things started right now."

And he had indeed run with the ball, he mused to himself, and quite successfully. He had cancelled his luncheon appointment forthwith and had quickly gotten in touch, using the secure phone in his office, with his CIA contact across the Potomac at Langley. He had relayed Marie's report, and had been told he would receive verification, or not, within the hour. In half that time the secure phone had rung, and his CIA contact had reported verification from a "mole" inside the Soviet Embassy.

With that, McGriff had asked the staff assistant to cancel his appointments for the rest of the day and for all of the next and had headed for the train station. Next early morning, once he had had his dramatic encounter with the Belton-Chapel couple in their Manhattan apartment, his work in the quasi-emergency was done. He guessed that Belton had driven immediately in the early-morning darkness to his lower-Manhattan detective agency and gotten on his secure transatlantic line with Rebecca and her family within 10 minutes of his having left the couple's apartment.

McGriff smiled. He had certainly earned his next cash payment from the CIA.

That thought led to a new one, one that quickly removed the smile. If Marie were to learn that he was in the employ of the CIA, how would she feel about that? And about him? Would she be horrified? Would she be impressed? And either way, what would he say to her if she somehow found out and asked him if it were true … a near impossibility, certainly, but …

And he knew immediately what he would say. He would simply say the truth: that he was a Christian and a U.S. citizen, a former chaplain in the U.S. Army with rank of captain at the conclusion of his active service, and that serving the Lord and his country at the same time had long ago become second nature to him. He would explain to her that when the CIA, having studied the makeup of his Washington congregation and his background as an Army officer, proposed this unusual arrangement —pastor *and* CIA employee —he had not hesitated.

Yes, he would simply say those things to her if she inquired.

He smiled again at this straightforward solution. Then he once more lost his smile at the thought that followed.

What if Marie responded to his neat explanation by pressing him on the twin ethical issues? First, it could be said that serving in the U.S. military was one thing; serving in a government spy agency, something else again. Relaying some of the privileged information given to him by trusting church members to the CIA would surely seem to Marie an obvious ethical breach.

And second, perhaps even more serious, what of his receiving payments from an intelligence organization which, as with all such organizations, used wholesale deception and, when necessary, calculated violence to achieve its ends.

What then?

The answer came to him as soon as he formed the question, but it played out in his mind less smoothly than his response to Marie's imagined initial question. His answer would be simply that the context was actually a military one, though not directly involving armies and navies. The Cold War was, in point of fact, a war, just as much as any other, he would note in his best expository style.

And certainly, as almost anyone would agree, in warfare one deceived the enemy in every way possible: landing one's armies on the coast of Normandy rather than on the Pas de Calais; striking with the First Marine Division at Guadalcanal instead of at Truk Lagoon; storming ashore at Inchon rather than … well … rather than anywhere else on the entire Korean peninsula. The defense of the nation required the subordination of certain conventions and individual rights, and this gave deception at times a higher priority than truth.

This was simply how the world worked, he would say to her. …

He shook his head. *This gave deception at times a higher priority than truth?* That sounded pretty lame —pathetic, even —when he imagined saying it to Marie. She had a fine mind. She was acutely sensitive to the Christian integrity of individual transactions: of trust between one person and another person, of confidentiality between a minister and a member of his flock.

Marie would simply note that if any of his parishioners knew that anything they might say to him could be relayed to the government's intelligence service, they would be appalled, and rightfully so. He shook his head again.

Then he sighed. This was simply going to be a part of his life that he would of necessity keep secret, even from this woman with whom he hoped perhaps to establish courtship. *To establish courtship?* Seriously? *Courtship?*

He shook his head, trying to clear his mind. He tried to refocus. All the intelligence agencies of the world were by nature secretive. He was no longer holding a chaplaincy position with the Army. If he were going to continue to serve his country in this semi-military way, secrecy would have to be maintained, secrecy even from —dare he to say this even to himself? —even from a wife, should he ever have one.

There. He had thought it. He had thought both things: secrecy … and wife.

He sighed. He was nearly 35 years old and hadn't the slightest idea how even to ask a woman for a date, much less how to conduct a courtship, much less how to ask a woman to marry him. And yet … he also knew that, right now, all he was thinking about was whether or not to pick up the phone and ask Marie to dinner.

That's all. Nothing huge. Just dinner.

But the thought terrified him. In the first place, he didn't like phone conversations. He couldn't see the other person's face, and the other person couldn't see his. Non-verbal cues were taken away from the transaction. There was no …

Suddenly he remembered where he was. He had a train to catch.

He looked up at the arrivals board and saw his train was expected in 10 minutes. And in that moment, he made his decision. That very evening he would go to Marie's home and invite her to dinner this weekend. He would just look up her address —he knew she lived in Bethesda, not very far from his own Northwest Washington address —and he would simply drive to her house, knock on her door, apologize for the unannounced visit, explain that he hated phone conversations, and ask her for a dinner date. Soon.

He knew it was the clumsiest possible approach to asking a woman to dinner. But once he had formed a picture of the two of them talking on her front porch *—did she even have a front porch?* —he was entirely relieved. He could to this. And she would forgive the adolescent stupidity of his approach.

He stood quickly, and, with a practiced shrug of his left shoulder, adjusted the position of the Beretta 9mm nestled tightly in the shoulder holster. Having thereby more carefully concealed the CIA-issued service weapon under his black, slightly oversized "priestly sport coat," as he liked to say, he walked briskly toward the gate.

He would go directly from the Washington, D.C., train station to his office at the church, and, with the staff assistant, catch up on everything that would have accumulated during his 24-hour-plus absence. Once the work had been completed, he would drive from the church to Marie's house and ask her out this weekend.

No matter how late, that's what he would do. She'd be pleased.

He was sure of it.

CHAPTER THREE

AT 8:45 THAT SAME EVENING, IN HER HOME LESS THAN 3 MILES to the northwest of the tiny Washington apartment occupied by her clergyman-counselor, Marie Campbell turned off the living room lights in her Bethesda flat. She had arrived home as usual at 6:15 p.m., having taken the 5:42 city bus from the embassy to her suburban Maryland neighborhood.

She had fed Penelope, her diminutive calico, and then herself, by 7:30. She had gone through the mail, written three checks, ironed the next day's skirt and several other pieces of her work wardrobe, and had read from her well-thumbed copy of *Surprised by Joy* until just before time for her 20-minute treadmill session, her habitual pre-bedtime activity on weeknights.

Wearing a green Western Maryland College tee-shirt and nondescript gray sweat pants, she laced on her blue Nikes, Penelope playing with the laces all the while, and stepped onto the treadmill, a commercial-quality machine that took up much of the space in the cramped 11-by-12 guest bedroom. Penelope jumped into her position on the arm of the one upholstered chair that could be squeezed into the room, and settled down to await the end of the session and her customary bedtime treats.

Marie started the machine, adjusted the pace and elevation, and —walking at a comfortable, brisk pace —began to reflect on the events of her yesterday. She focused immediately on the complications that her embassy colleagues had introduced into her well-ordered life, complications that had led to the disturbing noon meeting, the day before, with her pastor, and to the persistent angst she had experienced throughout the previous afternoon and, truth be told, throughout the 24 hours from then until now.

She knew that she had studiously avoided contact with her work mates, either the previous afternoon or, indeed, throughout the day just ending. She knew they had noticed. She knew they were connecting the dots.

But the fact remained that, even after the passage of a day and a half, she remained too confused and unsettled to have contact with them. She knew they would ask questions of her. Yet she was unsure how she should even *begin* to think about this Englishwoman, Rebecca Clark, and the woman's mysterious, cult-like following that somehow had come to be of interest to the Soviet Union's secret intelligence agency. So, what would she say to them, or to anyone?

Further confusing and unsettling to her was her pastor-counselor's less-than-helpful response: his seeming acceptance of Rebekka Yahalomin as a legitimate player in what appeared to be, however preposterous, this intersection of Christianity with competing American, British, Israeli, and Soviet national interests.

As she began to breathe more deeply and perspire lightly on the treadmill, she at length acknowledged that she had not even been aware that there *was* an intersection of Christianity with various competing national interests, and much preferred to continue to assume that there was no such thing. But, more than anything, she wanted simply to undo that conversation on the previous day with her work mates at the embassy, to erase the consequent session with Father McGriff, and to delete these two days of her life. The whole thing had been beyond mystifying.

And beyond disturbing.

But the thing *had* happened. And was still happening. And continuing to ignore her colleagues' reports and her pastor's response to those reports was not really an option. She was not a child; she had long ago put away childish things, such as pretending something had not happened, when it was obvious that it had. She was involved in this, despite very much not wanting to be. There were real people —this Rebecca Clark and her family and friends —who appeared to be standing into danger.

And she acknowledged grudgingly that her mental labeling of Mrs. Clark and her followers as "cult-like" had been unfair. After all, Father McGriff was the soul of Christian traditionalism and mainstream theology. He was the least likely clergyperson she had ever known to take seriously something that could be described as cult-like. He was also completely unlikely to shrug off something that was clearly Biblical, such as the possibility of divinely inspired dreams or messages. She saw that, to her pastor-counselor, such messages were nothing other than an advanced form of what Christian prayer life was *always* supposed to be: interactive.

There was something else, as well. Her experience of her Christian faith was that rarely had anything of significance been placed in front of her by accident. Her early-morning, daily devotions —solitary readings and prayers —included the explicit prayer that she might be obedient to God's will for her life, every day.

And, in this unexpected instance, obedience would seem to require that she not turn her back on this situation, despite the likelihood that the Clark woman and her "special messages" were stirred into a volatile mix of competing national interests. But, even so, what could she possibly do?

Indeed, why might anything be expected of her beyond what she had already done in reporting the embassy rumor to her minister? With her mind now beginning to work efficiently in concert with her well-tuned cardiovascular system, she allowed herself to travel back into her own recent history, looking for an answer to the question of how she could have had this kind of … strangeness … placed before her at this point in her life. Why her? And why now?

She thought about the fact that she had begun her work as an appointment counselor for the Soviet Embassy almost three years previous. The appointment counselor role had been immediately gratifying, placing her in routine contact with individuals of political or military importance from around the globe. Within a few months of beginning her embassy job, she recalled, she had transferred her membership from the suburban Episcopal church where she had worshipped for a decade to a larger inner-city church of the same denomination. Her reasoning had been that this new church would offer the chance to mix regularly with many of the same people she had come to know at work, both inside and outside the embassy, but in the explicitly Christian context of worship and service to an international community.

Had that change of churches been a mistake? Was that change, done for that kind of reason, somehow the wrong thing to do?

Right or wrong, that change had led her to a new clergy staff. And not just to a new clergy staff, but to a counseling relationship with the staff's family-counseling minister. And that counseling relationship had led eventually to the previous day's swift, almost panic-stricken half-mile walk from embassy to church, and to the unscheduled session —in her mind an emergency session —with Father McGriff.

And so, she concluded, as the treadmill's timer moved past the 15-minute mark, that would necessarily be the answer to her two questions: Why her and why now? Because ordinary Christian people will, inevitably at some points in their lives, be placed in situations in which they, and only they, can intervene.

In retrospect, her move from the suburban Maryland church to the Washington, D.C., church had been for *this* purpose, though she could not have known that at the time. And beyond that, she acknowledged, it could be said, not unreasonably, that her whole life had been a journey leading to this precise point: to *this* intersection.

She passed through the 20-minute mark on the treadmill without noticing. Her mind had already begun to move toward Father McGriff. Not the situation, the intervention, the intersection. The man himself.

She thought about something he had said to her at the conclusion of their session the previous day, something about: *I know whom to contact about this. I'll check on the report, and, if it's accurate, we'll get a warning to Mrs. Clark right away. You may have saved her life, Marie. I'll run with the ball.*

Why, she wondered, *was it only now, a day and a half later, is it occurring to me to ask what my pastor-counselor's words had really meant.*

How, exactly, would he know 'whom to contact' about this?

How, exactly, would he check on the report's accuracy?

Who, exactly, is the 'we' that will get a warning to Rebecca Clark in England?

How, exactly, would 'we' go about delivering such a warning?

What did her pastor-counselor mean when he said that I might have saved Rebecca Clark's life?

As she began to formulate these kinds of questions, she unconsciously began to work harder, and soon realized that she was outpacing the machine; her abdomen had begun to press against the treadmill's grab bar. She tapped the elevation button to increase the angle-of-climb fractionally.

So, she asked herself hesitantly, was Father McGriff more than he seemed? Or perhaps less than he seemed? Was he something other than the family minister of her church? What made him so apparently certain that he could check her report's accuracy and somehow get a warning to Rebecca Clark in London?

Those things would require more than simply being well connected to individuals in various government posts in the United States and elsewhere, by virtue of being their pastor. Father McGriff had spoken with *confidence* about the intersection of three nation's intelligence services —CIA, MI6, Mossad — with Rebekka Yahalomin, that Hebrew phrase that, all in itself, actually frightened her. Three secret intelligence services had actually invented a *name* for this woman, her family, and those that were part of her network. That led to new thoughts.

Was Father McGriff himself a part of Rebekka Yahalomin? Who was Father McGriff? Was he CIA? Did he carry a weapon? Could I actually trust him with this information? Could I trust him with anything at all? Was he even, in fact, an Episcopal priest? Were those framed diplomas covering his office wall authentic? Was he, in fact, a CIA agent who had been placed in the family minister role as a "cover"? Was he even an American intelligence agent? How do I really know anything at all about Father McGriff?

She tapped the elevation button to increase the workload yet more, as her mind continued to spiral outward in all directions at once. By the time she had competed nearly 30 minutes on the machine, she was certain of nothing other than the need to make a fundamental decision. Would she go back to Father McGriff the next day and interrogate him regarding every single component in this strangeness that had been placed in front of her? Or would she resign from her embassy post, return to her suburban Maryland church, and seek to distance herself from the whole perplexing, frightening mystery?

Having dialed the machine back to its cool-down speed and position, she reached for her towel and began to wipe the perspiration from her face, neck, and arms. She pulled the hair tie from the loose ponytail she wore for exercise, and let her brown hair fall free to her shoulders. She patted the towel at the dampness of her hair, and, after the three-minute cool-down phase, she switched off the treadmill and stepped thoughtfully back onto the floor.

"There, Penelope," she said softly to her waiting companion. "Sorry to have taken so long. You were good to be so patient."

Suddenly, she froze, the towel falling to her feet.

The faint metallic sound she thought she heard from the back of the house clarified itself into a recognizable series of delicate noises: the door to the back porch had softly opened and closed, followed by the unmistakable squeak of rubber-soled shoes on a linoleum floor.

Penelope flew from her perch and squeezed herself under the chair.

Marie's mind resisted the obvious fact: intruders, *inside my home.* But only for a moment. She stooped, picked up one of the five-pound dumbbells that rested next to the treadmill, and padded silently from the room. In the carpeted hallway she paused, holding her breath. She heard whispered words —male voices, not speaking English —from the kitchen.

She dropped the dumbbell, turned, and fled down the hallway toward the front door. She heard running steps behind her.

McGriff arrived at his church office mid-afternoon, dismayed —though not truly surprised —at the amount of work that had accumulated in his brief absence. The staff assistant had prioritized his tasks and, together, they worked steadily through the mountain of correspondence and phone calls to be returned until, well into the evening, they agreed that the rest could wait for the morning.

He bade the assistant good night and sat down heavily in the middle of the office sofa, his spot of choice when "taking his moments" at the end of any extremely long office day. He rested his head on the sofa back and thought about the day's events, starting with his 3 a.m. scramble from the Manhattan hotel bed and his 4 a.m. encounter with Belton and Dr. Chapel. After a few minutes of mental review, he returned to his subject of choice that day: Marie, and his decision, taken with all the seriousness of a solemn contract with himself, to present himself physically on her doorstep in Bethesda that very night, regardless of the hour, to make a dinner date.

You must be a lunatic, he said to himself, actually mouthing the words. *Yes,* he continued, admonishing himself silently, *but you've learned from hard experience that solemn resolutions, solemnly made in the light of day, are best acted upon when the time arrives for them to be acted upon, no matter if the day and time and circumstances have transformed the earlier resolutions into something now unrecognizable.*

He recalled days in his adolescence, when he would reach a decision to phone a girl for a first date, would make notes on paper, would stare at the phone for minutes on end, wrestling with the act itself. There had been times when it was too much, and he would crumple his notes, pick up his basketball, and retreat to the backyard to shoot at the basket mounted unevenly on the garage. But there had also been times when he watched himself dial the girl's number, staring at his hand as though it was being directed by someone else, then would wait, listening to the telephonic ring, hoping no one would answer.

But sometimes someone did answer, and sometimes it was she.

And "she" had without fail been kind to him. Pretending to ignore his nervousness. Thanking him for asking her out. Usually saying the *Yes* he had hoped — and not hoped —to hear from her.

Now, nearly two decades later, he wrestled with the same social timidity. It would be so easy to say to himself right now, *No, maybe tomorrow. I'm too tired. And Marie will be too tired. She may have already gone to bed. No, maybe tomorrow.*

Then he thought about the fact that she had sought him out the previous noon to report what she regarded as troubling news from her work mates. She had risked looking foolish in order to tell him something that she understood not at all, yet it seemed of possible importance. And he had not hesitated to act on her news.

He looked at the wall-mounted clock over the door to his office.

It read 9:15.

He stood quickly, strode to his desk, opened the top drawer, removed the Beretta 9mm, still nestled in its leather shoulder holster, and donned the CIA-issued carrying device. He removed the gun, checked the magazine, and reinserted the weapon into its holster. He snatched his oversized black sport coat from the hanging tree near the door, checked the side pocket of the coat for the keys to his year-old 1984 Jeep Cherokee —bright red, his favorite color —and exited the office, setting the church's electronic alarm as he did.

Having studied the Bethesda city map earlier that afternoon and having mentally charted the driving route to Marie's home, he pulled up in front of her modest two-bedroom a few minutes after 9:30. He turned off the Cherokee's engine and sat for long moments, introducing to his mind the same angst that had beset him from adolescence, throughout early adulthood, and on to this very moment. The voice in his head sounded just as it always had. *You're not committed to go in. She's probably on the phone with a friend. Maybe a boyfriend. She may be undressed and already in bed. You could come back another time. This is a very, very stupid thing to do.*

He forced his mind back to her courageous action of the previous day, making her unannounced visit to his office and insisting upon speaking with him. He took a deep breath, closed his eyes, said his five-word "companion prayer" to himself, the prayer he used many times a day and taught insistently to his parishioners —*Father, be present, be present* —and opened the car door.

He stood on Marie's front steps, still feeling unsure, awash with the certainty that he was a pathetically inept social misfit. But he took another deep breath, found the doorbell with his eyes, and raised his hand to the small round button. He hesitated, his finger an inch from the bell.

Suddenly he heard the muffled sound of a heavy object crashing to a carpeted surface, followed immediately by running footsteps coming toward the front door. Alarms went off in his mind and body.

The alarms transformed him instantaneously into something quite unlike the timid social animal he had been a moment before. McGriff was at home in emergencies. He was at home with danger.

Quickly he stepped to one side of the storm door, drew the 9mm, and, as he did, clicked off the safety. He saw the front door being drawn open violently, while simultaneously a tee-shirt-clad woman threw herself against the storm door, frantically hurling herself onto the front steps where he stood.

McGriff seized the woman's upper arm with his left hand, jerked her roughly to his side while raising the gun with his right, and, releasing his grip on the woman's arm, followed the muzzle of the Beretta across the threshold. As he did, two large, dark-clad men braked to a halt not 10 feet from him. He jabbed his finger at the floor, motioning them to the ground.

In fewer than five minutes, the family counseling minister had bound the men's wrists and ankles with duct tape and removed their doubtless false identification documents while his parishioner held the 9mm on them —"I've had training," she had said brightly. Then, after she had quickly changed out of her damp tee-shirt and into a red University of Maryland sweatshirt, and collected Penelope and her feline necessities, McGriff had moved to a wall-mounted telephone in the hallway. There he had placed a single brief call to a coded number at Langley. Aware that a listening device could have been placed in Marie's home, he simply spoke a series of numbers and letters to the emergency dispatcher.

Exactly eight minutes from the moment the coded phone call ended, two dull-black, unmarked high-performance Ford vehicles with 5.0-liter V-8s braked to a halt in front of Marie's house. Four plain-clothed men trotted up the walkway, each with a large handgun at his side, entered the house, received the faux identification documents from McGriff, handed him a set of keys to one of the Fords, and nodded their acceptance of the prisoners.

All this without a word being spoken.

Following the wordless example set by the men, Marie gestured to the key ring holding her house and car keys that was resting on a bookcase near the door. One of the men acknowledged her gesture, while McGriff handed the Jeep's keys to the same agent. Then he and his parishioner speedily left the house, she carrying Penelope in her pet taxi in one hand, and Penelope's travel kit in a grocery bag in the other. The pair wordlessly got into one of the black high-performance Fords and drove away, fast, leaving both their own cars behind.

Still, not a word was spoken between them as McGriff accessed the Washington beltway, headed for I-95 North. As he accelerated well past the speed limit, his companion finally broke the extended silence.

"What just happened? Why are you driving like this? Who *are* you?" Marie asked, speaking the words as a single sentence, syllables piling on top of each other.

He thought for a moment, trying to organize an answer that would fit the tightrope he had tread for years. The "moment" —perhaps 10 seconds —became too lengthy for his passenger, and she suddenly slapped the dashboard in frustration.

"Answer me, Jack McGriff!" she said, nearly shouting, seemingly unaware that she had used his first name for the first time. "Answer me now!"

And without consciously deciding to, he recovered in that instant the decision he had made almost 12 hours earlier in New York's Penn Station. He became a man simply wanting to be straightforward with the woman with whom he wanted so badly to begin a courtship.

That word again. *Courtship.*

Yet again, he had hesitated too long, perhaps another 10 seconds.

"I'm *waiting!*"

"I am a Christian minister, Marie. Ordained in the Episcopal Church. I'm a bachelor in his mid-30s, a bachelor who is good at speaking publicly, good at speaking from the pulpit, good at speaking in counseling sessions, but bad, very bad, at speaking socially —just plain casually —with anybody, especially with anybody whom I had hoped to ask to dinner this weekend."

He glanced at her in the semi-darkness of the Ford's interior. Her eyes had widened. Her jaw sagged.

Somehow encouraged, he decided to continue.

"I'm also employed by the United States Central Intelligence Agency. I'm not an agent, but the CIA pays me to assess talent, especially in Washington and New York City. I'm an evaluator and recruiter for the CIA, Marie."

He glanced at her again. Her expression had not changed. Her face reflected pure wonderment.

"That call I placed from your house a few minutes ago," he continued, "was to the CIA ready room across the river, at Langley. I sent a message in code to the emergency dispatcher there. The two cars were on this side of the river, on standby for emergencies. Those four agents were armed and ready, and they will take the two intruders over to Langley for interrogation. Your house will be sealed and treated as a crime scene by other agents.

"The two intruders may be Soviet KGB operatives, Marie, or they may simply be individuals on contract with either the KGB or the Soviet Embassy where you work. I don't know why they were in your house. I don't know if they intended you harm. We do not yet know anything, really, about what is going on with this report you brought me yesterday at noon.

"We just know the report has enough significance to be connected, almost certainly, to the fact that Rebecca Clark was pursued in her car on the streets of London yesterday and that the London-area Rebekka Yahalomin have assembled at their Lodge near Birmingham, following their established protocol for emergencies. It's also possible that a Manhattan-based couple who have a long association with Rebecca and her family, Dr. Eleanor Chapel, a famed Old Testament professor, and her husband, detective Sid Belton, may well be targets.

"Much of that information came to me in bits and pieces this afternoon via the CIA-installed secure line in my church office."

He glanced at her again. She had turned her head to stare out the passenger-side window.

"After you and I talked in my office yesterday noon, Marie, I took AMTRAK to New York to warn Dr. Chapel and Mr. Belton, face-to-face, about your report. They don't have a secure line in their apartment, and Mr. Belton does not go to his office, where there is a secure line, on a daily basis. I spent last night in New York —a smallish part of the night, I should say —and arrived at their apartment at about 4 a.m. Then I took the train back to Washington midday and worked in the church office until about an hour ago."

They were silent, the Ford now humming along I-95 toward Baltimore at more than 80 mph. He sensed her moving toward him, leaning nearer so as to view the Ford's speedometer.

He glanced at her again. Her unbound, still-damp hair had almost touched his shoulder as part of her effort to check the car's speed while constrained by her seat belt. Her large, brown eyes were luminous in the dim, red-tinged light emanating from the instrument panel. He tried to regain his concentration. At

80 mph on I-95, in the dark, there was no room for error. This was not the time to start focusing on the woman on the seat beside him.

Not now.

"The CIA works in cooperation with local law enforcement in situations like this," he said quickly, "and they will have cleared this vehicle all the way to New York to drive at whatever speed we need to. We won't be stopped."

"All the way to New York?" she said.

"Yes," he responded. "We need to get to Mr. Belton and Dr. Chapel, then, with them, establish communication with Rebekka Yahalomin in England via the secure phone lines they have in place at Mr. Belton's office. We need to meet face-to-face with Mr. Belton, Dr. Chapel, and Jaakov Adelman, Mr. Belton's partner, and put together an action plan, Marie. We can't just play defense on something like this. We need to get proactive."

"But … but …"

"I know, Marie. You didn't ask for this. One thing we have learned for certain. In working with Rebekka Yahalomin, it's obvious that God *selects* us for the work. We don't ask for it."

More silence ensued. McGriff steered the Ford onto I-895 to bypass Baltimore on the south, thence to re-connect with I-95 northeast of the city.

Finally, Marie spoke again. "So, you followed those men to my house, knowing they were going there to do something to me? The people at Langley had asked you to come to my house with your gun? To protect me?"

He smiled. "Marie, I had not the slightest idea those people were going to be at your house. Not the slightest idea."

"Then …"

"We have learned that, in this work, coincidences are rare. In fact, we're not sure there are *any*. It seems that God moves us around in the ways we need to be moved around. What looks like coincidence usually isn't. Not really.

"I wasn't there because I had information about those intruders."

"But, then …"

He smiled to himself and glanced at her again. Her liquid brown eyes met his.

"I was there, Marie, to ask you to dinner this weekend."

Silence again.

"I wasn't kidding earlier," he said, "when I said I had hoped to ask you to dinner. That's why I came to your house tonight. No other reason. Just to ask you out."

Extended silence, yet again.

Finally: "*What?*"

It was long after midnight —now Friday morning —when McGriff finally conformed to the posted speed limit. This he did in order to pass under the Hudson River via the Holland Tunnel, and onto the largely deserted streets of lower Manhattan. Marie, seemingly stunned into a contemplative silence by her counselor's series of revelations, barely stirred at the tollbooth.

Nor did she rouse herself to request an explanation of the fact that, just out of the tunnel and into the city, their vehicle had been met by yet another dull-black Ford, one of whose occupants took McGriff's place at the wheel of their own car while McGriff moved to the back seat. Nor did she ask why the driver dropped them off on Washington Square North. Nor did she inquire as to why McGriff escorted her briskly across the street to a nondescript building facing the square. Nor did she ask for information while he punched coded numbers into a keypad.

She simply stood silent, holding Penelope and the pet taxi in one hand and the grocery sack with Penelope's food and water bowl in the other. She did not even express amazement that, once inside the building's tiny, unadorned lobby, McGriff simply placed his hand on a particular spot on one wall, apparently causing the wall itself to slide open. And she said nothing about the fact that the small enclosure into which they stepped turned out to be an elevator.

But finally, upon reaching the sixth —and apparently the top —floor, as the elevator door opened, it seemed that Marie had had enough. When McGriff placed one hand lightly on the small of her back and gestured with the other hand for her to exit the elevator, she did not budge. Donkey-like, she planted her Nikes firmly and said, "I'm not getting off this elevator until you tell me …"

She stopped mid-sentence when, at that moment, a diminutive older woman appeared in front of them. She was wearing a two-piece gray suit, seasoned with an iridescent red scarf and a gold cross pendant over her off-white blouse. The bright red of the scarf and the gold of the pendant tended to take the eyes away from the badly worn, thoroughly scuffed, once-white tennis shoes. Her gray hair, apparently lengthy, was caught up in a tight bun.

Her penetrating blue-green eyes fixed themselves on Marie's large brown orbs just long enough to take in the obvious fatigue in the younger woman's face, coupled with the determination with which she gripped the pet taxi and the grocery bag. Then, to McGriff's utter amazement, Dr. Eleanor Chapel turned her gaze from Marie's face to his in a sudden fury.

"Jack McGriff!" she exclaimed in her musical, high-pitched voice, "What do you *mean* dragging this young woman all over North America at all hours of the day and night, and bringing her and her lovely little kitty to this *decrepit* office building where my husband has the unmitigated *gall* to suggest we stay in response to some *preposterous* rumor that the Soviet *KGB* suddenly has some interest in Rebecca and her family? What do you *mean?*"

Without waiting for a response from McGriff, Dr. Chapel stepped into the elevator, relieved Marie of her burdens, and, turning to McGriff, said tersely, "I'll thank you to step off this conveyance so that I may take this poor woman and her pet down to her sleeping quarters on the fifth floor."

She then stared at him with, McGriff hoped, good-natured hostility until he averted his eyes and stepped off the elevator, turning from the hallway to smile helplessly at his companion while the elevator doors closed. He then heard cackling laughter from down the corridor and turned his head to see Dr. Chapel's husband smiling gleefully at him, while Mr. Belton's much taller partner in the agency of *Belton and Adelman,* former Mossad agent Jaakov Adelman, watched the scene bemusedly, shaking his head sympathetically at McGriff.

"Delighted to see someone else the target of one of Dr. Chapel's tirades, Jack," said Adelman. "You should position yourself between her and me at all times."

Belton looked up at his partner.

"Don't pay attention t' Jaakov, Jack. Eleanor *never* yells at him. *Never.*

"C'mon t' th' conference room, you two," continued Belton. "Let's get some coffee.

"We got work t' do. It's already 8 a.m. in England. They've been waitin' fer us t' call. Let's get organized fer this, gentlemen. Right now."

His tone underscored what McGriff had concluded hours earlier: they were on a war footing.

CHAPTER FOUR

LATE THE PREVIOUS NIGHT, AS MCGRIFF WAS ACCELERATING along I-95 in his CIA-modified Ford with Marie on the seat beside him, most of England's populace, five hours ahead of U.S. Eastern time, had been asleep for hours. As McGriff and his passenger raced past Baltimore —just before 4 a.m. the next morning at the Lodge in England —Matt Clark was awakened by a sudden movement beside him.

Turning quickly from his left side to his right, he saw, in the semi-darkness, his wife sitting bolt upright in bed, her gray eyes wide. Instantly awake, he sat up and placed his right hand on the back of her neck, unsurprised to find her tresses damp with perspiration. Leaning into her, he found what he expected: her body covered in sweat, her skin clammy and cold, her breathing ragged.

"I'm freezing, Matt," Rebecca whispered. Then, before anything else, she added: "Check the twins, darling?"

Matt spun out of bed on the opposite side, crossed the room to the door, glided across the hallway, looked in on the sleeping children, and returned.

"Sound asleep," he whispered, before moving to their guest room's linen closet to retrieve one of the heavy woolen blankets. He enfolded her in its warmth, then returned to the other side of the bed. He slid across to her, lay down and, with his unimpaired right arm and hand, pulled her down to him, away from the dampness of the sheets on which she had been lying.

Now, with the side of her face resting on her husband's chest, Rebecca began to gather herself for what they both knew must come next. The passage of years had not dimmed the couple's memory of the requirements of this situation.

They knew that, when the dreamer had recovered sufficiently, she would recount for her husband every detail of the images she'd been given, so that both would possess the "data," as Rebekka Yahalomin always referenced these messages, and could thus be able to check and confirm, or not, each other's relay of the images to the others. They had learned from experience that delay could be fatal. The data demanded immediate action from all those involved.

Rebecca's breathing became regular as she warmed herself against her husband's body. After several minutes, he whispered, "Rebecca?"

He felt her nod against his chest.

She stirred, still struggling to recover her strength from the familiar vision-induced exhaustion. She moved her face up to his, so that her lips were almost touching his ear. And, in this position, his strong right arm supporting her, she began her report.

"A long, dimly lit passageway," she began. "An office building, I'd say. A slightly military feel to it. Gray, unadorned walls, the full length of the passageway."

He nodded.

She fell silent, remembering.

"Wood-paneled office doors, all along the way," she continued in a soft whisper.

Then, after a moment, "Ah, a name and number on each door. And … oh! The names are in Cyrillic, Matt."

She felt him turn his face quickly into hers, questioning, wanting verification.

She nodded. "Yes," she whispered. "Cyrillic."

Silence again as she searched her mind for details.

"Ah … yes … one name and number now readable: *Ivan Ivanovich 2044.*"

After a moment, he whispered, "Written in English, or Cyrillic?"

"Cyrillic," she responded.

He nodded his head against her face to indicate his understanding. They both knew the Russian alphabet well, and could read journalistic-level Russian passably, though they were hopeless in trying to hear or speak the language. The same could be said of other languages that they, together, had studied during their five years of married life. They had focused especially on Welsh, Gaelic, and Norwegian, always trying to stretch themselves —and then their children — beyond the usual Western European languages normally encountered in English schools.

Now, more silence.

At length Rebecca continued. "The dream then brought me *through* the closed door —the *Ivan Ivanovich 2044* door —into that person's office, and immediately across his office to a wall safe behind his desk. The safe appeared to be anchored in the floor, but built into the wall itself. Then … on *through* the safe's door and to its interior, to stop on a document: dark red binding … the title in both Russian and English."

Silence again, while she concentrated on the dreamed title.

Finally, "The title … printed in gold lettering … in both languages. In English, it reads … 'RY Proposal.'"

More silence.

Matt whispered, "RY … Rebekka Yahalomin?"

Shortly after 3 a.m. in Manhattan —8 a.m. in England —Belton, Adelman, and McGriff sat down with their coffee cups in the detective agency's sixth-floor conference room. Without preliminaries, McGriff efficiently delivered his report to the attentive detectives: the intrusion at Marie's Bethesda home; his arrival at her house at the critical moment; his use of the CIA-issued Beretta to interrupt what presumably was to have been a kidnapping, or worse; his summoning of a CIA ready team to the Campbell home; the CIA-furnished high-performance vehicle.

As McGriff was finishing his report, the bell to the secure transatlantic line sounded in the conference room. Belton pressed the button to activate the speakerphone, situated in the center of the oval conference table.

"Belton!" he shouted in his trademark guttural.

Matt Clark's voice filled the small room. "Detective Belton? Matt Clark, sir, from the Lodge."

The detective's voice softened. "Hey, kid. Good t' hear ya.

"But Matt," he continued, "we're not ready. We just sat down t' talk, an' we got nothin' put together fer ya yet."

"We have something for *you,* sir," Matt replied. "Rebecca dreamed, sir. Around midnight, your time. We know it's only 0300 hours, or so, in New York, but we felt you'd want her report now. Yes? If not, we can arrange …"

"Now!" shouted Belton. "Now!"

Jaakov Adelman held up his hand. "Hang on a second, Sid. Matt, Jaakov Adelman here. We have Father Jack McGriff, from D.C., in the room —the Episcopal priest whose report Sid phoned you about almost 24 hours ago —

and, downstairs in the dormitory, Eleanor and one of Jack's parishioners, Marie Campbell, who works at the Soviet Embassy. She's the person who contacted Jack about the report Sid relayed to you.

"Chances are Mrs. Campbell needs to be here, in the conference room, to hear any data you've got for us. If Rebecca's report is focused on the KGB or the Soviet Embassy, or both, I'd think she would want …"

"Hey, kid," interrupted Belton, "is Rebecca's report gonna have t' do with th' KGB or th' Soviet Embassy?"

"We think it probably does, sir."

The three men looked at each other. Adelman rose, saying, "I'll go down to the fifth floor and bring Mrs. Campbell back up. I'll try not to disturb Dr. Chapel."

"Neither of 'em is gonna be happy with ya," said Belton. "They gotta be in bed or almost in bed. Yer gonna get yelled at."

McGriff rose quickly. "I'll get Marie, Jaakov. I don't mind."

Something in McGriff's voice —or in his enunciation of the woman's name — caused both detectives to turn their faces to look at him carefully. McGriff saw this and, despite himself, smiled in obvious embarrassment. He dropped his eyes.

"I thought this woman was just another church member of yours, Reverend Jack," said Belton sardonically. "Sounds like she's a little bit more than that, hmm? Maybe *a lot* more than that?"

Belton turned back to Adelman, smiling his crooked smile. "I gotta think Mrs. Campbell is somebody *special* t' Jack here, Jaakov. Hmm? Know what I mean?"

Belton turned back to McGriff. But McGriff was gone.

Belton chuckled.

Fewer than five minutes later, during which time Matt and Rebecca Clark and others in their family had waited patiently on the other side of the Atlantic, McGriff escorted both women into the detective agency's conference room. Having been told by McGriff the nature of the request that they return to the sixth floor —that is, to hear a report from Rebecca concerning her overnight receipt of data —neither woman appeared irritated. Quite the reverse.

They appeared eager. Excited.

The three men, all well-mannered in the traditional sense, stood until the women were seated. Old-school gentlemen.

Dr. Chapel wore her tattered white bathrobe and slippers. Marie wore the only clothes she had with her: the red University of Maryland sweatshirt, the tired gray sweatpants, and her Nikes. She had a pale blue towel wrapped around her head, having apparently just washed her hair prior to McGriff's interruption. She no longer looked tired.

And they seemed completely unembarrassed by their bedtime appearance, both of them clear on priorities.

Having never seen Marie dressed in any way other than for church or for work until the previous night in Bethesda, McGriff had tried hard not to stare at her, either at her home, or in the Ford, or while escorting her across Washington Square North from the car to the detectives' office building. But now, seated at one end of the long, oval conference table, and with both women facing slightly away from him and toward the speakerphone in the center of the table, his eyes seemed unable to remain on the phone or on any of the participants other than Marie.

Are they noticing? he wondered. *Is she noticing?*

Adelman handled the introductions, and without further delay, Rebecca began. As soon as she described the dreamed corridor with its wood-paneled doors, with names and numbers on each, and with each name printed in Cyrillic, Marie gasped audibly, her hands flying to her face in astonishment at what she was hearing.

Rebecca, detecting Marie's gasp from across the ocean, paused.

"Shall I continue?" she asked after a moment.

"Yes, please," replied Adelman.

"What you heard, Rebecca, was Mrs. Campbell's reaction —a quiet gasp — to what you just reported."

"Really?" answered Rebecca.

"You recognized that corridor, Marie? *Really?*"

Rebecca had never become inured to the correspondences between the world depicted by those visions and the real world. Every fresh instance entranced her.

"I'm sorry I interrupted you," said Marie. "Please go on, Rebecca."

"Yes," replied Rebecca. After a moment, she resumed her account. "Out of all the doors and names and numbers," she said, "there was just one name and number —just one —made specifically visible to me in the vision. It read, in the Cyrillic alphabet, *Ivan Ivanovich 2044.*"

Rebecca paused in her narrative, reflecting.

In the pause, Marie turned involuntarily to look at McGriff, who, to his considerable embarrassment, was already looking steadily at her. Her eyes widened. She shook her head in amazement.

"It's just as you said," she said in a near whisper. "She is given … *data* … *exactly* as you said. I'm just …"

McGriff nodded and smiled.

And after a moment, he asked, directing his voice toward the speakerphone for the benefit of the listeners at the Lodge, "Marie, do you actually recognize that particular name and number?"

She nodded. "I do. I absolutely *do!*"

Adelman, anxious not to interrupt the dreamer's continuity of thought, interjected quickly, "Rebecca, is there still more?"

In response, Rebecca recounted for the group the details she had reported to her husband hours before, including the dreamed wall safe and red-bound document therein. When she finished, she said, "Matt, was there anything else that I described earlier? Was that everything?"

"Yes," he said, "and I'll just add that when I heard Rebecca say the document's title, I thought right away that the 'RY' could represent Rebekka Yahalomin."

After a lengthy silence from both locations, Marie said, "Rebecca, do you know this language? Do you have Russian?"

"Matt and I have worked," she replied, "to learn to read a number of world languages in our five years together, Marie. We have become passable readers of several, including Russian, although we can hear and speak none of them."

"I have modest Russian language skills, too," said Adelman, the former Mossad agent, "but If we run into something that requires a high level of Russian, I've got contacts here in New York that we can turn to. We'll be in good shape there."

The joint session turned immediately to next steps, and those steps materialized rapidly. Within an hour, the two groups were in agreement that, first, Marie would keep her half-day work schedule, both for that day and the next: that is, Friday afternoon from 1:00 to 5:30, and then Saturday morning from 8 a.m. until noon. She would enter Ivan Ivanovich's office around 6 p.m. that evening, half an hour after the time at which access to that section of the embassy would close.

CIA operatives at Langley would prepare and equip the quiet but self-confident and poised appointment counselor for her high-risk action: not just breaking, entering, and document-photographing, but breaking, entering, and document-photographing on what would be, technically and in fact, foreign territory.

Adelman, experienced in working with and among allied intelligence agencies, had, using a separate secure line to Langley, already arranged to fly Marie and Father McGriff to Washington in a CIA Learjet 35 at 8 o'clock that morning. There, she would receive two hours of training and practice with the instruments she would need, leaving perhaps 90 minutes to rest, recover, and dress in one of the two rooms provided for her and McGriff at a CIA safe house near Langley.

Father McGriff would arrive at his church office mid-morning and would keep his normal Friday schedule, which would include several afternoon counseling sessions and one clergy staff meeting to discuss final details for Sunday's services. As the family-minister clergyman on staff, Father McGriff presided and preached at Sunday services only occasionally, usually half-dozen times each year. This was not one of those Sundays, but his voice was listened to carefully as each service was prepared, since he, in a sense, "represented" the church's diverse range of families to the clergy staff.

CIA wardrobe personnel would transfer clothing and toiletries, as well as vehicles, from Marie and McGriff's homes to the safe house. Marie's room, she was astonished and grateful to learn, was set to include a litter box for Penelope's use, together with scratching post and two covered cat beds from which she might choose. Marie had made clear that Penelope's food and water dish were already in hand.

Marie would thus, that very evening in Washington, enter the cloak-and-dagger worlds of CIA, KGB, MI6, and Mossad with a grand total of two hours' training and perhaps three hours of sleep, about half of that sleep taken on the cramped front seat of the CIA-provided Ford that had whisked her from D.C. to New York. Strangely, however, once the plan was in place, she experienced an inexplicable calmness.

She had felt no discomfort whatever in speaking aloud her commitment to the plan and, thereby, to Rebekka Yahalomin. As a woman mature in her Christian beliefs, she had learned to trust her judgment of people. Trust preceded commitment; commitment preceded action.

The calmness she felt must be due, she thought to herself as she finally lay down at 4:30 a.m. in her fifth-floor dormitory bedroom across from Dr. Chapel's, not only to her trust in these people, but to the complete absence of choice she seemed to have in any of this. Once she had felt led, two days before, to report her embassy colleagues' rumors regarding Rebekka Yahalomin to her pastor-counselor, unseen hands seemed to her to have carried her away from her safe, quiet existence in suburban Maryland to this incomprehensible maze of intelligence-agency-driven hazards. Yet, as her eyes began to close in sleep, she found that it all seemed right to her, somehow.

Perhaps this was what the young people liked to call a God-thing. And on a different scale, she thought sleepily to herself, maybe this was what was really meant by the old Latin-derived word *vocation*.

A calling.

She stepped off a city bus near the Soviet Embassy at 12:35 p.m., 25 minutes before her first appointment on this June Friday. She wore a lightweight, beige suit, with conservative, color-matched low-heel shoes. Her shoulder-length hair was caught up behind her head by a tasteful gold barrette.

She carried a soft leather clutch —her everyday handbag —containing a coin purse with slots for driver's license and credit cards, a 3-inch can of pepper spray, an even smaller flashlight, and a few cosmetic items. The security personnel who would open her clutch —the guards at the interior checkpoint she would pass through to escort visitors to administrators' offices —were accustomed to seeing those exact items every day, and not just in Marie Campbell's handbag. The embassy's appointment counselors were all authorized to carry that same array in their purses.

One of the cosmetic items in Marie's clutch was obviously new. It was a Minnie Mouse compact mirror. The Disney figure's joyful face gave the hinged makeup-and-mirror combination the thickness needed to hide the compact's expected function during her upcoming incursion into the office of Ivan Ivanovich. One of the CIA's recent low-tech advances, the mouse's plastic face could be snapped off to release a listening device for simple combination safes, designed to allow unskilled operatives to open low-security safes with very little training and practice.

The CIA's two Soviet Embassy moles concurred in reporting to Langley earlier that morning that Ivan Ivanovich was a mid-level administrator whose office safe would contain nothing that the United States would term either Secret or Top Secret. Administrators at Ivanovich's level, they had explained, were given safes made to secure cash, together with documents that, in U.S. terms, would be graded no higher than Confidential. Consequently, they expected the safe would be of unsophisticated construction.

All of them assumed that the "RY Proposal" document would not —or would not *yet* —be classified higher than Confidential. If it were seen as being of higher security classification than that, it would not have been sent to a mid-level administrator. It would have been sent, instead, to an administrator whose office would be on a higher floor, a floor with much tighter security. The parties involved —CIA and Rebekka Yahalomin —accepted as fact the details of Rebecca's report: that is, the "data." The handful of CIA operatives entrusted with this type of data had long experience with the reliability of reports generated from this source.

Some of the CIA participants were Christians. Some were not. But each of them understood a long and impressive history of reliable reports when they saw them. And they valued such reliability far more than any skepticism they might harbor regarding the nature of the reports' origins. *That* topic was not even discussed among them.

The Minnie Mouse listening device had but three components: a small earpiece, a short, flat, acoustical cord, and a listening sensor the size of a quarter. It was, in effect, a tiny stethoscope. Marie had, that morning, received enough instruction and practice to feel confident that she would be able to hear the wall safe's mechanical pins sliding into place as she slowly manipulated the dial. As long as Ivanovich's wall safe was indeed of low sophistication mechanically, she felt she would almost certainly be able, with her Minnie Mouse stethoscope, to open its door in seconds.

The two moles had further explained to the Langley operatives that, in Ivan Ivanovich's section of the embassy, administrative offices were by policy left unlocked for the night cleaning crews, which began their work at 7 p.m. Offices were locked only when they had all been cleaned and inspected, usually long after midnight. And, because Ivanovich's section housed only low-to-mid-level management, there were no security cameras, either in the hallways or in the offices themselves.

As for the coin purse in Marie's clutch, it appeared to be the same one she carried every day. However, it had been modified that morning to serve both as coin purse and as a miniature document camera. Its operation was straightforward. As long as security personnel did not examine the coin purse or the Minnie Mouse compact mirror minutely, her everyday clutch handbag could be expected to pass through the embassy checkpoints without difficulty.

Her suit jacket had side pockets. In one pocket was her embassy photo identification card. In the other, there was a pair of thin rubber gloves and a plastic bag for dog waste. If questioned about the gloves, she would explain that she had walked her dog —the one she did not actually have —just prior to catching the bus for work.

Her walk from the bus stop to the embassy took fewer than five minutes, and she approached her entry door at 20 minutes before the hour. She drew her photo ID from her suit pocket, used its slender black cord to hang the ID from her neck, pulled her hair up and over the cord, careful not to dislodge the barrette, and proceeded to the entrance. The embassy's screening process at its entrance for appointment counselors and clerical-level American women was cursory: name badge with photo and a pleasant exchange of "good afternoon" with the three uniformed American men who staffed that particular entryway on weekdays. Passage into the more secure areas, something Marie was slated to do four different times this Friday afternoon, was to be, she knew, quite a different matter.

At 1 p.m. precisely, she walked into the waiting area where sat her first appointment, a Midwestern businessman and his young associate, both men looking uncomfortable. She quickly put them at their ease and, after several minutes of polite conversation, led them toward one of the interior security checkpoints —a significant screening upgrade from the checkpoint she had just used to enter the building —that would allow them passage into the low-to-mid-level administrative office corridors.

She escorted them through the checkpoint, handing her clutch to one of the Russian security men with whom she had a slight acquaintance. She returned his smile at the sight of her Minnie Mouse compact mirror, and stood aside to wait while the men's briefcases were opened and carefully scrutinized, one of the inspectors using a metal-sensitive wand to cover every inch of each briefcase, inside and out.

During her brief wait, she glanced down the intersecting corridors and confirmed that, in this relatively low-security portion of the embassy, there were no hallway cameras, as she thought was the case, but until now had never needed to note with any special care. She knew also, however, that she would not be able to confirm in advance another critical condition of her incursion, that, once this section of the embassy closed at 5:30 p.m., all office doors were left unlocked for the night-cleaning crews. Neither would she be able to confirm in advance that cleaning for this section began shortly after 7 p.m. and continued until all offices had been readied for Saturday or Monday appointments, depending upon the schedule for a given administrator.

She led her two guests through the maze of hallways and finally to the office of the administrator with whom she had made their arrangements. She introduced them to the administrator's assistant, then served coffee and chatted graciously with them during their 10-minute wait. Once the assistant took them into the administrator's office, she retraced her steps back through the security checkpoint and to the appointment counselors' office area, a large room with cubicles sufficient to accommodate the half-dozen American women who served as the hospitality team.

Since each administrator's own assistant had the responsibility of escorting visitors back to the general waiting area, she was free for the half-hour prior to her next appointment. She used the time to feign reading the Tolstoy she kept at her desk, while she, in fact, mentally rehearsed each step that would be required of her after her fourth and final appointment late that afternoon.

And the afternoon dragged, especially during the 90-minute gap between the finish of her 2 p.m. appointment, a little after 2:30 p.m., and the arrival of her 4 p.m. appointment. Finally, just after 5:30 p.m., her hospitality work completed for the day, she turned mentally, *very* conscious of the transition, to the first act in her new life as … what? A functionary for a government intelligence agency? A prospective member of something supernaturally mysterious called Rebekka Yahalomin? A pawn in an elaborate and danger-filled venture about which she knew almost nothing?

Perhaps all of the above.

Any one of the three would have been enough to send butterflies whirring through her stomach. The three combined led her to a level of nervousness just slightly short of nausea.

Regardless, she said to herself as she fought down waves of anxiety, she knew one thing. She knew that she was determined to embrace on faith the idea that her pastor-counselor and his detective friends and their English counterparts were Christianly and morally legitimate. She had committed to them and thereby to their cause, and had made those commitments on faith.

Oh … and perhaps she knew a second thing. She knew that a man whom she liked and admired had actually materialized on her doorstep late at night for the avowed purpose of asking her to dinner that weekend, an outlandish and hopelessly romantic thing for him to have done. She did not know exactly how she should think about that, but … well … she was certainly flattered.

More than flattered. Amazed. Fascinated. Intrigued.

And, given the fact that the same man had drawn a gun, faced down intruders, summoned CIA agents via a coded message, and then driven a high-performance vehicle at 80 mph at night along interstate highways … perhaps just a little fearful.

Following her final appointment on the afternoon of the same, interminably long Friday, Marie Campbell retreated to the nearest ladies' room, knowing that the 6 p.m. shift change at the security checkpoint would leave only a single night man on duty, someone routinely friendly to her. She knew that he would track and record the departures of embassy guests only, not of embassy employees, some of whom often worked well into the night or even into the next morning's office hours. There would be a final room-by-room canvass at 3 a.m., when the cleaning crews went home, but not before. Since the cleaning crews did not carry keys to administrative offices, all offices would be locked at that time, as part of the room-by-room canvass.

In the ladies' room, she dallied until the last woman had left, then retreated to the storage closet at the rear of the washroom. There she waited, standing motionless in the darkness until 6 p.m. She knew that by then the corridors would be mostly empty of departing employees, the security shift change would have been completed, and she would have an hour to finish her tasks before the cleaning crews' arrival.

When her digital lighted watch read 1800 hours, she said Father McGriff's companion prayer to herself one last time —*Father, be present, be present* —and stepped from the storage closet. She loosened the retractable shoulder strap on her clutch, placed the strap over her left shoulder to leave both her hands free, and swiftly exited the women's restroom. She walked briskly down one long corridor, a corridor silent and empty of traffic, and rounded the corner into Ivan Ivanovich's passageway. Immediately she saw an administrator and his assistant exiting their office partway down the hall and starting toward her.

She knew them both, and strode confidently toward them, with her explanation —a completely true one —at the ready. As they neared each other, the assistant said, in her heavily accented English, "Marie, tonight you have the evening guests?"

"No, Tatyana," she replied, "but I'm not ready for tomorrow morning's 8 o'clock. I want to have everything in place." The two women smiled their good-nights to each other and continued on their way.

With early-morning appointments, she liked to prepare the assistant's area the evening before as an "extra" touch: making sure the coffee pot had been rinsed, the creamer and sweetener and stirrer baskets filled, the reading material appropriate for the first guest, often one whose background and preferences were known only to her. It was the kind of gesture that endeared her to administrators and assistants alike.

Halfway down the corridor, she halted to rap softly on the door of office number 2038, heard nothing, and opened the door slightly. She called the assistant by name. Hearing no reply, she entered and prepared the anteroom for the 8 a.m. guest.

Her digital watch read 1813 hours when she finished tidying the anteroom. She paused to listen for voices or footsteps in the corridor, heard only silence, and donned the rubber gloves. She stood at the open door of 2038, and looked quickly, both ways, up and down the long passageway. She saw it to be empty. She snugged the shoulder strap of her clutch, closed the door, and walked rapidly to 2044. She rapped twice on the office door of Ivan Ivanovich and his assistant.

Hearing nothing, she opened the door with her gloved hand, whispered the assistant's name, and, satisfied that the office was empty, as expected, entered and closed the door behind her. No lights were on, either in the assistant's space or in the main office, but Ivanovich's west-facing office window, directly behind his desk, provided plentiful light from the gradually setting summer sun. She crossed both rooms to the administrator's wall safe, situated just to one side of the window.

The safe was actually anchored in the floor, protruded 5 inches into the room, and provided a total cavity depth of 15 inches, limited by the thickness of the exterior wall. The 15-inch depth gave ample space for standard 8-by-11 documents.

Marie knew that for the next half-hour she would be helplessly exposed to discovery, should anyone enter 2044. There could be no explanation of her actions from this moment until she exited Ivanovich's office.

Forcing herself to breathe normally, speaking her companion prayer repeatedly, she quickly knelt, removed the clutch strap from her shoulder, and pulled from the handbag the Minnie Mouse compact. The baby stethoscope worked beautifully, and she had the door of the wall safe open in less than 45 seconds.

Stooping still further, she inserted the miniature flashlight into the cavity, so that the light was not visible from outside the window, and immediately found the document. Turning, she shoved Ivanovich's wheeled chair out of the way and, still kneeling, placed the document on the floor under his desk. She saw that the indirect light from the window was adequate. She'd have no further need for her flashlight.

Using the document camera with increasing skill as she went, she quickly reached the point at which she was photographing four pages per minute. She made no effort to read what was on the pages, concentrating only on photography. The document was 72 pages in length, not counting front matter. As she turned page 66, her digital watch read 1840 hours. Twenty minutes to cover six more pages, to return the document to the safe, to exit the office, and to pass through the security checkpoint out of the administrative office section of the building.

Suddenly, she heard voices approaching. A man and a woman. They seemed to stop just outside the door to the assistant's anteroom. After a moment, she heard the door handle turn, sensed the door opening, and knew that she was no longer alone.

Sitting back on her haunches, hunched over the document, she gave thanks for the fact that the old-style desk had a skirt that shielded her, crouched under the cavity made for the administrator's swivel chair, from view. She opened her mouth wide, in order to breathe more silently than was possible through her nostrils. That had actually been part of that morning's lessons at Langley: increase the size of the airway; reduce the sound of one's own in-and-out breathing.

Motionless, she waited.

The sounds she heard, now that both individuals were inside the assistant's space, were at first not from spoken words. The sounds were those made by two people engaged in kissing: mouth noises, small moans.

Then, the woman, whispering: "I can't do this. I can't do this. I *need* this job."

The man, also whispering, though not quietly: "We're not gonna get caught. We got 20 minutes. C'mon."

The woman: "No. No. Maybe after work. No. Stop. Stop now!"

The man: "After work? Promise?"

The woman: "No. But maybe … maybe."

The silence of heavy breathing, but diminishing.

After another moment, Marie, still motionless on her knees, heard the door knob being turned slowly and carefully. She sensed the couple exiting on tiptoe.

She was alone.

Less than half an hour later, the sun now low in the sky, Marie stepped onto a city bus that would take her through the city, across the Potomac, and finally to the Langley area, within easy walking distance of the CIA safe house. Although the Friday afternoon traffic had thinned somewhat, the bus was standing room only. As instructed during that morning's lessons, she had removed the shoulder strap from her handbag as soon as she had exited the embassy, and now held the clutch "just like a football, if you were plowing through the middle of the Green Bay Packers' defensive front seven."

Having informed her instructor that she knew nothing about plowing through anyone's front seven, she had been shown exactly how to carry the "football." It rested in the crook of her right forearm, her left hand pressing down on the zippered top of the clutch. She found that the very act of holding the handbag in this fashion made her extremely nervous. To her, the football carry of her clutch radiated a signal that its contents were valuable and should be coveted by …

Suddenly, she became conscious of a large body pressing heavily against her from behind. A deep male voice spoke quietly in her ear, softly enough not to be heard by others over the noise of the bus's diesel engine, the outside traffic noises, and the conversations inside the bus itself.

"Release your grip on the bag," he said in heavily accented English.

"I have a 5-inch blade," he continued, "which I will insert between your ribs and into your kidney. I will leave the knife inserted in your body, and I will take the bag from your dying hands, and I will step off the bus at the stop, which is just ahead. You will sink to the floor, not noticed in this crowd, and you will die there.

"Or, you may release the bag … and live."

She immediately heard another male voice, this one familiar. The words were directed not at her, but at the figure leaning into her from behind.

"You are aware of the damage a hollow-point round from a 9mm will do to the inside of your torso. What you feel against your rib cage is the muzzle of my

Beretta. I will fire two rounds into you the instant you move that knife into this woman.

"You will die here, and painfully. You will not have secured her handbag. You will have died for absolutely nothing."

Then the familiar voice spoke directly to her. "Marie, go quickly to the front and step off the bus at this stop. Do it now."

CHAPTER FIVE

MARIE, TREMBLING, STOOD ON THE SIDEWALK, STILL GRASPING her handbag in the supposed football carry, and watched through a cloud of diesel fumes as the city bus roared away from the bus stop. Then it unexpectedly stopped.

She watched Father McGriff step off the bus, pause to make sure the bus door closed behind him, then turn to walk briskly toward her. He held something in one hand that she could not distinguish until he stopped just in front of her.

"Do you still have that empty bag for dog waste, Marie?" he asked.

She nodded, bewildered.

"Let me drop this knife into that bag."

He gestured to her handbag. She understood, opened her clutch, and Father McGriff deposited the assailant's knife, now encased in the plastic bag, into an oblong compartment in the side of the handbag.

"We'll run fingerprints when we get to New York," said Father McGriff. "Probably won't get anything, but worth a try."

He looked at her carefully. She was trembling visibly. Tears stood in her eyes.

And, then and there, in full view of Washington, D.C., pedestrian and vehicular traffic, Father McGriff broke one of his fundamental rules, the one about not hugging female members of his congregation. He stepped to her, placed both arms around her, and pulled her to him.

He was surprised at how small she felt in his arms, and it occurred to him that he probably outweighed her by at least a hundred pounds. He turned his face down and spoke into her ear. "You're going to be fine, Marie. I'm not going to let anything hurt you … understand?"

He felt her nod into his chest.

He also felt her begin to relax, muscular tension evaporating throughout her body as he continued to hold her. Finally, he stepped back and looked into her face.

She looked up at him and smiled. A small, hesitant smile. But a smile.

"Did you get the document, Marie?"

"Yes," she replied. "I mean, I have the camera, and I photographed every page of the document … so, yes," she said.

"Excellent. We're just a couple of blocks from the church," he said. "Let's walk."

They walked fast, without talking, and in fewer than 10 minutes he was unlocking the exterior door to the church's suite of offices. Once inside the vestibule, they paused while he punched numbers into a keypad. And once inside the hallway and away from the noise of rush-hour city traffic, they heard a tiny, distant meow from behind one of the closed doors. She looked at him inquiringly.

As they walked down the hallway to his office, Father McGriff said, "I've no time to explain right now, Marie, but that's Penelope. We need to load her into my Jeep and start for New York. Right now. We can't go back to the safe house."

She grasped both the urgency and the haste that was implied in his answer, and she immediately, without asking for an explanation, phoned one of her hospitality colleagues to arrange for a substitute next morning at the embassy. That done, she reassured Penelope as best she could, and they loaded the Jeep Cherokee for their second drive from Washington to New York City in just 24 hours.

As he navigated northwest through stop-and-go traffic toward the Washington Beltway, with Penelope comfortable and quiet on the back seat, her feline accoutrements stored in the Cherokee's luggage area, Father McGriff turned to business.

"Marie," he said, "do you want to tell me how your embassy experience worked out? Did everything go as we hoped?"

"I think it went well," she said, "but I want to hear from you, first, Father. What are we doing? Why are we not going back to the safe house?"

He braked the Jeep to a halt at a traffic signal and turned his face to her.

"Speaking as the man who appeared on your doorstep late last night to ask you to dinner this weekend, and as the man who just broke his decade-long rule not to embrace female members of the congregation, let me say that I'm no longer 'Father McGriff' to you. I'm Jack. You're Marie. Can we do that?"

"Well," she replied after a moment's thought, "I'm going to need to hear more about this dinner invitation thing, and about your showing up on my doorstep last night ... *Jack* ... but, yes, we can do that."

As the light changed, he glanced once more at her and saw a look on her face that he could only describe as quizzical. *That will have to do for now,* he thought.

He moved the Jeep forward through the intersection and began his explanation.

"First," he said, "the CIA people who are part of the document-photographing operation —the same people who provided the Ford, the Learjet, the safe house accommodations, Minnie Mouse, and the camera —will without question regard the photographed document as their property. Rebekka Yahalomin will, also without question, regard the document as *their* property.

"This is not a new conflict. When 'special messages' come to Rebecca, she and her family and the detectives have always regarded those messages as data provided specifically to them, for explicitly godly purposes. Whatever is in that document you photographed, Marie, it is, according to Rebekka Yahalomin, theirs to read, study, and interpret. Having done that, *they* will choose what will be communicated to CIA, MI6, Mossad, and other allies, if anything at all.

"Rebekka Yahalomin's tradition is to own the data, to choose what gets shared with anyone else, and, when needed, to ask for assistance without necessarily promising anything in return. A one-way street."

He glanced at her and raised his eyebrows.

"This makes the intelligence people quite unhappy, I'd think?" she asked.

"Oh, yes," he replied, "but they have always viewed the trade-off as, in the long run, worth it.

"However," he continued quickly, "had we returned to the safe house, we would have been greeted by an entire team of CIA people, every one of them determined not to let that camera go anywhere until they had processed the images and, thus, had their copy of the document in hand. We would have had a *very* hard time getting those images away from them and into the hands of Rebekka Yahalomin without their printing the images first. You and I, after all, do not have the status that Rebecca herself has with these people. We are not authoritative in their eyes."

She was thoughtful for a moment.

He waited.

"Yes," she said at length, "but it is a difficult issue, isn't it? I mean, it's not absolutely obvious that their position is wrong … Jack."

She spoke his name with difficulty, looked at him and laughed. "Oh," she said, "that's going to be hard."

"You just need practice, Marie. You'll have plenty of opportunities, I promise."

She smiled and continued. "Their argument in this case," she said, "would center on the fact that I would never have been able to follow Rebecca's vision to its real-life niche in the world … to office 2044 … to the safe … to the document … without their information —from their two moles —and especially without their safe-opening equipment and the training they gave me in using it. They can certainly argue that *shared* possession of the photographed document would be fair. Right?"

"Absolutely," he replied, "and without question … that would be fair."

After a moment's thought, he continued. "Well … forgive me for sounding preachy, Marie, but consider the points of emphasis in some of Jesus's best-known parables, like, say, the story of the lost son. In those kinds of parables, 'fairness' in the usual sense doesn't appear to have a high priority … you know … from the divine perspective.

"I mean … you'd have to admit," he continued, "that it wasn't really *fair* to the good son —the responsible, obedient son —for the lost son to be celebrated after squandering everything his dad had given him, after living a dissolute life for so long. But his dad wasn't thinking in terms of *fair* so much as in terms of love and generosity and forgiveness. Priorities … you know?

"Love … generosity … forgiveness. *Then* … maybe … fairness. Maybe there are times when fairness gets crowded out of the picture entirely."

He glanced at her again. She was focused, concentrating, much as he had seen her so many times in their counseling sessions.

He decided to continue. "And, in this case, we don't know … yet … what is at stake here. We'll probably find out as soon as we study this document you've secured for us. But my guess is that, once we find out, it'll be pretty clear that Rebekka Yahalomin will need to steer the ship. Intelligence agencies, whose basic currency is deception, can't be trusted to navigate in *these* waters, not from the perspective of the Source of our 'special messages.'

"We need to get your camera to the detectives, get the document analyzed and shared with Rebecca and the others at the Lodge in England, then form a plan. If we need MI6 or CIA … or even Mossad … we'll let them know.

"They'll understand who's at the helm. They know Rebekka Yahalomin has a tradition of giving them no choice in these matters. But also, a tradition of getting very good outcomes."

McGriff turned the Cherokee onto the entry ramp to the Beltway and found the traffic moving at moderate speed, almost 40 mph. Once he had maneuvered into the middle lane, he glanced again at his companion. She was obviously thoughtful, now looking out her side window.

Knowing she would speak when ready, he remained silent.

"Jack," she said finally, "would you have shot that man on the bus?"

"Without hesitation," he said firmly.

"But …"

"Yes, I know," he said in response to the question he knew was coming, as it had come to him innumerable times over the years.

"I know," he repeated, "but here's the thing. Combatants fighting combatants," he continued, "has always been honored as justifiable in mainstream Christian thinking. The commandment that is often spoken as 'Thou shalt not kill' is more accurately translated as 'Thou shalt not murder.'

"What you witnessed on that bus was combatant against combatant, armed man against armed man. What you were about to *experience* was murder: armed man against unarmed woman.

"Had I allowed that to happen, I would have violated what we participants in Rebekka Yahalomin regard as the blueprint of the universe: *my life for yours.*

"As we say —those of us who engage in this kind of spiritual and physical warfare —that blueprint applies at many levels, whether you're talking about the cosmic level embodied in Christ's sacrifice for us all, or intermediate levels such as the sacrifices we make for our families, or all the way down to the smallest courtesies.

"*My life for yours.* It's what we do, Marie."

After a moment, she offered, "Yet, to 'turn the other cheek,' in Jesus's words …"

"Yes," McGriff replied, "we must not return insult for insult against ourselves. That's quite a different matter than stepping forward to confront violent injustice against an innocent. If a combatant has a 5-inch blade pressing against the rib cage of an unarmed person, we must stop that action if we can, preferably without hurting the assailant, as was the case on the bus.

"I actually told that gentleman to 'have a nice day' after I'd disarmed him. He thought, no doubt, that I was just being sarcastic. In any case, Marie, we *must* stop violence against an innocent if we can."

Silence again descended on them, and the silence grew long as the Jeep moved, still at moderate highway speed, along the Beltway toward I-95 North.

"New subject," she finally said quietly.

"Okay," he replied.

"Is there a contradiction —a built-in contradiction —in your two roles, Jack? How can you serve our church members as their counselor and, at the same time, serve our national intelligence agency? What do you do when someone in your office, in a counseling session, says something to you that would be of value to the CIA? Given the international mix of our congregation, surely that must happen? Are you comfortable in these two roles, Jack?"

"No," he said immediately. "And," he continued after a pause, "believe it or not, I was playing this very conversation over in my mind in Penn Station in New York, just yesterday. I was actually imagining the two of us talking about this, and imagining what I would say when you asked what you just asked."

"You were? Really?"

He nodded. "Yes," he said, "and I came to no workable conclusion, Marie. I am *not* comfortable with my two roles. All I can say is that I have never yet faced a situation in which I felt tugged in opposing directions by something a counselee told me.

"Let me say that better. More directly. I have never had a counselee say anything to me that I thought should be repeated to anyone … not just to the CIA … but to anyone at all. Not a single instance."

"But," she objected, "you can imagine one, yes?"

"Yes, I can."

"And?"

"And I don't know, except to say that, because of you, I'm going to need to think through my roles and decide something. If I had to decide right this minute, I think I would formulate some kind of policy that would make clear to our church members that, like other professional counselors, there are some topics that I cannot promise to keep private. That's true of all counselors, of course: threats of murder, or suicide, or other criminal activity … we are obligated not to keep quiet on some issues. This would fall under that umbrella."

"Can you imagine," she replied, "being *comfortable* with that kind of policy?"

"Well, I don't know," he said.

He thought for a long moment, then decided on a U-turn. “It may be that, in the end, I will resign my post with the CIA, and you and I will open a Washington branch of the Belton and Adelman Detective Agency, Marie. How does that sound? Has a certain ring, yes?”

She laughed her happy laugh, as he had hoped she would.

He joined in her laughter, but then he glanced at her and continued. “It sounds funny, but think about it. I’m not really comfortable accepting payments from the CIA. I’m guessing you’re not really comfortable accepting paychecks from the Soviet Union.”

He looked at her. She was shaking her head slowly, thoughtfully.

“With Mr. Belton and Mr. Adelman, there’s no subterfuge. They’re internationally respected as men who unearth complicated mysteries, step-by-step. We’d be great at that: *Campbell and McGriff, private detectives and pastoral counselors.*”

Suddenly she emitted a squeal. “Ohhhhh,” she said, letting her head fall back against the headrest.

“You are *impossible,* Jack McGriff. I cannot tell from one minute to the next whether you are in your clergy role, your intelligence role, or your standup comic role. I don’t know how I’ve managed to get mixed up with someone like you. You’re a horrible human being.”

He smiled and reached for her hand. To his mild surprise, she took it.

Silence again enveloped the car. A comfortable silence.

His heart had begun to sing so strongly he imagined she could hear it.

Minutes passed, their hands entwined.

Finally, she turned her face toward him once more, clearly ready to resume the discussion. She removed her hand from his.

McGriff steeled himself.

“Jack,” she said finally, again forcing herself to speak his name, “do I have any clothes in this car?”

He laughed. “Well,” he replied, “I had to load the Jeep at noon right in front of CIA security people at the safe house. They understood why I’d need to take Penelope and her stuff with me —or pretended to understand, since they’re probably not cat people —and why you might want your University of Maryland sweatshirt instead of your suit jacket to go to a fast food place for dinner, but I wouldn’t have been able to explain packing all our stuff in the Jeep. That wouldn’t have gone well.”

She considered his response for a moment. "So … no," she said, shaking her head incredulously at his explanation, and at his obvious self-satisfaction with the explanation he'd provided her. "You're saying I don't have any clothes in this car."

He felt her staring at him.

He kept his eyes straight ahead.

After a long sigh, she launched a detailed review of her clandestine penetration of Ivanovich's office and wall safe, answered McGriff's questions, and then, the conversation on pause, announced that she was famished. Accordingly, they stopped for food at an I-95 service plaza.

Once back to the Cherokee, Marie removed her suit jacket. As she pulled on the sweatshirt, she said, "You know, Jack, I don't feel as if I've slept in a week. I'm going to get on the back seat with Penelope and try to catch up. Okay?"

McGriff had to drive much more slowly in the "civilian" Cherokee than he had the previous night in the CIA-owned, high-speed-cleared Ford. So it was that they arrived in the New York City area an hour after midnight: early Saturday morning. And, rather than using the Holland Tunnel, thence to lower Manhattan, they crossed Staten Island to reach the Verrazano Narrows Bridge into Brooklyn.

Marie sat up at the tollbooth on the Staten Island side of the bridge, rooted around in her clutch to retrieve her travel toothbrush and toothpaste, and proceeded to brush her teeth without recourse to running water. McGriff looked at her in the rear-view. "No need for water? Very military, Marie."

"No," she said, "very emergency. No one thought to bring any of my clothes or toiletries, and this is the result. Of all the CIA persons I've ever ridden to New York City with, twice in 24 hours, you are, far and away, the most inconsiderate."

He laughed long and delightedly. "Ms. Campbell," he responded after catching his breath, "you're easily the funniest Soviet Embassy appointment counselor I've ever driven to New York City twice in 24 hours in my entire life."

Returning the toothbrush to her handbag, she looked out the window at the moonlit water and asked, "Why the Verrazano? Why not the tunnel?"

"Because I am so thoughtful of your needs, ma'am."

"I *need* to cross this bridge?"

"Before I left the church office this afternoon to come to your rescue," he said, "I used the secure line to speak with Mr. Belton, Dr. Chapel, and Mr. Adelman in New York. I explained everything to them.

"They said they'd arrange with a long-time NYPD partner of Mr. Belton's, a Pete Bronkowski, now retired, and his wife, Jean, to put together two gym bags full of clothes for each of us: basic stuff like jeans and shirts and workout clothing and running shoes, plus the toiletries you'd be so miserable without. Dr. Chapel said she'd guess at our sizes, and they assured me that the Bronkowskis would have everything ready.

"We're headed for their home in Brooklyn Heights, Marie. Should get there in about 15 minutes. We'll get a taxi into Manhattan. The Cherokee will stay in the Bronkowskis' two-car garage until we need it again."

After a moment, now holding Penelope in her lap, she spoke. "Well … I must say I'm impressed, sir. You're not nearly as horrible as I thought you were. Not *nearly* as horrible."

It was after 2:30 a.m. Saturday when the taxi carried them over the Brooklyn Bridge and into lower Manhattan. Minutes later, they entered the detective agency's tiny lobby. The two of them rode the elevator to the fifth-floor dormitory level and stepped into its small common room.

McGriff carried both the gym bags that the Bronkowskis had packed for them, and Marie, the pet taxi and Penelope's food and water dish. They placed their belongings in their sleeping rooms and together took the elevator up to the conference-room floor where the two detectives and Dr. Chapel awaited them.

As they stepped onto the elevator, McGriff said, "Marie, you may as well go ahead and get the camera out of your handbag. They'll want to dive right in."

They walked into the conference room together and Marie placed the faux coin purse on the table in front of Belton before taking her chair. "I photographed every page, Mr. Belton, all 72 pages," she said. "It should all be there."

Adelman then introduced the sixth person in the room, a small, somber, black-haired man wearing plain, dark clothes and with a yarmulke perched on the back of his head. "This is the Russian language expert I mentioned before," Adelman said to the newcomers. "By mutual agreement between my former organization and Rebekka Yahalomin, he will remain anonymous. In fact, he'll be with us only long enough to determine if we will need his services.

"He and I both," Adelman continued, "will work through our Sabbath. We will not pause for Shabbat."

"Welcome, you two," added Belton to the newcomers. "England is on th' speakerphone with us. As much as we'd all like t' get th' details of what happened in Washington, we're gonna postpone all that. We gotta get t' work on th' document."

Belton paused and glanced around the room. "Know what I mean? Hmm?"

Heads nodded.

He continued. "But … is there somethin' we *gotta* know, somethin' that'll help us get t' th' bottom of it all a little faster?"

"Yes, sir," replied McGriff immediately.

"Although Marie conducted her incursion at the embassy beautifully," —here McGriff actually found himself blushing, to the undisguised amusement of Belton and Adelman —"there was an attempted assault on her, at knifepoint, on the city bus, after she left the embassy. An attempt to steal her handbag, which, of course, contained the camera. I was there with the 9mm, and so she got away unscathed.

"I relieved the assailant of his 5-inch knife, and we have protected it so that fingerprints might be run, if you think it might be productive."

As he said this last, Marie pulled the doggie-bag-clad knife from her clutch and passed it around the table to Belton. He accepted it, saying, "Can't hurt t' run this past th' boys at th' precinct. Nice work, you two. Anything else?"

The newcomers shook their heads in the negative, and Belton, addressing the speakerphone, asked, "Anything from England?"

The sound of applause came clearly through the device, followed by a male voice saying, "Well done, *you!* Well done!"

"Thank you, England," said Adelman, speaking for McGriff and Marie.

Then, speaking to everyone, Adelman continued. "Our Russian-language guest and Sid and I," he said, "will spend what I expect to be the next three to four hours printing and analyzing the document —that's my best guess at the time it will take us to go carefully through 72 pages. Let's set 9 a.m. New York time for reconvening. England, will an early Saturday afternoon session work for you over there at the Lodge?"

"Yes, fine," said the same male voice over the secure line. "We've sent all the Lodge's guests home. We're clear."

The authoritative, "*We've* sent all … home," signaled to the New York listeners that the male voice was that of Jason Manguson, who, with his wife, Elisabeth, was the Lodge's co-owner.

"Good," said Adelman.

"Eleanor," said Belton after a moment, "I think you, Marie, an' Jack here should hit th' sack fer these next four hours. Maybe longer. Whaddya think?"

"I think 'maybe longer' is exactly right, dear. Maybe *much* longer." Saying this, Dr. Chapel began to rise from her chair, as did Marie.

McGriff walked the women to the elevator and, as its doors slid open, he said, "I'm going to go back to the meeting for a few minutes. Rest well, if you can. I'll see you at some decent hour this morning."

He returned to the conference room and, as he resumed his chair, he gestured inquisitively with his eyes toward the speakerphone. Adelman nodded.

"It's off, Jack," he said.

"So," said McGriff, "have you given any more thought to the concerns I expressed yesterday afternoon about the possible leak we have somewhere, a problem that was made even more plausible by this knifepoint attack on Marie?"

Adelman and Belton nodded vigorously.

"Yeah, we have," said Belton.

"Yes," said Adelman, "especially to your hypothesis that we're being naïve to think that these 'secure lines' in this room, and in your office at your D.C. church, and at the Lodge in England, all of them installed by CIA and MI6, are, as we have been assuming, iron-clad impenetrable. We fear you're right, Jack.

"We fear that CIA and MI6 and, maybe, Mossad, too," Adelman continued, "are listening around the clock. And, beyond that, we have to acknowledge that the KGB can place its own mole within the allied intelligence agencies, just as we've managed to place two moles within the Soviet Embassy in D.C."

After a brief silence, McGriff asked the obvious question. "So," he said, "other than shutting off the secure line here in the agency, what can we do about that problem, if it's true?"

Belton looked up from the coin-purse camera at McGriff and smiled his crooked smile. Then he chuckled and said, "Whaddya think, Father Jack?"

Belton's nearly black, deep-set eyes somehow twinkled with amusement. "C'mon, Jack," Belton repeated. "You're a smart guy. Whaddya *think* we'd do? Hmm? Whaddya *think?*"

McGriff, understanding that the detective's lopsided smile should be telling him something obvious, shrugged and shook his head.

"Jack," said Adelman, "we're going to have a surprise for you at our 9 a.m. session this morning."

"A surprise?" he asked. "What kind of surprise?"

"Well," said Belton, "if we told ya that, it wouldn't be a surprise, would it?"

Adelman continued. "You should go down to the dormitory, Jack. Try to rest. We're going to need you at your best."

"What about you two?" McGriff asked. "When do you sleep?"

"We don't," replied Adelman.

CHAPTER SIX

AS THEY FINISHED THE BREAKFAST FRUIT THAT DR. CHAPEL HAD brought down to the fifth-floor common room for them, Marie looked at Jack and said, "Thank you for yesterday."

Seeing her seriousness, he replied with equal earnestness, "You're welcome … but you were amazing. This is all new to you, and you handled yourself like a seasoned pro. That applause from England over the speakerphone was well deserved. I understand from Mr. Belton and Mr. Adelman that those people are not easily impressed."

"Well … thank you … but they were mainly applauding your rescue of me on the bus, you know," she replied.

"No," he said, "these folks are results-oriented. *You* got the document photographed and clear of the embassy. *That* is what drew the applause."

Minutes later, as they exited the elevator on the sixth floor at nearly half-past ten on a June Saturday morning, Marie looked up into McGriff's light blue eyes, smiled her bright smile, and said, "And thank you again, Jack … seriously … for getting me something to wear.

"Dr. Chapel and Jean Bronkowski worked wonders to get us these clothes."

They walked down the short hallway to the conference room, conscious of the fact that they were wearing well-fitting, nearly matching outfits. The Bronkowskis had supplied them with white Adidas running shoes, nicely tailored jeans, and knit, collared, short-sleeve shirts, hers in a bright yellow and his in a dark blue. They had already joked that they should be photographed for the apparel makers.

As they turned into the conference room, they halted in the doorway. The room was so completely silent that their entrance felt to them like an intrusion.

No one looked up. Each participant's eyes were fixed on her or his copy of the printed document.

McGriff's attention was drawn to the pile of scribbled-upon legal-pad sheets surrounding Belton, presumably notes the detective had been taking as the document revealed itself to him, page by page. Marie's eyes, however, were busy scanning the room. In seconds, her eyes fixed on a person sitting at the far end of the conference table. She knew instantly who it was.

Rebecca Clark.

Rebecca Clark was, *impossibly*, present in the conference room.

Rebecca looked up from her document just as Marie recognized her. She smiled and rose gracefully from her chair. She wore a white, high-necked, sleeveless blouse over a dark, mid-calf-length skirt. Her bare, sinewy arms were toned and tan from a near-lifetime of outdoor tennis, and her low-heeled shoes pushed her six feet of natural height slightly higher, adding to a picture of feminine athleticism rarely encountered in the ordinary course of life.

Rebecca's notorious facial scar struck Marie as being exactly as advertised. It did not detract from her beauty, but simply made that beauty more interesting, intriguing, idiosyncratic. Rebecca moved quickly around the conference table and walked straight to Marie. Upon reaching her, she enfolded the smaller woman in an embrace notable both for its strength and for its obvious genuineness.

Dr. Chapel, whose chair Rebecca had just circled past, and who, thus, viewed the embrace from behind the Englishwoman, smiled as Marie, more than a half-foot shorter and much more slight of build than the former internationally ranked tennis player, disappeared completely from her view. But she saw that, at length, Rebecca released her captive, stepped back, and offered her hand, which Marie, still stunned by the unexpected presence of a woman of such legendary status, accepted hesitantly, as though unsure that the fabled woman was not an apparition.

"Marie," said Rebecca in her British-accented English, her voice low, for a woman, "I am so pleased to meet you. You cannot *imagine* how impressed I was to hear of your successful exploits at the Soviet Embassy yesterday. We are so grateful to you … just so thankful."

Seeing the American's dumbstruck response to her presence, Rebecca continued gracefully, "Here, Marie, come and sit by me at the end of the table. We can share my copy of the document."

With that, Rebecca took the right hand she had just shaken in her own left, and led Marie to the empty chair next to her own. They sat down just as McGriff looked wonderingly at the detectives, his mystified expression begging for an explanation of Rebecca's presence.

Adelman supplied it immediately, looking alternately at McGriff and, at the far end of the table, Marie.

"You may recall, Jack, that both Kory and Luke Manguson remained in the Royal Navy as reservists after their active duty was completed?"

McGriff nodded.

"Luke, through the Royal Navy," continued Adelman, "has maintained his contacts within the Royal Air Force, and has from time to time arranged, through those connections, to hitchhike on scheduled RAF flights to all points around the world, his exact destination depending on his agenda at a given time. Yesterday, Luke arranged for his sister to board a late-evening flight —late evening in England, but roughly the time frame during which you, Marie, were starting your heroic work on our behalf at the embassy —from Brize Norton RAF base in Oxfordshire, home of the RAF strategic and tactical Air Transport arm, to McGuire Air Force Base in New Jersey.

"Rebecca's four-engine transport refueled at Harmon Air Force Base in Newfoundland and arrived at McGuire at 0700, Eastern Time. Elapsed flight time was altogether about 10 hours, plus the refuel-and-rest stop in Newfoundland, but the flight gained five hours via the time change.

"It's a 90-minute drive, New York City to McGuire, so I left here at about 0500, picked up Rebecca at the air base, and had her here in the office by 0900."

"We'd got th' document printed by 4 a.m. and me an' th' Russian," Belton said as he gestured toward the still-anonymous Russian language expert seated near Rebecca and Marie, "kept workin' at it while Jaakov was gone t' get Rebecca.

"We got it pretty well sorted by now, Jack."

McGriff nodded again, but his continued puzzlement was obvious to the detectives, and Adelman addressed his curiosity.

"You're wondering about security of communication, right, Jack?"

"Yes," he replied. "If we needed Rebecca's movement from England to New York to be kept secret from our adversaries, whoever they may turn out to be."

"Right," said Adelman.

"Have you, Jack, or you, Marie, ever heard of something called the Simple Mail Transfer Protocol?"

They shook their heads.

"It's a means of communicating," explained Adelman, "that grew out of research and development in the U.S. and the U.K., starting with efforts in the 1950s to link primitive computers together into networks. About 20 years ago, in the mid-60s, researchers at the National Physics Laboratory in Teddington —part of the London metro area —developed a test bed that has accelerated rapidly from then until now.

"The state of the art," he continued, "at the moment, is SMTP —Simple Mail Transfer Protocol —but the field is developing so rapidly that by … let's say … roughly 1990 … only five years from now, or so … there may well be a worldwide web of communication networks that use none of the current communication systems. All current systems of communication will be on their way to becoming obsolete. Pay phones, for example, will simply fade away."

He paused while McGriff and Marie processed this information.

"So," asked McGriff, "you're saying that we have SMTP now, here in this office, allowing communication with England without use of the secure line?"

Adelman nodded. "Yes," he replied, gesturing toward his desktop computer, off to his left. "Kory Manguson," he explained further, "Rebecca's sister-in-law, works at the same international consulting firm as do Rebecca's husband and brother-in-law."

Here Adelman looked toward Marie, wanting to make sure she was clear on the familial relationships. "Marie, that's Matt Clark, Rebecca's husband, and Luke Manguson, Rebecca's twin brother … Kory's husband."

She nodded appreciatively.

"Kory," he continued, "specializes at the consulting firm in scientific and technological applications to worldwide communication systems. She has begun using the SMTP in recent months, and her immersion with that and with older 'secure systems,' like the ones installed here by CIA and MI6, has led her to question our reliance on those soon-to-be antiquated systems … that is, led her to question the reliance of Rebekka Yahalomin on systems installed by national intelligence agencies, even these two 'friendly' intelligence agencies."

"So," asked McGriff quickly, "she wanted us to shut down the CIA and MI6 installations long before I mentioned doing that very thing?"

"Yes," answered Adelman. "She sent a classified packet to me four days ago by RAF courier, Brize Norton to McGuire Air Force Base," Adelman explained, "containing a message detailing use of the SMTP and, as well, containing a compact disc —a CD —for installation in my desktop computer here in the agency. The SMTP CD in my computer then allowed Kory to message me 18 hours ago to say that Rebecca was en route and would be arriving at McGuire in New Jersey at 0700."

"We kept that under our hats," said Belton, "until she got here. No need fer anybody else t' know until th' thing actually happened. Know what I mean?"

There was another pause, the detectives again giving the newcomers time.

Finally, Marie shook her head. "Mr. Adelman ..."

He interrupted her.

"Please use my first name, Marie. I'm Jaakov."

She smiled, looking at Jack.

Jack said, "I'm working on her to do exactly that with me, Jaakov. She still thinks she's being rude to call me Jack."

Smiling, they all turned back to Marie, who acknowledged the accuracy of McGriff's statement with a shy smile of her own, then moved on with her question.

"I'm sure I'm missing something obvious," she said, "but I just don't see the connection between the SMTP compact disc installation in your computer, Jaakov, and Rebecca's needing to travel to New York. What is it that I'm missing?"

"Not much," said Adelman. "The word 'simple' in the SMTP acronym means just that," he explained. "The messages that the SMTP can handle are grammatically and structurally simple. The SMTP system, by means of the CD installed in my computer, allowed Kory to tell us that Rebecca would be coming, and exactly when and where she would arrive, but nothing beyond that. Just the barest facts of her itinerary.

"Think for a moment," he continued, "about trying to decipher the subtleties of any 'special messages' Rebecca may receive, going forward, with that kind of limitation on the complexity of the transmissions. As we've said, we think our secure lines are probably not, and we *know* that the SMTP can't handle complex messages. It just doesn't have that kind of capacity as yet.

"Rebecca realized," Adelman concluded, "that she would eventually need to be face-to-face with us. And, so did we, after we digested all this. And sooner seemed better than later."

Marie nodded and turned her head toward Rebecca, seated next to her.

Bright smiles from both.

By noon, the group had completed its study of the document. The 72 pages had been written and then photocopied in both languages, and in facing-page format: Russian on each left-hand page, and the corresponding English on each right-hand page. The Russian-language expert had spent nearly all his time confirming or challenging the accuracy of the translation, Russian-to-English.

He was confident that the original document had been written in Russian, and that the English text was a translation by an embassy employee. The expert had made numerous changes in the employee's translation, though none of the changes was substantive, each change designed only to enhance the accuracy and readability of the English text.

Minutes after noon, the group declared a 45-minute break during which most members visited the kitchen, just down the hall from the conference room, and individually put something together for a midday snack. When they reassembled after the break, they found that the Russian-language expert had been dismissed, with effusive thanks, by Adelman, anxious to allow the still-unnamed gentleman to observe properly the remaining hours of Shabbat.

With the group reassembled in the conference room, Belton —aware of his own limitations and quirks as an oral communicator —invited Adelman to provide the overview and summary. He began immediately, speaking in his brisk, precise, Hebrew-accented English.

"I should mention first," he said, looking at McGriff, "that your Jeep will remain in the Bronkowskis' garage indefinitely. As soon as we became convinced that the secure line was no longer reliable, we messaged the Bronkowskis by bicycle courier that their evacuation plan should be effected immediately. That's a simple arrangement that calls for them to take their go-bags and move temporarily to one of several NYPD safe houses further out on Long Island. They were to call a taxi right away and leave their own vehicle and the Cherokee in their garage."

McGriff nodded. "Good," he said. "I'd wondered."

Adelman turned to his overview. "Our major *source* conclusion regarding this document," he began, "is that the 'RY Proposal' is not an official government plan. This proposal has not been produced by KGB officialdom, nor by government officials at any of the higher levels within the Soviet regime. This is, to that extent, a rogue document.

"That is not the same, however, as saying that it has not been *endorsed* at high levels throughout the Soviet government and its intelligence community."

Belton caught Adelman's eye.

"Sid?" he said.

"Yeah," said Belton. "I gotta think, though, that th' top people mighta *created* a little group t' put this plan together … ya know … t' do th' dirty work fer 'em. Th' thing might be just a cover fer all th' higher-ups that wanna protect their backsides in case th' plan goes belly up.

"But Jaakov's exactly right. This thing's got none a' th' earmarks of Soviet official stuff. This is too loose. Informal. Messy."

Heads nodded.

Adelman continued. "As for the *content* of this plan, the document obviously contains a biblical section. I'd like to defer either to Dr. Chapel or Father McGriff, as the two among us with Christian academic backgrounds. May I ask one of you please to begin for us?"

McGriff nodded in the direction of Dr. Chapel. "Dr. Chapel?"

She returned his nod and dropped her eyes downward for a moment, either collecting her thoughts … or praying … or both. After several comfortable seconds, she looked up and began.

"The document is disturbing, but not because it lays out a plan of action. In fact, it's disturbing in part because it does *not* lay out a plan of action. Although its title includes a word translated as 'plan,' this is not a plan. It's a mix of three elements, none of them clearly tied in to the other two.

"The first section is the kind of thing only an auditor might decipher. It's about money, of course, but it's coded so that, I should think, only an 'insider' could say what these money sources are and what they mean."

She looked toward her husband.

"Yeah," said Belton, "it's gobbledygook. Money gobbledygook. It's a lotta money, but I'm thinkin' that it's a bunch a' money trails that, five'll getcha ten, all lead t' th' Russian Mafia. Ya know?

"Th' arms trade. Th' drug trade. Th' child prostitution market. You name it. If it's against th' law, and if it makes a lotta money, it's prob'ly in here somewhere, an' it's prob'ly gonna feed somethin' we're gonna hafta deal with."

"Jaakov," said Dr. Chapel after a moment, "I see that the money figures on the left-hand pages are given in rubles, whereas we see dollar figures on the right-hand pages. Do you think our translator has confirmed these dollar figures?"

"Yes, Eleanor. He used an up-to-the-moment multiplier to confirm the right-hand page figures. We've got accuracy in numerical translation."

"Are there any suggestions, then," continued Dr. Chapel, glancing around the table, "regarding how these enormous sums of money connect to anything else in this document? Or to anything at all?"

Silence.

She nodded and continued. "The second section of the plan consists entirely of New Testament verses. I have struggled to understand the sequencing of the verses, with no success. And I've struggled as well to identify the translation, but I can't. Father McGriff?"

He shook his head. "My guess is that these verses have been translated from their original languages into contemporary Russian, and that the right-hand pages show someone's translation of *that* translation into English. And, of course, our Russian translator would have made further emendations, as he saw fit."

More silence.

"So," asked Marie helplessly, "what is this then?"

"Well," said McGriff, "other than a mysterious arrangement of New Testament verses into page after page of Russian and then English translation … we don't seem to have any idea, Marie."

Yet more silence.

Finally, Belton, frustrated and impatient. "Y' mean we got nothin' we can explain about either these dollar figures or these Bible verses? I can see how we can't get much from all this money stuff, but how's it possible th' wizards in this room can't figure out what these Bible passages mean? Huh? How's that even *possible?*"

"Well, dear," said his wife quietly, "these are Bible *passages,* you understand. These are collections of verses in no recognizable order, and the translation itself, first into Russian and then into English, makes it even less intelligible.

"But we're not giving up, Sidney," she added. "We're just going to need more time with the whole document, I think."

Still more silence.

"We do recognize this last section, of course," said Rebecca suddenly.

"Well, yes," said Dr. Chapel. "That does need noting, doesn't it? This is the United States Declaration of Independence —or parts thereof —but it just starts suddenly, immediately after one of the New Testament verses, without an introduction or break in the manuscript of any kind. It just begins … just materializes … as if it were part of the New Testament … as if it were an extension of the Bible itself."

Rebecca nodded, smiling. "Yes," she said, "and the phrases are intimately familiar to many of us who are not Americans: 'We hold these truths to be self-evident, that all men are created equal, that they are endowed by their Creator with certain unalienable rights, that among these are Life, Liberty and the pursuit of Happiness.'"

Rebecca quoted the passage without reference to the document.

"That sentence has always *sounded* rather scriptural to me," she added. "I would love to have chatted with Mr. Jefferson about his document.

"But," she added quickly, "I don't want to distract us. Recognizing the scriptural source of this middle section, and recognizing the Declaration of Independence as comprising the final section, doesn't get us closer to the mystery, does it?"

Discussion continued by the group for some time with little progress other than to acknowledge that, since extraction of the document from a wall safe at the Soviet Embassy was driven by one of Rebecca's "special messages," and since the title of the plan was "RY Proposal," further scrutiny of the document would be an obligation, not a choice. Participants were all prepared to maintain the assumption that "RY" referenced Rebekka Yahalomin, despite the fact that nothing in the document made mention of the group. Further, all were prepared to admit that they saw no connection among the three sections, any one section to any other section, and no connection of anything in the document to Rebekka Yahalomin.

The session began to drag.

Finally, Dr. Chapel slapped the table with both hands and stood up, pushing her chair back so quickly that it nearly toppled. "We're sleepwalking through this, people," she said, her high-pitched voice strong with accusation. "Where does it say we're allowed to bring anything less than our best to these periodic incursions of 'divine messaging' into our midst?

"Let's each go to our sleeping rooms on the fifth floor and pray, think, rest … whatever recovery approach seems right to each. As for me, after I do all three of those things, I'm going to go to the kitchen at six this evening and start making sandwiches. Anyone who wants to help, meet me there and then. We can have something to eat and begin afresh here in the conference room at seven. Yes?"

"Well," said Rebecca immediately, "I think best while in motion, Dr. Chapel. I understand we have a gym on the fourth floor? I'll take my praying and thinking respite there, I think."

Thus, the afternoon passed with each of the six isolated from the others, employing her or his own approach to prayer, rest, recovery, and problem solving. And when the six reassembled in the conference room, having grazed their way through the evening meal either standing in the small kitchen or sitting in the lounge area that extended off to one side of the conference room, a new energy was indeed present. This, despite the fact that, for Rebecca, her "body time" was midnight.

Belton, acting as informal host in his and Adelman's multi-purpose building, called the session to order in his inimitable fashion. "Awright, everybody," he said as he took his chair at the head of the long table, "who's got th' first genius thought fer us? Hmm?"

Seeing smiles but hearing no actual words, he turned his face to his wife. "Eleanor," he said, "I *know* you've got a genius thought. Gimme one or two of 'em. Hmm? Whatcha got?"

"Sidney," she said, rolling her blue-green eyes theatrically, "you're like a four-year-old child chairing a meeting of grown-ups. Where on *earth* is your sense of decorum?"

He cackled delightedly. "So *that's* why y' married me, huh? My decorum? C'mon, Eleanor," he persisted. "Let's hear it. I know ya got somethin'."

"In fact, dear," she responded sweetly, "I believe I do."

She looked down at her copy of the document. "After laboring over this middle section of the proposal for another hour or so this afternoon after my nap," she began, "it came to me out of the blue, so to say. I read and reread these assorted Bible verses, and then reread them yet again, until the thing suddenly called out to me.

"Finally … clarity. These verses," she said with a certainty borne of decades of study and analysis of scripture and related texts, "comprise excerpts from what is commonly called the Jefferson Bible. Once I was reasonably sure, I went downstairs, to the street, and used the pay phone at the corner to talk with our friend at the downtown library, and she and I read and compared a number of passages from her copy of that book.

"What we have is near-verbatim, once you allow for peculiarities in someone's translation, first, into Russian, and then, someone else's translation back into English, and then, our own expert's additional touches early this morning. There is no doubt. These are whole-cloth excerpts from the Jefferson Bible."

She looked triumphantly at her husband.

He beamed with pride.

She continued. "Thomas Jefferson's actual choice of title," she explained, "was fulsome, in the style of the times: *The Life and Morals of Jesus of Nazareth extracted textually from the Gospels in Greek, Latin, French and English.*

"His original 'Bible' consisted of verses actually cut with scissors and pasted with glue into columns in parallel. The verses were re-ordered to conform to an overall sequencing that Jefferson thought plausible. While the translations are defensible for the most part, you must understand that he excluded anything clearly supernatural from his new version of scripture.

"Nothing overtly miraculous, in other words, appears in his reconstructed representation of the Four Gospels."

After a moment, McGriff asked, "You say nothing *overtly* miraculous, Dr. Chapel. Anything *implicitly* miraculous?"

"Oh, yes, lots," she replied. "For example, the Lord's Prayer, known in the Roman Catholic tradition as the Our Father, is here. And that prayer, of course, includes Jesus's words, 'Thy Kingdom come. Thy will be done, as in heaven, so in earth,' which obviously comprises a reference to God, the Father, acting supernaturally to bring about His kingdom here on earth.

"And there are the references to the day of judgment, with 'the Son of Man' coming in judgment with 'all the holy angels.' Another thoroughly supernatural reference, then, even though it's not presented with emphasis.

"But the most dramatic miraculous actions of Jesus Himself, such as His healing of the woman who had hemorrhaged continually for years and, minutes later, bringing back to life the 12-year-old child … these are carefully excised.

"As are, of course, the accounts of Christ's own resurrection, the central event in all history from a classical Christian viewpoint."

She paused while the group worked to absorb her account of the document's middle section. At length, she took up her narrative again. "Like many … certainly not all … of this country's founders," Dr. Chapel continued, "Mr. Jefferson was not 'Christian' in the sense in which you and I use that term. He was by most standards and definitions a deist, a believer in a God who created the universe and then stood back from His work, allowing it to move under its own steam. Often the 'watchmaker' metaphor is used to approximate the deist idea.

"In that kind of system, Jesus of Nazareth is the world's foremost teacher and exemplar, but since from Jefferson's perspective Jesus was operating in a deistic universe, Jesus could not, as I've suggested, work anything that could be termed supernatural, and could not therefore experience resurrection from the dead.

"And this is why, as I said, Mr. Jefferson could not be termed 'Christian' at all, from our point of view."

McGriff could not contain himself. "Brilliant, Dr. Chapel!" he cried. "Absolutely *brilliant!*"

Belton turned his face to McGriff and scowled playfully. "Ya gotta tone it down there, Father," he said with exaggerated severity. "She's hard enough t' live with already … know what I mean? Hmm?"

Smiles, then silence once more.

"Dr. Chapel," said Rebecca quietly after some moments, "does your uncovering the source of this middle section of the document lead you to understand how the three sections are meant to go together, or what any of this may mean for us?"

"No, Rebecca," she replied simply. "It does not."

More thoughtful quiet.

After a pause of perhaps another full minute, the group heard a small noise — something like a soft moan —from Rebecca.

Faces turned to her.

Rebecca's gray eyes were closed, her head down, presumably in prayer. She looked up to find everyone looking questioningly at her, and she smiled. She sat up straighter in her chair and took a deep breath before speaking.

"Dr. Chapel's analysis has led me to a small epiphany," she said softly. "Actually, two of them … or, I suppose … one, but paired with another. I'd like to lay these two realizations before you … for everyone's consideration.

"May I, Detective?"

This last was directed to Belton, the informal host.

"Well, I gotta tell ya, ma'am," said Belton, "I'd like t' hear a couple epiphanies."

He gestured disgustedly at the document copies that lay strewn around the conference table. "We been starin' at this thing since 4 a.m. an' we still got nothin'," he added, glancing uncomfortably at his wife. "No offense, Eleanor."

"Of course not, dear," she said, smiling. "You knew all along this was the Jefferson Bible."

Belton erupted again in his cackling laughter, but was cut short by Adelman, who good-naturedly but forcefully pointed out to his partner that Rebecca was waiting to offer her 'realizations,' which would presumably be followed by a plan of action, something badly needed at this point.

"Yeah," said Belton. "Right. Sorry. Go on, Rebecca," he said.

Still smiling at the couple's irrepressible banter, Rebecca began. "Over the years," she said, "our varied experiences with 'special messages' —dreams, visions —have repeatedly centered on fraudulent or corrupted documents. There was the Creed of St. David, for example. There was the Matheson Mental Health Curriculum for Children, for another."

Belton, who had lived through both, nodded in quick recollection.

"Having listened to Dr. Chapel's observations just now," continued Rebecca, "I sense that this is yet another campaign of that kind. Surely it is. It *must* be.

"We have in our hands Jefferson's scriptural potpourri, something we traditional Christians must label honestly for what it is: his superficially appealing, and yet destructive, *corruption* of the Four Gospels."

She shook her head is dismay. "The *effrontery* of it!" she said with a vehemence that startled and frightened Penelope, dozing in Marie's lap in the chair next to Rebecca's. Marie then lifted the small calico onto the table, where she curled up immediately, almost exactly where she'd been placed, and resumed her post-dinner nap.

Rebecca paused during this brief transaction, murmuring, "Sorry, dears," in the direction of Penelope and Marie. Then, seeing the pet settle, she continued. "Seamlessly following this array of Bible verses," she said, gesturing *seamlessly* with a smooth sweep of one hand, "we have Jefferson's true masterpiece, the Declaration of Independence. We see that those two sections of this document follow an opening section which is a maze of numbers, a maze that suddenly suggests itself to me as the financial ingredients in a stupendous war chest designed to underwrite a publication-and-distribution scheme, much like our former adversaries' projects."

She scanned the room questioningly.

"How then is this 'RY Proposal' *not* laying the groundwork for the printing and worldwide distribution of this Jeffersonian corruption, a corruption that would stand an excellent chance to play favorably with an American populace forever ready to think reverentially, and appropriately so, of the Founding Fathers?"

Rebecca again looked around the table at the faces that were each deep in concentration.

"If we were to walk into any hotel room here in New York or almost anywhere else in this country and in numerous other countries, as well," said Rebecca thoughtfully, "we would find a copy of the King James Bible in a drawer next to the bed, courtesy of the Gideons. Now, imagine something similar, yet on an even larger and more grandiose scale, with literally millions of copies, all featuring an attractively bound volume that opens with the words of promise in the Declaration —'We hold these truths to be self-evident …' —followed by the Jefferson Bible."

Extended silence. Concentration. Furrowed brows.

"My goodness," Dr. Chapel said in wonderment, "the title itself —the title given by its publishers, as distinct from the lengthy title Mr. Jefferson chose — invites a reader's naïve acceptance of the idea that this is indeed *the Bible*, rather than one deist's revisionist distortion of scripture into a 'life and morals' compilation."

More thoughtful silence.

Then Marie. "Rebecca," she said tentatively and a little apologetically, "I just can't seem to pull this together in my mind. I'm so sorry.

"But this document," she continued, "was secreted in the office safe of Mr. Ivanovich at the Soviet Embassy. It has sufficient importance that you were sent one of your *staggering*, to me, 'divine intrusions,' the substance of which allowed me to extricate the document and then photograph every page.

"I can't understand why the Soviet government or its intelligence agency would care, one way or the other, about any of this. The original embassy rumor that led me to seek my pastor's counsel at our church" —here she glanced toward McGriff —"was that the KGB had developed an interest in Rebekka Yahalomin.

"*Why* is this of interest to the KGB?"

Rebecca nodded, and responded without hesitation. "Well done *you*," she said. "Marie, you've just provided the perfect segue to my second epiphany —as I mentioned, *two* 'realizations' materialized in my mind as Dr. Chapel spoke her revelation about this middle section —and here is the second.

"I think it entirely possible," continued Rebecca, speaking louder and more rapidly now, "that this document is *not* actually of interest to the KGB for its own sake. I think it is quite likely that this is nothing but misdirection on their part.

"Suppose they —the proposal's authors, whoever they may turn out to be — simply want us to focus *here*, on the Jeffersonian corruption aspect of the proposal, while their *primary* objective is elsewhere."

Rebecca looked down, organizing her thoughts, then continued. "Long before we were given our Hebrew name, Rebekka Yahalomin, by some creative person at Mossad" —here she smiled at Adelman —"we were called upon repeatedly, via the 'special messages,' to intercept publication and distribution of documents designed explicitly to weaken or destroy traditional Christianity.

"Now … *these* adversaries," Rebecca continued, "those who work within the Soviet Union's government and military, likely place little credence in the divine origins of our messages, as is the case, surely, with some of the individuals in our own allied intelligence agencies.

"But, like those skeptical allies, they know that *something* gives Rebekka Yahalomin access to high-impact plans and actions before anyone else knows anything about them. They know that *something* allows us to find out things that others can't. They may shrug their shoulders at the 'something,' but they see the results.

"And so … they want us stopped, and they know that creation of a plan like this … this 'RY Proposal' … and making sure it gets into our hands … is the surest way to activate Rebekka Yahalomin and bring us into the open."

"Rebecca!" said Marie quickly, "are you suggesting that the proposal's authors *expected* us to photograph the document … to extract it from Mr. Ivanovich's wall safe … to do exactly what we have done … and to have this kind of conversation about it?"

Rebecca, smiling at Marie's quick mind, nodded in assent. "Yes," she said simply.

"And does that mean also," continued Marie, "that that knife against my ribs on the city bus was part of an elaborate act? That my assailant was simply playing a part? That he had no intention of using that knife on me? That these people *expected* Jack to be there to intervene?"

"They expected *someone* to be there to intervene … possibly they expected *me* to be there on that bus," replied Rebecca.

"They *wanted* us to have this document, Marie, but they wanted us to be convinced otherwise. Thus, the document was sequestered in that wall safe. Thus, they feigned the attack on the city bus.

"They *wanted* us to see that publication and distribution of a document like this would call for our forceful intervention. Our group has reacted in all the ways our adversaries might have hoped and expected, right from the start."

Rebecca smiled and looked toward McGriff.

"That does not mean," she added, "that Father McGriff's actions on the city bus were any less heroic than we have assumed. He fully expected that knife to be driven into your ribs, Marie, just as you did.

"And," she added, "he might have been right. But I have begun to doubt it."

She turned her eyes inquiringly toward Dr. Chapel. "Dr. Chapel?" she said.

Dr. Chapel stood suddenly, pulled herself up to her full 4 feet and 10 inches of graying beauty, circled her chair, and, standing, faced Rebecca, who, though seated, was nearly eye-to-eye with the diminutive scholar.

"Suppose," said Dr. Chapel, excitement lighting her face, "that this 'RY Proposal' is, insofar as the Soviet government and intelligence agency are concerned, exactly the red herring you just suggested, Rebecca, a means to lure you away from the protections afforded you in England. Suppose even the original car chase in London was planned by this document's authors at the Soviet Embassy in D.C., then staged in London merely to push Rebekka Yahalomin into action.

"Suppose that even the incursion into your home, Marie, was for no purpose other than to add to the confusion … to add to the urgency of drawing Rebecca out … to pull her away from the Rebekka Yahalomin fortress in England.

"Suppose all this was to make clear that Rebecca would need to get face-to-face with Rebekka Yahalomin's U.S. contingent —Sidney, Jaakov, me, and now Marie and Jack, too —and thus ready to give up-to-the-minute reports and disclosures the instant those were given her … given her by whatever means, supernatural or other."

"But Dr. Chapel," protested Marie quickly, "does that not mean they are pulling the ceiling down on their own heads? If they expect Rebecca to be directly involved, does that not mean they are asking to be defeated?"

"No," replied Dr. Chapel immediately, "not at all. Over the years, Marie," continued Dr. Chapel, "almost everyone involved with Rebecca, including Rebecca herself, has been wounded, and some of the wounding could easily have been fatal. Matt Clark's left arm and shoulder will never be functional again, and, except for Rebecca's heroism, he would have died that same night on the Welsh coast. Jaakov was once absolutely riddled with automatic weapons projectiles, and then, while recovering in hospital, he was attacked again, but saved at the last instant by Sidney's intervention.

"In other words, Marie," Dr. Chapel concluded, "when God summons us to step into these conflicts, He absolutely does *not* guarantee our safety. Rebecca may not survive this. Nor may I. Nor may you. Nor may any of us.

"Our adversaries are confident that pulling Rebecca into their physical orbit will put them in position to capture, drug, torture, and kill her at their leisure. The rest of us, too. They do not fear Rebekka Yahalomin."

She paused and looked toward the head of the table, at her husband, furiously scribbling on his note pad, his lifelong habit as one of the world's best-known and most respected law enforcement figures. He looked up at her.

"Well, Eleanor," said Belton after a moment, "it worked, huh?"

"What worked?"

"Well … Rebecca's here … right here. So, the Soviet bigwigs' plan worked. The Soviet bigwigs got her here. Trouble is, fer these dirtbags, she's not gonna go back 'til she's whipped 'em like scrambled eggs. We'll see how these lowlifes like what they've brought down on their thick skulls. They're gonna be wishin' they'd had some *other* kind a' bright idea … know what I mean? Hmm?"

In the now-comfortable silence that followed, Marie leaned forward, elbows on the table, almost touching the still-sleeping Penelope. She turned to Rebecca.

"Rebecca," she said, smiling slightly at the thought, "Mr. Belton is suggesting that you're seen by the Soviet Union's 'bigwigs' as a sort of *strategic weapon* that could be used against them. Do you *feel* like a strategic weapon, Rebecca?"

Rebecca smiled. "Sometimes … I find myself feeling like a strategic *instrument,* Marie. Yes."

CHAPTER SEVEN

JUST AFTER 9 P.M., INDIVIDUALS BEGAN TO TRICKLE OUT OF THE conference room in ones and twos, tired, but nevertheless gratified at the long day's progress. Good-nights were said by all.

But a mere 90 minutes later, five of the six sleepily emerged at almost the same moment from their respective sleeping rooms, spilling into the fifth-floor common area. Looks of puzzlement were exchanged.

"What *is* that sound?" inquired Marie of anyone who might offer an answer.

"It sounds like somebody throwin' baseballs against th' gym wall down on th' fourth floor," suggested Belton.

They listened again to the strange, repetitive noise from under their feet.

"Where is Rebecca?" asked Dr. Chapel.

After a moment, Marie said, "I'll just peek in her room."

She looked in, then closed Rebecca's sleeping-room door. She turned to the group and shook her head. "Her bed is still made up. She hasn't been to bed at all."

Without further discussion, they moved as one toward the elevator. They descended in complete and extremely uncomfortable silence.

Suddenly Dr. Chapel exclaimed, "Sidney Belton! You brought your *gun?*"

"'Course I did, Eleanor. Ya think I'm gonna whip some dirtbag with my cane? Hmm? That what ya think?"

The elevator ground to its ponderous stop on the fourth floor. After what seemed an eternity, the doors finally opened. Since the elevator opened directly into the gym, they saw immediately the source of the unsettling noises.

Rebecca stood 25 feet from the wall to the elevator's left, and, just as the door opened, her colleagues saw her stride forward with her left leg and, in a powerful underhand throwing motion that engaged her right shoulder, arm, wrist, and hand, she released a Barringtons Swords 12-inch competition-grade throwing knife at a sheaf of newspapers tacked to the south wall. The terrifying blade flew like an arrow —a no-spin throw of enormous technical difficulty — and penetrated the 5-inch sheaf as if it were gelatin, thudding into the wooden wall —the wall fronting Washington Square North —with a sound like a small explosion.

The group stood transfixed, astonished at the grace, fluidity, power, and lethality of what they had just witnessed.

Nothing was said.

Rebecca was clad in her standard all-white tennis garb: tennis shoes, tennis skirt, sleeveless monogrammed tee-shirt, and pony tail to control her long tresses. She studied the placement of her throw carefully before turning to face the group.

"I'm so sorry," she said. "I know this noise is terrible. I had thought the newspapers would muffle the sound of each impact, but I'm wrong. Just give me another 10 minutes, if you would. My brother has taught me never to go more than 48 hours without practice, or my skill level will fall.

"Can you forgive me, everyone?"

The group seemed collectively so stunned by what they had just witnessed that no response was forthcoming until, after a full ten seconds of silence, Marie finally ventured, in a very small voice, "Can we watch?"

Four hours later, in the small hours of that Sunday morning, Rebecca Manguson Clark was, yet again, visited in her sleep by the Source. When the vision at length departed, she struggled from her bed, perspiration-soaked, as always. She slipped from her room and padded barefoot across the fifth floor's common area, then rapped softly on the door of the sleeping room occupied by Dr. Chapel and Belton.

In just seconds the door opened and Rebecca heard a whispered, "Did you dream, dear? Yes? Come in and tell us."

Hours later, Father McGriff led a worship service for the three women and three men assembled around the sixth-floor conference table. The worshippers included Adelman, who observed mildly, "Well, I missed my Sabbath service yesterday, so I'll just be part of yours, if no one objects."

Five broad smiles welcomed him.

Following worship, the hours fled past on this working Sunday. First, Rebecca reported her "special message" to the group, verified in detail by the Chapel-Beltons, who had listened to her summary immediately after it had been sent her. Second, plans were put in place for the next several days.

Those plans included a Sunday night AMTRAK trip from Manhattan's Penn Station to D.C.'s Union Station for Rebecca, Marie, McGriff, and Adelman, while the Chapel-Beltons remained at the New York City detective agency's office to communicate with the Lodge in England by means of the SMTP CD in Adelman's desktop computer —technology which had been mastered quickly by Dr. Chapel —and to care for Penelope, something Eleanor had also quickly and happily mastered. Movement of the four from the detective agency to Penn Station would be accomplished, in male-female pairs, by after-dark movement through the building's back alleyway that connected to Washington Mews, the tiny street that ran parallel to Washington Square North, one block away. Taxis would transport each pair to the train station.

Both men would be armed with 9mm pistols carried in shoulder holsters, but Marie had as yet only minimal training in use of weaponry, and carried no weapon of any kind. Rebecca was never armed in the way most others chose to be, but she was indeed armed.

Her armament was carried in three draw-string pouches, each containing a set of three Barringtons Swords 12-inch throwing knives. While six of the throwing knives were emplaced deep inside the small gym bag that she carried easily by its shoulder strap, one three-knife set was lodged in the bag's quick-open side pocket. Thus armed, she was well prepared to intervene in the way she was most able and willing to engage physically: to disarm and wound an assailant from moderate distance.

Messaging between New York and Washington would be carried out by unavoidably cumbersome arrangements to be set up between Belton's long-time NYPD precinct, located near the detective agency's building, and a precinct office near Union Station in D.C., whose captain was a Belton protégé and eager always to assist his mentor whenever he could.

The foursome would book two rooms —one for the women and one for the men —in one of the older, stately hotels within walking distance of the Mall, near the Museum of Natural History. They would not return to the CIA safe house across the Potomac in Virginia, nor contact that agency at any time.

They planned to refresh their wardrobes from the hotel lobby's clothing stores on Monday morning. With a new suit and shoes paid for by the Belton and Adelman Detective Agency, Marie would report to work at the Soviet Embassy, as scheduled, at 1 p.m. that afternoon.

The group would travel only by taxi.

At the completion of her embassy responsibilities on Monday late afternoon, Marie would reenact her Friday office incursion in detail, using the same Minnie Mouse compact and its enclosed implement, along with her coin-purse document camera. The difference would be that this clandestine office penetration would take place directly across the hallway from 2044. Rebecca's Saturday night dream had identified office number 2045 as the new target, along with the wall safe not of the administrator, but of the assistant, Tatyana Kuznetsova, the woman with whom Marie had exchanged pleasantries Friday evening in that same hallway.

According to Rebecca's reading of her vision, the document to be photographed Monday was thin —one or two pages —and, thus, presumably, not truly a document but merely a list. The group assumed that the list would disclose the identities of those involved with leadership of the rogue group, and, perhaps as well, others who were less directly involved or yet to be approached. They hoped that the group's primary leader or leaders would be indicated, but declined to speculate.

If the pages indeed provided the identities of key adversaries, then, they knew, next steps could conceivably require the physical capture of one or more of them, followed by interrogation, and, depending upon the outcome of the capture-to-interrogate process, the eventual involvement of the U.S. Federal Witness Protection Program to provide a permanent safe haven for any rogue group member who might choose to give assistance. Belton's legendary record in law enforcement had often made such inter-agency arrangements readily workable.

It was also assumed by the group that, at some point, assistance would be requested from one or more of the three still-active Mossad agents —two in D.C. and the other in New York —whom Adelman had said he could call upon informally for help. That sort of borrowed muscle and experience would almost certainly be required should there be a need for any sort of capture-to-interrogate activity.

By mid-afternoon on Sunday, all six participants in New York City's Rebekka Yahalomin group were once more in the fourth-floor gym, engaged in whatever fitness regimen each had previously incorporated into her or his life. The treadmills and the recumbent exercise bikes received the most use, though Belton's battered body and consequent physical limitations permitted him use only of the weight machine, speed bag, and heavy bag.

Belton attacked each in sequence with his usual enthusiasm.

By late afternoon, only Rebecca, Marie, and McGriff remained, the latter determined to launch his self-styled weight-loss program aggressively. And once Rebecca had completed 20 minutes of knife-throwing practice under these less-populated conditions —she, firing her knives into the south-facing wall while her two companions exercised against the north —she saw immediately that the other two were lingering, hoping for time alone.

Rebecca excused herself forthwith.

As the gym door —actually, the elevator door —closed, McGriff, just finishing 30 minutes on the heavy bag following 60 minutes on one of the recumbents, turned his face toward Marie, who was well into her second 20-minute treadmill session, the two sessions having been interrupted by an hour of yoga. She felt his gaze and quickly turned her face toward his.

Without speaking, each stopped, cooled down, began to towel off, and moved toward the worn, two-person sofa that occupied one corner of the gym. It was the only piece of furniture the detectives had placed in the room, and received little use under normal circumstances. Standing together at the sofa, they tried to complete their efforts to dry the sweaty dampness from their bodies, Marie focusing on her hair and neck, and McGriff on his face, neck and forearms.

They each wore togs selected by the Bronkowskis two days earlier. For Marie, that included a pair of fitted, dark-blue yoga pants and a light blue *I Love New York* tee-shirt. McGriff wore loose gray sweatpants and an absurdly stylish white-and-black, pin-striped, New York Yankees sweatshirt, its sleeves rolled up above the elbow.

She took a seat on the right-hand cushion and pulled her legs up and under her, turning toward him from the waist, the towel draped around her neck. He sat beside her, leaning forward with his elbows resting on his knees.

After a moment, McGriff turned his face toward her. They smiled at each other bashfully and looked away. Resolved to plunge in somehow, he sat back and extended his right hand toward her. She took his hand in her left.

He sighed deeply. "I really don't know how to do this, Marie," he began.

"How to do what?" she said, searching his face with her naturally sad brown eyes, knowing what he meant but wanting to hear him say it.

"Start a relationship with a woman," he replied. "I don't know how to start a relationship with a woman."

He looked away, but continued. "In high school," he said, "I was bigger than nearly everybody, and good only at football and the debate team and studying. If there was a girl I liked, she was always 'taken' already by some guy who knew what he was doing. College was the same. Seminary was sort of the same, except many of the women were married."

"And there was no football or debate team," she added helpfully.

"Well," he said smiling, "no football, certainly, but lots of debating … *lots* of debating, just not in a team format."

He paused, thoughtful, still cradling her small left hand in his large and muscular right, before continuing. "I've always had friends who were girls — women — but not girl*friends*.

"And I was okay with that," he added. "I've felt God's hand on my shoulder for a long time, Marie. In college. In seminary. Even training as an Army officer and during my military service as an officer-chaplain. Then, after the Army, assignment to my church —our church —in D.C. God's hand has been right there on my shoulder … always."

"Even in your CIA involvement?" she asked, not unkindly. Simply wanting to know the answer.

"I thought so," he said. "I've become less sure of that. I'm going to need you to help me think about that, once we've gotten through this."

He left the sentence unfinished.

She nodded, and he continued.

"But," he said, "as you and I have gotten to know each other through two years of counseling sessions, I've gradually found, for the first time, that I truly *wanted* a relationship with a woman. A particular woman. And not just a date or two. Something ongoing. Something with depth."

She laughed. "You want a *girlfriend*, Jack McGriff?" she said.

He turned away, embarrassed.

She saw, and squeezed his hand. "Oh, I'm sorry. I didn't mean to be flippant, Jack. Really. I'm sorry."

He was silent still, his face averted, and she became fearful that her *faux pas* was growing in importance.

"Jack? Please … I'm sorry."

He turned back to her. "No," he said, "not a girlfriend, Marie. That sounds too high school.

"I want to … *invest* in a relationship with you. I want to skip from the boyfriend-girlfriend thing that kids do, Marie, all the way to *investment* in a man-woman relationship. The kind that has a chance for … permanence."

He looked away again. He shook his head.

There. I've said it. I'm pathetic.

The gym was quiet except for the soft hum and hiss of the building's air conditioning system. He realized he had begun to hold his breath.

And he felt her stirring, and feared she was preparing to leave.

Suddenly he felt her damp hair on the side of his face. He turned toward her and their lips met immediately.

The Sunday evening AMTRAK to Washington had gone smoothly. For once, each member of the foursome experienced an adequate night's sleep. They had awakened, breakfasted in their hotel rooms, and shopped quickly and efficiently at one of the hotel's clothing stores.

An hour later, they assembled, looking fresh, in the men's hotel room for their final briefing prior to Marie's starting to dress for her afternoon's work at the embassy. She had already scheduled her taxi for a 12:30 pick-up.

Adelman began the meeting by summarizing the steps he foresaw for Marie that afternoon and evening, including the plan for McGriff and himself to be stationed outside the building at the time she was expected to exit. Both would be armed, as always, in anticipation of a repeat of Friday evening's attempted interception —whether it was staged or real —by the rogue group. This time, Marie would not be using a city bus. The men would have a taxi waiting, ready to transport the three of them back to the hotel.

Rebecca would remain at the hotel throughout, her whereabouts to remain unknown to the adversary for as long as possible.

As Adelman completed his overview of the expected course of that afternoon and evening's events, he saw Rebecca shake her head almost imperceptibly. "Rebecca?" he said.

She did not reply immediately. The group waited courteously.

"I do not think we are giving our adversaries enough credit," she began.

"I do think that you, Marie, will be safe during working hours inside the embassy, since nothing has happened to make hostile action against you *today* any more acceptable in the eyes of most embassy employees than on *Friday*. It may well be, in fact, that the rogue group's members do not expect to see you at the embassy today at all … or ever … after Friday's scare.

"And since we have carefully avoided further communication with our CIA liaison unit, the double agent —the mole —whom we suspect to be operating from within that unit cannot know anything about your whereabouts or about our plans.

"But I do *not* think that we should proceed on the assumption that the rogue group is not preparing for exactly the kind of office penetration that we have in mind for this afternoon and evening. We cannot afford that assumption.

"I think we must assume," she continued, "that the security arrangements at your exit checkpoint will be strengthened, Marie. If even a single member of the rogue group is a security guard on one of the higher-security floors —and I would expect this group to recruit several of those guards —I should think that nothing would prevent that individual from stationing himself at the exit point for your floor, Marie.

"He could simply explain that such-and-such management team executive asked him to help. He could even offer to *relieve* one of his security-guard colleagues, suggesting there would be no need for them both to be late getting home.

"Easily done."

They fell silent, each considering Rebecca's observations.

Finally, McGriff spoke. "What do you suggest, Rebecca?" he asked.

After another moment, she replied.

"I suggest that I go downstairs and purchase an inexpensive coin purse for Marie's use today. I suggest that she leave the faux coin purse here with us, so that she has no document camera with her at all.

"She will need the Minnie Mouse, of course, in order to get into the assistant's wall safe, but once she has extricated the list —surely we are right that this tiny document is nothing more than a list of names —she must memorize as many of the names as she can in, let's say, 15 minutes. Then she must, I think, return the list to the safe, lock the safe, walk to the ladies' room to rid herself of the implement —the tiny stethoscope —and move to the checkpoint with nothing in her handbag other than a plain coin purse, a compact with nothing enclosed that would be viewed as incriminating, her flashlight, her pepper spray … just the things the guards expect to see.

"While still in the ladies room," concluded Rebecca, "she should wrap the stethoscope in wet paper towels, along with her rubber gloves, and push them well down into one of the waste bins."

Rebecca looked at Marie. "And Marie," she added, "I think our adversaries might also station a female guard at the checkpoint. I think she may take you into a private room and pat you down rather thoroughly."

She stopped and looked at Adelman. "Jaakov?" she said.

He nodded his head thoughtfully. "Yes," he said finally. "Yes. I'm afraid so."

Silence.

Suddenly McGriff found himself speaking with a level of anxiety in his voice that he rarely experienced.

"I think you must be right, Rebecca, that Marie will be safe during working hours this afternoon, just as she was on Friday, but …"

"Yes," said Rebecca, interrupting, "but what about the 15 minutes she will spend in Ms. Kuznetsova's office with the list in her hands, fully exposed to anyone who might choose to enter? We know the cleaning crews will not be expected until later, but suppose Ms. Kuznetsova herself decides to return?"

"Or," said McGriff, interrupting, "the amorous couple from Marie's intrusion into 2044, this time choosing 2045, just across the hall?"

"Or," said Rebecca, interrupting, "*any* member of the rogue group who is aware that the list is in Ms. Kuznetsova's wall safe?"

"Stop!" said Marie, interrupting them both. "Just stop. I'm going to do this," she said, looking at McGriff. "I'm going to do what I did Friday, except that I'm going to be memorizing names rather than photographing pages. Rebecca is not sent these visions for trivial reasons," she continued.

"She is sent these visions for reasons that matter. She's been given the image of this thin document in Tatyana's office, and I'm going to get it, read it, and memorize as much as I can. If our opponents *expect* this, then they will be prepared to take my camera at the exit checkpoint, as Rebecca has anticipated, and presumably place me under arrest. But now they will find no camera.

"And, really, that's all there is to it," she concluded, blushing with embarrassment at her own assertiveness.

The group looked at her with surprise. It was the first time any of them had heard her speak with such defiance.

Rebecca and Adelman nodded their heads, small smiles on their faces.

McGriff did not.

He rose from his chair and strode to Marie's, leaning over her and gently touching the side of her face with his fingertips. They looked at each other from close range, not speaking or smiling.

"Marie," he said, his fingertips still on her face, "I get it. I do. But I want you at least to handle this differently. Please."

He stood erect, taking her hand as he did.

"Extract the list," he said. "Close the safe door firmly, without locking it. Walk into the larger office space —the administrator's area —and stand in his coat closet or in his private bathroom or at least behind a curtain. Anywhere that keeps you from being immediately visible, should *any* of those possible intruders open the door. Just hide yourself for the 15 minutes … or however long you take to do the memorization … to reduce the risk.

"When you have memorized all you can, cross into Tatyana's office, replace the list, lock the safe, and get out of there. Please."

He held her hand for several seconds more. Finally, she smiled up at him and said simply, "Yes."

McGriff returned to his chair and sat heavily. A worried expression remained on his face. At length, he looked up, first toward Adelman, then toward Rebecca, inquiring with his eyes.

Rebecca spoke in response. "Yes. Good," she said simply.

After a moment, Rebecca continued with her commentary. "Marie now has only two hours before time for her taxi," said Rebecca.

"While I run down to the lobby to buy a coin purse for her, Jaakov, why don't you give her a crash course in the fast memorization of lists?"

"Right," replied Adelman. He then looked at McGriff. "Jack, you should bring the Epson 20 with you when we pick Marie up from the embassy," he said, "so you can record the names while we're still in the taxi, as soon as Marie begins speaking them."

Seeing the questioning looks from both women, McGriff explained that, as part of his arrangement with the CIA, he had been given a battery-powered computer that was so small and so light that he could fit it into his briefcase. He stood, reached for the briefcase, and extracted the device.

"This is the Epson HX-20," he said. "Developed four or five years ago —late 1970s, early 1980s —in Japan. It's the first, or one of the first, truly portable computers. Weighs almost nothing. This model has been enhanced, especially for my purposes, by the CIA's technology people. The manufacturer licensed the changes."

Rebecca and Marie gazed curiously at the small machine.

"So, Jack," said Marie, eyeing him suspiciously, "you're telling us that, on top of everything else, you're a techno-wizard?"

"No," he replied, smiling at he thought. "But I know how to turn this thing on," he said, laughing. "And I'm a very good typist."

At nearly 6:30 that Monday evening, Marie emerged from the Soviet Embassy. She was quickly joined by McGriff and Adelman, who steered her briskly down the street to their waiting taxi, its air conditioning running at full blast in the sweltering June heat.

The driver was a Sudanese graduate student, by way of the U.K., who doubled as a paid informant for the local police. He had been hand-picked for the evening's work by the police precinct captain, Belton's long-ago protégé. Adelman had already prepared the young man to take a circuitous route around the mall —at least twice —before taking them to the hotel.

The threesome sat on the back seat, Marie between the two men. As soon as they were seated, Adelman reached forward and handed a set of high-grade earplugs to the driver. He, having been prepared for the importance of his not hearing the conversation, immediately worked the earplugs into place.

As the taxi moved off from the curb, McGriff opened the Epson 20 and, in seconds, indicated to Marie his readiness to take dictation. Adelman had prepared her to ascertain, first, as she examined the list in Tatyana Kuznetsova's office, whether the list was simply alphabetical, or whether there appeared to be some sort of hierarchy.

"There were two lists," she began, turning her head to the right where McGriff was poised, his hands on the Epson's keyboard.

"The first one was short. Just six names, but the second was much longer and ran onto the second page. That second list had maybe three dozen names, all in alphabetical order.

"The first list was *not* alphabetical."

She closed her eyes, picturing the list.

"Ready?" she said to McGriff.

"First name, Artur Volkov … second name, Ivan Ivanovich … third, Egor Alexeev … fourth, Pyotr Nikolayev … fifth, Randy Simpson … and last, Mr. Volkov's assistant, Tatyana Kuznetsova."

She paused, while McGriff, lightning-fast on the Epson, tapped out the names and then checked them to make sure his fingers had done what his mind intended. He lifted the Epson to Marie so she could check the names on its small screen.

"Spellings?" he inquired.

"They look right," she said after a moment.

"And the alphabetized list?" asked McGriff, his fingers again on the keyboard.

Marie shook her head.

"No," she said. "When I realized that the first list was —it seemed to me — rank-ordered, with Tatyana listed last and with her administrator, Artur Volkov, listed first, I made the decision to memorize that list perfectly and to ignore the second."

She turned her head to the left to address Adelman. "I was too frightened to think about that second list, Jaakov," she said.

"The first list screamed out to me that these were the leaders, and that the names on the long second list were … well … not part of the inner circle. Maybe not part of anything at all. Maybe just some people who might be asked for assistance without even knowing the purpose of their assistance.

"I'm sorry, Jaakov," she continued, "I just wanted to get that first list in my mind to perfection, and then to get out of Tatyana's office. I know we said I could take as long as 15 minutes, but I think I was in that office maybe *three* minutes, once I had the safe open and the pages in my hands. I didn't even move away from the open safe. I just couldn't function, except to focus on those six names. And I couldn't make myself concentrate longer.

"I'm sorry," she said again.

Adelman raised his hand to stop her. "No, no, Marie," he said. "You did right. Exactly right. Don't apologize. What you've given us is precisely what we needed most."

She took a deep breath and it became a long sigh. "Do you mean it?" she asked.

"I do indeed."

"Thank goodness," she said.

McGriff reached for her hand. He found it was trembling. He raised her hand to his lips and kissed it, beaming at her.

"You were brilliant, Marie," he said.

"Yes, you were," said Adelman, "but I'll leave all that kissing to the other guy."

They laughed gladly, and a sense of something like jubilation fleetingly ran through them. They had perhaps not fully realized, until now, how tense they had been throughout the long afternoon.

After several moments, Marie startled. "Oh!" she said, "I completely forgot. There was a title at the top of the list! It was a Russian word, but printed in our alphabet, not Cyrillic.

"The word was *Ataka,"* she said carefully, then spelling the word.

"Really?" said Adelman. "That's Russian for attack."

He smiled to himself. "Interesting," he added thoughtfully. "So, the rogue group's name for itself," he mused, "is attack. And the group's chief appears to be Tatyana Kuznetsova's manager … Artur Volkov.

"And that," he added, "would account for this list being placed in Ms. Kuznetsova's wall safe, right there in the same suite with the leader of Ataka."

He smiled again. "It fits," he said.

Stopping and starting in the slow-moving traffic, the taxi began its second loop around the Washington Mall. Fifteen minutes before, after Marie had emptied her brain of the six names she had stored there from the Ataka list, Adelman had instructed the driver to alter the positions of both of the taxi's side-view mirrors, positioning each so that he and McGriff, each leaning forward from the back seat, could track whatever vehicles might be behind them. That done, Adelman had then directed the driver through a number of turns, using all available side streets, thereby providing ample opportunity for the two men to detect trailing vehicles.

There were none.

After considering for several minutes the fact that they were not accosted on the embassy grounds or sidewalk as they moved to the taxi, together with the fact that they were not being followed by other vehicles, Adelman said, mostly to himself, "Well, I don't understand it. No one has attempted to interfere.

"Why the Friday evening knife-brandishing on the city bus," he continued, "and yet, this evening … nothing?"

"Maybe our speculation was right," answered McGriff quickly, "that Marie's coming to work *at all* today was unexpected, and they had no time to do anything to prepare … maybe just time to beef up the security at her final checkpoint?"

"And, beyond that, of course," added Adelman, "it's quite possible that they were, and are,100 percent unaware that Marie entered Tatyana Kuznetsova's office —or any office at all —after working hours."

He was thoughtful for another moment, and then, an idea coming to him, he said, "Marie, were you separated from your handbag at any point during your passage through the last checkpoint?"

She thought for a moment.

"Yes," she replied. "When the female security person took me into an adjoining room to do her pat-down, my clutch stayed with the others."

Adelman reached for the handbag. "Please?" he said.

Opening the clutch wide, he ran his long fingers over every square inch of the interior surface of the handbag, probing the soft leather for any irregularity. After some 30 seconds of this, he carefully pulled open an interior seam and extracted a small, flat, silver object barely larger than a quarter.

He showed it to his companions.

"Electronic tracking device," he said simply.

After a moment, he reached forward and handed the driver —the young Sudanese graduate student who had been hand-picked for the evening's work by the police precinct captain —both the tracking device and an amount of cash easily equal to twice the amount of the expected fare.

The young man removed one of the earplugs, turning his head slightly, while keeping his eyes on the traffic.

Adelman said, speaking both to the driver and to his companions on the back seat, "We're going to jump out of the car at the next traffic signal. This additional cash is to pay you to drive, without us, across the bridge to Arlington National Cemetery. I want you to wait there in the main entrance area for at least five minutes, then drop this thing into the nearest storm drain.

"I'll let the precinct captain know you handled everything just as we asked. I'm sure he'll have something extra for you. Understood?"

Ten minutes after their scrambling exit from the first taxi, the threesome had completed their trip to the hotel, having quickly hailed a second taxi. They swiftly changed into their workout clothes in anticipation of a late session in the hotel fitness center. But they first assembled in the men's hotel room for debriefing with Rebecca and for further planning.

Once all four were seated, McGriff powered up the Epson 20 and called up the six names Marie had dictated to him. He handed the open Epson to Rebecca.

She studied the names as Adelman began.

"Rebecca," he said, "you were exactly right about the security level at the exit checkpoint tonight. If Marie had had the document camera again, and if she had not rid herself of the safe-opening paraphernalia …"

"Yes," said Marie. "I can't thank you enough for not letting me go through that exit checkpoint with the coin-purse camera, Rebecca. I honestly don't know what would have happened."

Rebecca, focused on the six names displayed on the Epson's small screen, waved away the expressions of gratitude with a quick smile and a slight dismissive movement of her hand. She then asked, "Who is Artur Volkov? Do we want to assume that he is in command of the group … of Ataka?"

A half-hour's vigorous discussion led the group in a straight line to several conclusions: first, that the most likely implications of the title and of the ordering of the six-person list were that Artur Volkov was indeed the rogue group's leader; that Ivan Ivanovich was his second-in-command; that Tatyana Kuznetsova served as administrative assistant for Ataka activities; and that the apparent American in the list, Randy Simpson, was likely the long-suspected mole in the CIA group designated to coordinate with Rebekka Yahalomin, and, thus, to spy on them for Ataka.

Their second conclusion resulted from a short debate focused on the advisability of simply turning over to Soviet officialdom both the Ataka list and the Ataka document. If, after all, the rogue group members' names and their 72-page planning document were given to Soviet government and KGB officials, would not Ataka simply cease to exist, their members punished and their plan swallowed up by the Soviet monolith?

Five minutes' examination of the question resulted in the obvious response: the rogue group was being *encouraged* to operate by Soviet authority, an authority providing a silent, behind-the-scenes endorsement likely to go very near the top of the government and the KGB.

And the final conclusion reached in the intense half-hour was that certain immediate actions were called for that very night. Those actions would necessitate Adelman's traveling by taxi to the residence of one of his two D.C.-area former Mossad comrades-in-arms.

There, he would ask the agent to arrange an urgent data extraction from the Mossad files in Tel Aviv on all six Ataka leaders, on the financial portion of the 72-page Ataka document, and, as an afterthought, on the Sudanese graduate student and taxi driver, whose name Adelman had carefully recorded from the identification-and-licensing certificate clipped onto the vehicle's visor. Adelman, it was decided, was to go to his former Mossad colleague's residence immediately, thence to the Israeli Embassy in downtown Washington.

There they would use that embassy's uniquely secure communication system to request the data extraction in Tel Aviv's international Mossad headquarters. At midnight that night in Washington, the Mossad office in Tel Aviv would just be opening for business Tuesday morning, given the seven-hour time difference. An hour later, by 1 a.m. Tuesday in Washington and 8 a.m. Tuesday in Israel, the data would be arriving at the Israeli Embassy in D.C., and Adelman and his Mossad colleague would be there to receive the response and to print it out for the others.

Priority in the data extraction would be given to Artur Volkov and to the financial data section of the document, but all six names —seven, counting the Sudanese —would be researched: their histories, their organizational connections, their families' locations. Full reports on each component could be expected to be produced in Tel Aviv in 30 to 60 minutes from time-of-request.

Adelman and the Mossad agent would then send an Israeli Embassy car for Adelman's other local Mossad comrade-in-arms, and the three of them would rendezvous at the hotel, there to awaken Rebecca, Marie, and McGriff. By 2:30 a.m., at the latest, the six of them could expect to begin detailed planning for next steps.

All were aware of the urgency in the situation.

They knew that Ataka would be positioning itself that very night to move forward on the overriding priority in their tightly-focused reason-for-being: drawing Rebekka Yahalomin into the open, capturing, drugging, torturing, and killing Rebecca herself and any other members of the group who could be secured as well, resulting ultimately in the destruction of Rebekka Yahalomin.

CHAPTER EIGHT

LATER THAT SAME MONDAY EVENING, ANOTHER SMALL-UNIT meeting began several miles away from the hotel. This meeting, with six individuals present, was held in a nicely appointed conference room just off a well-lighted, recently completed underground tunnel located directly under the Soviet Embassy building.

The tunnel and the conference room had been constructed, ironically, under the direction of the U.S. Central Intelligence Agency, for the purpose of emplacing state-of-the-art listening devices under the embassy while the building was still under construction. The project, when near completion, became the casualty of a Soviet-CIA double agent who tipped off his Soviet handlers that the project existed.

When confronted by Soviet officials, the U.S. government abandoned the project and sealed off the end of the tunnel that extended beyond Soviet Embassy property. The underground facility, thus secured from U.S. access, was subsequently redesigned, structurally reconfigured, and finally completed by Russian construction workers, thereby becoming a useful site for some of the embassy's most secure planning sessions, product development work, and storage of technological apparatus.

The Reverend Father Artur Volkov, influential Russian Orthodox priest and Soviet political operative, chief of the Ataka leadership team, and the senior KGB agent in North America, was speaking on this evening to the other five leadership team members. Volkov was a heavy-shouldered man, paunchy in his mid-40s, but exuding bullish strength. His wide, flat face was punctuated by small, black eyes, over which bushy, black-to-graying eyebrows fell like unruly nests. He leaned forward on the conference table, his heavily veined, enormously muscular hands clinching and unclinching as he spoke.

He wore the same, unexceptional brown suit, with narrow black tie over unstarched white shirt, its collars turning upward unchecked, that he had worn to work that morning.

He had not worn his priestly collar that day. He rarely did.

His dark eyes swept the tidy conference room.

He spoke in English, rather than in his native Russian, since one of his listeners, Randy Simpson, raised in the American Midwest, had only a smattering of Russian, and, as well, because routine use of the "American language" was part of Ataka leadership team policy. Volkov addressed Egor Alexeev.

"I must congratulate you, Alexeev," said Volkov in his rasping monotone, "on the outcome of today's work, despite your catastrophic bungling of everything else that has happened in a week's time. It would appear you have managed to salvage something from the ruins, although the next several hours will be decisive."

Alexeev nodded unhappily. "Yes," he said quietly, "I think we will have the opportunity we hoped for."

"For your sake," replied Volkov, "I trust that will be the case.

"Certainly," he continued, "nothing *whatever* has yet been accomplished."

Volkov allowed the tense silence to lengthen while he studied the two pages of typed notes in front of him.

"Let me review," he said at length.

"The two men," he noted sourly, "that you, Alexeev, selected to capture Mrs. Clark and her children in London, failed so utterly that she and they, and her husband, and her brother, and her sister-in-law … *all* escaped to their Birmingham fortress.

"And the two you selected," he continued, "to take Mrs. Campbell from her home in Maryland were not only defeated by the woman's *counselor*, if one can imagine, but were themselves taken into custody by the CIA.

"I do acknowledge that your man, selected by you to feign the attack on Mrs. Campbell on board the city bus on Friday, did his work convincingly. We wanted Rebekka Yahalomin to have the photographed document, while thinking, all the while, that we were willing to kill the woman to prevent its loss. Now they have it. And they think they rescued Mrs. Campbell and the document. Good.

"They will *never* make sense out of that document."

He turned to Randy Simpson.

"Well done, Mr. Simpson, letting us know of Mrs. Campbell's planned treachery, and helping to prepare her for her document thievery in the embassy on Friday. Very, very good."

Volkov turned from the first to the second page of his notes, and, after scanning the notes, turned again to Alexeev.

"Earlier this afternoon," he said, "after you, Alexeev, chose to place the tracking device in Mrs. Campbell's purse, rather than taking her directly into our custody, you allowed the same *counselor* and the former Mossad agent, Adelman, to drive away with Mrs. Campbell in their taxi. You made no provision for the likelihood that it might occur to a former *Mossad agent* that there might be a tracking device in her purse, once he saw no one trying to interfere."

Alexeev, a seething anger growing inside him, felt his face redden and heard the bluster in his voice despite his efforts to retain his self-control.

"We had no information whatever" —here he turned an accusing glance toward Randy Simpson, their mole in the CIA —"that Mrs. Campbell would even be at work today. When she appeared at the embassy this afternoon, we were thrown into emergency tactical planning mode. We did well under the circumstances. I challenge anyone to have done better."

He glared at Volkov, then continued, his face still contorted in anger.

"The tracking device," he said, speaking as fast as his second-language English would permit, "gave us our best chance to find out where these people are staying. You'll remember, surely, that our New York informant had reported to me that on Sunday night two couples boarded AMTRAK to Washington. He recognized the men.

"He knew the detective —the Mossad agent —and had photos of the politically meddlesome priest. He did not recognize the two women. One of them, he noted, was tall and athletic, and appeared to be in her early 30s.

"And so, even though Mrs. Campbell's very presence at the embassy was not expected, and even though we were rushed to enhance our exit security, and even though we do not know whether she attempted *anything* unlawful this afternoon and evening," concluded Alexeev, "we succeeded with the main goal. We now know their hotel, and the probable fact is that Mrs. Clark is there with them in that hotel. My assignment was completed satisfactorily."

"Well, yes," interrupted Volkov, "it was completed satisfactorily in the sense that you recovered from your blunder —your *series* of blunders —and we now have the hotel's name and location, and we have the *possibility* that Mrs. Clark is actually there with the others. But your capturing and interrogating the Sudanese driver was nothing other than an act of desperation and good fortune.

"We could easily have had nothing."

Alexeev shook his head angrily.

"We had our best chauffeur and best car at the ready this evening. When Mrs. Campbell departed with the two men in the taxi, we were never more than a quarter-mile behind them. And, though we were too far away to see her and the men exit the taxi, we immediately saw —using our electronic tracking-companion device —that the taxi driver was headed for the bridge," he said, his voice rising.

"Pyotr and I had our chauffeur go *hard* across the Potomac, to the Arlington Cemetery entry area, and we were able to trap the driver before he could toss the device and get away. He gave us the name of the hotel in 10 seconds, once I showed him the blade."

Volkov appeared to consider this for a moment. "Yes," replied Volkov, "but you let him live. Why?"

"The Sudanese is an informant," said Alexeev, "for the police precinct captain, Sidney Belton's old friend. I knew that it would be better to have him listed by the police as 'unaccounted for' than 'murdered.' The police response will be less urgent.

"We have him here. Here in the underground complex. We will have time to interrogate him further, and at our leisure."

Volkov considered this last, then seemed to lose interest.

"What do you propose to do at the hotel tonight?" he said to Alexeev.

"Pyotr and I have laid our plan," replied Alexeev, looking across the conference table at Nikolayev.

"We expect the rooms to be listed under the names of Adelman or McGriff, or perhaps under the name of the local precinct captain. We also expect the billing arrangements to have been set up by that same police precinct captain. Regardless, we will *extract* the room numbers from the staff. With three of our backup gunmen plus our best chauffeur, we will approach the hotel a half-hour before midnight.

"The night staff comes on at 11 p.m.," he continued.

"At 11:30, a half-hour later, on a weekday night, only the bookkeeper and a front-desk intern, probably a student, will be present. Our chauffeur, plus one of the backup gunmen, will control the entryway to the lobby, while Pyotr and I and the other two gunmen take care of the lobby itself and the two staff people. We will incapacitate them, obtain keys to the rooms, and surprise our adversaries in their beds.

"We will have Mrs. Clark here in the embassy's underground interrogation chambers by 1 a.m. tonight," he concluded.

"And the other three?" inquired Volkov.

Egor Alexeev smiled and shook his head, glancing at Nikolayev.

Pyotr Nikolayev returned the smile.

Both turned their eyes to Artur Volkov.

After a moment, Volkov responded.

"I think," he said evenly, "that there are a dozen ways this plan of yours may result in yet another failure. Its best feature is its speed. Our enemies are almost certainly convinced that they have reached their hotel undetected. Whatever their plans, they are not expecting visitors in the middle of the night. Not *this* night.

"So … if they are in fact at this hotel, and if you in fact can control the front desk and the lobby quickly and before anyone can trigger an alarm, and if in fact our targets are in their rooms and not expecting visitors of our sort …"

Volkov looked steadily at Alexeev, and then at Nikolayev.

"Are you prepared," he said, looking from one to the other, "for the likelihood that yet another failure will result in your immediate return to Moscow? Are you prepared for the long-term consequences of that?"

"Da," they both said at once, and with more confidence than either of them felt.

Volkov nodded.

"I will expect to see you back here, with Mrs. Clark in hand, by 1 a.m. tonight."

He turned to Ivan Ivanovich. "Go with them, Ivan," he said quietly, but within earshot of the others. "Report your impressions to me tonight, regardless of outcomes."

The three men rose and hurriedly left the room.

Randy Simpson and Tatyana Kuznetsova remained seated.

After the door to the conference room closed, they turned their faces anxiously to Artur Volkov, each of them acutely aware of Volkov's multi-faceted positions of strength within Soviet hierarchies: highly influential priest in the Russian Orthodox Church, chief of the Ataka task force, sworn enemy of Rebekka Yahalomin. And, they knew, the senior North American KGB agent, as well.

His power over the two of them was absolute.

Volkov scowled as he watched the conference-room door close. He shook his head grimly, his visage darkening.

McGriff looked at his watch, calculating.

Adelman had been gone from the hotel for more than a half-hour, and by this time, just after 11 p.m., he would probably have arrived at his former Mossad colleague's home in Maryland. The two of them would soon be on their way to the Israeli Embassy to begin making arrangements for the data extraction in Tel Aviv, at midnight in D.C. and early morning in Israel.

Adelman had said he expected to be back at the hotel by 2:30 a.m.

Now, McGriff paced through and around the room occupied by Marie and Rebecca. Several times, as he circulated around the room, he shook his head without noticing he had done it.

The women sat on the room's small sofa, talking softly to each other, but also watching him orbit through the room. He was clad in his black ministerial garb, the shoulder holster and Beretta bulging slightly against the left side of his oversized coat. Incongruously, to Marie's eyes, he wore his Adidas running shoes.

Finally, Rebecca cut her eyes toward McGriff, then back toward Marie, and gave Marie a small nod.

Marie rose immediately and intercepted McGriff as he neared the sofa. She stepped directly in front of him, forcing him to stop and look down at her.

"What?" he said, surprised.

"Yes," she replied. "What, indeed?"

Seeing him hesitate, she gently pushed him two steps back, her hands against his chest, until he found himself sitting on the edge of one of the beds. She then turned and resumed her seat next to Rebecca.

"Talk to us," Marie said.

He recognized this as an order, playfully given.

He smiled at her gratefully and then looked down, trying to organize worries into words. After several moments, he leaned forward, placed his elbows on his knees, and looked up at Marie.

"If I had been Artur Volkov, or Ivan Ivanovich, or Randy Simpson, or any of those six whose names you memorized this evening, Marie, I would have been waiting this evening in one of the Soviet Embassy's chauffeured vehicles, engine running, ready to move. And when your taxi pulled away, I would have instructed the embassy driver to remain within a quarter-mile of the tracking signal coming from your purse.

"And," McGriff continued, "when I eventually realized that the taxi was leaving the Mall area, near which so many hotels are located, I would have guessed that the tracking device had been discovered. I would have guessed that you had found the device, left it in the taxi, paid the driver to leave the area, and jumped from the cab, to walk to the hotel or to flag another taxi.

"And once I saw that the tracking device was being carried toward the river, I would have directed the chauffeur to go hard in pursuit. I would, in fact, have expected to come upon the empty taxi and its driver soon after it came to a stop."

Marie stared at him, wide-eyed, while Rebecca looked down, thinking.

"And what would you have done with the driver, had you been any of the people whose names I memorized?" Marie asked after a moment.

"Well, I'm not sure what I'd have done with the driver after speaking with him, Marie," replied McGriff, "but I'm certain —had I been one of the Ataka people —I would have threatened him with his life unless he told me immediately the name and location of the hotel.

"*This* hotel.

"And then… now that I think about it… I'd have kidnapped the driver. I'd either have had one of my associates take him to the Soviet Embassy in his own taxi, or I'd have tossed him in the embassy car and had my associates dispose of the taxi. Either way, I'd have taken the driver."

There was a lengthy silence.

Finally, McGriff looked from Marie to Rebecca.

Rebecca nodded.

"They're coming," she said quietly.

All three rose immediately.

Egor Alexeev, Pyotr Nikolayev, and four KGB gunmen —one of them in the role of chauffeur —pulled into the hotel parking lot in a black, unmarked, tinted-window, eight-passenger Soviet Embassy limousine. They sat in the vehicle, engine running, 50 yards from the entrance to the hotel lobby, watching.

Another 50 yards behind the limousine, Ivan Ivanovich sat alone in a dark blue embassy sedan, waiting unobtrusively for the action to develop. As they waited, both he and the limousine occupants saw a four-person American Airlines flight crew step from the hotel's airport shuttle a moment after it came to a stop under the hotel portico. Its driver and the flight crew, their wheeled luggage trailing along, entered the lobby.

Alexeev waited 10 minutes for the flight crew to check in and the van driver to leave for home. At that point, he uttered the single word, "Go!"

At the command, he, Nikolayev, and the two gunmen assigned to enter the building with them moved their face coverings up and over their mouths and noses.

Sixty seconds later, the limousine was positioned under the hotel portico, and professionally lettered signs reading, "Lobby closed for cleaning; please use side doors," were in place on each side of the entryway. Meanwhile, Ivanovich had pulled his sedan into an empty parking space 25 yards from the limousine, ready to take command of the operation, should an emergency develop.

The two outside men, one of them the chauffeur, both of them wearing workmen's uniforms and their faces uncovered, stood near the signs to enforce the signs' directives. The other four, pausing momentarily behind the portico pillars to confirm that the flight crew and van driver had exited the lobby, quickly entered and forced the two night clerks into the small office that connected to the front-desk area itself. Both employees, unresisting, cowered against one wall of the office.

Pale with fright, the two, a university student and the night bookkeeper, faced Glock 17s in the hands of Alexeev and Nikolayev. Before being herded into the office, they had seen the two inside gunmen setting up their positions to command both the lobby and the ground-floor corridor.

Each wielded a Kalashnikov AK-47 automatic rifle.

Alexeev addressed himself to the middle-aged, bespectacled bookkeeper, enunciating carefully through his mask in his heavily accented English, "There are two rooms whose charges are to be billed to the local police precinct, correct?"

The bookkeeper's eyes fluttered involuntarily before he stammered, "Y-yes."

"Give me those room numbers, and if you touch anything that could produce a signal, we pull the triggers and kill you both. Understood?"

Alexeev gestured for the trembling man to approach his desk and its wide-open ledger. As he did, Alexeev said, "Place your hands behind you. Touch nothing."

His hands behind him, the bookkeeper peered down at his ledger.

After a moment, he said, voice trembling, "I n-need to turn this p-page."

"Do it," said Alexeev.

Hands shaking, he turned the page and studied the lists.

After a moment, he said, "R-rooms 404 and 406. P-please don't hurt us."

"Do those rooms have a connecting door?"

The man studied the schematic next to his ledger and nodded.

"Y-yes."

Alexeev turned to the young student. "Keys to 404 and 406. Now!"

In another 60 seconds, the two employees were down on the office floor, their wrists and ankles tied with strapping tape, their mouths covered with duct tape. As the four assailants raced to the stairwells at each end of the ground-floor corridor, one of the men stationed outside moved into the lobby to deal with any hotel guests who should be unfortunate enough to appear.

On the fourth floor, Alexeev and Nikolayev emerged from the stairwells, each accompanied by one of the masked gunmen. The four men converged quickly on rooms 404 and 406, room keys in hand, guns up.

Minutes before the Soviet Embassy limousine, followed closely by Ivanovich in the embassy sedan, moved into the hotel parking lot, Rebecca, Marie, and McGriff stepped from a taxi in a residential neighborhood a half-mile from the hotel, carrying with them their few belongings and those of Adelman. At the curb, they waited casually, chatting, until the taxi had rounded a corner, no longer in sight.

McGriff turned to the two women.

"We'll pass through the alley between these two lots," he said, gesturing, "then we'll cross the street at the end of this alley and pass on through another alley, really a continuation of this one. That will bring us to the street, two blocks from here, where my friend will be expecting us."

"So," said Rebecca, "this address was a diversion, yes? So that the taxi company dispatcher would not have our actual address?"

"Exactly," replied McGriff.

"*This* home appears to be for sale," observed Marie, looking at a discreet sign near the front porch. "Clever of you, Mr. McGriff," she added, smiling at him.

"Thank you, Mrs. Campbell," replied McGriff, mirroring her teasing compliment. "I was here just two weeks ago, wishing the family a good move. They've been with us at church for a decade. Now they're moving south. I was sure this house would be empty, should Ataka come looking for us."

Carrying their luggage, they moved through the two alleyways toward their actual destination. Rebecca and McGriff carried everything the four of them had brought to Washington, or had purchased in the hotel clothing stores, except for McGriff's lightweight briefcase. Marie carried that.

The Epson 20 modified prototype rode comfortably in the briefcase.

As they passed rapidly through the consecutive alleyways, Marie protested to them both, "You're not letting me carry my share, you know."

She heard the plaintive tone in her own voice and rolled her eyes. "Sorry," she said, partly to herself. "I'm whining."

Rebecca turned her face and smiled broadly at her, the sort of smile that caused the V-shaped scar on her cheek to move slightly. The subtle change was visible to Marie even in the shadowy light provided by nearby street lamps.

"Father McGriff has twice your size and strength, Marie," replied Rebecca. "And I am a much larger woman than you. Let us take care of you just a little. You have taken immense risks on our behalf. I can assure you we do not feel put upon."

Marie appeared to be thinking about this when McGriff interrupted her thought, gesturing across the street. "There," he said, "two houses to our right, on the other side.

"That's it."

"This is the friend you phoned as we left the hotel?" asked Rebecca.

"Yes," replied McGriff. "He was a member of the search committee that brought me here years ago. We've been close, all along. And we bang heads year-round on Monday nights in the 30-and-over basketball league.

"His wife and daughter have flown to the west coast for a relative's graduation. They're going to extend the visit to include a little sightseeing. And he's driving to Charlottesville tonight for some kind of alumni event.

"I just caught him with that phone call as he was leaving, Rebecca. He has a late-arrival reservation tonight and through the weekend. He's just going to give us the house keys and then take off."

Minutes later, the threesome had been welcomed, given keys to the house, and left to "make yourselves at home." McGriff, who had been a guest in the house many times, showed Rebecca and Marie the daughter's vacant bedroom and the ample guest bedroom, saying he would make up the sofa bed in the family room for himself.

"All set?" he said to them, as soon as he had given them the bare-bones tour.

Rebecca and Marie looked at him with questioning glances.

"I'm going to jog back to the hotel," he explained. "It's less than a half-mile. That's why I've kept my Adidas on. I want to see if Ataka does what I think they will do, and I want to be there, later, when Jaakov and his two Mossad friends get there. I need to let them know what has happened since Jaakov left us earlier tonight."

He looked at his watch. "I need to start out," he said. "The Ataka people could already be moving on the hotel."

"But …" said Marie.

"No," he said to her over his shoulder as he strode toward the front door of the house, "I don't intend to interfere with the Ataka incursion, Marie. I just want to see what level of force they'll bring against us."

"You're *not* going to try to stop them?" Marie said, insistently, to his back.

He continued, not replying, toward the front door.

Rebecca, standing just behind Marie and watching over the smaller woman's head as McGriff departed, smiled down at her companion's brown, shoulder-length hair and asked softly, "Do you remember the 'blueprint of the universe,' Marie?"

Marie turned around and looked up into Rebecca's face. "My life for yours," she said, her brown eyes widening.

She spun around again, but only in time to see Jack McGriff carefully closing the front door behind himself.

Ivanovich, from his sedan, watched Alexeev, Nikolayev, and the others exit the hotel lobby and side doorways at a run, toss their signs into the limousine's trunk, and leave the parking lot at speed. Conscious of the hotel's security cameras, Ivanovich pulled his face covering up, jumped from the sedan, and ran into the hotel.

Seeing no one at the front desk, he moved quickly into the small office and saw the two employees, bound hand and foot, on the floor.

Ivanovich was a kind man, a believer who, much like Jack McGriff, was not entirely comfortable with his association with his country's intelligence agency. He had already begun privately to reevaluate that connection. He gazed down at the two hotel staff members and shook his head.

They stared back at him, their eyes wide.

"Are you hurt?" he asked, speaking carefully through his mask.

They did not respond.

He looked quickly around the small office and saw a pair of scissors on one of the desks. He seized the scissors and moved swiftly to the young woman's side. Seeing the terror in her face, he said to her simply, "No. You're safe."

Kneeling beside her, he said, "Roll to your side, so I can free your wrists."

She did, and he carefully cut through the strapping tape and then helped her move into a sitting position.

"Here," he said, giving her the scissors. "Free yourself and your companion. Call 911. You'll be fine."

He left the office and exited the lobby. He had accomplished what he knew Artur Volkov wanted, in case of failure of the raid. Volkov wanted the damage minimized, so that nothing about the incident would need to be sensationalized, either in the media or within the various law enforcement agencies.

Volkov wanted the incident, if a failure, to appear to the various Washington-area publics merely as an intrusion focused on two fourth-floor rooms. No property damage. No information about the occupants of those two rooms, other than the fact that the reservations had been made by the local police precinct. Front-desk people tied and gagged, but released unharmed.

An uninteresting, though unexplained, incident, hardly worth pursuing in a sea of more serious inner-city crimes.

Ivanovich jogged to the sedan, which he had left unlocked for quick access in the event of need for an even faster departure than was proving necessary. He pulled his face covering down, glanced back at the hotel, and slipped behind the wheel.

As he started the sedan's engine, Ivanovich calculated that he had at least three minutes to exit the hotel parking lot before the employee's 911 call would bring the nearest squad car. Leaving the headlights off, he drove to the parking lot's rear entrance and then accelerated through a zigzag pattern of side streets until he became confident that he was clear.

Ivanovich pulled into a shuttered office building's parking lot and stopped. He turned off the engine, leaned back in the seat, closed his eyes, and said a small, silent prayer of thanksgiving that no one had been injured or killed —or even captured —in the raid. As he completed his prayer, his eyes sprang open.

He felt the muzzle of a gun, cold steel, against the back of his head, just behind his right ear. Then a man's resonant voice, just inches away.

"Both hands on top of your head," said the man quietly. "Lace your fingers together. Otherwise, no movement."

Ivanovich complied. He then felt the assailant, without moving the muzzle of the gun, reach with his left hand over Ivanovich's shoulder to remove the Glock 17 from his shoulder holster. He sensed his captor checking the gun's safety mechanism, and then heard the Glock thump to the floor behind the front seat.

He then heard the man slide across the back seat so that he was leaning against the right-side, rear-seat passenger door. Ivanovich kept his fingers laced on top of his head, certain that the weapon remained trained on him.

"Do you have another weapon in the car?" asked the man.

Ivanovich shook his head. "No. Just the Glock."

"Fine," said the man.

The voice sounded increasingly familiar.

"Relax, Ivan. Let's chat for a couple of minutes."

Ivanovich cautiously removed his hands from the top of his head and turned in his seat. The face he encountered was one he knew well. Ivanovich smiled hesitantly, noting that Father Jack McGriff's Beretta had not been lowered.

After a moment, McGriff clicked on the safety and holstered the 9mm.

"How are the girls, Ivan?" asked McGriff pleasantly.

Ivanovich took a long, slow breath, and then shook his head, smiling.

He had a nice, bright and genuine smile. It was set in a narrow face, one that looked every one of its 36 years, though his early-onset baldness sometimes led others to think him older. His long, straight nose produced a military severity in the face, except when he smiled. McGriff returned Ivanovich's smile with his own.

"You know Annika, Father, we just hope she'll actually get promoted to fifth grade. She's smart enough, but … you know the story … 'excessively talkative' is the only thing her teachers ever say about her."

McGriff laughed, picturing the little girl squirming through church services.

"Khristina, though," continued Ivanovich. "Smartest child in either of our countries, Father. She is sure to become president of something or other by the time she's our age."

McGriff nodded. "Please give my best to Katina, Ivan," he said.

"I haven't seen her in a month or so, I think. She and I had a good chat about Khristina's confirmation classes."

"Yes, Father. I absolutely will."

A pause while McGriff shifted mental gears. "No luck back at the hotel, I gather?" asked McGriff.

"None," said Ivanovich.

"And no injuries," he added, "to hotel staff, happily."

"That was a formidable crew," said McGriff, "that I witnessed fleeing the hotel minutes ago. Can you give me a sense of what your people would have done with us, had we been in our rooms when they arrived?"

Ivanovich looked down, obviously trying to decide how much he could say without violating commitments to his country and his organization. He was quiet for some time before looking up to answer.

"Some of our higher-ups are obsessed with Rebekka Yahalomin's capabilities, Father," he said finally. "If Mrs. Clark is, in fact, with you —and we don't actually know that she is —then it is she who would have been the focus. Had she been present, she would by now be on her way to the embassy. Once there, I don't know what form her interrogation would have taken.

"Above all, our higher-ups would like to *co-opt* her visions. Failing that …"

Ivanovich shook his head.

"And the rest of us?" asked McGriff.

"Jaakov Adelman is certainly a worry," he said. "It is especially his old contacts with Israeli intelligence that are a concern. I don't know what would have been done to him, had he been captured as well."

"And the rest of us?" repeated McGriff.

"You and Mr. Adelman are armed," Ivanovich answered, "and so I can't answer for what might have happened back at the hotel if gunplay had erupted. I just know that our men carried Kalashnikovs."

McGriff nodded. "That's about what I assumed," he said.

"Oh!" added Ivanovich, a new thought coming to him. "Do *not* allow Mrs. Campbell to return to the embassy, Father," he said emphatically. "Katina and I have come to know Marie fairly well at church. Don't expose her to these people again."

"Right," said McGriff. "Thank you, Ivan."

The two men fell silent at that point, both thoughtful.

Finally, McGriff ventured one more question. He wanted to word the question carefully, wishing to keep Ivanovich and the Ataka leadership unaware that Tatyana Kuznetsova's safe had been opened and the six-person Ataka leadership list memorized by Marie. He wanted Ataka to assume that only Ivan Ivanovich's name was now known to Rebekka Yahalomin, and that that was the case only because the 72-page "RY Proposal" had been housed in Ivanovich's office safe.

"Ivan," said McGriff thoughtfully, "Sidney Belton, the New York detective who, as you know, has a long-standing relationship with Mrs. Clark and Rebekka

Yahalomin, has been told by one of his sources that a Soviet Embassy executive named Artur Volkov has a particular interest in Mrs. Clark and her group."

This was, of course, not precisely true. The source of the information about Volkov was Marie's memorization of the list in Tatyana Kuznetsova's wall safe. This kind of falsehood was one of the many discomforts McGriff routinely experienced in his dual role as Christian minister and CIA employee.

"When you made reference," continued McGriff, "to higher-ups being obsessed with Mrs. Clark and her capabilities, were you including Mr. Volkov in a *group* of higher-ups? Or is he *the* higher-up whom you mean?"

Ivanovich turned slowly away, now staring determinedly out the front windshield of the sedan. McGriff waited, but no reply was forthcoming.

"Ivan," said McGriff, "I need to know.

"Is Artur Volkov just another mid-level manager in the embassy? Or something more than that?"

Ivanovich turned back to McGriff.

"Or is he what, Father? What do you want to ask?"

"Ivan, is this man with special interest in Mrs. Clark—this Artur Volkov—is this man someone you regard as *evil?*"

Ivanovich stared at McGriff, stone-faced.

He did not answer.

CHAPTER NINE

AS HIS WRISTWATCH REGISTERED 0200 ON THIS MONDAY NIGHT/ Tuesday morning, McGriff, seated on the front passenger seat, directed Adelman, now at the wheel of one of the Israeli Embassy's dark-blue Lincoln Town Cars, to the address where McGriff had left Marie and Rebecca hours earlier that same night. The car carried four men —McGriff and Adelman, plus the two Mossad agents. They cruised slowly past the house, circled the block once, and, on a second orbit, stopped to let the agents out on opposing ends of the block, enabling them to approach on foot from opposite directions.

After yet another circuit, Adelman and McGriff again drove slowly toward the house. They could see in the dim light of the street lamps both agents, each carrying Uzi submachine guns, standing on guard in front. Adelman pulled the Lincoln quietly into the driveway.

Adelman nursed the Lincoln up the driveway while the agents took positions in the shadows cast by two mature trees in the front yard. As the car neared the one-car garage, now empty with the owner's departure to Charlottesville, McGriff slipped from the front passenger seat, moved swiftly to the garage, and manually opened the overhead door. Adelman moved the Lincoln into the garage as McGriff closed the overhead door behind him.

They exited the side door of the garage, stopped in the shadows of the garage's overhang, and listened for long minutes. Finally, they heard the barely audible footfalls of the two agents as they moved from the front yard to the side of the house.

The four men came together at the back door and McGriff used his house key to gain entrance to the kitchen. They passed quietly through the kitchen into the main hallway and again paused to listen. Almost immediately, they heard bare feet padding down the carpeted stairs. McGriff, in the lead, looked up in the dim light provided by the hallway floor lamp to see Marie creeping down the stairway, her face displaying all the anxiety that had built over the tense hours since McGriff had wordlessly closed the front door behind himself, leaving her and Rebecca standing in that same hallway.

Seeing him, she skipped down the remaining steps and ran into his wide-spread arms. His robust bear hug lifted her off the ground with ease.

Behind them, Adelman motioned for the men to follow him into what appeared to him to be a sitting room. All three collapsed into upholstered chairs, tension and fatigue writ large on their faces. After long moments of silence, McGriff led Marie by the hand into the same room and together they sat down on a wing of the L-shaped sofa, Adelman already occupying the other wing.

Marie, dressed once more in her workout clothes, sans running shoes, and wearing the household's daughter's sweatshirt over her tee-shirt, pulled her bare legs and feet up under herself. She maintained a tight grip on McGriff's hand, both her hands encompassing his left.

After a moment, Adelman addressed Marie. "Rebecca?" he said simply.

"She was asleep, I think, as soon as she got into bed," replied Marie.

"Good," said Adelman in reply. "Marie," he continued, "the data extraction from Tel Aviv is not as decisive as we had hoped. It does confirm what we thought regarding the financial elements in the document. That is, it appears to be a coded summary of funding sources and funding estimates, much of it originating from arms trade operations run by the Russian Mafia. Hundreds of millions of dollars altogether, possibly more than a billion.

"However, without the necessary conversion keys and multipliers, we can't go further than that. We can't tell, from these reports, who controls this financial … this financial *empire* … or how to interfere with, or redirect, the use of this money.

"The Russian Mafia is not a monolith. We need more than we have."

Adelman paused, reflecting.

"Regarding personnel," he continued, "the Mossad report notes that Alexeev and Nikolayev are security specialists, that Simpson is a fledgling CIA-KGB double agent, and simply that Ivanovich is a member of your church … yours and Jack's.

"We do learn," he continued, "that Artur Volkov is a priest and an influential figure in the Russian Orthodox Church: that is, a high-level church bureaucrat. The report notes that Volkov *may* be a KGB operative, as well, but that is not known with any certainty. And finally, Marie, and maybe the most intriguing bit of all, the report states that Tatyana Kuznetsova appears to have connections that run through all strata of Soviet authority, possibly including the KGB, but certainly including the government itself. She is more than she appears.

"And," he concluded, "regarding the Sudanese graduate student, our part-time taxi driver …"

Just at that moment the atmosphere of acute fatigue in the room was jolted. The men suddenly sat straight and then began to rise.

Marie and McGriff, sitting with their backs to the hallway, turned their heads toward the doorway.

Their eyes widened.

Then they, too, rose to their feet.

The Ataka leadership team assembled for the second time that night in the underground conference room as soon as Ivan Ivanovich returned to the embassy an hour after midnight. This was at almost the same time Jack McGriff would make his unscheduled rendezvous with Adelman and the two Mossad agents at the now-abandoned hotel.

Meanwhile, Tatyana Kuznetsova and Randy Simpson had been sitting anxiously in Tatyana's office —actually Artur Volkov's office number 2045 —until Volkov buzzed them from the underground conference room.

"Come," he said brusquely.

Tatyana and Simpson entered the conference room and took the chairs indicated, opposite Volkov and Ivanovich. It was obvious to them that neither Alexeev nor Nikolayev was going to be present, and they immediately assumed, correctly as it turned out, that the hotel raid had failed and that the two Ataka toughs were on their way to Moscow and a career of bureaucratic paper shuffling, if they were fortunate.

Volkov, in ill humor, began the session. "Jack McGriff, this troublesome priest, has just had … shall I say … an uncomfortable conversation with Ivan, following tonight's failure. As one of Ivan's pastors, McGriff misguidedly used no violence toward Ivan, although he was in position to do so. He will soon regret his misplaced generosity, but I am pleased to have Ivan back with us, safe.

"You will not see Alexeev or Nikolayev again," he continued, tersely. "Thanks to their carelessness, we have lost track of the prey. We cannot even know with certainty whether the Clark woman is, in fact, here in Washington with the others. Incredibly, we do not know with certainty whether she is even in this country."

He looked at Randy Simpson. "Mr. Simpson, here, tells me that his CIA liaison unit with Rebekka Yahalomin has received no information … no communication of any kind … since last Friday, and reports that they —our enemies — have apparently stopped using the secure telephone line jointly installed by CIA and MI6. It is as if these people simply disappeared from the face of the earth between the time Mrs. Campbell stepped off the city bus Friday evening, and the time she reported for work at the embassy Monday afternoon, a little more than 12 hours ago.

"We had no idea she was coming here to the embassy, ever again, after her known treachery, and after what she certainly must have perceived as her near-death experience on the bus."

He shook his head and actually snorted his disgust.

He waved his hand dismissively.

"We will go forward without additional delays," he said.

He turned to Randy Simpson. "Mr. Simpson," he said, "immediately return the Sudanese driver's taxi to the taxi company's garage. Make some excuse to the dispatcher. Tell him his driver became ill and asked you to return the vehicle.

"Any excuse will do. Turn in the keys and leave that area of the city. We'll have one of our town cars follow you there.

"Understood?"

"Yes, sir," responded Simpson, relieved to be given a relatively simple task.

"Ivan," Volkov continued, turning to his long-time associate, "interview the taxi driver. If necessary, turn the interview into an interrogation. He *must* know something about the Clark woman.

"Our patrolman friend at the precinct station tells us that this young Sudanese student was hand-picked to drive that taxi. If he was specifically chosen for the task, he was probably given considerable information about why the job had particular importance. Push him hard.

"We need to know the whereabouts of Mrs. Clark," said Volkov. "We need to know *tonight.*"

"I'll see what I can do, Artur," replied Ivanovich calmly. "Shall I go now?"

Volkov nodded and turned to Tatyana Kuznetsova, while Ivanovich collected his notes and rose to walk down the hall to the room in which the Sudanese was held.

"Tatyana," said Volkov, "get the KGB agent coordinator out of bed and have him set up a stakeout in the residential neighborhoods near the hotel. Give him descriptions of the three, and of Mrs. Clark, and inform him that they may have drawn upon Israeli intelligence —the Mossad —or the Israeli Embassy for assistance.

"Look for the four people," he continued, "but also for vehicles that appear to be embassy vehicles. Look for any activity that appears to be unusual for the neighborhoods near the hotel."

She nodded. "Right away, sir."

"And as soon as the stakeout arrangements are underway," continued Volkov, "begin preparations for the transfer of funds from our special sources into the publication-and-distribution fund.

"Alert our publications arm to prepare for mass printing of our version of the Jefferson Bible, with its introductory excerpts from Jefferson's *Declaration,* and with the added elements which we will give them, within the week. Confirm by midday today that all preparations are satisfactorily underway."

"Consider it done, sir," she replied.

Marie, McGriff, Adelman, and the two Mossad agents stood frozen, staring at the figure in the doorway. And Rebecca stared back at them, equally motionless.

Her regal face was alight. Her startling gray eyes seemed to communicate a kind of authority that none of the room's occupants had seen. The V-shaped scar across her right cheek, just under the prominent cheekbone, somehow accentuated this silent, yet utterly commanding, presence.

She appeared to have just risen from her bed, for she had not taken time to brush her usually shimmering black hair. She had simply pulled her hair around and over her right shoulder, so that it fell, mildly tangled, over the right side of her chest, almost to her waist. She was barefoot, and was clad, over her sleepwear, only in a woman's raincoat taken apparently from an upstairs coat closet.

Marie felt an unaccountable urge to curtsey, if she but knew how. And she felt vaguely embarrassed to be dressed only in workout clothes and sweatshirt. *I should be wearing my suit. And my good shoes.*

But she and McGriff, without signal to each other, simply reached for each other's hand. They had formed the same thought: *This is how the angels looked.*

Minutes seemed to pass, though only a single actual minute had lapsed.

It was Adelman who first recovered. "Rebecca," he said quietly, "you've dreamed?"

She nodded.

"Marie," Adelman said, thinking quickly, "would you mind going upstairs to your and Rebecca's rooms and finding the Epson 20 machine? If you'll bring it down here, Jack can record the dream in detail.

"This will be too complex," he said, "to use with the SMTP CD in my computer in New York, so we will not be able to send it electronically to the Lodge, but we can print Rebecca's report later, and send it to England by military courier. All that may take 36 hours, but it will be so much better than anything else we might do."

Marie, still barefoot herself, trotted past Rebecca and up the stairs. She returned in seconds, carrying the briefcase. She handed it to McGriff, who, hesitant to sit while Rebecca stood, looked his question to her.

Rebecca, suddenly realizing the men's dilemma, said simply, "Please, everyone … you should sit down."

With all seated, she, still standing in the arched door to the hallway, said to McGriff, "Tell me when you're ready, Father."

McGriff set up the Epson with practiced efficiency, and, seeing Rebecca intended to speak to them from the doorway, nodded to her over his shoulder. She began, still standing motionless, closing her eyes to maintain focused recall of the vision, her hands clasped together in front of her chest.

Her voice, as always, was low, soft, and redolent with British dialectical nuance.

"I saw in my dream," she began, "another corridor, similar to the one in the previous vision, but this corridor felt more sinister than bureaucratic. The walls and floor were unpainted, untreated concrete … there were no wall hangings … lighting came solely from naked overhead bulbs … metal doors were interspersed at considerable distances from each other, and appeared only on the left side of the corridor. The numbers all started with double-ought: 002, 004, 006, and so on."

She paused, concentrating.

"Father?" she asked.

"Yes … go on," he responded after taking a moment to check his work.

"As before," she said, "the dream took me *through* one of the doors, the one marked 004. The room I saw was fairly large, probably more than twice the size of our hotel rooms … there was furniture, but my mind was not drawn to any of it, and the furnishings remained hazy and shapeless around the edges of my periphery.

"No one was present in this room, but the vision pulled my mind to one of two doors in the opposite wall … the two doors were widely separated from each other, so that I assumed they were leading into two different rooms beyond the room in which I found myself. But that impression was wrong.

"There was but one room, not two, beyond the immediate one, and it appeared much, much larger than the first one. This second room was the size of … I should think … a half-dozen standard-sized hotel rooms of the sort we occupied last night … perhaps even larger than that.

"There were no windows in either room."

McGriff held up one hand, lowered it, continued to tap on the Epson's keys for several seconds, then held up his hand again while he checked his work. Finally, he turned his head and nodded in Rebecca's direction.

"The vision," she continued, "gave me two distinct images from within the second room. The first was of banks of computers against all four walls: long tables, all around the outside of the room … each table with at least one computer and, I think, with a separate printer for each computer."

She paused. "Father?"

"Wait … go."

"The second image was that of a person. He was tied to a chair that was centered among the computer tables across the back of the room … his ankles were bound … his hands were bound behind the chair back … his mouth was covered with tape … his eyes were not covered, and I could see his face rather clearly.

"He was a person of color… darker than brown … a rich, dark skin color … rather than pasty white like most of us here."

McGriff interrupted.

"Rebecca," he called out, without turning his head, "would you mind repeating that last sentence … your description of his skin color, please?"

She repeated her description, paused, then continued when McGriff nodded.

"He was handsome … a high forehead, prominent cheekbones. Youthful in appearance, but no longer a teen, either … possibly mid-20s.

"He was perspiring and seemed extremely uncomfortable. It may be that the bindings around his ankles and wrists were so tight that they cut him … or it may be that he was simply afraid for his life. …

"Let me correct that," she said immediately.

"He was *certainly* in fear for his life, because there appeared, as I watched, just to one side of him … perhaps 5 feet away … a disembodied hand. That hand was holding a pistol … the muzzle of the pistol was pointed directly at the young man's head."

McGriff's fingers tapped for several more seconds, flying across the keyboard. Then he paused, held up one hand, reviewed his notes, then lowered the hand and nodded to Rebecca.

When she did not continue, he turned his head far enough to see her. She looked back at him and nodded. "I think that's the end," she said. "Would you read back, Father?"

He read slowly from the machine's small screen, covering Rebecca's entire report, word-for-word.

He turned to look at her, and they nodded to each other.

"Good," she said. "Thank you, Father."

Then her eyes scanned the small group.

"Who is this young man? Where is he being held?"

Adelman spoke in response.

"The captive," he explained, "is almost certainly the young Sudanese who drove our taxi, Rebecca. We —Marie, Jack, and I —were with him for a short while Monday evening. I recorded his name in my notepad from the taxi's identification certificate clipped to the vehicle visor. His name is Kazim Deng."

Adelman picked up a file folder from the sofa arm. Opening it, he looked down at a printout.

"According to our data extraction from Tel Aviv's Mossad headquarters tonight," he said, "Mr. Deng's family escaped from Sudan when he was a boy, traveling by commercial shipping from the Suez, and eventually to London.

"There they achieved British citizenship by the time young Kazim was ready for what we consider high school in the U.S. He received an academic scholarship to attend a private boarding school in New Jersey, then majored in mathematics at Georgetown University, also on an academic scholarship. He eventually achieved a Master's degree in computer science from American University, and is now enrolled in that university's computer science Ph.D. program.

"He lives alone in grad-student housing, according to our data, and drives the taxi to help support himself. He is also paid by the local police precinct to help them on a part-time basis with criminal data analysis, which explains why he is in the Mossad data bank in the first place. He was selected explicitly by the precinct captain to be our driver following Marie's incursion into Tatyana Kuznetsova's office."

Rebecca nodded. "And his place of captivity?" she asked.

Four people tried to speak at once: the two Mossad agents, McGriff, and Marie. The men laughed and deferred to Marie, who declined by indicating her own deference in the direction of the older of the two Mossad agents, a tall, wiry, leathery, salt-and-pepper-haired man in his 50s or 60s.

"I've no doubt," he said in a raspy monotone, "that Mrs. Clark was seeing in her dream the underground complex at the Soviet Embassy. The CIA secretly began work on the tunnel when the building was first under construction, but a double agent exposed the project for what it was, an effort to emplace high-quality listening devices under the embassy. After being confronted, the CIA closed down the project and sealed up the end furthest from the building. The project was redesigned and eventually completed by Russian construction crews. Your taxi driver is in imminent danger, probably because his captors assume that he knows more than he does."

After a moment's thoughtful silence, Adelman spoke again. "This is my fault," he said gloomily. "When we left the embassy after picking Marie up, and when I saw we were not being interfered with, I realized that a tracking device in her handbag was a possibility. And there it was.

"I gave it to our driver, Mr. Deng, and asked him to let us out at the next traffic signal, and then to transport the tracking device across the Potomac to the entry area at Arlington National Cemetery. I did not think through the possibility that our adversaries might follow the signal to Arlington and accost the driver there.

"But the three of you sorted that out that while you were still in your hotel room, as my colleague and I were going to the Israeli Embassy at midnight. That's, of course, how you knew to evacuate the hotel as fast as possible.

"Mr. Deng was obviously caught at the cemetery," continued Adelman, "forced to give up the name and location of the hotel, and taken to the Soviet Embassy for additional questioning. Rebecca's vision tells us that he's being interrogated right now in that underground, and possibly will be killed at any moment.

"Certainly," he concluded, "if the KGB is doing the interrogating, and if they believe Mr. Deng knows anything about Rebecca's whereabouts —and he does not —they are likely to kill him and dispose of his body at their leisure."

Adelman shook his head sadly. "I'd give anything to have my spur-of-the-moment decision back. I should have simply tossed the tracking device out the window. That would have served our purposes just as well, and would not have exposed Mr. Deng to capture, torture, and, I fear, execution."

Rebecca, after a thoughtful pause, addressed Adelman. "Jaakov," she said, "we need to be conscious of the fact that the time sequences in my visions have never been contemporaneous with our moment-to-moment lives. I don't recall ever being shown, in a vision, an event that was actually in progress at the same moment as my dream of that event. What I was shown in *this* dream, within the last half-hour, especially the portion of the vision that showed a pistol aimed at Mr. Deng by a disembodied hand, is more likely to be future than present."

She scanned the room. "On the other hand," she added, "the timing of my visions has always had great urgency to it. We have always needed to move fast.

"I can recall no exceptions to *that.*"

CHAPTER TEN

AT 7:30 A.M., MCGRIFF TELEPHONED IVANOVICH —HIS POLITICAL adversary and church parishioner —to ask permission to visit him at his home immediately, before Ivanovich left for the Soviet Embassy to begin his workday. There was a long pause on Ivanovich's end of the line.

"Why?" he said finally.

"I have information for you, Ivan, and questions, too … and both have great immediacy," answered McGriff.

Another pause ensued. Finally, Ivanovich replied.

"Are you going to bring your gun?" he said evenly.

"Of course not, Ivan," said McGriff.

"You know that I had the 9mm at the hotel because of the circumstances. Your people were conducting an attack on me and my colleagues. The attack failed, but it was an *armed* attack. Obviously, I needed to be armed myself. Simple prudence.

"I'm asking to visit you in your home, Ivan. Just information and conversation."

Another pause followed. Finally, this.

"I'll need to leave for work by 8:45," he said, "but come ahead."

Then, as an afterthought, he added, "Katina and the girls are in North Carolina on the annual week-long math camp for girls. They'll be sorry to have missed you."

McGriff, accompanied by Rebecca, left the temporary lodging quickly, he at the wheel of the Israeli Embassy's Lincoln Town Car. He had been mildly surprised to see that she brought her overnight bag with her, tossing it in the back seat before getting into the vehicle's front passenger seat.

He looked his question at her.

"Oh, I almost never go anywhere without my workout clothes and shoes and my … umm … my weaponry, Father," she said.

"I've found that when I'm not at home I often need to seize the odd opportunity to stay as fit as I can. I know we're planning to come back here, to the house, after our interview with Mr. Ivanovich, but our plans could change quickly, it seems to me, depending on his response."

She smiled. "When the dreams are upon me, Father, I really never know what will come next … or when."

McGriff already knew the location of the Ivanovich home, having visited with the family on several occasions when they first arrived in D.C. and were making their decision about a church home. Once they were face-to-face with Ivanovich, McGriff and Rebecca hoped to confer with him as Christian brothers and sister.

They planned to open themselves to the chance that Ivanovich would respond in charity to the extraordinary fact of being entrusted with the contents of one of Rebecca Clark's legendary visions, legendary as much to the Soviets as to the allied intelligence agencies —Mossad, MI6, and CIA.

They knew the risks. They knew that Ivanovich might not cooperate. They knew that he might immediately report Rebecca's presence in his home to his Ataka comrades, or, of even more dramatic consequence, directly to the KGB.

Ivanovich had, after all, just hours earlier that same night, closed himself off completely when McGriff had pressed him for his impressions of Artur Volkov. His loyalty to his country and to his organization, and, indeed, to his old friend and administrative superior, might well prevent his even agreeing to hear Rebecca recite a single sentence of the details of the new vision, assuming he allowed the two of them into his home at all.

The risk was substantial.

But Rebecca had prayed about their next steps, and this utterly radical idea —disclosing details of one of her visions to an active adversary, and, beyond that, offering herself in person to the adversary —had formed itself in her mind during prayer. She had at length become certain that her vision should be presented to Ivan Ivanovich, if he would agree to hear it, and that she herself should make the presentation.

It was almost, in her mind, as though the presentation to Ivanovich had itself become a component of the vision.

Meanwhile, as McGriff and Rebecca drove away, a driver from the Israeli Embassy in a nearly identical vehicle picked up Adelman and the two Mossad agents from McGriff's hastily arranged sanctuary. They proceeded to the embassy to begin the process of converting the Epson 20's record of Rebecca's dream into an encrypted transcript to send by courier, along with a paper copy of the complete Ataka "planning document," to Israeli officials in New York and London, thence to the Chapel-Beltons in Manhattan, and to Kory Manguson at the Lodge. Rebecca had insisted that all members of Rebekka Yahalomin have full access to the transcript of her most recent vision and to the Ataka document.

At almost the same moment at which Adelman and his companions pulled up to the gate at the Israeli Embassy, McGriff and Rebecca came to a stop at the home of Ivan Ivanovich, fewer than two straight-line miles from the Israelis. Knowing that Ivanovich would be looking out his living room window expectantly, McGriff, stepping from the Lincoln, made an elaborate show of removing his "priestly sport coat" and tossing it on the back seat of the town car, thereby revealing to their host, before approaching the home, that he was not wearing his shoulder holster and would enter the home unarmed, as promised.

Ivanovich, who had nearly finished getting dressed for work when McGriff phoned earlier, noted McGriff's gesture, smiled briefly, but then froze in astounded recognition as Rebecca stepped from the Lincoln.

Anger surged within Ivanovich at McGriff's duplicity.

He was immediately torn between his obvious and overpowering obligation —to telephone Artur Volkov or Tatyana Kuznetsova and urge an armed embassy patrol or KGB unit to take both of his guests as captives —and an equally powerful urge to meet with, and to be in the presence of, the famed Rebecca Clark, who was at that moment advancing up the walkway to the door of his home. For 10 full seconds he stood, immobile, unable to form a coherent thought, and by then it was too late.

They were knocking on the door.

Ivanovich still did not move. From Ataka's perspective, the opportunity to accomplish the one absolutely necessary step in their grand plan was actually presenting itself at that very moment. He had but to contact Volkov or Tatyana, and Rebecca Clark could be taken into custody in minutes.

He saw that his visitors had stepped back from the door, just enough to see him through the large front window. He stared at Rebecca, and she smiled.

He dropped his face into his hands and found himself saying a prayer of desperation, a prayer for the presence of God's hand on his shoulder and in their midst. He breathed deeply, then looked up, locked eyes with McGriff, shook his head in an unspoken rebuke, and strode to the front hallway.

He breathed deeply yet again, and looked down at himself as he prepared to invite the adversary —the apparition —into his home. Ivanovich was clad in lightweight, dark-color dress trousers and white shirt, the collar still open, awaiting his usual dark-colored tie. His hand now on the doorknob, he glanced down and to one side of the doorway, where his own shoulder holster rested on the small entryway table, the Glock snugly but visibly in place.

Ivanovich opened the door and looked at the twosome through the glass of the storm door, still uncertain whether to invite them in or to pick up the Glock and order them to the floor of his living room. He stared at Rebecca, still fighting himself.

She wore the same clothes she had worn on the AMTRAK from New York to Washington: a dark skirt, the hem of which fell just below her knees, and a sleeveless, white cotton blouse. Draped over one arm was a lightweight, maroon windbreaker she carried against the morning chill, one borrowed from the coat closet of their absent hosts. Before they had left the house, Marie had declared that Rebecca, her hair now brushed and glistening, looked "just right."

Ivanovich opened the storm door and stepped onto the small front porch. He extended his hand to Rebecca. "Welcome, Mrs. Clark," he said with genuine warmth in his voice. "It is a pleasure to have you here, and I'm only sorry that Katina and the girls are not here to meet you and to chat with Father McGriff, who is one of *their* favorite people, though he is not one of mine at the moment."

She smiled again and shook his hand. "You're very kind to allow us to visit on short notice, Mr. Ivanovich. And I apologize that Father McGriff said nothing about his intention to bring me with him. He said the thing seemed impossible otherwise. I don't know if he was right about that, but I am sorry."

Ivanovich's eyes moved to McGriff's and a frown of suppressed anger directed itself at him. "This is wrong," he said to McGriff.

"You failed," he continued, "to mention your intention to bring Mrs. Clark. You knew I would decline. That constitutes, as you say, deceit by omission, Father."

McGriff nodded. "Yes," he said, "it does."

Rebecca, standing just arm's length from Ivanovich, said softly, "You may still decline, Mr. Ivanovich. This is *your* home."

Ivanovich blushed in the presence of such grace and courtesy. He turned and gestured toward the doorway, stepping aside for Rebecca to enter. He followed her across the threshold, McGriff trailing.

As they passed into the front hallway, McGriff inquired hastily about Katina, Khristina, and Annika by name. And, at the same time, his eyes took in the holstered Glock on the entryway table.

Have I been colossally stupid to do this? Have I brought Rebecca into a trap from which neither of us can possibly escape?

The tension between the two men was palpable, yet Rebecca appeared either oblivious to that tension or utterly unconcerned about it. Ivanovich, uncertain as to how to serve as host to *this* guest, took in the tanned, sinewy strength in her upper arms and the radiance of her scarred face, suddenly unsure of himself in his own home.

He asked clumsily, "Mrs. Clark, may I … ah … may I take your jacket … or … ah … perhaps get you something to drink? I'm not sure what we have, but …"

She smiled and shook her head, turning to take a seat on the nearest living room chair. As she sat, so did the men.

As soon as they were seated, Rebecca engaged Ivanovich again with her stunning gray eyes and her captivating smile —not seductively, he sensed fleetingly, but in a kind of forthright, unspoken kinship between believers, a kinship that implied they rise above the tension —and said simply, "Mr. Ivanovich, overnight I was given a new vision, one which, we think, involves your group and your embassy. I would like to speak it to you.

"May I?"

He nodded vaguely, caught between clear, practiced obligation, on one hand, and an eager anticipation of being addressed in this way by Rebecca Clark, who, incredibly, was offering to give him a firsthand report of a vision only hours old.

In response to his nod, Rebecca recounted her vision just as she had, during the long night, to McGriff and the others. When finished, she sat quietly, her eyebrows raised expectantly.

Ivanovich responded by dropping his eyes.

He said nothing and did not appear to intend any response at all.

After a lengthy silence, McGriff asked, "Ivan, do you recognize the dreamed corridor and the dreamed computer room … and the dreamed captive?"

Ivanovich suddenly rose from his chair. As he strode from the room, not looking at either guest, he mumbled, "Excuse me, please." Rebecca and McGriff listened to his footsteps in the main hallway, then heard a door slam at the far end.

They looked at each other.

Neither felt certain what response was called for, and so they sat quietly, not conversing, for several minutes. Finally, without a word to each other, but mutually cognizant of the fact that Ivanovich could be on the phone to his embassy at that moment, they rose to leave. As they neared the front door, Rebecca suddenly turned, said to McGriff, "Just a moment, please, Father," and walked down the hallway toward the closed door to —she assumed —the master bedroom.

Through the closed door she called, "Mr. Ivanovich, before we leave your home, I'd like to know that you're going to be all right. Do you need anything from us? Would you like to talk about what I've just described?

"I know this is a fearful thing, Ivan," continued Rebecca. "Please let me see that you're going to be all right after we leave."

Rebecca stood, still and silent, for perhaps 30 seconds. Then she stepped closer to the door, raised her right hand, and rapped softly.

"Mr. Ivanovich," she said quietly, "I would like to enter the room, please. Just say 'Yes' or 'No,' and I'll do as you say.

"Mr. Ivanovich?"

Another 15 seconds passed, and then she heard faintly a muffled "Yes."

She looked toward the front door where McGriff had just taken a step toward her. She raised her hand, palm toward him, to indicate to him that he should remain there for the moment. Then she placed her hand on the doorknob and turned it slowly.

She pushed the door open and caught her breath at what she saw. Ivanovich sat on the side of his bed, his face buried in his hands. Beside him on the bed, just to his right, was another Glock, and just to his left was an open Bible.

He did not look up.

Rebecca stood quietly in the doorway, not speaking or moving.

Finally, Ivanovich lifted his face from his hands and looked at her. His face was that of a man stricken. His cheeks glistened with drying tears. His mouth was set in a grimace. He struggled to speak, but no words emerged.

What came from his throat was a sound that could be described as something between a croak and a moan. As he uttered the small noise, he slowly moved each hand, his right to the Glock, his left to the open Bible. There each hand remained, one resting on the firearm, the other on Holy Scripture.

Rebecca took in the movement of each hand, and, after a long moment, said quietly, "Ivan, what Scripture passage do you have under your left hand?"

He turned his head and looked down at his hand as it rested on the open Bible. He replied, his voice tightly constricted, "Hebrews … Hebrews 10:31."

She smiled. "'It is a fearful thing to fall into the hands of the living God.'"

He nodded slowly, his eyes still on the Bible.

"Ivan," she said, "is that how you feel right now? That you are falling into the hands of the living God?"

He looked toward her, his face contorted in pain. He cleared his throat. "I was talking … I was talking … to this young Sudanese… just a few hours ago," he said, shaking his head. "He seemed … such a good, trusting, faith-filled man. And he was perfectly well … *perfectly* well … when I spoke with him, Mrs. Clark."

"Do you imagine that he is perfectly well now?" asked Rebecca softly.

Ivanovich pulled his hands into his lap and looked down at the floor. He remained silent. His shoulders slumped.

Rebecca sensed that McGriff had arrived behind her in the hallway. She moved to one side and he stepped forward into the room. He spoke quietly to Ivanovich.

"Ivan, last night you warned me not to allow Marie Campbell to go to work at your embassy today … in fact, not to allow her to return to the embassy at all.

"Why, Ivan, did you warn me in that way?"

Ivanovich shook his head.

"You and Katina know Marie, from church," continued McGriff, "and you both know her to be a good person, Ivan. And you've just said that the young Sudanese seems 'such a good, trusting, faith-filled man.' And you *know* Rebecca's visions are divine in their origin, and you *know* that they are true in every detail, and you *know* that that is why Ataka was formed in the first place: to *destroy* Rebecca Clark."

Ivanovich's head snapped up at the mention of Ataka, his eyes wide in astonishment. "You *know?*" he asked in wonderment.

"Ivan," continued McGriff, "you have in your home, in this very room, at this very moment, a woman repeatedly chosen by God to be His messenger on earth. Time after time she has been used as His right arm to intervene in the face of terrible threats to Christianity. She stands here beside me, *in your home.*"

McGriff paused, then softly walked to the bed, picked up the Glock, lifting it by its barrel, saw that the safety was still in the "on" position, and opened a drawer on the night stand. He placed the weapon in the drawer, closed it, and walked back to the door, now standing beside Rebecca again.

"Holiness has entered your home and your life, Ivan," he said.

"The group you work for, and with, is at best corrupt. You need to decide. And I think you have very, very little time to do so. I think Mr. Deng has very little time. I fear that Rebecca Clark … and Marie Campbell … and possibly I, myself … and possibly you, yourself …

"We have very, very little time."

McGriff, the car keys in his hand but not in the ignition, sat in the Israeli Embassy town car, parked with Rebecca in front of Ivanovich's home, for nearly 15 minutes, both of them confident now that Ivanovich, though torn, would not report their presence to his embassy nor to the KGB. Ivan Ivanovich's prayerful angst, they now understood, had been directed specifically toward his own future … and that of his family.

The Glock beside him on the bed had been intended for use against himself, if at all, but suicide had never been a realistic choice for this Christian man.

And so, McGriff and Rebecca remained silent, thinking about what had just transpired. At length, he looked inquiringly at her.

She nodded, and he started the engine. McGriff drove slowly to the end of the dead-end street, made his U-turn, and drove back past the Ivanovich home. He continued 50 yards further, to the stop sign at the corner.

As McGriff began to move the Lincoln across the intersection, he glanced in the rear-view mirror and saw Ivanovich striding quickly from the sidewalk in front of his home to the center of the street, waving what appeared to be a small envelope over his head. McGriff gestured for Rebecca to look back while he continued across the intersection, negotiated another U-turn when traffic permitted, and returned.

Ivanovich was standing at the curb in front of his house. Rebecca lowered her window and Ivanovich stooped to hand her the envelope. He looked across her to McGriff. There was residual anger on his face.

"I'm placing my life, and the lives of my wife and daughters, in your hands by giving you this note, Father. And after I meet with you this afternoon, as my note says, all bridges will have been burned. If I cannot get to the rendezvous I've proposed in the note, then life on this earth will be at an end for me. In that case, go to North Carolina, rescue Katina and the girls, and hide them.

"Hide them for me, Father," he said again, his voice cracking. "It's all I ask."

He wheeled and was gone.

After another U-turn and a short trip of three blocks to a small, residential park, McGriff parked the town car and turned off the engine. He nodded at Rebecca and she worked the envelop open, extracting a folded, single-page note. She unfolded the note and held it open for them both to read.

The note was handwritten in a masculine scrawl. It read:

1. *I will attempt to see Kazim Deng today. I will bring him with me, if I can, to meet with the two of you at church at 4 p.m. Just you two. Bring no one else. No Mossad. No former Mossad.*

2. *Randy Simpson is a double agent, CIA and KGB. He keeps Ataka informed about Rebekka Yahalomin. Any communication you make to your CIA contact unit at Langley is relayed by Simpson to the Ataka unit at our embassy.*

3. *If I cannot get to the church at 4 p.m., that will mean that I am being sent to Moscow. Or that I am already dead. Save Katina and the girls.*

The two of them needed no discussion. They both knew that they needed to get to the Israeli Embassy quickly, while Adelman and his colleagues were still there. In minutes, they were at the embassy gate, where they found that the name Jaakov Adelman itself served as an adequate password. And within 15 minutes of passing through the gate, they found themselves seated in a conference room with Adelman and the two Mossad agents with whom they had met overnight.

As soon as Adelman read and digested Ivanovich's note, he punched in a number on the conference table's secure telephone. He was immediately connected to his contact person with the small CIA unit that had been set up specifically to deal with, and to assist when needed, Rebekka Yahalomin.

"We have independent confirmation," said Adelman into the phone, "of a Tel Aviv headquarters report regarding Randy Simpson's status as a double agent. Call me back as soon as you've decided on the course of action you prefer. Bear in mind that our agents are on standby to collect Simpson and transport him to a permanent location, as you and I previously discussed."

That done, Adelman explained to the new arrivals that paper copies of the Epson 20's encrypted transcript of Rebecca's overnight dream, plus a complete copy of the Ataka document —the financial statements, the passages from the Jefferson Bible, and the portions of the Declaration of Independence — were already en route, as Rebecca required, to the other members of Rebekka Yahalomin, both in New York and in England. A chartered Israeli Embassy flight would handle the Washington-to-New-York leg, and a Royal Air Force transport would take care of the transatlantic portion. Full decryption would take place at the Israeli United Nations office in New York, and, later, at the Israeli Embassy in London, prior to delivery of the material to Sid Belton at his office, and to Kory Manguson at the Lodge, respectively.

No sooner had Adelman finished bringing Rebecca and McGriff up to date than the conference-table phone rang. Adelman picked up, listened, said, "Agreed," and hung up. He looked at his colleagues around the table.

"Randy Simpson was placed under arrest moments ago at CIA headquarters at Langley. One of our Mossad units will collect him within the hour. He will be in Israel by noon tomorrow. His entire future life will be spent on a work farm there."

"A *kibbutz?*" asked one of the Mossad agents at the table.

"Yes," answered Adelman, "but one that has Israeli soldiers and police posted, 24 hours, around its perimeter. Mr. Simpson will need to work hard, but he will live."

The group silently processed this information.

"Well … doesn't sound too terrible for a spy," said McGriff finally.

"Right," said Adelman.

"Compared to the alternatives —Guantanamo Bay, Siberia, or worse —it's going to be a livable life. Neither Simpson's CIA bosses nor, I would think, his KGB bosses, have any interest in severe punishments in this case. Simpson has not been involved in anything qualifying as high-level treason, in either direction, nor in violence. He has been a low-level operative for a few years, and life on a kibbutz will likely prove, in some ways, a relief to him."

"Perhaps a nice Jewish girl," added the older Mossad agent with a chuckle.

The others looked at him with good-natured disapproval.

He feigned confusion. "What did I say?" he said, smiling. "What greater happiness could I wish for the poor man?"

Quiet, indulgent laughter.

After several more moments of comfortable, thoughtful silence, Adelman looked at McGriff and said, "Jack, let's evacuate the house we used last night and set up occupancy for you, me, Rebecca, and Marie here in the embassy's third-floor guest quarters. Much, much safer."

McGriff looked at Rebecca, who, after a moment, nodded her ascent.

"I'll head over there now," McGriff said.

"Marie and I can pack up our things in 15 minutes. We ought to be back here in 45 minutes or so.

"We can then start to strategize," he continued, "about this 4 p.m. meeting with Ivan at the church. I need all of you to help us think about how to approach that session. Ivan's note says only that he hopes to bring Mr. Deng with him — having somehow freed him, *alive,* from the situation depicted in Rebecca's dreamed portrayal —and that, if he cannot meet us at church, we should assume the worst and rescue Katina and their daughters in North Carolina.

"There are dozens of problems … dozens of risks … attendant to that proposal. Rebecca and I need to be prepared for any eventuality."

"Yes," said Adelman, "you do.

"And so do the rest of us. We're not sending you two alone to this rendezvous, Jack. We'll want to be tightly organized. As you say, ready for *any* eventuality.

"And, in fact," he added, "let me give you this right now, before you head out to pick up Marie, rather than giving it to you later this afternoon."

He turned to the younger Mossad agent, who reached into his pack and handed Adelman a small, soft-leather bag, held closed by a drawstring. Adelman removed a circular device the size of a quarter in diameter, but thinner than a dime. He examined it briefly and, standing, reached across the table to hand it to McGriff.

"This is our latest tracking device, Jack," he said, "similar to the device the Soviet Embassy people placed in Marie's handbag so that we could be tracked in our taxi.

"Before you leave the room, place the device under the arch of one of your feet, against the skin. Peel off the transparent covering, and that will activate the device. It will adhere to your foot for about 72 hours, even after you get it wet.

"After that, it will continue to send its signal, so don't discard it. Just use a band-aid to affix it to your foot. We want to know where you are, Jack, not just when you go to today's 4 p.m. meeting, but starting right now, just for the drive across town to pick up Marie and your belongings."

McGriff examined the small device, then turned in his chair, leaned over, and began the process of removing a shoe.

After a moment, Adelman continued. "I'll ask for two of our agents to drive you to Marie's location," he said, "and to bring the two of you back here after you've collected your things. Meanwhile, my colleagues and I —and perhaps others now in the building whom we should involve —will begin to map out contingencies for that 4 p.m. meeting."

He turned his face to Rebecca.

"Will you need to go with Jack to get Marie, Rebecca? You need to collect your things from the house, as well, do you not?" asked Adelman.

She gestured toward a corner of the conference room. "I brought my overnight bag with me this morning, Jaakov. I tossed it over there in the corner when we arrived here in the conference room. And I didn't bring anything else with me from England."

The two Mossad agents looked at each other, smiled, and nodded. They seemed inordinately impressed by this.

Adelman noticed and said to Rebecca, "My colleagues thought only their own women agents traveled that light, Rebecca. They'd like to sign you up."

She smiled politely at them.

After a moment, McGriff, having affixed the tracking device to the underside of his foot and re-tied his shoe, turned to her. "Rebecca, do you want to try to get some rest while I go over to the house to collect Marie and our things?"

She shook her head and turned to Adelman. "Jaakov, may I have access to the embassy's workout room for the next hour?"

"Of course," he said. "I'll arrange for that as soon as you're ready. You'll want to take your overnight bag upstairs to your room and change clothes first, I assume."

"Yes, please," she replied. "Oh," she added, "could a target be placed in the workout room for my use?"

Both Mossad agents' eyes widened. The older man spoke. "I'm afraid our workout room is not a firing range, Mrs. Clark," he said, smiling at the thought of handgun practice in the small embassy gym, usually occupied mid-morning by agents and administrators using the various weight and cardio machines.

Adelman looked at him and shook his head. "You misunderstand, my friend," he said.

"She throws knives."

CHAPTER ELEVEN

AS THE CONVERSATION IN THE ISRAELI EMBASSY'S CONFERENCE room drew to a close, Dr. Eleanor Chapel, on the sixth floor of the Belton and Adelman Detective Agency's building in New York City, heard Adelman's computer emit its unique chirping noise. She moved from the sitting room into the conference room and sat down at the machine. There she saw that a special message had just come in via the SMTP CD, sent to Adelman from Kory Manguson in England. Eleanor tapped the keys to call the message onto the small screen.

As with all transmissions sent and received by this novel method, the message was short and to the point: *Luke overnight RAF to Andrews AFB Washington D.C. Scheduled arrival now.*

"Sidney!" she called to her husband, who was puttering in the detective agency's kitchen, just down the hallway from the conference room where the computer was situated. Something in her voice led Belton to move with unusual alacrity, thumping along with the heavy cane, down the hallway and into the conference room.

Eleanor gestured to the screen.

They took a moment to digest the message.

"Sidney," she said, "this means that the Lodge must have decided that Luke should join his sister and the others in D.C. soon after we notified them on Sunday night of Rebecca's and the others' movement from here to Washington. They wouldn't have seen that SMTP message until Monday morning —just yesterday —their time."

Belton nodded. "Right," he said.

"An' ya know, Eleanor," he continued after a moment, "this makes sense. T' leave our best weapon —Luke Manguson —on th' other side of th' ocean when things are comin' t' a boil isn't really … ya know … very … ah … circumspect."

She looked up at him. "*Circumspect,* Sidney?"

The crooked smile worked its way across his lined face. "Hey," he said, "I know some words, Eleanor.

"You may be th' smartest person in th' room, but … I got some *words!*"

She laughed her tinkling laugh, then turned serious again. "How should we think about this, dear?" she said softly.

"Well," he said, "fer right now … just let 'em know we got th' message.

"Then we can put on our thinkin' caps an' put somethin' t'gether."

They knew that Luke's arrival in the U.S. was a game changer. Rebecca's twin and Kory's husband, Luke, was the family's premier warrior, a former Royal Navy boarding-party leader skilled at moving his navy's most nimble vessels in close against ships suspected of transporting contraband. In his active-duty years —a not-so-distant past —he and his combat units would force passage onto an opposing ship, almost never with the use of firearms. Because this form of combat was conducted in such close quarters, and because Luke's team would engage the enemy so quickly, pistols and rifles were of little use to either side.

Fists, knives, ropes, and clubs were the weapons of choice.

Those, along with sheer physical intimidation.

And Luke had the prototypical build for this kind of fighting. A trifle shorter than 6 feet in height —and, thus, slightly shorter than his twin sister —he was astonishingly broad of shoulder and heavy of chest and upper arm. Furthermore, whenever he prepared for action, he wore a shoulder holster superficially similar to that worn by McGriff, Adelman, and Belton, but Luke's included no fittings for any type of firearm. Instead, the elaborate leather device had been handcrafted to Luke's specifications, so that it contained numerous niches individually tailored to hold edged weapons, restraining devices, small tools such as lock picks, and more.

Luke, like his wife Kory, had maintained status as an active reservist with the Royal Navy, and that, along with his combat reputation, gave him ready access to Royal Air Force transport flights to any destination in the world. It was this access that had allowed Rebecca to fly to New Jersey the previous Friday-Saturday overnight.

Given Dr. Chapel's SMTP CD message to the Lodge, sent on Sunday evening, that Rebecca and her companions had taken AMTRAK to Washington, Luke had made the decision the next day to fly into Andrews Air Force Base, just

10 miles southeast of the city proper. He actually knew that base's transportation officer as a result of previous flights into Andrews, and he was immediately provided with an unmarked high-performance Ford roughly comparable to the one that the CIA team had loaned to Jack McGriff the previous week.

The Ford boasted the same 5.0-liter V8 engine: a *pursuit* vehicle.

Now, having acknowledged to the Lodge in England her receipt of the SMTP message, Dr. Chapel gestured for her husband to sit down next to her at the computer table. He pulled a chair from the conference table and faced her.

"How can we help them, Sidney?" she asked after a moment.

"We can stay outta their way, Eleanor," said Belton without hesitation. "We got nothin' t' add t' what they got now," he added. "They got Rebecca; they got Luke; they got McGriff; they got Jaakov. An' they got Marie's knowledge of th' Soviet Embassy, if they need that kinda thing.

"We just stay here and handle th' computer stuff, Eleanor," he concluded.

"*We* handle the computer stuff, dear?" she asked mischievously.

"Yeah. You an' me, Eleanor. We *got* this techno-stuff."

As Luke was working through the paperwork and signatures necessary to be given use of one of the base vehicles, McGriff and Rebecca, at the Israeli Embassy, were being escorted from the conference room to the embassy's third-floor guest quarters. Their escort, a mid-level staff member, mistook them for a couple, and opened a single guest-room door, handing the single key to McGriff. Upon hearing his explanation that they would actually need two rooms and four keys, the escort excused herself to retrieve more keys.

She returned quickly.

McGriff went into his room with his key and Adelman's, closed the door, freshened up quickly, and with difficulty resisted the urge to lie down for a quick nap. His eagerness to retrieve Marie, to return to the embassy, and to join with Adelman and the others in planning for the 4 p.m. session with Ivanovich, overrode the need for rest. He sat on the edge of one of the two beds, leaned over, removed a shoe, and checked the adhesion of the tiny tracking device nestled under the arch of that foot.

He re-tied the shoe, stood, and looked at himself in the full-length mirror. He adjusted the shoulder rig and the loose fit of his black priestly sport coat.

Satisfied, he strode to the door of his room, placed his hand on the doorknob, and bowed his head in prayer. Standing at the door, he said his five-word "companion prayer" to himself, the prayer he used many times a day and taught insistently to his parishioners —*Father, be present, be present* —and opened the door.

He then headed down the hallway, descended the main stairwell, and walked into the conference room. Adelman was waiting for him there with two agents whom McGriff had not met previously.

After confirming the address where Marie would be waiting, south of the embassy in a mixed-use neighborhood just off of Connecticut Avenue, the two agents, both armed, escorted McGriff to one of the embassy's town cars. Once inside the vehicle, the driver activated the Lincoln's tracking device and pulled out of the garage, through the parking lot, and onto Connecticut, driving south toward city center.

Meanwhile, back inside the embassy, having moved to the operations center, Adelman and others watched the wall-mounted electronic grid of D.C. and its environs, as the pair of blinking dots moved down Connecticut. The larger dot represented the Lincoln's own tracking device; the smaller, the device carried in McGriff's shoe.

The group watched silently as the town car continued south, stopping and starting in Washington's mid-morning traffic. After several minutes, as the car turned off Connecticut, someone said, "I'm wondering if we shouldn't have sent an escort vehicle behind them."

"No reason to think there'll be a problem with this," responded another.

A pause ensued.

"Yeah," said Adelman a minute later. "We probably should have."

Rebecca resisted, as did Jack McGriff in the adjacent room, the temptation to lie down and rest. Instead, she opened her overnight bag and changed into her all-white tennis outfit: tennis shoes, tennis skirt, and sleeveless monogrammed tee-shirt. She pulled her hair into the pony tail —always her choice when preparing for vigorous activity of any kind —and dropped all three of her three-knife sets of Barringtons Swords 12-inch competition-grade throwing knives into their slender leather carrying sheath.

She then removed her Bible from the book-sized pocket on the inside of her overnight case and took it to the single, straight-backed wooden chair the room offered its overnight guests. Moving the chair to the window, she turned to Ephesians 6, and read the entire chapter, pausing on its concluding passages: "Put on the whole armor of God. … Take the helmet of salvation, and the sword of the Spirit, which is the word of God."

She then dropped to her knees at the window and prayed for the strength and clarity to act in obedience to God in the maelstrom that she expected to face in the coming hours.

She stood, picked up the sheath of throwing knives and the small passport-sized folder in which she carried not only her passport but also U.S. cash and detailed contact information for her family in case she was severely wounded or killed in what was to come next. She left the room and descended the same stairwell McGriff had transited earlier, arriving quickly at the small gym on the second floor.

The same escort who had taken her and McGriff to their third-floor rooms was waiting for her.

"We've set up a target on the wall farthest from the workout machines, Mrs. Clark," she said hopefully.

"It's an archery target that some of our agents use on the outdoor range. We hope it will work for your purposes."

Within 15 minutes the small gym was filled with amazed onlookers crowding into the constricted space to watch something they had never seen before and never imagined. Here was a 6-foot-tall woman in tennis garb firing terrifying-looking foot-long knives at a target mounted on one wall of the gym. Each of her nine knives was released with a powerful underhand motion using a technically difficult no-spin release that sent each missile flying, exactly like an arrow, but in a slightly rising trajectory from her hand to the target.

Observers could not help but imagine, with each *thud* of the knife into, and through, the target, the effects of such a weapon on a human adversary. They stood transfixed as Rebecca repeatedly fired her nine knives, walked to the target to extricate them, then returned to her release point nearly 30 feet from the target.

At no point did she appear to notice the onlookers.

Her concentration was total.

Suddenly there was a stirring at the door as Adelman pushed his way through the crowd.

"Rebecca!" he shouted.

She turned and read his face.

Tatyana Kuznetsova had wasted no time taking action on Artur Volkov's order to awaken the KGB agent coordinator and to have him immediately set up a stakeout in the residential neighborhoods nearest their adversary's hotel. The coordinator's response was not what she had hoped.

Appearing to be offended that Volkov had delegated this instruction, rather than doing it himself, and appearing further to be offended to be given an order by a mere woman, the coordinator had sleepily cited the "saturation point" that had been reached on high-priority agent assignments, had talked about his agents' lack of sleep and rest, and had suggested that he arrange for a limited surveillance network, to be in place "perhaps" by noon that day. She responded furiously and profanely, leading to a series of grudging compromises that resulted in a six-car, 12-agent KGB stakeout of several hotel-area neighborhoods by 9:30 a.m. that morning.

The actual neighborhood to which McGriff, Rebecca, and Marie had gone by taxi, taking the last hundred yards on foot through alleyways, was indeed covered —fortuitously for the KGB agent coordinator —by his limited stakeout. The surveillance coverage was, however, put into place too late to detect McGriff and Rebecca departing in one Israeli town car before 8 a.m., or to see Adelman and his two colleagues as they were picked up in another shortly after that.

Now, just before 10:30 a.m., the Israeli Embassy town car carrying McGriff to collect Marie and their belongings turned into the neighborhood in which she had been waiting anxiously for … she did not know what. She was actually standing near the front door of the house, peering through the sitting room window when the town car pulled into the driveway. She turned and ran back through the house, out the back door, and into the side door of the garage. She was there in time to see one of the Israeli agents manually raising the overhead door for the town car's entry.

Her welcoming embrace for McGriff was enthusiastic … and lengthy.

Nevertheless, as McGriff had predicted, he and Marie were packed and seated comfortably in the Lincoln's back seat in just 15 minutes. The unwieldy vehicle edged back out of the driveway and had started toward Connecticut Avenue when the Israeli driver suddenly realized that the black Mercedes S-Class sedan approaching from the opposite direction was actually steering a collision course.

The Mossad agent braked sharply, spun the wheel to the left, and began a sluggish U-turn that would quickly prove impossible, given the length and turning radius of the town car and the narrow width of the small residential street. In seconds the Lincoln was sandwiched on each side by identical Mercedes-Benz sedans that pinched the town car tightly between them.

McGriff's eyes widened as he saw eight heavily armed men spring from the two Mercedes sedans. As eight Kalashnikov automatic rifles opened from close range, he sprang on top of Marie, forcing her down onto the floorboard with his full weight.

In seconds, the firing stopped. Both rear doors of the town car were ripped open and at least four AK-47s focused on the black-clad priest whose bulk completely covered the small woman lying under him.

In less than one minute the thing had been done. The two Mossad agents were dead, and McGriff and Marie were being driven away from the area by one pair of the Soviet murderers, the other six riding in the accompanying vehicle.

McGriff had been stripped of his 9mm, and Marie of her purse containing the pepper spray. They were thus without weapons of any kind. They now had real handcuffs on their wrists and blindfolds over their eyes, as they sat next to each other on the back seat of one of the Mercedes sedans.

Before the blindfold was applied, McGriff had seen that the vehicle had been set up to transport captives: a cage-like device separated the front seat from the back, and doubtless an auto-lock system was in place to make the rear doors impossible to open from the inside.

Marie had been shocked to her core by the murders. Although she knew neither of the Mossad agents, she did know they were her protectors, that they had not initiated the violence, and that they were clearly dead. It was her first such experience. She felt weak, drained, faint. She leaned her shoulder into McGriff's side.

He was thinking hard. There were two positives.

First, though they had been roughly handled, neither of them had been injured. Second, the tracking device affixed to the arch of his foot was in place and surely active, allowing Adelman and the others at the Israeli Embassy to follow their movements.

He guessed that their captors —certainly KGB agents acting under orders from Ataka —had expected Rebecca Clark to be in the Israeli town car, and guessed further that only the capture of Rebecca would have justified, in their enemy's minds, the unhesitating daylight slaughter in a quiet Washington neighborhood, an act certain to stir a hornets' nest of law-enforcement and possibly military activity. After all, McGriff and his colleagues had determined to their own satisfaction, while still in New York City, that the capture and, probably, the subsequent murder of Rebecca Clark would have to be the ultimate goal of Ataka's leaders, regardless of whatever other elements might form some part of their overall plans.

Had the KGB agents in the Mercedes sedans known that the woman in the Israeli town car was Marie Campbell, McGriff suspected, they would simply have threatened the Mossad agents and then taken Marie and himself without violence.

If, that is, the two Mossad agents would have acquiesced to such intimidation, a doubtful proposition, McGriff realized on further consideration.

Even now, he was not certain that their captors understood that they did not have Rebecca. Although the two women —Rebecca and Marie —were not similar in stature, they were the same age and, except when exercising, always carefully coiffed and dressed. But eventually, he knew, these men would come to realize that they did *not* have Rebecca Clark in their hands.

McGriff tried to imagine their captors' plans. Doubtless the KGB, and perhaps the Soviet Embassy, had at least one safe house in the D.C. area. Perhaps one of those was their destination now. And, whether or not, these men would upon arrival get in touch with Ataka … with Artur Volkov or Tatyana Kuznetsova. At that point the KGB agents would come to understand whom they had kidnapped, and would receive instructions.

What would those instructions be?

He could only imagine that this would then become a hostage crisis, with Marie's life, and possibly his, offered in exchange for Rebecca … and her life. And he found it easy to imagine that Rebecca Clark would be a willing participant in such an exchange as that one: *The blueprint of the universe: my life for yours.*

He turned his face to Marie as she continued to lean into his shoulder. He kissed her sweet-smelling brown hair.

"Father," he prayed softly to her and for her, "be present, be present."

Interrupted in her knife-throwing practice by Adelman's shout of alarm, Rebecca ran to the target, collected all nine of the knives, slipped them into the leather sheath, and, as the crowd of observers parted, ran for the door of the gym. She and Adelman then sprinted side-by-side from the gym to the embassy's main stairwell and, descending at a run, arrived in 30 seconds at the central operations room.

Once they were admitted, Adelman gestured immediately toward the wall-mounted electronic grid of the city and its environs. Ignoring the others in the room, the twosome focused their attention first on the large blinking light indicating the position of the town car in which McGriff and Marie had been riding. They saw that that light was now stationary, while the smaller blinking light representing McGriff's specific position was moving rapidly away from the immobilized town car, eastward toward the Anacostia River and southeast Washington.

The senior operations-room manager addressed them. "We've called the D.C. police and asked for assistance immediately, where the vehicle is stopped," he said. "They're on their way, but no report yet."

As he said this, one of his phones rang and he picked up. His face drained of color. He struggled to speak, and finally said grimly to all in the room, "The police report they're dead, both of them.

"Both shot and killed. No perpetrators in sight."

The room fell completely silent.

Rebecca and Adelman stared long at each other, then turned and looked again at the grid and at the small blinking light still moving away steadily toward the Anacostia River. Adelman turned back to the operations-room manager, who was still holding the phone to his ear.

"A description of the dead?" he asked quietly.

The manager relayed the question, listened, and said, "Both of our agents."

Just then the intercom buzzed. The same manager hung up the telephone and picked up the intercom receiver. He listened, and addressed Rebecca and Adelman.

"Our chief security guard says there is a Lieutenant Luke Manguson, Royal Navy Active Reserve, at the embassy gate, driving a white Ford interceptor registered to the automotive pool at Andrews Air Base. The lieutenant is asking if either of you is here in the embassy building and, if so, if he might speak to one of you.

"What should I tell him?"

Within minutes, Luke strode into the operations room and embraced his sister. As he did, he extended his right hand to his companion in previous Rebekka Yahalomin conflicts, Jaakov Adelman.

Luke was wearing military-issue fatigues, including a billed camouflage cap that came low over his eyes. But the attention of the Mossad agents and administrators in the room focused —through the pall that had been cast immediately upon receipt of the news of the murder of their two associates —on Luke's shoulder rig and its myriad edged weapons, tools, fastening devices and more.

They'd never seen anything like it.

Conscious of the effects of the tragedy on others in the room, Adelman quietly conducted necessary introductions and an explanation of Luke's identity and capabilities. The reputation Adelman had built in his days as a Mossad agent gave him instant cache in any Israeli operations room.

Adelman quickly briefed Luke on the situation, and turned immediately back to the wall grid, calling Luke's attention to the in-motion blinking light, as it moved across the Anacostia River toward the Maryland suburbs along the left bank of the river.

"That's Jack McGriff, Luke, and, we assume and hope, Marie Campbell, as well," said Adelman.

Luke nodded, then asked after a moment, "Do we assume the presence of a KGB safe house along the left bank of the Potomac?"

"We do," said the operations-room manager, "but we don't have a location."

After another moment, Luke asked, addressing anyone in the room who might offer an answer, "Do we think they realize that Marie Campbell is not Rebecca Clark? Do we think they know they do not have my sister in that vehicle?"

There was a thoughtful silence, then Adelman responded. "They may not yet realize it, but once they get to their safe house and communicate with … with their command unit …"

Adelman was reluctant to name Ataka or Artur Volkov in front of the group. The long-established protocol within Rebekka Yahalomin was never to discuss what they knew or suspected in front of those not part of the group, whether the information came from Rebecca's "special messages" or from more conventional sources … except when authorized by Rebecca herself.

"Agreed," said Luke in response to Adelman's observation.

"They soon will know that they do not have Rebecca in their custody. They'll clear that up as soon as they get to their safe house."

"And at that point," said Rebecca, "they will understand that Father McGriff and Marie will serve as excellent and effective hostages, because they can be used to draw me to them. I'm the one they have wanted from the start."

Luke turned to his sister. "You'll not go," he said authoritatively. "We do not respond to hostage threats."

Rebecca turned to her brother, placed her hands on her hips, and affixed him with a steely, withering stare that said more than words could.

The gray eyes could turn hard and cold.

Adelman considered this wordless face-off, and smiled in spite of himself. He'd never seen the twins confront each other in quite this way. He looked from one unsmiling face to the other, and began to feel somewhat unsettled.

Major force against major force, he mused to himself, *and yet none of it verbal, and none of it physical.*

The wordless, motionless confrontation was fearsome.

And prolonged.

Suddenly, the operations room manager broke the silence.

"It looks as if Father McGriff's tracking indicator has stopped," he said.

They all turned to look at the wall grid.

As the tense scene continued to develop in the Israeli Embassy's operations room, Belton in New York City responded to his detective agency's street-level buzzer. "Yeah?" he growled into the two-way speaker mounted on the wall in the agency's sixth-floor conference room.

"Courier from the Israeli UN office, sir," said a male voice. "Urgent delivery."

"Who sent ya?"

There was a pause.

The courier, who sounded like a young man, but not an adolescent, cleared his throat nervously and said, "Sir, the names on the origination lines are: Jaakov Adelman and Rebecca Clark, both of them in Washington D.C."

Belton responded quickly. "I'll buzz ya in."

Two minutes later the young Israeli courier, carrying Israeli Army identification, stepped off the elevator and handed the packet to Belton.

"My instructions are to remain with you, sir," he said to Belton, "while you review the material. I am to say that, if you wish, I will drive you across the Hudson to the Teterboro Airport in New Jersey, where an Israeli Embassy Learjet will fly you —and Dr. Chapel, if she wishes —to Washington … to Andrews Air Force Base."

They walked together from the elevator to the conference room where Dr. Chapel waited, seated at the long table. Belton took a seat next to her, the courier standing with practiced formality in the doorway.

Having studied the Ataka material previously, the couple skipped to the freshly decrypted transcript of Rebecca's overnight vision. They read of the mysterious underground corridor, the no-windows computer room, the bound captive, and the disembodied pistol.

They finished at the same moment, looked briefly at each other, and turned their faces to the young Israeli officer. It was Dr. Chapel who spoke for them both.

"Give us 15 minutes," she said, "and my husband will be ready to go with you to that New Jersey airport."

Belton looked at his wife inquiringly. Not in disagreement. Just seeking her thoughts, but without needing to form a question in words.

"I need to stay with the SMTP, dear … and with Penelope," she said.

"We could bring Penelope with us," he said.

"We can't bring this computer with us," she replied.

He was thoughtful.

"I'm still not sure," Belton said carefully, "what I can add t' what we already got there in D.C., Eleanor."

"Your brain, your decades of experience, and, especially, your contacts, dear," she said. "You know, Sidney, and are known by, every law enforcement officer in this part of the country … and beyond. There is no one else in Rebekka Yahalomin that can even *approximate* what you will bring to the group. You need to be *there,* not here."

In minutes she had packed his overnight bag for him, while he had loaded his big Springfield .45 pistol, its shoulder holster, a box of .45 ammunition, and the documents just delivered by the courier, into a soft-sided briefcase.

Then, a tender kiss between husband and wife —they had outlawed perfunctory kisses long ago … no "pecks" allowed —and he and the courier were gone.

"Well, Penelope, dear," said Dr. Chapel inquiringly to Marie Campbell's adaptable feline, lounging near the center of the conference table, "things seem to be nearing the edge now, wouldn't you say?"

Penelope looked at her.

Eleanor nodded in response to her own question.

"*Very, very* near the edge,"

CHAPTER TWELVE

AS THE ISRAELI EMBASSY'S CHARTERED LEARJET ROSE FROM Teterboro Airport and leveled off at 17,000 feet, taking a heading for Andrews Air Force Base just southeast of D.C., the co-pilot removed his earphones and turned to the aircraft's only passenger.

"Mr. Belton," he called through the cockpit door to the small seating area, "what can we do for you in transit to Andrews? Our radio has a satellite connection that is as secure as air-to-ground transmissions can get, if you'd like to use it."

Belton looked up from the legal pad on which he had been scribbling since he and the courier had first pulled away from the detective agency's building on Washington Street North in Manhattan.

"Gimme about five, Captain," he said, "an' I'll be ready."

In less than five, Belton had been fitted with a set of headphones and connected to the operations room in the Israeli Embassy in Washington. Huddled around the speakerphone there were Rebecca, her brother, and Adelman, having been notified minutes earlier by the Israelis' New York City UN office of Belton's decision to fly to Washington on the charter. Also in the room were the operations-room manager and other Mossad agents and support staff.

"We'll be touchin' down at Andrews in less than an hour," said Belton over the Lear's radio. "Gimme whatcha got."

"Sid," said his detective-agency partner, "we've got a new crisis."

Adelman then outlined what the electronic grid-map had shown, and what the D.C. police at the murder site had reported, regarding the interception of the embassy's town car, the slaughter of the two Mossad agents, and the subsequent kidnap of McGriff, and, presumably, of Marie.

"Sid," Adelman asked, "is there a good map of the D.C. area on board?"

Belton looked up and saw that the co-pilot was already pulling from the Lear's map compartment the very chart he had just heard requested. He spread the large map out on the jet's fold-down table for Belton.

"Okay, people," said Belton into his mic. "I'm lookin' at the city."

Adelman then described the precise point at which McGriff's individual tracking indicator had stopped moving. He noted that it was continuing to flash its regular signal, but was now stationary. Adelman added that McGriff and, all assumed, Marie with him, appeared to be sequestered in a structure nestled in a sparsely settled area along the Potomac, on the Maryland side, not far from an inlet called Swan Creek. The area was, at that point in its mid-1980s development, still in the process of becoming a bedroom community for the city proper.

The exact location of the structure, presumed to be the Soviets' Maryland safe house, was actually nearer Andrews Air Base —no more than five straight-line miles —than it was from downtown Washington. The safe house had, it appeared, been carefully chosen by the Soviets so as to be difficult to approach by vehicle without being observed at considerable distance by those stationed in and around the house.

After an extended silence while all parties examined their maps, especially the thoroughly unsatisfactory vehicular approaches available, Belton barked into his mic, "Okay, people, we got about half-hour t' touchdown at Andrews. How fast can y' get t' th' base from where y' are now? Hmm? How fast?"

"Mr. Belton … Luke here … it took me exactly that long … 30 minutes … to drive from the base to the embassy."

"How fast did ya drive, Lieutenant?" asked Belton.

Belton prided himself on having learned to pronounce Luke's military rank in the British fashion, something that always made his British colleagues smile.

"Fast," replied Luke.

"Okay. You three get started. I'm gonna get in touch with D.C. police an' with th' state patrol offices in both states … Maryland an' Virginia … an' I'll have somethin' fer ya by th' time I see ya at th' base."

Adelman signed off, and he, Rebecca and Luke stood immediately to run for the embassy parking lot, when Rebecca stopped and looked down at her attire: white tennis shoes, short white tennis skirt, sleeveless white tennis top.

She turned to the operations-room manager and the others present … all of them men. "Would any of you gentlemen," she said, speaking rapidly in her low, lovely, Oxford-flavored dialect, "be willing to loan me a long raincoat, preferably dark in color, for the rest of the day? I don't want to take time to go up to my guest room, and I brought nothing like that with me, in any case."

One of the agents, who happened earlier to have witnessed the start of Rebecca's knife-throwing practice, jumped from his chair and strode quickly to a bank of lockers along one side of the operations room. "Ma'am," he called over his shoulder, "I've got the perfect thing for you."

He pulled a lightweight, knee-length, dark-colored raincoat from a locker and held it up for her to see.

"It was manufactured just for our agents, Mrs. Clark," he said. "It has two 20-inch-deep pockets on the inside. One pocket is designed to hold an Uzi machine pistol with the stock collapsed and the magazine removed. The other pocket is for as many magazines as we want to carry into a fight.

"That knife-sheath of yours will fit easily into either of these pockets."

She accepted the garment gratefully, slipped it on, pulled her long ponytail out from the raincoat's entrapment, and dropped the throwing-knife sheath into one of the interior pockets. She then turned and ran for the door, where the two men awaited her.

With Luke behind the wheel of the Andrews Base 5.0-litre Ford, Adelman beside him in the front passenger seat to assist with directions, and Rebecca seated on the back seat, they were pulling out of the embassy lot four minutes after sprinting from the operations room. During the half-hour drive, the threesome did not speak except for Adelman's occasional directional suggestions.

There was a reason for the atmosphere of studied silence.

Rebecca, outwardly quiet, was internally churning her way through prayers that were borne of a turmoil of intersecting urgencies.

As Luke cleared the embassy parking lot and started south on Connecticut, Rebecca leaned forward from the back seat and said quietly to the two men, "I'll be in prayer for a while, please, gentlemen."

The men turned their heads slightly toward her and nodded.

Rebecca pulled the knife sheath from the raincoat's Uzi-capable pocket and placed the heavy sheath carefully on the floorboard. She then lifted herself, turned, and knelt sideways on the rear seat, her body facing the left side of the vehicle.

She pulled her arms out of the raincoat and lifted the oversized garment up and over her head. She bent forward at the waist to lower her center of gravity against the stop-and-go of the Ford. She tucked her chin nearly to her chest and clasped her hands together in classic prayer pose.

Thus, she closed herself off from the visual and auditory distractions that pressed on her from the teeming city traffic. In her makeshift prayer room —the back seat of a Ford pursuit vehicle, a Mossad-designed raincoat covering her head, and in a kneeling position in the semi-darkness and semi-quiet created by the coat —she began to pray.

The prayer was necessarily complex, for her needs at the moment made up a confusion of at least three elements. First, she needed to regain clarity of focus in circumstances that had transformed themselves rapidly from that of a diabolical, but seemingly straightforward, publishing-and-distribution threat, to an urgent need to plan and execute two separate rescue missions, one, of Marie and McGriff, her Rebekka Yahalomin colleagues, and two, of the Sudanese graduate student.

Underlying all this was the certainty that she herself, whether captured or killed, was always the number-one objective of her adversaries.

Second, she needed to prepare herself for a situation in which she was likely to be the lone woman in the presence of perhaps a dozen powerful men, all of whom were accustomed to being in charge of everyone and everything around them, only three of whom even knew who she was. And one of those was angry at her, and she at him.

And that led to the third. She needed to transform the brother-sister disaster that had just erupted in the embassy's operations room. Rarely in their lives had such anger boiled up between them in that way, and this mutually felt anger formed a burning, toxic stream that seemed to flow through and around everything else that passed through her mind and heart.

That being the case, she began her prayer there, with the third issue. She "spoke" her prayer phrases silently, yet moving her lips so as to form each word without use of the vocal cords that would convert think-speech into audible-speech. She mouthed the phrases slowly and emphatically, pausing between each phrase.

Father, speak, please, to my brother … Father, speak, please, equally to me … Change us, Father, in the name of Thy love … Change us, Father, for the sake of Thy love … Change us, Father, for the sake of the mission which Thou hast given to us. …

Change us now, Father … Change us now … Please. …

And then she waited, not going further.

Seconds passed. Then minutes.

As the minutes passed, she repeated her prayer, over and again.

At length, she felt movement against the edge of the raincoat, and realized her brother was reaching back over the driver's seat with his right hand, driving with his left, seeking her hand under the garment.

She covered his hand with hers. He turned his hand upwards, so that they were palm-to-palm. Their hands —hands that had shared their mother's womb together —gripped hard and tight.

Then mutually released.

Immediately, Rebecca found herself smiling.

She called to mind, as she often did, Blaise Pascal's "magnificent dictum" —C. S. Lewis's encomium of choice for the mathematician's famous observation —his observation that God had instituted prayer in order to confer upon humankind what he called the "dignity of causation." And she found her whole body beginning to relax, her breathing returning to normal, her mind now freeing itself to focus on the other elements in the immediate crises before her.

Thus, cleansed in spirit by her brother's and her own mutual acts of forgiveness, she renewed her prayer, this time adapting phrases from the 23rd Psalm.

Father, in the coming hours of trial on this day, lead me in the paths of righteousness for Thy Name's sake … Though I walk through the valley of the shadow of death, strengthen me to fear no evil … Help me and my brother and our colleagues to free these captives —Marie and Jack now, young Kazim Deng this evening —while causing no injuries that will threaten the life of any person, friend or foe. …

And, Father, please stand with me in the face of both my allies and my adversaries, many of whom will seek mortal injury to the other. …

She stopped and allowed the Presence within her makeshift prayer room to wash through her, to tell her what she needed to hear. And God's words as written in Jeremiah played into and through her mind:

Call to Me and I will answer you. …

More minutes passed.

And it was done.

"Thank you, Father," she whispered aloud, as she straightened herself, removed the raincoat from over her head, slipped her arms back into the sleeves, turned, and resumed her seat. She reached forward and lifted the sheath from the floorboard, inserting it carefully into an interior pocket of the coat.

Her brother, sensing her movement, reached up to the inside mirror of the Ford and turned it so that he could see her face. She nodded to him.

She was ready.

As was he.

As Rebecca, Luke, and Adelman walked into the charter-flight hangar's conference room at the base, they saw Belton's Learjet, as if on cue, taxiing to a stop less than 100 yards away. And almost immediately afterward, neither Rebecca, nor her brother, nor Adelman was surprised to see that, within 10 minutes of the four of them —Belton now present —having taken their seats at the hangar's conference table, they were joined by a parade of senior officers from the D.C. police, the Maryland State Police, and the Virginia State Police, all arriving separately, but in such tight sequence that the thing felt as though it had been choreographed.

The three Rebekka Yahalomin members not named Sid Belton had worked with Belton many times before. They knew the esteem in which he was held. They knew that, upon being summoned urgently by Sid Belton, any local-area officer would run for the nearest patrol vehicle or patrol helicopter, and then proceed hard and fast to the specified rendezvous point. Rebecca, Luke, and Adelman were seeing exactly what they expected to see, but they were nonetheless impressed.

Rebecca caught Belton's eye and smiled her congratulations to him. The familiar crooked smile crept over his face.

I'm pretty impressed myself, ma'am, he thought to himself.

He got the meeting underway without preliminaries, other than to thank the men for coming so quickly. He then introduced Rebecca, Luke, and Adelman to the law enforcement officials from the three jurisdictions represented: D.C. police, and state police from the two states involved. Each jurisdiction had sent two of its top law officers, plus one underling, presumably to record the discussions.

Seeing the focused attention the nine newcomers were giving to Luke's military-issue fatigues, billed camouflage cap, and shoulder rig, with its edged weapons, tools, fastening devices, and other accoutrements, Belton spoke several additional explanatory paragraphs about Luke's Royal Navy combat background. He then added, but without detail, the fact that Rebecca Clark, without being an actual member of CIA, MI6, or Mossad, was nonetheless considered a high-value asset by all three intelligence agencies, and, in all likelihood, it was she the KGB agents had hoped to kidnap that morning, rather than the woman they did take. He then moved on swiftly, obviously discouraging any questions that might have been asked about either Luke or Rebecca.

Thus, Belton had assembled and had called to order an emergency session comprising a dozen men, counting himself, and a single woman.

In his description of the morning's emergency, he focused on the near-certain involvement of KGB agents and, as well, of officials at the Soviet Embassy. He explained carefully who the kidnapped pair was; he noted Jack McGriff's dual roles as Episcopal priest and part-time CIA recruiter.

He left Marie Campbell's identity unexplained, other than to note her status as a member of McGriff's church in D.C. He noted that two Israeli Mossad agents had been tasked with transporting and protecting the couple and that both had been murdered in a Washington residential neighborhood while they were taking the pair to the Israeli Embassy. And finally, he noted the current location of the small tracking device that the Israelis had provided McGriff before his and the Campbell woman's kidnapping.

One of the senior D.C. officers then added that his three squads' immediate canvass of the neighborhood in which the murder-kidnapping occurred had yielded reports of as many as eight armed men in two vehicles. This led to Belton's assumption that McGriff and Marie were being held by at least eight KGB agents at what was presumed to be a KGB safe house in Maryland, near the Potomac and, in fact, probably within five miles of the base.

Receiving Belton's nod, Adelman then rose and moved to a large, wall-mounted map of the area. Knowing what Adelman would need to do, Luke quickly extricated from his shoulder rig a curious-appearing extension device, probably designed to pick up small objects lodged in confined spaces, but in this case perfect for pointing out features on the wall map. Adelman extended the device and pointed to the D.C. neighborhood in which the murder-kidnapping had occurred. He then traced the approximate route taken by the KGB agents, stopping finally at the point at which McGriff's personal tracking device had become stationary.

The senior Maryland State Police officer rose and walked around the long table to the wall map, standing beside Adelman and looking up at the area just indicated.

"Not much there," he said after a moment's thought. "A few older farmhouses, probably gonna be torn down in a few years to make way for the developers to put up dozens of matchboxes."

"Captain," said one of his Maryland colleagues, speaking from his chair, "I was over in that area recently. I think you're right. Probably the Soviets bought one of those old farmhouses. It'd be a good place to hide somebody. *Really* good sight lines from those old houses out toward the roadway. We wouldn't be able to get within a half-mile of those places without bein' seen, easy, from the second floor."

"Or from the woods that line most of those entry drives," added the captain.

From that point on, the discussion flowed in the expected direction.

What levels of firepower will we need?

How many vehicles?

How many choppers?

Which agency's negotiator will we use?

And if the Soviets are really interested in Mrs. Clark —right here with us in this room —how can we use that to our advantage in a tactical situation?

At some point, Rebecca quietly stood, and, as most of the men crowded into the space between the conference table and the wall map, she made eye contact, first with Belton and then with her brother. The three of them moved unobtrusively to one of the exits, while Adelman inquired of them with his eyes whether or not they wished him to come. Rebecca shook her head, and he nodded and turned back to the map.

Outside the door to the conference room, in a vacant corridor leading to the hangar space itself, they stood close, speaking in low voices. They were a strange-looking threesome, Rebecca wearing the dark, knee-length raincoat over her white tennis skirt and top, Luke with his elaborate shoulder rig worn over the full-body camouflage outfit, and Belton with his shoulder holster covering his rumpled, pinstriped shirt and lightweight, dark-colored dress trousers and shoes.

Nor could they have been physically more unmatched, with Rebecca the tallest, Luke the broadest, and Belton the short, stooped, wizened warrior, leaning heavily on his multi-purpose walking cane.

Rebecca addressed the detective with her always top-of-mind question.

"Mr. Belton," she said softly, "has Dr. Chapel had success in her efforts to trade messages over the SMTP each day? Are Matt and the children doing well?"

He reassured her on both counts, and she thanked him, emphasizing her appreciation with a heartfelt hug in which she seemed actually to envelope his slight figure. Then she stepped back and moved to the immediate situation.

"This will not do, gentlemen," she said.

"We're not going to permit a gun battle here. Aside from the strictures of our long-established Rebekka Yahalomin principles, a gun battle would be tactically the worst possible approach to getting Marie and Father McGriff out of there safely.

"We've seen the map," she said, "and we know where the tracking signal stopped. That appeared to be in a structure —presumably a farmhouse —no more than 100 yards from a small jetty, not far north of the inlet labeled Swan Creek. There must be a good-probability, low-violence approach that the three of us can engineer.

"Luke?"

He nodded. "Yes, Rebecca," he said, "and I think I've got the outline pretty clearly worked out in my head. How does this sound?"

Rebecca smiled to herself as she listened to her brother. No longer was he insisting that she stay away from the danger. He needed her.

And she needed him.

As always.

Marie and McGriff, their wrists handcuffed behind their backs, the handcuffs looped through each chair's seatback slats, watched silently as a heavy-set man wearing priest's clothing entered the KGB safe house kitchen and pulled up a chair opposite them. As he did so, he tossed a thick file folder onto the small kitchen table that separated the captives from the captor.

After a moment, he leaned forward, hands clasped on the table, and spoke. "I am Artur Volkov," said the Ataka director, Russian Orthodox priest, and senior KGB agent. "You are Father Jack McGriff. And you, Mrs. Campbell, I already know from your work at our embassy."

Volkov and McGriff wore nearly identical all-black ministerial garb, their white dress shirts and clerical collars standing out visually from the blackness of shoes, trousers, and oversize suit jackets. McGriff assumed that Volkov's suit jacket was loosely fitted for the same reason his own was: to accommodate an under-shoulder holster and weapon.

McGriff's Beretta and shoulder holster had been taken from him at the time of his and Marie's capture by the same agent who, after arrival at the safe house, had ushered them into the kitchen, handcuffed them to their chairs, and remained there, standing, from that moment until this.

The agent had not holstered his Glock at any point, which led Volkov, after his cursory self-introduction, to look at the agent appraisingly. "Why do you not holster your weapon?" he asked gruffly in his clipped English.

The agent did not reply in words. He simply looked at McGriff, smiled slightly, raised the weapon, and took aim at McGriff's chest. McGriff stared impassively at the agent's face, neither speaking nor acknowledging the threat.

Marie, in contrast, involuntarily gasped, whereupon the agent slowly moved the barrel toward her, and smiled more broadly.

"You are enjoying this," said Volkov, not smiling.

"Where is your professionalism, my friend?" Volkov added, still speaking English and still not smiling.

The agent lowered the Glock and nodded slightly at Volkov, but he continued to hold the weapon at his side. He clearly intended not to holster the firearm despite the presence of the most senior Soviet intelligence official in the United States, an official who had just openly questioned his professionalism.

This agent wanted Volkov to know he would not be cowed by mere authority.

Volkov shrugged, turned back toward the captives, and leaned toward McGriff. "Where is Mrs. Clark, Father McGriff?" he asked pleasantly.

McGriff did not reply immediately. But after the passage of perhaps 10 seconds, he said, "I don't know, but if I did, I would not be at liberty to tell you."

Volkov nodded and said simply, "Of course."

He turned his face toward Marie. "Mrs. Campbell," he said, matter-of-factly, "you must feel some embarrassment, sitting here with me, a person who is aware that you have used your employment at our embassy as a means to break into two different safes: Ivan Ivanovich's, first, and then Tatyana Kuznetsova's, my own administrative assistant.

"You feel much shame at this treachery, do you not, Mrs. Campbell?"

She smiled. "Yes, Mr. Volkov," she said, taking her calmness cue from McGriff, "as do you, no doubt, to have sent intruders into my home last week, and, this morning, to have sent gunmen to murder our guards and then to kidnap us."

Volkov returned her smile, although his, to be fair, translated more as a grimace in the eyes of the captives sitting across the small table from him.

"Yes," he acknowledged to her, "I do admit that some of what I have done is shameful. Sometimes there is … conflict … between what our Christian values require —yours, Father McGriff's, and mine —and what our countries' national interests require. There will be times we must choose the latter."

He smiled at McGriff. "Is that not the case, Father McGriff?" he asked, not unkindly.

Rather than answering the question directly, McGriff asked his own question. "Tell me, Father Volkov," he said, "what are your real plans? We know that your overriding goal is to capture Rebecca Clark, and that everything you have done to this point has been done with that objective in mind. You hoped that she —Mrs. Clark —would be in the car with me this morning, rather than Mrs. Campbell.

"As for the so-called planning document Ataka has produced," continued McGriff, "the more I have considered that document, the less I see that there is anything truly sensationalistic about your plans to publish and distribute some phrases from the Declaration of Independence, along with Thomas Jefferson's rationalistic excerpts from the Gospels. Jefferson's homemade version of the New Testament has been available for centuries, and to little effect.

"And, of course, there is nothing unlawful about your republishing and distributing some version of all that, as long as you follow guidelines for attribution."

Volkov started to speak, but McGriff spoke over him.

"Please, Father," said McGriff, "let me finish."

Volkov nodded indulgently. He was in no hurry.

"I've been thinking," continued McGriff, "that the ease with which you allowed Marie to obtain access to your documents —although you made her work for it and even feigned a knife attack on a city bus —and, as well, to obtain access to a list of Ataka members, suggests that your actual publication and distribution plan must be considerably more ambitious, and considerably more potentially destructive, than what we have been allowed to see so far.

"It has, in fact, occurred to me that, while you have used the Jefferson documents effectively as a means to bring Mrs. Clark's … um … associates … into the conflict, you have more ambitious plans for the documents."

Volkov smiled. "What might those plans be, Father?" he asked, still indulgently.

"When I realized several years back," replied McGriff, "that our Episcopal church in Washington was attracting Christians from many embassies, including the Soviet Embassy, I did some deep reading into the various national and religious traditions represented by those embassies.

"As a result, when I read several days ago the document you allowed Mrs. Campbell to photograph —excerpts from the Jefferson Bible and the Declaration —I kept thinking that there had to be more. And that has led me to recall some of the articles I studied when I was acquainting myself with Russian perspectives on Christianity.

"I've become as certain as I can be, in advance of actually seeing your final product," McGriff continued, "that you're going to bring in Marx himself when you piece together the final version of your document, with the objective of blurring the lines between Christian ethical obligation, such as revealed in Christ's words, 'Inasmuch as ye did it not to one of the least of these, ye did it not to me,' and Marx's theories of the redistribution of wealth. And you'll do this under the umbrella of Thomas Jefferson's name, without any actual mention of Marx, thereby making the completed document all the more volatile and all the more dangerous.

"I keep thinking, Father Volkov," said McGriff, "about Matthew 25, before the sentence I just quoted, where we read, in a more recent translation, 'I was hungry and you gave me no food, I was thirsty and you gave me nothing to drink, I was a stranger and you did not welcome me, naked and you did not give me clothing, …' and how you will no doubt couch your doctrines in ideas so familiar to Christians, that your slender, readable volume will fly off the bookstore shelves. And I now think you'll entitle your little book something like, *An American Bible for the New Century: A Jeffersonian Declaration for Our Times*."

Volkov's eyes were wide in astonishment.

McGriff had seen Volkov visibly blanch at the mention of Marx, confirming in that instant McGriff's hypothesis, and, in fact, confirming it more strongly than any words of denial could have done. McGriff felt he could actually see the gears shifting in his adversary's mind, as Volkov sorted through his options in the face of this astonishing statement by his ordained Christian enemy.

This Christian enemy had somehow seen through his carefully worked-out plan to publish and distribute a document so seductive that its inversion of the Christian message would creep through undetected by the average uncritical reader.

Ingenious and diabolical, in equal measure, thought McGriff to himself.

He watched as Volkov recovered, and he realized that it was like watching the black clouds of a storm front as it built up and approached over the prairie. Suddenly Volkov raised both fists and in a powerful downward motion struck the small table so hard that the wood actually cracked down the middle. Marie flinched at the forcefulness of the action and at the sound of the wood spitting, while McGriff simply held Volkov's eyes, a welcome calmness flooding his mind and muscles.

And he smiled in spite of himself.

Volkov, perhaps as infuriated by McGriff's smile as by McGriff's analysis of his planned Jeffersonian Gospel-distortion documents, leaped from his chair. He stood so violently that the chair tumbled noisily backwards across the floor, clattering to a stop near where the KGB agent still stood, holding his weapon in silent readiness.

Volkov snatched the file folder from the cracked surface of the table, wheeled away from the captives, and strode from the kitchen, motioning for the agent to accompany him. The instant the two men left the room, McGriff once more scanned the room and its exits.

An hour earlier, when his and Marie's blindfolds had first been removed, he had seen that the old farmhouse appeared to be "loose," with old-style windows open against the summer heat, and with thin screens in place in each of the two kitchen windows. There appeared to be nothing substantial that would be likely to prevent the two of them from breaking out, as long as they were left unguarded, even for two minutes, and as long as they could manage to free themselves from the flimsy wooden chairs to which they were handcuffed.

In addition, McGriff saw that the rear exit from the kitchen appeared to lead toward the back door of the farmhouse. The kitchen itself and the back door were apparently connected by a passageway of indeterminate length, a rectangular space that was probably used by the original farmhouse occupants as an elongated coat closet, mudroom, and laundry area.

He could not actually see the back door from his position, but there was no other obvious way out of the rear of the house.

He tested the strength of the chair's slats to which he was handcuffed, and could feel weakness in the slender and aging strips of wood. He immediately twisted and pulled hard against the chair back, hearing the wood creak and moan against the pressure. Focused as he was on this effort, he did not immediately realize that Volkov and the armed agent had reentered the kitchen.

Volkov laughed. "Seriously, Father McGriff?" he said scornfully. "You think you can actually escape from this? Neither of you will *escape*. You can, however, *bargain* with us."

Volkov paused for effect, wanting his captives to fondle the idea.

"As you know," he continued, still standing in front of them, "we desire to converse with Mrs. Clark. You can begin by telling us where she is. We suspect that she has flown to this country within the last several days.

"And we further suspect that she has traveled to Washington along with you two and the former Mossad agent, Adelman. If she is indeed here in Washington, Father McGriff, and if she is willing to trade her life for yours —as any good Christian ought rightfully to be —then you and your friend and parishioner, Mrs. Campbell, can be on your way home within the hour. Absolutely free. Completely uninjured.

"*Comfortable,* in your own homes."

He looked at Marie for several seconds, then returned his gaze to McGriff.

"I suspect, Father," he said, "that you *may* be brave in the face of torture to yourself, but how brave will you be when you find yourself watching your … ah … your *friend,* Mrs. Campbell, here, undergoing torture?

"Knowing that you can stop her torture at any second, simply by supplying me with information regarding Mrs. Clark."

He picked up his chair, moved it back to the table, and sat down heavily across from his captives. He raised his formidable eyebrows inquisitively to McGriff, and then looked first to one and then the other.

Then he looked away, his eyes moving toward the front of the farmhouse.

Neither Marie nor McGriff spoke, but both noticed the change in Volkov's expression. And then they began to hear what he had heard.

CHAPTER THIRTEEN

THE 19-FOOT STARCRAFT HAD A SMALL CABIN, FORWARD, AND A 25-horsepower Mercury outboard on the stern. The boat's high gunwales and diminutive cabin were expected to be useful when the three-person crew — comprising Rebecca, Luke, and the Maryland State Highway Patrol officer who regularly handled the boat —grew to five with the hoped-for addition of Marie Campbell and Jack McGriff.

The large Mercury could provide considerably more power and speed than was assumed to be needed for the operation that was planned. However, both Luke, experienced with watercraft of all sizes and types, and the state highway patrolman, insisted to the patrol supply and equipment officers that "more is better," noting that available speed was always an advantage, whether it was actually used in a given operation or not.

The patrolman carefully backed the state's utility truck-and-trailer rig down the boat ramp until the StarCraft's stern entered the water and began to float. Rebecca, her tennis shoes and long coat already removed and tossed into the boat, waded into the water barefoot, in her short tennis skirt, and released the boat from its fastenings to the trailer. The truck then pulled the trailer from under the boat, while Rebecca held the boat in place by its mooring line. The truck then moved briskly to the parking area.

Rebecca, having tossed the line to her brother, climbed into the craft and donned her white tennis shoes and borrowed long coat. In minutes the threesome was moving slowly into Broad Creek, near its confluence with the mile-wide Potomac.

Things had come together quickly after the meeting in the Andrews Base charter-flight conference room, so that it was still early afternoon as the StarCraft swung left and reduced its speed to something just above idle, moving with the river's current toward the small jetty that marked the rear of the KGB safe house property. The rescuers expected to cover the mile-and-a-half in about 15 minutes, using low power and the steady current to creep along the secluded shoreline.

They would have much preferred to launch the operation at night, but knew that their adversaries had no compunction about either torture or murder. Nightfall's arrival was a luxury they could not afford.

During the quarter-hour transit, all three checked their weapons. Rebecca selected what she considered the two best-balanced throwing knives from her nine-knife array, and removed the other seven from the sheath, leaving them loose in the borrowed coat's elongated pocket, which she would leave on board the StarCraft when she and Luke went ashore.

She would carry the two knives in the sheath, and the sheath in her hand. She knew that an extended firefight with Russian AK-47s against an individual using only Barringtons Swords throwing knives would come to a bloody end long before a third knife could be drawn from its sheath and actually used. One throw —two, at the most —and the usefulness of her weaponry in this engagement would end.

She would wear only the tennis outfit during the rescue attempt.

Luke pulled the small lock-pick from his shoulder rig and handed it to Rebecca, who tucked it into a small pocket on the side of her tennis skirt, a pocket designed to hold a single tennis ball. The pick was likely to prove crucial, since they expected the captives to be handcuffed to household furniture or appliances.

Luke checked his array of edged weapons, implements, and bindings, loosening the snap-covers on those he considered most likely to be used in the upcoming fight. Then, while he took the wheel of the StarCraft for several moments, the state patrolman checked the readiness of his two weapons: a Winchester 20-guage shotgun and a Remington .223 bolt-action rifle. Although he would stay with the boat while the siblings approached the farmhouse, all three knew that, especially in broad daylight, a rifle, a shotgun, or both, might be required to keep a well-armed enemy at bay during what they hoped would be the escape phase of the operation.

And even at that, a single bolt-action rifle and a single shotgun would be thoroughly overmatched against what could be as many as eight automatic rifles.

The rescuers' disadvantages were both obvious and formidable, but their advantages were not negligible, either. First, the area behind the farmhouse was thickly wooded, providing good cover for the boat while it lay at the jetty, and for Rebecca and Luke, as they made their approach. Second, the KGB agents were unlikely to be anticipating a rescue attempt at all, having by now discovered that the twosome they had so murderously captured were mere ciphers —nonentities —in comparison with the *visioner* they had expected to secure.

There might be a negotiated hostage exchange for Rebecca Clark, but a straight rescue effort to save Jack McGriff and Marie, no.

Third, the KGB agents' precautionary defenses would be oriented toward the roadways fronting the house, not toward the river in back, given their natural assumption that in the unlikely —in their view —event of an attempted rescue, such an operation would be organized by police or highway patrol, and that any such rescue attempt would be launched from vehicles, not watercraft.

And fourth, even if there were to be token KGB surveillance at the rear of the farmhouse —perhaps one agent with an AK-47 —Belton's plan was almost certain to redirect the attention of the agents, no matter where they were originally stationed.

Suddenly the three men and the lone woman in the KGB safe house kitchen fell silent, listening intently to the indistinct sounds they were beginning to hear from the direction of Andrews Air Force Base, five miles distant. They quickly recognized the far-off, but distinctive, whump-whump-whump of a helicopter rotor, and then began to realize they were hearing the sound of more than one such machine.

Volkov rose again from his chair, looked at his ever-attentive agent, and then returned his gaze to McGriff. "Any attempt by your friends to rescue the two of you will prove suicidal," he said evenly and confidently. "No helicopter can get anywhere near this structure, given the thickness of the woods here, and no wheeled vehicle can get even 50 yards down the driveway without being cut to pieces by AK-47 fire."

Suddenly there were shouts from the wooded areas toward the roadway, arriving in the safe house kitchen in the form of faint, lengthy strings of verbiage in Russian. Volkov shouted his replies in that language, then turned to the agent, stepped close to him, and said just a single word.

"Ubiystvo."

The agent nodded.

Volkov pivoted and looked back at the two captives for a final time. He shook his head at them in a silent statement filled equally with pity and contempt, and then stalked out of the kitchen and through the main hallway of the farmhouse, once more beginning to shout staccato orders to his agents as he moved toward the front.

McGriff glanced at Marie, whose face had drained of color. She knew enough Russian to understand Volkov's *kill* order to the agent.

McGriff read her face and resumed his desperate efforts to break the flimsy slats that bound him to his chair, but he knew there was no hope. He ceased his efforts after a moment and turned back to Marie.

"Marie," he said tenderly, "may God be with us, now and forever."

"Amen," she whispered, as a single, lonely tear trickled down her cheek.

The agent was now standing close to their table, facing them, the Glock in his right hand, but not yet aimed at them. In passable English, he addressed McGriff, saying, "Your preference, Father? You first, or the woman?"

Just at that moment, the three of them heard a new sound, rising quickly in the medium distance, that of numerous sirens, all of them seemingly moving along the roadway fronting the farmhouse. Almost immediately, AK-47s opened up, so that, combined with the percussive "whumps" of the approaching helicopters and the wail of the converging sirens, a mountain of invasive sound built steadily, all of it from the wooded areas in front of the safe house, and beyond, toward the base.

Through it all, Volkov could be heard, shouting in Russian to the agents.

The agent in the kitchen had turned his back to the captives momentarily, stepping to the center of the room, a position that enabled him to see down the long hallway toward the front door of the structure. He watched as Volkov exited the front door and broke into a run, still shouting.

The agent's back was now to the kitchen table, his head turned toward the violent cacophony emanating from the front of the house. His right arm and hand, holding the Glock, now hung relaxed at his side. Somehow the fact registered on the edges of McGriff's mind that the firearm was now exposed to the kitchen's rear exit, and thus to its opening into the elongated coat closet, mudroom, and passageway leading to the back door of the house.

Suddenly, faster than eyesight could follow, the Barringtons Swords knife flew from somewhere deep in that passageway and thudded heavily into the right bicep of the agent, slicing cleanly through muscle tissue and nerve pathways.

Several sounds followed in near-instantaneous succession.

The thumping, tearing sound of the knife's penetration of human tissue was followed by the wounded agent's indistinct moan, an inarticulate "uhhh" that cut through the noise of helicopter rotors, vehicle sirens, and shouted Russian from outside the farmhouse, and finally, the Glock's unceremonious crash to the kitchen floor.

The agent staggered to one side, looking down in stunned confusion at the terrifying weapon protruding from the muscle of his upper arm. Only in his periphery did he see the camouflage-clad figure that hurtled toward him and the rock-hard fist that smashed into his temple. The agent fell, fully unconscious, to the floor, with a fierce Luke Manguson riding him down.

In a flash Luke had slapped 3-inch-wide strapping tape across the agent's mouth, while Rebecca, having followed her brother at a run, swiftly extracted the knife from the bleeding bicep. Luke then applied a second strip of tape across the wound to staunch the blood flow, while his sister turned to the captives, the lock-pick in her hand.

As the four exited the kitchen, McGriff snatched Marie's purse from a kitchen countertop, where her captors had carelessly tossed it upon their arrival, looked fruitlessly for his shoulder holster and weapon, then turned and ran back through the passageway to overtake his colleagues.

Their exit from the farmhouse was swift and at first unnoticed. They avoided the rough, irregular pathway that led from farmhouse to jetty, so as to follow the thickly wooded, overgrown, and somewhat concealed route Rebecca and Luke had used in their approach. But they soon found that Marie, wearing low-heel casual shoes and a knee-length straight skirt, was forced to pick her way so carefully through and around the prickly vegetation that their progress had become excruciatingly slow.

Although Rebecca's legs were bare, she was able to bound —almost to fly —over the tangled vegetation, so that, while her calves picked up superficial scratches, her pace was actually faster than that of the men. Halfway to the jetty, Rebecca looked back, assessed the situation, and called to her brother, "Luke! Fireman's carry!"

Without a word, Luke wheeled, ran back to Marie, ignored McGriff, who had been trying to help her navigate the vegetation, and drove his shoulder into her lower abdomen. He lifted her over his right shoulder as easily as if she were a small child and turned to continue his swift, crashing pace toward the jetty.

As they approached the water, they saw that the Maryland State Patrol officer had stepped onto, then away from the jetty, and had kneeled, the rifle to his shoulder. As the two rescuers and the two rescued piled into the StarCraft, they heard a single report from the .223, followed five seconds later by the roar of the 20-gauge shotgun.

Luke gunned the engine as the patrolman, both weapons in his hands, leaped into the stern and wheeled again toward the farmhouse, working the bolt-action rifle as he did. The boat roared away, upriver, toward Broad Creek, hugging the shoreline, while the patrolman fired the rifle repeatedly back toward the jetty.

"I'm just keeping them away from the jetty, Luke," shouted the patrolman over the engine noise. "They were beginning to come down the path just as you were approaching the jetty. I think the shotgun, especially, gave them second thoughts."

Luke nodded, concentrating on speed and navigation, wanting to run as close to the shoreline as possible without risking a gash to the StarCraft's hull from a submerged rock. At nearly 30 mph, he succeeded in putting half a mile between the boat and the jetty by the time a full minute had passed.

They were by then fully out of accurate range of the AK-47s.

Luke slowed. The entrance to Broad Creek was in sight in the distance, the boat ramp just around the bend from the creek's intersection with the Potomac.

Rebecca moved to the stern and leaned close to the Maryland trooper so she could be heard. "Thank you, officer," she said, giving him a grateful pat on the shoulder and showing her brilliant smile.

"You're welcome, ma'am," he said. "Did things go smoothly at the house?"

She nodded. "I don't think either of them is injured," she said, turning her head back toward the small cabin, inside of which Marie huddled in the arms of McGriff, her face turned into his chest, her body wracked with sobs.

Rebecca patted the officer's shoulder once more, and then crept forward to make eye contact with McGriff. She raised her eyebrows inquiringly.

McGriff smiled grimly and nodded.

He mouthed his response. "We're okay."

At the boat ramp they found a spacious, 15-passenger van waiting, with *Virginia Highway Patrol* lettered on the side. Inside the van were Belton, Adelman, and a Virginia highway patrolman serving as van driver.

As soon as the rescuers and rescued were seated, the driver moved the vehicle out briskly, heading north toward the Woodrow Wilson Memorial Bridge across the Potomac. Belton and Adelman explained to the newcomers that they were headed to the CIA safe house at Langley, Virginia.

"Langley? The CIA house? Seriously?" said McGriff skeptically.

"With Randy Simpson having been exposed," replied Adelman, "and carted off to a kibbutz somewhere in Israel, that small CIA unit assigned as liaison to Rebekka Yahalomin is again secure, Jack. We've checked.

"They've tightened the unit now so that there are only three agents who are a part of it. You and I know all three. And that safe house in Langley where you and Marie were quartered last week has much better accommodations than our embassy does."

"And my clothes are there!" exclaimed Marie, suddenly brightening, dabbing at her still-wet eyes with a handkerchief from her purse, and smiling for the first time since their town car had been stopped and shot to pieces that morning.

Adelman, on a front-row seat, turned and called back to Rebecca and McGriff. "That reminds me," he said, "that when I realized we'd not be going back to the embassy, I asked the receptionists to go to your rooms, Rebecca and Jack, and repack your overnight bags. They're on the overhead rack just above our heads."

"Thank you, Jaakov," they replied in unison.

"You're very thoughtful," added Rebecca.

The van then became silent while each turned to her or his own thoughts.

McGriff, reviewing the escape in his mind, soon turned to Belton. "Did you set up all those noisemakers to distract the KGB people and provide cover for us, Mr. Belton?" he said. "Was that all your doing?"

"Well, mostly, I guess," answered the detective. "But th' Maryland State people did all th' work of gettin' those three choppers an' those six siren-blastin' vehicles t' converge on that farmhouse at pretty much th' same time. An' th' Virginia State people took care of gettin' this van all th' way from their headquarters over in Virginia, then t' th' embassy t' pick up yer bags, then across th' bridge, an' then down t' th' boat ramp on Bear Creek in time t' pick us up.

"Oh, an' Luke," Belton said, turning to Luke, "a couple of th' Maryland troopers volunteered t' get yer Ford from th' Air Base an' drive it t' Langley fer ya, so ya got wheels if ya need 'em."

This brief exchange supplied a kind of soft closure to the drama of capture, rescue, and escape, and the vehicle gradually became quiet once more under the steady sounds of air-conditioning and well-tuned, 250-horsepower engine. The passengers, emotionally drained after the hours of murder, seizure, threat, and still more violence, continued to process the whirlwind they had just survived.

The driver and the two detectives understood that the rescuers and the rescued, exhausted, would want to be undisturbed for a time in order to decompress and recover. Adelman and Belton were themselves veterans of numerous danger-laden relief missions, having experienced such missions both from the side of the rescuers and of the rescued. They were familiar with the enormous sense of relief and gratitude that falls quickly upon survivors.

Rebecca sat alone, distanced from the others, her borrowed long coat again covering her skimpy tennis garb. She busied herself cleaning the bloodied knife she had pulled from the KGB agent's upper arm, then reassembling the full array of throwing knives, then placing the nine-knife sheath in her overnight bag. Finally, she dabbed antiseptic from the vehicle's capacious first-aid kit onto the angry array of scratches along her sinewy calves.

Having finished these after-action tasks, she leaned against the window and closed her eyes in prayerful thanksgiving for their deliverance. Her actual prayer was unusually brief, for her mind moved irresistibly back to the moments just before, during, and after her successful knife attack.

Her throw, she recalled with satisfaction, had been pinpoint accurate, as it needed to be, and delivered at maximum force. She knew that, without the knife strike, her brother could not have succeeded in his rush to overpower the KGB agent. Luke had required seven or eight pounding, running strides to reach the agent, but the agent would have needed but a single second to raise the Glock and fire, had the Barringtons Swords knife not severed muscle and nerve in his upper arm.

And the agent's shot, could he have taken it, would have been delivered at point-blank range. Aiming would have been unnecessary.

The bullet would have gone home.

And so, *Yes*, she thought, her knife strike had been an absolutely essential component in the rescue of Marie and McGriff. And yet, she thought somberly, necessary or not, she found herself horrified at the memory. It was the first time she had ever used a weapon against flesh and blood. Her concentration on her aiming point —the KGB agent's right bicep —had been so complete that the throw felt no different from the countless daily practice throws at paper targets.

It was the bloody withdrawal of the 12-inch-long Barringtons Swords throwing knife that sickened her, then and now. The sight, the feel, and the miniscule sucking sound of the blade's excision from the agent's upper arm had imprinted themselves powerfully on her mind.

Yes, she had succeeded in enacting Rebekka Yahalomin's treasured *blueprint of the universe: my life for yours*, risking her life to save another's, and had done so without taking the life of the adversary. In this case, without even crippling him.

The KGB agent would recover.

But she *felt* nauseated by the memory of those 15 seconds that raced through her life: the violent knife-throw; the desperate sprint, just behind her brother, to the stricken agent; the slow, careful removal of a blade that had fully penetrated the agent's muscular upper arm, possibly grazing bone but not stopping until it had contacted his rib cage. She recalled yet again how, as she had withdrawn the knife, the wound had insistently yielded the man's lifeblood, if only during the seconds prior to her brother's administering the strapping tape to cover it.

Rebecca's emotional distress —an uncommon experience for her —forced her mind, yet again, back into prayer. *Father, please help the adversary whom I have wounded to heal, in body and in mind; to recover physically; to recover mentally and spiritually so as to understand how a Christian could hurt him in that way; to understand how a Christian could stop him from killing, yet without attempting to take his life in return; to know that You are with him always. …*

As for Marie, she, too, found herself in prayer. But her prayer was grounded in such a different form of experience than Rebecca's that her emotional distress was of a different order as well.

Marie had assumed her own death when the eight enemy agents had stormed the Israeli town car, even while McGriff was covering her body with his own. And she had again assumed her own death just hours later, in the farmhouse kitchen, when she heard and understood Artur Volkov's Russian-language *kill* order to the agent guarding them.

And she had sensed, yet again, her own imminent death when she found herself unable to negotiate the formidable undergrowth that ripped at her shoes, legs, and skirt as she tried to keep pace with her three colleagues during their escape to the river.

And finally, she had experienced an overwhelming sense both of relief and of embarrassment when Luke had turned, had run back to her, and had tossed her over his shoulder. By the time she had broken down in sobs in McGriff's arms, once on the StarCraft, further humiliation seemed impossible.

It seemed to her that only she had failed in every way possible during these hours of testing, that only she had been unable to contribute to the rescue in any way, that only she had collapsed in tears once they had reached safety. And she was acutely aware that every element of her failure had come in full view of the person who had been falling in love with her, and she with him.

She suddenly understood how it was possible for a distressed person to tumble into a kind of self-loathing. And with that realization came an awareness that she was no longer praying. She had begun in prayer, focused on thanksgiving to God for her deliverance from what had seemed near-certain death.

But in seconds her mind had slipped into un-prayer. She had swiftly descended —plummeted, really —down a chute that leads to despair. Sitting next to McGriff in the van, but no longer touching him, she held her face in her hands while a soft moan escaped her lips, unintended and scarcely audible.

Suddenly McGriff's arm was around her shoulders and his face was pressed into her ear. "Stop it, Marie," he said quietly. "This self-blaming and self-pity is not you. It's nothing to do with our faith. It's nothing to do with anything, really. Just stop it.

"Recognize what has happened today for what it has actually been: a tapestry woven of equal parts Good and Evil. And Evil predominated early on, with the murders of our two protectors this morning. But Evil has been overcome as the day has advanced, Marie. You and I have been rescued, and we have been rescued without loss of life to friend or enemy.

"Recognize God's hand in this. And be thankful. Just be thankful, Marie."

He kissed her hair while she wiped the drying tears from her cheeks with her already damp handkerchief. She nodded and turned her face away from him, toward the window, as they approached the bridge over the wide Potomac. She looked upriver toward the vista of gleaming government structures, all overseen by the Washington Monument's majestic spire.

Suddenly she rose, stepped across her surprised companion, and moved back two rows to where Luke sat, also peering upriver at both the natural and the manmade beauty. At his seat, she leaned down and embraced this stranger to whom she had not yet even been introduced.

"Thank you, Luke," she said, her eyes now bright with thanksgiving.

"What you and Rebecca did —and what Mr. Belton and Mr. Adelman arranged —is beyond amazing to me. You risked your life to save mine, and you and I don't even know each other.

"I know that's not really how you think about this … but I do.

"I'm so grateful," she continued, "that you've given me a chance to live longer than I had any right to expect, just hours —and just minutes —ago. I hope to honor God with every day you and He have managed to give me.

"Thank you, Luke."

She stood, saw that Rebecca was looking at her from near the back of the van, and returned Rebecca's brilliant smile with her own. "Thank you, Rebecca," she mouthed to her new friend.

"Thank you so much."

CHAPTER FOURTEEN

AN HOUR AFTER THE VAN'S SIX PASSENGERS HAD BEEN DROPPED off at the Langley safe house, a new planning conference began. The time was 4:15, just a quarter-hour later than the scheduled meeting at the church … the meeting Ivan Ivanovich had requested in his hand-scribbled note to McGriff and Rebecca that same morning, at his home in Maryland. Since his note specified a meeting with just Rebecca and McGriff, the conference began with no others present.

Ivanovich, driving his personal car, had been intercepted —recognized by his Maryland license plate number —by the D.C. police on his way to the church. The patrolman had approached Ivanovich's car, identified himself, and asked Ivanovich to walk back to the police cruiser in order to speak with "a Father Jack McGriff" by means of the police radio.

Ivanovich had been uncertain for a moment, but realized quickly that this was exactly what he would have expected —a D.C. police officer asking him to talk on the police radio band to Jack McGriff —if there were any sort of change in the plan he had suggested in his note. He walked from his car to the passenger side of the police unit, where he was handed the unit's long-cord handset.

"Ivan," McGriff had said through the crackling, noisy radio, "I'm talking to you from the CIA safe house at Langley. Let me start by saying that Randy Simpson has been whisked away by Mossad agents, and the CIA unit assigned to work with us has been reduced to three individuals whom we know well. I'd say the CIA safe house is a 'safe house' once more. Thank you for helping us with that.

"We've had an eventful day, my friend. …"

Minutes later, Ivanovich was sitting down with Rebecca and McGriff in the safe house meeting room. McGriff began the session by reviewing Ivanovich's early morning note. He read the short missive in its entirety.

1. *I will attempt to see Kazim Deng today. I will bring him with me, if I can, to meet with the two of you at church at 4 p.m. Just you two. Bring no one else. No Mossad. No former Mossad.*

2. *Randy Simpson is a double agent, CIA and KGB. He keeps* Ataka *informed about Rebekka Yahalomin. Any communication you make to your CIA contact unit at Langley is relayed by Simpson to the* Ataka *unit at our embassy.*

3. *If I cannot get to the church at 4 p.m., that will mean that I am being sent to Moscow. Or that I am already dead. Save Katina and the girls.*

McGriff looked up from the note. "What happened today, Ivan?" he said quietly.

"First," replied Ivanovich, "tell me how it's possible that you are here, Father. I learned this morning of the violence done by eight KGB agents —the murder of your two protectors —and of their kidnapping of you and 'a 30-something woman' whom we assumed to be Rebecca. I've been barely able to function today, not having any information other than that, and unable to find out anything."

McGriff then sketched the details of the capture, and Rebecca filled in the details of the rescue operation. Ivanovich nodded his head throughout, appreciative of their willingness to bring him up to date. When Rebecca completed her overview of the rescue, Ivanovich responded thoughtfully.

"It seems to me, then," he said, "that others should be here with us to hear my outline of what has transpired back at the Soviet Embassy. If I give an overview just to you two, we're going to need to repeat the story to others in just a few minutes."

Rebecca and McGriff readily agreed, and in fewer than five minutes the conference room felt crowded. Belton, Adelman, Luke, and the three-person CIA liaison team seated themselves quickly. Adelman, the only individual who actually knew all the others, handled the introductions.

Everyone turned then to Ivanovich, but he said simply, "I don't think we should continue without Marie Campbell. While she is not a combatant, so to speak, in the sense that the rest of us are, to varying degrees, she has worked at the Soviet Embassy for quite some time, and she knows many details of the embassy's operation that only a well-regarded person handling inside-outside logistics can know."

He looked his question to the group.

Seeing heads nodding all around, one of the CIA agents rose, punched in a number on the internal-communications wall-mounted phone, spoke Marie's name into the device, and sat down.

"Three minutes," he said.

They waited in complete silence until Marie, looking remarkably fresh after a quick shower and a change of clothes in the room she had occupied on her and McGriff's previous stay, came into the conference and sat down on a chair that had just been brought in from the hallway by one of the agents.

Ivanovich began.

"When I got to my office this morning after giving you my note" —here he nodded first to Rebecca and then to McGriff—"Tatyana Kuznetsova buzzed me and asked me to step across the hall to her office, saying she needed to confer about something urgent and didn't want my assistant to hear. So, I crossed the hall and she met me at the door, indicated 'silence' with an index finger to her lips, and gestured for us to walk toward the elevators.

"We waited," he continued, "for elevator number three, the only one that can travel all the way to the embassy's underground. I understood, without Tatyana saying so, that we were going to the computer room where Kazim Deng was being held."

Here Ivanovich explained that he had interviewed —not interrogated — Deng in the early hours of the morning, focusing in that interview on the whereabouts of Rebecca Clark. Ivanovich said that he had concluded quickly that Deng not only did not know Rebecca's whereabouts, but that he had no idea who Rebecca was, or why any of us wanted to know her location.

"Mr. Deng said repeatedly," continued Ivanovich, "that, in his taxi, he had carried Mrs. Campbell, Father McGriff, and Mr. Adelman from the Soviet Embassy to an intersection on the Mall, where they left the vehicle. This was after one full loop around the Mall. He insisted throughout the interview that he knew nothing about a fourth member of their party.

"I found his account believable," concluded Ivanovich.

Here he paused in his report and looked a question toward McGriff. McGriff understood, and replied to Ivanovich that everyone in the meeting, not just the individuals with whom Ivanovich was familiar, understood who Deng was: a Sudanese native, a Ph.D. candidate in computer science, a part-time analyst with the D.C. police and, as a result of his being selected by the police to drive the taxi carrying the threesome now present in the conference room, presently a captive in the Soviet Embassy's underground computer center.

Ivanovich continued. "In the elevator," he said, "Tatyana explained that young Mr. Deng had been scheduled to be interrogated by Father Volkov earlier that morning, but the interception of the vehicle carrying Father McGriff and, we all assumed, Rebecca Clark, made that interrogation unnecessary. It actually did not occur to anyone that the '30s woman' taken with Father McGriff was anyone other than Mrs. Clark … such was the Ataka fixation on the visioner."

Ivanovich scanned the room to see if anyone had questions for him. Seeing only heads nodding, he continued.

"Tat told me, as we exited the elevator, she intended to follow her orders from Father Volkov: to get the conversion keys and multipliers that would allow her to send instructions authorizing the movement of millions of dollars from their holding bank in New York City to their printing and distribution center in New Jersey. She explained that the conversion keys and multipliers could be accessed only by means of a particular password-protected computer located in the underground computer center.

"This was new information for me," Ivanovich continued. "Not, you understand, the knowledge that Ataka needed to authorize the movement of funds from the New York City holding bank to the printing and distribution center in New Jersey … but that the conversion keys and multipliers were accessible by means of a particular computer located in the underground computer room."

Seeing Marie Campbell's frown, he simply looked to her and said, "Marie?"

She smiled a thank-you to him, and said, "But Mr. Deng, Ivan? Is he not being held in that same computer room?"

"Ah," replied Ivanovich, "you have anticipated me, Marie.

"Yes, he is," he said.

"And I realized that what I most needed —not what Tatyana, Father Volkov, and Ataka needed, but what I needed —was time alone with Kazim Deng. You see, everyone … I have … since my early morning session with Father McGriff and Mrs. Clark … tried to … ah … rethink my own priorities.

"No … more than that …" he continued, struggling, "more than that. I have tried to rediscover who I am … and who I want to be … for my family … for my country … my *old* country, not the one it has become … for my church."

Here he looked across the table at McGriff.

"When you asked me this morning at my home to consider my own caution to you *not* to allow Marie to return to our embassy … and to consider my own evaluation of Kazim Deng as a good person … and, above all, to consider that, at that very moment, in my own home, Rebecca Clark was *risking her life* to help me know that the world's understanding of our Christian faith stood to be damaged by the Ataka project … I suddenly understood the position I was in.

"That's what led me so quickly to write the note that I gave you as you were leaving. That's what led me to realize that Katina and I —and our daughters — would soon be in danger."

Here he paused again, still struggling with his emotions, and dropped his eyes to his hands, clasped together and resting on the table. He signed audibly, then looked up once more at McGriff.

"I realized," he said, "as Tat and I approached the computer room that I was the only person who could act meaningfully, first, to save Kazim Deng; second, to interrupt Ataka's printing and distribution project; and third, to prevent Father Volkov from achieving his long-standing goal: capture, conversion, and, failing that, execution of the person on whom he had become fixated, Rebecca Clark."

Marie gasped audibly.

Ivanovich looked at her, a woman he knew well, both from her work at his embassy and, more so, from their shared involvement in Jack McGriff's church.

"I know, Marie," he said, "that it's possible I'm exaggerating my own ability and my own importance when I say that I realized that I was the only person in position to interfere with those three things —especially the third, about Mrs. Clark —but in the few seconds I had to think while Tatyana and I walked from the underground elevator to the computer room, those certainties overwhelmed me."

McGriff was startled to see tears welling in Ivanovich's eyes. He rose quickly from his chair, circled the table, strode to Ivanovich, and, standing behind him, placed his hands on his church member's shoulders.

Leaning down, McGriff said quietly, but audibly to all present, "Ivan, you have traveled a very long way this day. Now tell us what we can do to help you."

By this time, Marie, too, had circled the table from the opposite direction. She stood next to her pastor and placed a hand on Ivanovich's arm. Leaning around him, she offered him a tissue packet and, speaking even more softly than McGriff, said, "I know your first concern is Katina and the girls, Ivan. I have learned, just before coming into the room, that they are being brought here now, as we speak, by CIA Learjet. They are expected here within the hour."

Ivanovich turned his face toward her, astonishment and joy on his face. Marie looked toward Adelman, who seemed to be informally presiding, and said, "Jaakov, should we take a short break to allow Ivan to process all this?"

But Ivanovich intercepted Adelman's response to the question. "No, Marie," he said kindly, looking up at her, "I need to continue with this.

"There is no time to waste, as you will hear. But thank you, Marie.

"Thank you."

Ivanovich composed himself while Marie and McGriff returned to their seats across from him. Then he looked up, breathed deeply, and continued.

"Outside the anteroom that leads to the computers, I told Tatyana that I needed 10 minutes alone with Kazim Deng before we focused on the master computer and its codes and multipliers. I said that, in view of Father Volkov's not having had a chance to interrogate Deng, and given the fact that my late-night session with Deng was simply information-gathering, not interrogation, I wanted to approach him from a completely new angle. I wanted to present a different face to him.

"At first," he continued, "I thought she was going to insist that she accompany me for the interrogation, but then it occurred to her that she wanted to hear the chief of the underground guard unit give her an overview of what had been done with Deng overnight and thus far, this morning. And she wanted to know of Deng's response.

"So, she looked at her watch, said '10 minutes, Ivan,' and headed back down the underground passageway to the guard office.

"I passed through the anteroom and entered the computer room. I found Deng bound tightly to a chair near a bank of computers at the rear of the room. He was not blindfolded and his mouth was not covered. My overall impression was of a young man who was sleep-deprived and exhausted, but not really … um … defeated … not … ah … terrified … He struck me as a person not readily intimidated."

"Ivan," said McGriff quickly, "I would imagine that those characteristics account, in part, for the D.C. police precinct captain's choice of Mr. Deng to serve as a part-time computer analyst for the local units, and, later, to serve as driver for three of us as we left your embassy for the last time."

Ivanovich nodded. "Yes, Father," he said. "I think you must be right, but I had not thought about him in that way. In any case, after asking him if he was injured —he said he was not —I turned up the computer room's ventilation system to max, in order to mask our voices against any listening devices the room might have, and I pulled a chair up close to his. Speaking as softly as I could, I told him I intended to save his life, but I needed information from him. I asked him to tell me in five minutes what had happened since he had been placed there, and to tell me what he had learned about the importance of any particular computer in the room.

"He looked surprised, but apparently decided he had nothing to lose. He told me that the guards threatened him repeatedly with their handguns, but that they did not hit him or hurt him in any way, perhaps not wanting to leave visible marks on his face or torso. I suspect this is due to Father Volkov's instructions to the guard unit that only the leadership team of Ataka would be allowed to interview or interrogate the captive.

"Deng went on," said Ivanovich, "to tell me hurriedly —before Tatyana was expected back in the computer room —how the computer personnel, many of them Americans or foreign nationals on contract, came and went, hour by hour. He said that they seemed eventually to forget that he was in the room, of no more significance than the furniture. And so it was that he had learned that computer number three, on the center table just behind him, was the master unit, and presumably the one containing all of the conversion keys and pertinent multipliers that I was interested in.

"At that point, one of the guards burst into the room and said that Ms. Kuznetsova needed me immediately in the second-floor operations center. The guard left as soon as he delivered that message, and so I took a moment to loosen Deng's constraints and to assure him that I or my colleagues —the ones he transported in his taxi, plus others —would return for him in a matter of hours.

"I think," concluded Ivanovich, "that he took very little comfort from this. I think he expected to be killed long before a rescue of any sort could take place, and to be candid, he had no real reason to believe me … that we would rescue him."

One of the CIA agents shook his head in irritated confusion. "Why do we care about the Sudanese guy?" he blurted.

He turned his face to Adelman. "I understand, Adelman," he continued, "why you feel badly about the way you handled that tracking device, since Deng could probably have just gone back to the taxi garage and then to the D.C. police station, if you'd just thrown the device out the window or tossed it in the bushes somewhere.

"But seriously," he added, "the young man has nothing to do with the issues we're facing —big-money transfers, publication and distribution of fraudulent material, the safety of Mrs. Clark and of other members of the group —and it seems crazy to me to risk anything or anyone to try to get him out of that embassy building.

"We don't even know for sure that they're going to do anything to him."

Adelman started to respond, but saw Rebecca looking at him closely. The deep, penetrating gray eyes could stop most people in their tracks when Rebecca focused them steadily and insistently on a single face.

Adelman closed his mouth and nodded to her.

Rebecca carefully and deliberately pushed her chair away from the table, and, in characteristic fashion, began to pace around the room, circling the conference table and thereby passing behind those seated at the table, and in front of those whose chairs were pushed against the wall. Thanks to Adelman's thoughtfulness in having her overnight bag packed by Israeli Embassy personnel and eventually loaded into the Maryland State Patrol van, she had taken the minutes needed to change from her short tennis skirt and sleeveless top, and into the plain, straight, dark skirt and sleeveless cotton blouse she had worn to Ivanovich's home early that same morning.

She had not changed her hair as the eventful day had passed. It was still configured tightly in the long, action-ready ponytail she had set earlier as she had prepared that morning to use the embassy's workout room for knife-throwing practice.

She strode nearly halfway around the meeting room before she began.

"You three gentlemen of our CIA contact unit," she said carefully in her British-accented contralto, "have always inspired wonderment among those of us who —thanks to Jaakov —have been given the Hebrew name for Rebecca Special Communications Unit or Rebecca Special Messaging Unit … Rebekka Yahalomin.

"We have been continually amazed at your generosity in giving credence to these messages which have over the years been sent to me as images … dreams … visions … that are, we have no doubt, divinely authored … God-sent messages on the basis of which we have been called upon to take action.

"I say generosity because you are trained to search for hard evidence for everything on which you take action. Nonetheless, you —like some of your colleagues at MI6 and Mossad and, apparently, now at the Soviet Union's intelligence organization —concluded at some point that, regardless of *how* these messages originated and were received, you would need to treat them with utmost seriousness."

She paused in her pacing of the room, and, standing still, looked from one agent's face to another … at each one of the three.

"We have never asked you … or anyone … to believe that these messages were, in fact, God-sent. And yet you have created this specialized unit at CIA for the sole purpose of cooperating with us whenever it seemed appropriate and necessary.

"I think you understand that, to us, these messages are *not* particularly astonishing. We think, for example, of the passage in First Samuel: 'The word of the Lord was rare in those days; visions were not widespread.' And then, in just seconds, in that Old Testament account, everything changed for the young Samuel.

"We feel that ancient kind of Truth-messaging coming to us, in the present day, just as it has done to —and for —others, for millennia.

"Whether or not you believe, with us," Rebecca concluded, "that my 'special messages' are God-sent, I want you to know how much we appreciate your acceptance of the validity and importance of these messages, whatever their probable origin in your eyes. We are very, very grateful."

She smiled at each agent, the smile causing the dramatic scar along her right cheek to compress slightly, yet noticeably, as always. Then, her eyes now scanning the room to encompass the others present, Rebecca resumed her pacing.

"Having said all that," she continued, "I want you to know that my most recent special message featured young Mr. Kazim Deng, and only him. Since that is the case, we of Rebekka Yahalomin can only conclude that the young Sudanese has importance well beyond the mere fact of his imprisonment in the Soviet Embassy underground. We conclude that he is, in fact, destined to have importance to the mission to which we are apparently being summoned: to stop or substantially redirect the funding, printing, and distribution of the material being referenced by Father McGriff as *An American Bible for the New Century: A Jeffersonian Declaration for Our Times.*"

She stopped and again looked at each of the agents.

"For us, gentlemen," she said, both kindness and firmness in her voice and manner, "there is no choice about this. We *must* rescue Mr. Deng, and we *must* do it quickly, before our chief adversaries, Father Volkov and Ms. Kuznetsova, return to their embassy and turn their attention once more to him."

With that, Rebecca quietly resumed her seat at the table. She looked back to Ivan Ivanovich, wordlessly signaling him to resume his account of his long and eventful day. He understood, and began again.

"I went upstairs from the underground computer room," said Ivanovich, "to the operations control center, and found that Tatyana and Father Volkov were both there. I found that the focus of the entire operations command was on the just-then-reported capture of Mrs. Clark —so they assumed —and of Father McGriff. It was obvious to me that nothing else was going to be attempted until the outcome of that presumed capture of Rebecca and Father McGriff was known.

"I didn't have long to wait to find out what was next," he continued, "because within a half-hour, Father Volkov, Tatyana Kuznetsova, and a number of KGB agents departed for the Maryland safe house, where Mrs. Clark —actually, of course, Mrs. Campbell, not Mrs. Clark —and Father McGriff were being taken and held."

Ivanovich paused, and McGriff interjected a question. "Ivan," he said, "the apparent priorities here, on the Soviet end, appear to place capture and … ah … control … of Rebecca Clark and members of Rebekka Yahalomin at a higher level than the funding and distribution of the document I've been calling privately *A Jeffersonian Declaration for Our Times.* Am I correct about that?"

Ivanovich nodded. "Absolutely, Father," he said, "especially in the eyes of Father Volkov. I think the word 'obsessed' applies to his attitude toward Mrs. Clark. I honestly think there is *nothing* that has a higher priority in his mind that the capture and … to use your discreet word … control … of her and of the others in the Rebekka Yahalomin group. But especially of Mrs. Clark herself."

"Well," said Belton after a brief silence, "since Mrs. Clark is sittin' here in th' room with us, an' since others in th' Rebekka Yahalomin group are sittin' here, too … what's next, people? Hmm? What's yer thinkin'?"

Ivanovich replied without hesitation. "Kazim Deng is next, in my view," he said. "Now that Father Volkov and Tatyana have discovered that Mrs. Clark was never in their hands at all, and since Father McGriff and Marie have been rescued and are here with us, there is nothing to prevent Father Volkov, Tatyana Kuznetsova, and others from going straight to the embassy and doing their worst to Mr. Deng."

Belton shook his head and made a sort of rumbling noise designed apparently to register his disagreement. Heads turned to him in time to see the crooked smile spread across the craggy countenance.

"See," he said, "I mighta made a little suggestion t' th' Maryland Highway Patrol people out at th' KGB safe house that they oughta keep all those Highway Patrol vehicles in place, right there, blockin' th' exits, all around th' perimeter of that KGB house, t' make sure *nobody* tries t' leave an' come back t' th' city.

"Know what I mean? Hmm?"

One of the CIA agents shook his head incredulously. "Those state troopers have no jurisdiction over those people from the Soviet Embassy, Mr. Belton," he said respectfully, but authoritatively. "They can't just secure that perimeter and hold all those people in place. You are aware what 'diplomatic immunity' has always meant, sir."

"I told 'em not t' worry about bein' polite t' th' Soviets, see," Belton replied. "I told 'em that those murderous dirtbags killed two Israeli nationals in broad daylight, in a Washington neighborhood, earlier t' day, an' that they'd prob'ly not get in trouble with anybody at any level if they held 'em all in there, at least fer a few hours.

"I even said that I figured th' Soviets would be tryin' so hard *not* to have th' thing blow up into an international PR disaster, that they'd just make a lotta noise an' sit there at th' safe house screamin' into the telephone, until some U.S. senator or the U.S. Attorney General or somebody else like that tells 'em t' stand down.

"When I explained about th' murders of th' two Israelis, I got th' impression that they were actually gonna bring in another half-dozen of their state mobile units t' make sure that perimeter stayed sealed tight as a drum.

"Know what I mean? Hmm? Know what I mean?"

The CIA agent who had challenged Belton's action smiled and shook his head, apparently in disapproval mixed equally with admiration.

There were no other comments about Belton's ploy.

Rebecca eventually broke the silence. "Mr. Belton," she said sweetly, "you have done your magic wonderfully today, but I personally feel no less anxiety about young Mr. Deng than I did when I dreamed his capture in what seems many nights ago."

After brief discussion, it was agreed that Ivan Ivanovich would act alone to attempt to free Kazim Deng. No one at the Soviet Embassy could plausibly be aware of the self-described conversion that Ivanovich had undergone that same morning. Even Tatyana Kuznetsova, who had chatted with Ivanovich that morning once he had arrived at the embassy, could be expected, surely, to continue to count on Ivanovich's long-established commitment to Ataka and its priorities.

A taxi was summoned immediately to transport Ivanovich to the embassy.

Minutes before the taxi's arrival at the CIA safe house in Virginia, Belton spoke by police radio with the senior officer overseeing the blocking units at the KGB safe house in Maryland. The officer reported that their seal of the perimeter was still tight, but that pressure was mounting at several political levels to back off. The officer guessed that by 7 p.m. the blockade would have to be abandoned.

Ivanovich's taxi driver, moving smoothly into the city at the evening rush hour, when 90 percent of the traffic was moving in the opposite direction, was able to drop his passenger at the curb in front of the embassy just before 6 p.m. Ivanovich paid the fare, sat back against the seat, lifted his lightweight briefcase, and paused, the vehicle door partway open.

There, suspended between the safety of the vehicle and the dangers that awaited him inside the building, Ivanovich mouthed quietly McGriff's companion prayer: *Father, be present, be present.*

He stepped onto the curb, closed the vehicle door, and turned to the walkway that led toward the lobby. In his third stride he heard a familiar voice from somewhere down the street.

"Ivan!" called Tatyana Kuznetsova. "Wait for us!"

He turned and saw her walking briskly toward him.

Two steps behind her, he saw the dark, angry figure of Artur Volkov.

CHAPTER FIFTEEN

"WHAT A DAY WE HAVE HAD!" EXCLAIMED TATYANA, AS SHE caught up to Ivanovich on the walkway to the embassy lobby. She fell in step beside him, while Volkov continued to walk sullenly behind them, clearly not interested in talking.

"As it turned out," she said, "the woman captured by our agents was not Rebecca Clark at all. It was our friend, Marie Campbell, who, it seems, may have become our enemy, but who is of no interest to us at all, in comparison to Mrs. Clark. We were busy setting up an exchange of Marie and Jack McGriff for Mrs. Clark, when, somehow, they were stolen from us … taken out the back of the property … rescued by what seemed to us, watching from a distance, to be a Maryland Highway State Patrol boat."

They entered the embassy lobby, showing their IDs as they passed through security. Tatyana then continued her story as they walked toward the elevators. "After that, we were illegally blocked in by state law enforcement people, prevented from getting to the roadway, but Father Volkov eventually got in touch by phone with two of the executives who are here to negotiate the trade agreement."

The three of them stepped into the elevator and pressed "2" to go to their offices on the second floor. Volkov remained silent, his anger boiling at the wasted day, ready to erupt at any moment.

"Those two executives arranged the lease of a small cabin cruiser from the James Creek Marina on the Anacostia," said Tatyana, "near its intersection with the Potomac. The boat, with a crew of two, made the trip down the river to our safe house in about half hour. They arrived before 5 p.m., and brought the two of us back to the marina. We caught a taxi and got here just in time to see you exit your own cab.

"What a day!" she concluded. "I'm just exhausted."

The threesome paused in the hallway between offices 2044 and 2045. Volkov looked at his watch and scowled. Then he spoke for the first time since their arrival.

"I must phone Moscow now," he said. "Eight hours difference. I must awaken the chairman. He will not be pleased."

With that, he wheeled and strode into his office.

"I'll need to set up that call for him, Ivan," said Tatyana over her shoulder, as she followed Volkov into 2045. "I'll meet you in 15 minutes. We'll go together to the computer room. Yes?"

Ivanovich nodded, and turned to enter 2044.

He entered, closed the door noisily, waited behind the door to hear Tatyana close the door to 2045, then quietly opened his door again and crept into the empty corridor. In the minutes since hearing Tatyana call to him on the sidewalk, his mind had been working furiously as he pretended to listen to her account of her adventures that day.

The utterly unexpected presence of Volkov and Kuznetsova more than two hours in advance of his expectations of their arrival had reduced from hours to almost zero the amount of time he had counted on to extricate Deng. Now, padding as softly as possible down the carpeted hallway, he walked past the elevators and continued to the far end of the second-floor corridor. He paused, glanced behind him once, saw no one, and quietly opened the fire door that led to one of the emergency stairwells.

Ivanovich entered 004, passed through the anteroom, and looked into the computer center beyond it. To his immense relief, only Kazim Deng occupied the spacious room. When Deng saw him, he immediately stood and, raising his hands in a questioning gesture, asked, "Where have you been? You promised …"

Ivanovich interrupted him forcibly. "Stop!" he said as he crossed the room to the captive. "We must get you out of the building immediately."

Then, still processing what he was seeing, he added, "How are you free of your restraints? I loosened them, but …"

"You should stop, yourself!" Deng said irritably, his anger at the hours of being regularly threatened by embassy guards and bound tightly to the upright chair suddenly bursting through his usual calm reserve.

"The day guards have not been in the room for hours," said Deng, "and I think the night shift may not yet have started. Meanwhile, some of the computer guys and I have been talking a lot today. None of us, as it turns out, likes the Soviets, and the guys were happy to undo my constraints once it appeared that the day shift had gone home.

"They were also happy to get me into that master computer you're so interested in, and this floppy disk is a complete copy of that computer's hard drive. Open your briefcase, Mr. Ivanovich. Hide this thing in there and get me out of this building."

With that, Deng unbuttoned his shirt and pulled out a thin, 4-inch diskette.

Ivanovich, astonished, could barely respond, but seeing Deng's insistent waving of the diskette in his face, he quickly placed his briefcase on the nearest computer table, opened it, and inserted the disk in the middle of one of the thick policy documents he happened to be carrying with him.

Still too stunned to think clearly, Ivanovich closed the briefcase and simply stood motionless, trying to formulate a plan to get both Deng and the disk out of the embassy.

Deng was impatient. And assertive.

"There's no time to do anything complicated, sir. Just get me to a fire exit and let me run for it," he said, urgency in his voice. "There are people here who, I'm reasonably certain, will kill me if you let them have their way. Which way do I go?"

Ivanovich lifted the briefcase and crossed the room briskly, motioning for Deng to follow. They exited the computer center, crossed the anteroom and, at the doorway leading out of 004, Ivanovich pushed the door open enough to see down the full length of the corridor.

"Come," he said, and led the young Sudanese-American back toward the stairwell Ivanovich himself had used to descend from the second floor. They climbed the stairs rapidly and paused at the exit that opened into the main lobby.

"When I open the door," said Ivanovich, "walk straight across the lobby toward the entrance. Become part of the horde rushing to get to the busses. Hold my ID in your hand and just wave it toward the guards if one of them asks. Don't stop.

"With any luck, a dozen employees and another dozen guests, some of them foreign, will be moving through the security line at the same time you are. They don't check IDs very often when we leave the building; only when we enter.

"Don't stop. Just go. At the sidewalk, turn right onto Wisconsin.

"I'll catch up with you at some point. Don't turn and look for me. I'll overtake you when it looks safe."

Ivanovich cracked the stairwell door and looked into the lobby, where he saw what he had hoped: employees and guests, mixed together, briskly passing through the security exit line, waving their IDs … or not … and in any case not slowing. He stepped aside and Deng, without urging, glided quickly into the lobby and fell in with the crowd.

The employees were mostly ethnic Russians —white —but the guests were as likely to be people of color as not. Deng's dark skin looked appropriately ordinary as he moved across the lobby and passed unchallenged through the main doors. He did not look back at any point.

Ivanovich then followed, waved casually at the guards, all of whom knew him on sight, and passed into the late-afternoon sunlight. He saw Deng, 50 yards ahead, continuing toward the street, still not looking back.

Ivanovich knew that if anyone was watching him —anyone at all —the one thing he must not do would be to appear to be in a hurry. He forced himself to walk in leisurely fashion all the way to the street, where he turned to the right and then began to walk more quickly. At the first intersection, Wisconsin and Calvert, where Deng waited with others for the traffic signal to change, Ivanovich moved up beside him and said, without turning his head, "We can get a ride over there."

He gestured to his right, where a line of parked cars sat, facing the other way, and apparently not occupied.

As they strode together along the line of cars, Ivanovich saw, several cars ahead, a white Ford interceptor. He watched as a familiar black-clad figure rose from the passenger-side front seat. Jack McGriff opened the back door and gestured for Ivanovich and Deng to enter.

They did.

Luke Manguson pulled away from the curb and into the rush-hour traffic, heading back toward Langley, Virginia.

Promptly at 8 p.m., the late-afternoon group assembled again in the CIA safe house conference room: Belton, Adelman, McGriff, Luke, Ivanovich, the two women, the three CIA liaison agents, and Kazim Deng. All had eaten something and appeared eager for the next action steps, whatever they might be.

All sensed that progress, however undefined, was being made.

"Welcome back, everybody," said Belton. He turned to Ivanovich. "Ivan, whatcha got fer us?"

Ivanovich turned to Deng, seated beside him at the conference table. "This is Kazim Deng," he said. "You are all familiar with his resume, and you all understand why, as Mrs. Clark explained to us this afternoon, his rescue was viewed by her and her associates as essential to their mission. Kazim, will you give us your account?"

Deng nodded and began to speak, apparently neither intimidated nor even uncomfortable addressing an array of individuals most would consider imposing. "First," he said, turning his eyes to Rebecca, "thank you, Mrs. Clark. Mr. Ivanovich has explained to me how you were led to envision me in a dream, and how you insisted that I be rescued immediately this afternoon. I'm very grateful."

She smiled. "We are so glad," said Rebecca, "to have you here with us, Mr. Deng. We have been quite fearful on your behalf."

He returned her smile, and said, "You and I must speak to each other about visions sometime, Mrs. Clark. I have had some … experiences … I'd like to share with you."

"That would be my pleasure, Kazim," she replied.

He nodded his gratitude to her, and then began. "In my hours in the Soviet Embassy's computer center," he said, his voice strong, his Sudanese accent noticeable but mild, "I at first assumed I would be killed.

"You see, when I stopped my taxi at a parking area at Arlington Memorial Cemetery, following Mr. Adelman's instructions, I was almost immediately threatened by a Soviet agent who placed a large knife at my neck and demanded information.

"I'm afraid I gave him that information without hesitating. I was not brave enough to die, sitting there in my taxi. The information they demanded was simply the hotel where you" —here he looked from Adelman to Marie to McGriff —"were staying. I told them.

"I'm so sorry."

Here he paused, looking down in apparent embarrassment. Ivanovich placed a hand on the young man's shoulder.

Deng smiled at the gesture, swallowed, cleared his throat, and looked up. "They forced me into their vehicle," he said, "and took me to the Soviet Embassy, where I was taken to the computer center and tied to a chair.

"At first, I expected to be interrogated, tortured, and killed, because I knew I had absolutely no information to give them, other than what they already had.

"As time went on," he continued, "I became less certain of my captors' purposes in holding me there … or holding me at all. Even now, I'm not certain of their purposes, and, I suppose, it's possible that they were not clear themselves, but were just doing something to me more or less spontaneously.

"Random persecution of a convenient target …"

His voice drifted off, then he regained focus.

"In any case," Deng resumed, "from time to time, guards would come into the room and toy with me, waving their pistols in my face, pulling the trigger to cause the firing pin to snap, shouting at me in Russian, threatening to strike me … though they never actually did anything to me at all."

Ivanovich interrupted gently. "Kazim," he said, "tell them about the computer."

"Yes," he replied. "What you will all want to know is this."

Here he reached over to Ivanovich's briefcase, which was resting, closed, on the edge of the table, between the two men. Deng opened the top enough to reach inside, and removed the 4-inch floppy disk. He held it up for viewing.

"Some of you will know," he said, "and some will not, that this is called a floppy disk. This particular floppy is a duplicate of the hard disk drive that functions as the 'brain' of the master computer in the Soviet Embassy's computer center. In other words, this floppy disk contains every bit of data that is held by that master computer.

"Several of the embassy's computer technicians," continued Deng, "who spent much of today in the computer room with me, are foreign nationals: one, a man of color, like me, from Nigeria; another, a white man, like you, from South Africa. In other words, the three of us were all from Africa, and we felt a certain kinship among ourselves.

"At first, I assumed they were employees of the embassy, under contract to work with the computers. However, when the guards were not in the room making threats toward me … when the three of us were alone in the room, which was most of the time during the day … I found that their status was actually much the same as mine. They were more like prisoners than contract employees. They explained to me that, when they were not working in the computer center, they were routinely escorted to one of the upper floors in the building, and held there under guard.

"Furthermore," said the young Sudanese, "they had both been brought to the U.S. under duress from Eastern Europe, arrested essentially for being highly expert, but foreign … and therefore, not necessarily loyal … technicians in a country under Soviet control. Their skills and, as well, their independence of mind, became apparent to the Soviet officials there, and they were simply arrested and shipped to D.C. … to the Soviet Embassy … to work as forced labor.

"As one of them put it at some point today, 'It was really no different from being arrested as a spy, which we were not, and sent off to Siberia; Washington is not Siberia, of course, but we are no more free here than we might have been there.'

"With each conversation," said Deng, "it became more apparent to me that they were on my side, so to speak, and wanted to assist me, if they possibly could."

Deng paused, took a deep breath, and continued, emotion beginning once more to surface in the timbre of his voice.

"This morning," he said, "after Mr. Ivanovich came through to tell me that he would be back later to free me, the two Africans came back in the room and I spoke to them about that and about the master computer —number three, it was —and about how there was data on that computer that Mr. Ivanovich needed badly.

"Then, this afternoon, after these new friends had decided to release me from my bindings … just because it came to seem absurd to them that I was constrained … and after we had shared a snack … I asked them if they would look the other way while I made a floppy-disk copy of computer number three's hard drive … the entire hard drive. They not only agreed, they actually served as lookouts while I took a blank disk from a shelf and did the work of copying the hard drive. I think they felt honored, actually, to be asked to do something that would help me, and would, they hoped, hurt their captors.

"They did not hesitate … not for an instant.

"Here it is."

Four individuals in the room appeared to understand immediately what this could mean. Their obvious astonishment self-identified them as Adelman, whose role in his and Belton's detective agency had extended and expanded his technology-heavy work with Mossad; Luke, whose consulting role in England had become increasingly technology focused; and two of the three CIA agents. The others turned to those, inquiring with their eyes.

The senior CIA agent offered. "If I understand the nature of what you have been engaged with —those who are included in Rebekka Yahalomin — you have had in your possession for some days now a partial document that includes some obscure financial data, some passages apparently taken from the cutting-and-pasting Thomas Jefferson did with the New Testament, and certain portions of his Declaration of Independence.

"Yes?"

All nodded.

"The group has collectively deduced," continued the agent, "that the obscure financial data requires mathematical keys to unlock their meaning and import, and that these keys have been hidden in a password-protected master unit housed in the Soviet Embassy's computer center.

"Yes?"

More nods.

"And now we have on this floppy disk the full data array from that master computer, and, we think, by analyzing its contents, we will be able to unlock the full meaning and relevance of the financial data, as well as to review the final, complete version of the Jeffersonian documents. You noted, Mr. Deng, that the computer was password protected. Since you have managed to copy the hard drive, you obviously learned the password … or your friends did.

"Yes?"

"Yes," said Deng.

"The technicians needed that password to begin work on something that had been assigned to them, something different from what we are interested in here."

The agent nodded. "And so, in summary," he said, "we have in our hands what is presumably a full and complete and detailed description of, first, the sources of unlawfully generated millions of dollars; second, the methods used in securing the unlawfully generated millions; third, the names of at least some of the principal players in these schemes; fourth, the place or places in which the millions are being held; and fifth, the completed Jeffersonian-derived, edited, and rewritten documents. And we expect the principal players in all this to comprise units of the Russian Mafia in the U.S.

"Yes?"

Nods from Deng, Adelman, Luke, and one of the other CIA agents.

Deng signaled he had something to add. "I'd just add, sir," he said, "that one further expectation is that the 'principal players' in this scheme must include at least one —possibly more —of the individuals who are employed by the Soviet Embassy. I don't think there is some other way to account for the fact of the financial data's having been transferred from the Russian Mafia to the embassy's computer center. Someone, or a number of someones, in the embassy had to be involved in that."

Silence reigned for a full three minutes. Some participants scribbled notes on their notepads. Others simply sat and thought.

Finally, the senior agent again.

"I propose that several of us, including Mr. Deng, spend the next two hours examining the financial contents and implications of this disk, carrying in the forefront of our minds this question: *Is there any reason not to contact the Director of the United States Federal Bureau of Investigation tonight and invite him and his minions to descend upon the individuals or units responsible and, in addition, to confiscate every dollar of these unlawfully accumulated millions?*"

Suddenly the magnitude of Kazim Deng's accomplishment became clear to everyone present. They now began to grasp the critical importance of Rebecca's earlier insistence that Deng be rescued immediately —not "merely" to save his life —but because he was central to the mission that continued to infuse the decisions and actions of Rebekka Yahalomin.

As each individual absorbed the agent's summary and his recommendation for an immediate analysis of the disk's contents, the room began gradually to clear. Deng, Adelman, Luke, and all three of the CIA agents left the room first, taking the diskette with them, on their way to the adjacent building which housed the computers they would need to read the data from the disk.

While the most technologically, financially, and mathematically savvy members of the group left to begin their analysis of the material, the remaining five — Ivanovich, Belton, McGriff, Marie, and Rebecca —repaired to their sleeping rooms to rest and relax in preparation for what would presumably be yet another late-night session. As the five began to collect their things and move out of the conference room, Marie turned to Rebecca quietly and asked if she might speak privately with her for a few minutes.

"Of course, Marie," replied Rebecca. "Give me 10 minutes to change into more relaxed clothing," she added. "I'm in room 210, at the end of the hall."

McGriff heard the exchange, smiled, and left the room, trailing Ivanovich and Belton down the hall to the stairway to the second floor.

Marie changed clothes herself, waited 15 minutes to make sure she was not rushing Rebecca, and walked to room 210. She knocked softly, and heard footsteps moving across the carpeted floor. Rebecca opened the door and stepped aside, motioning for Marie to enter.

Marie saw that Rebecca had taken down her ponytail and had brushed her glistening black hair, which now fell far down her back in Rebecca's preferred style. She had also changed into dark slacks and a light blue "I love New York" tee-shirt like the one Marie had been wearing earlier, though she had retained the white tennis shoes. Marie had never seen Rebecca wearing anything other than skirts, blouses, or tennis garb, so this was a substantial departure in her eyes. Marie herself was dressed similarly, in slacks and a lightweight sweatshirt.

"We only have two chairs to pick from, Marie," said Rebecca. "Your choice," she added.

Marie chose, while Rebecca moved to the room's compact refrigerator. She opened its door and said, "Well, Marie, someone has stocked our little refrigerator with soft drinks —most of them sugar-free, it would appear —and bottled water. Interested in either?"

"Yes, Rebecca," said Marie. "I'm parched. Water would be nice."

The two women drew the chairs close to each other.

Marie took a deep breath and began.

"Rebecca?"

"Yes, Marie."

"Should I say 'Yes' if Jack asks me to marry him?"

Rebecca's contralto laughter immediately filled the small room.

Seeing the humor in her no-preamble, out-of-the-blue question, Marie's lighter, higher laughter joined Rebecca's in a lengthy vocal cascade that only gradually subsided. Finally, Rebecca managed a response.

"Well, Marie," she said, working to suppress more laughter, "Father McGriff is a *believer*, and one who clearly likes being in your company. And he is a courageous and versatile professional: thus, an admirable man.

"And, importantly," she added after a short pause, "he is an *adult.*"

Marie took several moments to absorb Rebecca's impromptu commentary, immediately aware that the short statement was ocean-deep with meaning, and, thus, ocean-deep with implications.

Finally, she managed to utter a small "Hmm."

Rebecca took the indistinct sound as a signal to continue.

"Have the two of you," asked Rebecca quietly, "talked at all about the future, Marie? About his vocation? About his work with the CIA? About your work with the Soviet Embassy? About children?"

Given the weight of that list of questions, Marie found herself thinking so hard and so long that Rebecca began to wonder if Marie had finally succumbed to exhaustion. Rebecca had begun to turn her mind elsewhere when Marie spoke.

"We have talked a little about his work with the CIA. We have not yet talked about children, Rebecca," she said.

"I think you know," Marie continued, "that my husband was killed in an accident on his Navy warship. We'd not been married very long. Just three years.

"We had planned to start trying to have a baby as soon as that WestPac deployment was over, but he didn't come back."

"I'm so sorry, Marie."

"It was so sad, Rebecca, and for both reasons. My husband didn't come back, and our child didn't get conceived. But I knew, of course, that I was only mid-20s, still a young woman … a young widow … and, if a second husband and then children were intended to be in my life, they would eventually be.

"I still feel just that way: that if children are to be in my life, that will come.

"And that will come, if it does, as a result of my marriage to, to use your own phrases, Rebecca, a man who is a *believer,* a man who loves being with me, a man who, as you said so elegantly, is a 'courageous and versatile' professional, and, thus, admirable. And, as you also said with intriguing emphasis, an *adult.*

"Those are the very qualities in Jack that lead me to feel that the question of children will be answered early and easily, Rebecca. I really don't think we will struggle with that question. We will pray and talk and the answer will come."

Marie paused.

"But the other thing," she continued thoughtfully, "his employment by the CIA … that's quite different.

"I'm not at all comfortable with that, and I don't think he is, either, Rebecca. In fact, we jokingly told each other last week that maybe we'd start a Washington D.C. branch of Belton and Adelman Detectives. We were joking about that, but we were serious about our discomfort with an organization whose mission involves deceit … treachery … sometimes murder … as core elements in its *modus operandi.*

"It's hard to fit Christianity, we think, to that kind of thing," she added.

"We know we might be looking at it wrongly, but it seems to us so different from service in the military. Or from work as part of a detective agency. Or from other areas of law enforcement.

"All those roles seem to us somehow more … more honest … and yet I know that misleading an adversary is standard practice: you want the adversary to think you're going to attack over here, but you're actually going to attack over there.

"Look, for example, at what we ourselves have been doing," Marie concluded. "We have gone to great lengths to keep the Ataka people from knowing where you are, precisely because we want to deceive them.

"It's confusing. …"

"Well," replied Rebecca after a moment, "our family has a tradition of military service, but none in our family has ever chosen service with any of the intelligence agencies. So, I do understand what you mean, Marie.

"And I'll add my impression that Jaakov left his employment with Mossad for reasons related to his Judaism. He still has relationships, obviously, with some of his former colleagues in the agency, but he is no longer a Mossad agent.

"Whereas, my husband, my brother, my sister-in-law, Detective Belton, your deceased husband, and Father McGriff, as a U.S. Army chaplain … all served, and served with pride, in the military organizations of our two countries.

"We have always seen that as a good thing. But the other …"

The two women fell silent, thinking.

"But Marie," offered Rebecca after a half-minute, "it sounds to me as if you and Father McGriff are not in disagreement about his engagement with the CIA. It sounds to me as if you two are already thinking about how things might work, if you were truly a couple … a married couple … and about how you might even work together.

"I, for one," she continued, "think that the two of you launching a branch of Belton and Adelman here in Washington is a brilliant idea. Just think, Marie: Belton, Adelman, Campbell, and McGriff."

The two again joined in the easy laughter of new friends talking about important things and looking at those important things through the same lens.

"It sounds like a law firm, Rebecca," said Marie, "and I think I like it."

It was shortly before 11 p.m. when the group reassembled in the CIA safe house conference room. The kitchen staff had prepared late-night snacks, and the participants, several of whom had not eaten since midday, attacked the array gratefully and enthusiastically.

Aside from the food, the center of attention for the several minutes prior to resumption of business were three new feminine faces in the room: Katina, Khristina, and Annika Ivanovich.

Ivan Ivanovich beamed with happiness and pride as he made the introductions, assisted by Maria and McGriff, already well acquainted with the Ivanovich family from church services and church projects. After several minutes, Katina and the girls took their plates and cups out of the room and across the hallway to the reception area.

By then, all had sated their hunger, or nearly so, and had turned to their beverages: coffee, soft drinks, and, in a gesture that the Englishwoman and her brother found stunningly thoughtful, tea for Rebecca and Luke. At that point, the senior CIA agent began his report of the two hours of analysis the tech group had completed.

"The first section of the disk ferreted out of the Soviet Embassy by Mr. Deng and Mr. Ivanovich gives us exactly the clear-cut financial picture that we had hoped for. Let me summarize the finance-related details.

"First," said the agent, "the Russian Mafia —that is, its U.S. wing, which is based in New York City —has accumulated hundreds of millions of dollars via arms trafficking, drug trafficking, and prostitution. Second, Artur Volkov, the top KGB agent in North America and, *de facto,* in South America as well, has negotiated a deal with the mob to facilitate dramatic increases in the revenue spreads from all three of those sources, especially from their South American satellite operations, in exchange for funneling a substantial portion of current and prospective cash-on-hand to the Jefferson Bible and Declaration of Independence project, if I may refer to it in that way.

"Third," continued the agent, "the senior decision makers in the Russian Mafia —that is, the mob bosses —both those in New York and those in Moscow, are identified by name, with addresses and other contact information for each one. Fourth, hundreds of illegal transactions are listed in detail and in chronological order. And fifth, the financial institutions agreeing to hold the cash here in the U.S. are listed, as well as their actual cash-on-hand as of *yesterday's* close-of-business, if you can imagine."

He paused to allow the five who had not been part of the analysis —Ivanovich, Belton, McGriff, Marie, and Rebecca —to process what they had just heard.

"This is stupendous, Kazim," said Rebecca after a moment. "We cannot possibly thank you enough for this. Well done *you!*"

And she started applause, which quickly consumed the room.

Deng smiled shyly and responded by saying, "Without Mr. Ivanovich's intervention, you know, Mrs. Clark, I would be …"

"Yes," said Rebecca, "we do know."

She turned her face to Ivanovich. "We are so grateful to you, Ivan," she said. "Just think how you and I and Father McGriff were with each other, just this morning, and how we are now. You have been so incredibly brave today, Ivan."

"I don't feel so much brave, Rebecca," said Ivanovich, "as grateful and blessed to have been reached … finally … in this way.

"You and Father McGriff risked a great deal this morning when you came to my home. The whole thing has a feeling of inevitability to it now, looking back over these 15 hours, but at the time you made that decision, you were taking an enormous chance."

The senior CIA agent waited to see if there were further observations, then, hearing none, he offered his proposal. He directed his statement to Belton, the only member of the group whose connections to FBI leadership were likely to be even stronger than were the agent's own, and those of his two CIA colleagues.

The FBI and CIA had, after all, something of the inherent tension traditionally underlying that relationship in all nations which housed both kinds of agencies: one that focused on domestic issues, and the another that focused on foreign issues.

Overlap was inevitable. Tensions were unavoidable.

But tensions could be overcome when larger issues superseded competition.

"Mr. Belton," said the agent, "I suggest that you or I —or both of us together —contact the Director of the FBI right now, probably getting him out of bed, and strongly recommend that he and his top people get over here immediately. We'll explain that the FBI needs to arrest the principal Russian mob figures in New York City *tonight,* and to confiscate, also *tonight,* all Mafia funds prior to the impending transfer of those funds to their New Jersey printing and distribution firm.

"If the fund transfer is allowed to happen, we'll explain, then everything — the arrests and the confiscation process —will become so much more difficult.

"What do you think, Mr. Belton?"

"I got the Director's all-hours number right here," said Belton.

"So do I," responded the agent.

"I say we gotta do it," Belton said, the crooked smile creeping across his face, his delight in arriving at the point of no return obvious to all.

The agent looked at his watch.

"No time like the present, Detective," he said cheerily.

"I get t' be th' one t' wake 'im up," said Belton.

CHAPTER SIXTEEN

THE GROUP WAITED EXPECTANTLY WHILE THE CIA AGENT AND Belton left the room to make their call to the director of the FBI. They did not have long to wait. In fewer than 15 minutes, the two of them returned to the room to announce that the director had agreed with great enthusiasm, and had promised that he and several of his highest-ranking deputies would be there, at the CIA safe house, in less than half an hour.

The FBI director had further promised, reported the senior CIA agent, that he would awaken his New York City FBI chief and order him to get the entire metropolitan organization out of bed and ready for a 2 a.m. full-organization preparation session for an armed, pre-dawn raid on the Russian Mafia chieftains.

Belton added, "I can tell ya that I've never heard th' director that excited. He sounded like a kid with a new bicycle. I think he wants t' come over here an' pin a medal on every one of us before midnight. He doesn't get this kinda chance very often an' he *really* doesn't wanna to miss it."

Expressions of gratification, verbal and non, ensued, all around the conference room. Then, the agent spoke again.

"Mr. Belton and I also took it upon ourselves, Mr. Ivanovich," he said, "to roust yet another senior U.S. government official from his bed. We telephoned the director of the U.S. Federal Witness Protection Program. His approval of our request to relocate you and your family —new location, new identities, new employment —was as immediate as the FBI director's, based upon the verbal agreement I gave him that we would supply the Witness Protection Program with a copy of the floppy disk.

"It was obvious, you understand," he continued, addressing all in the room, "to the Witness Protection Program director that Mr. Ivanovich, having helped Kazim Deng remove the disk from the Soviet Embassy's computer center, as a Soviet government employee —well … as of this night … a *former* Soviet government employee —would be at substantial and ongoing risk if he and his family were not given a new location, new identities, and new employment. This is exactly what the Witness Protection Program is cut out to do.

"Oh … and Ivan," he added, "the director said that you and Katina and the girls should not return to your home at all. A U.S. Marshals Service team will pack up the house, put it on the market, and transport all your family's belongings to your new home, somewhere in the United States. They will meet with you and Katina tomorrow, here, to discuss all details with you. You'll be given some attractive choices."

The agent looked at Ivanovich expectantly.

Ivanovich leaned back in his chair and breathed deeply. "That has been our prayer," responded Ivanovich, "for all the months that Katina and I have wrestled with our family's future. We have longed for this outcome, but were never confident that we knew how to get it to happen … or confident that we were brave enough to get it to happen.

"Thank you, sir, from the bottom of my heart.

"Thank you."

At this juncture, the group began gradually to realize, with a combination of amazement, relief, gratification, and, oddly, a touch of disappointment, that their work was finished. The culminating intervention would be handled by the one U.S. authority —the FBI —with both the statutory power and the armed strength to step in and bring the Russian mob to its knees. The Russian Mafia would be stripped of its power to operate in the Western Hemisphere in any meaningful fashion for years, its leadership behind bars and its funding gone.

It was a colossal and comprehensive stroke.

After more than a full minute of an unspoken but strongly felt sense of wonderment filling the room, it was McGriff who ventured to articulate the obvious. He worded his summary as a question to all the others present. And when he completed the summary, he looked alternately to the senior agent and to Belton.

"So," said McGriff, "do I seem to have it right? Have we, in fact, completed our work? Is it now the work of the two agencies —the FBI and the Marshals Service —to handle everything from here on in? Do we all pack up and go home?"

The senior agent and Belton looked at each other.

"Well, Father McGriff," said the agent, "I'd say *yes* to that. You, Sid?"

The crooked smile spread once more across the rugged face. "Well," said Belton, "you an' I can stay here an' meet with th' two directors when they get here in a few minutes. An' Ivan, you an' your missus will wanna be part of th' conversation with th' Witness Protection director.

"Otherwise, yeah … I'd say we're done."

Rebecca and Luke had become immediately aware, as they listened to the reports from the CIA agent and Belton, that indeed their work in the current crisis had been completed. With the involvement of the FBI and its extraordinary power —with the diskette in its hands —to put an end to the looming publication-and-distribution threat, a threat that had called to Rebecca through her visions in England, New York, and Washington, their charge was fulfilled.

And so they began to say their good-byes without delay, suddenly overcome with the desire to arrange transatlantic military transportation for themselves that very night, and to reunite with their families, if possible, the following day.

No member of Rebekka Yahalomin ever regarded good-byes to each other as final. They knew their work would never be finished. And so, all farewells had the feel of "until next time," and a sense of a specific mission accomplished quickly and efficiently.

The two fatalities —the murdered Mossad agents —comprised heart-rending collateral damage, but the only wounding inflicted by Rebekka Yahalomin itself was a knife injury to one KGB agent's upper arm, plus whatever bruising Luke's fists had inflicted on the same agent's face and cranium.

The shots fired back toward the jetty during the waterborne escape from the KGB safe house, shots fired by the patrolman on the StarCraft, were not actually aimed at anyone. They had been designed to discourage the KGB agents from taking aim at the escaping craft, and had been successful in accomplishing exactly that.

Rebecca's tenderest good-bye was awarded Sid Belton. The two of them had by now been working together, and in much the same way each time, for nearly a full decade. They had known each other before either of them had fallen in love with and married their spouses, and had seen weddings and, in Rebecca's case, children, enter each other's lives.

As always, Rebecca's hug of the diminutive detective seemed to swallow him up in her vigorous embrace. He groaned playfully.

"Hey, Ms. Clark," he said, speaking into her shoulder, "lemme get a breath b'fore ya squeeze th' life outta me. I'm gettin' too old t' be hugged by anybody as strong as you, ya know. Eleanor's more my size an' speed. Know what I mean? Hmm?"

Rebecca stepped back and looked down fondly at the gnome-like features of Sidney Belton. "I have *always* known what you mean, Mr. Belton," she said tenderly, "but I will expect you to give Dr. Chapel exactly that kind of hug when you get home.

"Promise?"

"Yes, ma'am," he said obediently. "I'll do my best."

Rebecca and Luke's good-byes with Ivan Ivanovich were less fulsome, but similarly heartfelt. He reiterated, emotion filling his voice and his eyes, that he and Katina had been moving to this decision for months. The events of that day had brought to conclusion a long process of prayerful examination of their lives.

"This is the right outcome for us, Rebecca," said Ivanovich.

"It had become inevitable," he continued, "that sooner or later Katina and I and the girls would have to leave our heritage behind. Thank you for pushing the decision to its climax today. I am so very grateful."

The good-byes, all done briskly, ended shortly before midnight. Without hesitation, Luke then phoned the transportation service at Andrews Air Force Base to inquire about immediate RAF flights to England. He was told that an RAF transport aircraft was scheduled for departure in just a few hours —0400 Eastern —and that there would be plenty of space for him and his sister.

Luke told the late-night Andrews office clerk, a civilian contract employee, to log himself, Royal Navy Lieutenant Luke Manguson, and his sister, Rebecca Clark, on that flight, and that he would park the Ford just outside the transportation office by 0330. He would push the car keys through the slot in the office door, since the office was not scheduled to be staffed between midnight and 0600. The employee made the proper notations in his log and signed off.

After closing up the office, the clerk walked 20 yards to the pay phone housed in a person-sized shelter along the outside of the building. Using that phone, he made two calls before walking to his car and heading for home.

Earlier that evening, Artur Volkov and Tatyana Kuznetsova rendezvoused in their shared office, number 2045, in the Soviet Embassy. It had been clear to them for several hours that Ivan Ivanovich was gone, and that he had taken Kazim Deng with him. They had queried the security personnel in the main lobby, and had found that two of the guards had seen Ivanovich leave by that exit—an exit not normally used by administrators at his level—and both of them remembered a young man fitting the description of Kazim Deng. The two guards agreed that Deng had exited the lobby about 30 seconds before Ivanovich, and confirmed that they did not closely check IDs of departing employees and guests at that time of the afternoon.

"Ivan has defected, Artur, and taken Deng with him," said Tatyana, shaking her head in sad incredulity. "No other explanation is plausible. And they've hidden themselves, surely, with that CIA unit—the one Randy Simpson has been part of—at Langley. Randy missed his daily check-in this afternoon, which is surely a result of Ivan's having exposed him to the CIA. Randy is gone, too.

"And with Randy exposed and removed," she continued, "we'll have no way to gain information, or to retrieve Ivan or Deng … or to get to the Clark woman. All we can do is green-light the cash transfer that I have set up, per your instructions, in New York, for tomorrow, and have the New Jersey people prepare to print and distribute the document as soon as practical. Everything is at the ready; they're just waiting for a copy of the disk, which I will have flown up to New York before noon.

"We have allowed the Clark group," she said carefully, wanting to emphasize the bright side of the situation, "to see a few bits and pieces of our Jefferson Bible project, Artur, but they have such incomplete information, they'll have no chance to do anything with it. We may have lost whatever chance we had to get at the people—the Rebekka Yahalomin people—but the project will go forward just as we have planned all along."

She stood up, walked to Volkov, and stood beside his chair, looking down at him.

"I know you're disappointed, Artur, but the project is a huge blow to our enemies. It will have destructive effects on their traditions for years … decades … and even more … perhaps centuries. It's your masterwork, Artur. You must focus your mind on the project and its extraordinary outcomes. It is truly a triumph."

Volkov had been listening with his back to his assistant, his own chair swiveled to face the window. Slowly, he turned the chair toward her as she stood next to him.

"Yes," he said, finally, his brow furrowed and his heavy eyebrows cascading down over his hooded lids. "Yes, the project will be a triumph," he agreed, "but it is not enough.

"And I do not think you are correct, Tatyana, that we have lost the chance to get at those people. We have lost Ivanovich and Deng, almost certainly, but they are nothing in the larger picture, Tat. They are less than nothing."

He gestured for her to resume her chair.

"Think, Tatyana," he said.

"Ivan and Kazim Deng are now, as you suggest, most likely sequestered at Langley with the CIA unit. And their group … the Rebecca Clark group … knows by now that Ataka has been decimated. After all, four of the six members of our leadership unit are gone. Only you and I remain.

"Their group," continued Volkov, "may well be under the impression that, having crippled our leadership, they have crippled the Jefferson Bible project. They may well think it is time to declare victory and go home. Back to New York for the detectives. Back to England for the brother and sister. Back to the church for McGriff and his friend … your own embassy friend, Mrs. Campbell.

"Back to business as usual, you see?"

"Yes," she replied dutifully.

"But I think," Volkov resumed, "that we can still get our hands on Mrs. Clark, and, if we can, we can regain control of *everything.* As you have said, Tat, our project will go forward regardless, because we have let them see so little … certainly not enough for them to understand who is doing what.

"But I want more, Tatyana. I want Mrs. Clark. I want to remove any chance that we might be faced with her repeated efforts to interfere with our largest and longest-term plans and projects. I want us to rid ourselves of this annoying mystic … this ubiquitous interferer … and her propensity to confound our work worldwide.

"I want *her.*"

"But Artur," protested Tatyana, "how can we …"

"Listen," he said, interrupting.

"You have a paid informant, Tatyana … a civilian clerk … working in the transportation office at Andrews, yes?"

She nodded.

Volkov looked at his watch.

"It's 9:30 p.m. now. Call him. Tell him four figures in cash awaits him if he will let you know the instant Mrs. Clark, or her brother, or the detectives, or anyone connected with their group, schedules a departure from Andrews, whether it be to New York or to London or to anywhere on earth. Tell him that you must be notified instantly if any such plans are made. Tell him you will need details as soon as he has them."

She nodded, making notes as he spoke.

"And Tatyana," added Volkov, an ominous smile starting, "tell him something else … tell him to contact the Russian snatch-and-remove unit. Tell him to instruct the head of the snatch-and-remove unit —he is Eremenko, yes? —to stand by. Say that we may need Eremenko's unit, possibly this very night. Say that he, the clerk, will be paid a percentage of what we will pay the snatch unit, if it is successful. Tell him we will pay him 10 percent of a six-figure payout to Eremenko and his men.

"Call him now … the Andrews transportation clerk … and tell him that he, and they —Eremenko's unit —will be very, very well rewarded.

"And remind the clerk not to use the transportation office telephones to call you. Tell him to use pay phones only."

Volkov smiled … his smile indistinguishable from a grimace.

A frightening smile.

"I will get her yet, Tatyana," said Volkov. "You *know* me. I will get her yet."

At 2:45 a.m. Rebecca and Luke tossed their overnight bags onto the back seat of the Ford and pulled out of the CIA safe house parking lot in Langley, headed for the Woodrow Wilson Memorial Bridge across the Potomac to Maryland, thence to Andrews AFB for their scheduled 0400 departure on Royal Air Force transport to England.

Rebecca, sleep-deprived though she was, found herself nonetheless excited. She had been counting the hours since leaving her children behind at the Lodge with their father and their grandparents. That number of hours had grown much too large, far larger than at any other time since the twins' birth four years prior.

She found herself smiling, picturing the twins' happy faces. She only wished the flight were not so lengthy. It would be at least 12 hours from takeoff at Andrews until she was actually with Matt and the children at the Lodge.

Long, long hours.

Once they had crossed the Potomac into Maryland, Luke took the Andrews exit off I-495, and brought the Ford to a stop at an intersection that seemed utterly desolate after the relative busyness of the interstate. As he prepared to turn left onto Allentown Road toward the AFB entrance roughly 300 feet to his left, he saw two sets of headlights speeding toward him from that direction.

As they neared, he tensed.

Suddenly he shouted "Down!"

Rebecca, her hand already in position, instantly hit the release catch to her seat belt and hurled herself onto the floorboard, her head nearly under the steering wheel. Luke, a fraction of a second behind her, released his seat belt and threw himself over her body just at the instant a Dodge Ram pickup truck with a heavy-duty front-bumper winch extending three *massive* feet forward from its nose plowed into the Ford's left front fender, crushing the fender as if it were tissue paper and collapsing the left front wheel into a shapeless mass of steel and rubber.

The Ford's front end flew more than 35 feet to the right, spinning the sedan almost 90 degrees from its original position, and pushing the front of the Ford well off the roadway and onto the dirt along the side of the exit ramp. The vehicle was instantly and permanently disabled.

As the sedan flew, skidded, rocked and finally stopped, Luke pushed himself upright and shouted to Rebecca, "Out and run!" while he worked the handle on the driver's side door and pushed the door open far enough to extricate himself.

As he did, he saw the Ram first backing and then cutting its wheels to the left and roaring away, bouncing back onto Allentown Road, its wheels throwing up dirt and debris as it went. He also saw the trailing vehicle, another large truck with a crew cab —four doors and a passenger seat behind the front seat —braking to a halt just feet in front of him. All four doors of the truck popped open and large men, all of them masked, ran toward him from both sides of the truck.

Luke chose the nearest of the four dark-clad figures and drove his shoulder into the man's midsection, driving him back into his companion. Luke then stood and spun around to face the other two. As he did, he felt the shock of a high-voltage Taser as it was slammed into his neck from behind. Losing control of his muscles as the electric shocks raced through his body, he fell, his limbs twitching helplessly.

Rebecca had not hesitated after her brother's order. She reached for her door handle, flipped the handle and in the same instant kicked the passenger-side door open with her tennis shoe. She rolled out onto the ground, stood, and began a sprint in the direction opposite the action behind her.

She found herself in a stumbling run across uneven ground in the faintly moonlit darkness, but had nonetheless opened a 50-yard gap between herself and the others when she heard gunshots behind her and saw puffs of dirt kicking up around her feet. Then she heard a voice shouting, "Stop! Stop! Stop now, or the next shots will be fired into your brother's brain!"

She stopped.

Breathing deeply, she turned and began to walk back toward her brother and the enemy that had entered their lives from yet another direction. And she knew, as she walked, that this was the *other* part of the twin goals of their adversaries: eliminate Rebecca Clark, her family, and her colleagues … eliminate Rebekka Yahalomin.

Marie and McGriff, by pre-arrangement, slept late and met for breakfast at the CIA safe house dinette at 9 a.m. Belton and Adelman had already done the same, and were just finishing their coffee.

"You two headed for New York pretty soon?" asked McGriff as he took a seat next to Marie, their cereal bowls and toast in front of them.

"Yeah," said Belton, "we got our eyes on a 11:14 a.m. AMTRAK express that gets t' Penn Station in Manhattan about as fast as we'd get t' our office if we went t' th' trouble of gettin' a flight up there. An' we got no need t' use th' CIA's or the Israeli Embassy's airplanes. We've spent enough of their money already.

"Know what I mean? Hmm?"

After a moment, Marie asked the detectives, "Have we heard anything this morning about the FBI raid in New York?"

The detectives shook their heads.

"No," said Adelman, "and I doubt we will.

"They have no need to keep us in the loop on this unless there is some huge failure … an unlikely prospect."

"Well," said McGriff, "they'll report something to the CIA people here, and we can check with them later today and get at least a cursory report on the outcome."

Belton nodded, thought for a moment, and then asked, "When are we gonna see you two again? Marie, ya gotta come up an' get yer cat, and Jack, ya gotta come up an' get yer car, ya know. Yer Jeep is still sittin' in th' Bronkowskis' garage over in Brooklyn."

An hour after saying their good-byes to the detectives, Marie and McGriff, telling the CIA safe house room coordinator that they expected to use their rooms for another few days, took a taxi into D.C., to the church. As they walked into the office area, one of the assistants rose quickly and walked to McGriff, anxiety written on her face.

"Father," she said, "we've just received a call from the transportation office at Andrews. The car they checked out to a Lieutenant Luke Manguson, Royal Navy, was to be returned during the night. It was not. The lieutenant left your name and the church phone as his local contact. Should we be concerned?"

Blood drained from McGriff's face as he stood, stunned, his mind suddenly on fire with danger signs.

Marie's hands went to her face.

"Oh, no," she murmured.

After a moment, McGriff forced himself to focus, and said to the assistant, speaking rapidly, "Please contact our friend … the chief of the D.C. police precinct. Get him on the line personally, if you can. Say it's urgent.

"I'll run to my office and pick up in there."

He seized Marie's hand and together they ran down the corridor.

McGriff picked up his desk phone and heard the precinct chief, Belton's long-ago protégé, coming onto the line.

"Chief," said McGriff, "Father Jack McGriff here. I need to ask an urgent favor."

Minutes later, Belton and Adelman, walking briskly through Union Station, carrying their overnight bags, heard their names over the public address system: *Attention: Mr. Sidney Belton and Mr. Jaakov Adelman, please come to the Information Office for an urgent message from the District of Columbia police precinct chief.*

Belton and Adelman's taxi dropped them at the police station just moments after Marie and McGriff's taxi had done the same. The four of them were escorted together into the precinct captain's office. The captain, Horace Johnstone, was standing at his desk and speaking into his phone as the foursome entered.

He said into the phone, "Wait a moment … he just walked in."

He held the phone out toward McGriff and said, "It's your office."

Then he turned to Belton and a broad smile creased his face. "Sidney!" he said happily. "What a privilege to have you in my office, sir, at long last."

Johnstone walked around his desk and shook hands warmly with Belton.

Johnstone then playfully stepped back, eyeing Belton's cane.

"Just keep that spring-loaded walking stick of yours away from my feet," he said. "I've seen that knife pop out of the base of that thing. Just keep your distance, sir, and I won't need to bring my SWAT in here to handle you."

"Like they *could,*" replied Belton.

The captain then introduced himself to Marie and Adelman. They exchanged pleasantries briefly until McGriff hung up the phone.

They looked inquiringly to him.

"That was one of our assistants at church," he said.

"She said that the Andrews transportation office had phoned again to say that Lieutenant Manguson's Ford had been found just a hundred yards from the base entrance, and had just been towed to the transportation office. She said the office reported that the left front of the car looked like it had been crushed by a tank.

"Our assistant also said," continued McGriff, "that the caller reported that there was no sign at the scene of the lieutenant or his sister. Also, that the transportation log showed that the two of them were scheduled to fly out of Andrews at 4 a.m. on RAF transport, headed for a Newfoundland refueling stop, then on to England. The flight left exactly on time, but without either of them on board."

Johnstone motioned for his guests to be seated, then looked at his longtime mentor and asked, "Sid, what can I do to help?"

Belton's response was immediate. "We need t' get a look at that log. An' we need crime-scene people —yours or a Maryland State Police unit —t' look at th' car and th' scene around th'… attack.

"I started t' say th' 'accident scene'," he added, "but this was no 'accident'."

Captain Johnstone pressed an intercom button and said sharply, "I need a transportation cruiser out front in *two minutes* to take Mr. Belton and his associates out to Andrews, and to stay there to take them wherever they need to go after that."

Thirty minutes later, Belton, moving as fast as his cane-limited gait would allow, led Adelman, Marie, and McGriff into the transportation office at Andrews Air Base. At Captain Johnstone's request from his position as D.C. precinct chief, the base logistics officer —a lieutenant colonel —was there to lend weight to the importance of opening the base transportation log to civilian scrutiny. Earlier, the same officer had arranged for the Maryland State Patrol Crime Scene Unit to rush to the site of the collision.

It was not yet noon when Belton opened the session with the lieutenant colonel and the senior member of the crime-scene unit in the conference room with him and the others. Belton looked up from the transportation log.

"Right here," he said, pushing the logbook in front of the logistics officer, "ya see yer civilian clerk entered a phone call he got just before midnight. He shows th' call was from Royal Navy Lieutenant Luke Manguson, a person you know pretty well, I believe, sir, an' th' notes show that Luke got himself an' his sister Rebecca booked on th' 0400 RAF flight t' Newfoundland and on t' England.

"As ya know, th' Ford never got here. Appreciate yer gettin' th' crime-scene crew over there so fast, sir."

Belton stopped and nodded to the crime-scene unit's head.

"Ma'am?" he said.

She replied carefully, looking at her notes as she went.

"We've completed a fast run-through. We'll continue with a more thorough examination during the afternoon, but I can give you preliminary outcomes now.

"The Ford apparently came to a halt at the stop sign where the exit ramp from I-495 feeds Allentown Road, which leads to the base entrance in about a hundred yards. The Ford appears to have been rammed by the extremely heavy front end of a vehicle —not just an ordinary front bumper of a car or pick-up —but something heavy enough to move the Ford's front end about 35 lateral feet, and to crumple the front end and left front tire and wheel into nothing that is even recognizable.

"We could see," she continued, "that the point of impact appeared to be made by something not very wide … possibly by something like a heavy-duty towing winch … something that would protrude from the front end of a commercial-grade pick-up truck … something that was driven into the Ford at perhaps 40 miles per hour.

"Although the frame was twisted, the passenger compartment of the Ford was not compressed," she explained further, "and we conclude that the occupants —there were two —were not injured, or not much, by the impact. There appears to have been a fight on the driver's side of the Ford. The dirt and vegetation on the ground are seriously disturbed, and there appears to have been at least one body … not necessarily a 'dead body' … that was driven to the ground just a few feet from the driver's side's door.

"No blood on the ground."

"*None?*" interjected Marie hastily.

"Absolutely none," repeated the crime-scene unit's head.

"On the passenger side of the Ford," she continued, "that door was also standing open. There are running footprints that lead from the Ford to a point about 50 yards away, where they stop, and then return to the scene at a walk. There are traces of bullets having been fired at that person, but probably not actually aimed to hit the person. The bullet traces plow up the dirt on each side of the runner's tracks. Back at the point from which those rounds appear to have been fired, there is no brass on the ground, so the assailants picked up their brass carefully after firing their weapons.

"We could not find the rounds themselves, and, since they were apparently fired for the purpose of getting the runner to stop, rather than to hit that person, the rounds could have continued, skipping and skimming the ground, for 200 yards or more. We may never find them. There were probably three or four shots before the runner stopped and returned to the Ford.

"There was no luggage in the Ford, either inside the passenger compartment or in the trunk. There was, in other words, nothing whatever that could help us identify either the assailants or the occupants of the Ford, though we assume Lieutenant Manguson and his sister must have been in the car."

"They had identical overnight bags with them," offered Marie.

"Yes," responded the crime-scene unit's head.

"We had assumed something like that, and we looked carefully for that kind of luggage, but also for anything much smaller, like travel kits. There was nothing.

"The assailants, other than the driver of the ramming vehicle," she continued, "must have arrived in a second vehicle, just behind the ramming vehicle. It appears that that vehicle came to a halt about 10 feet short of the wrecked Ford, and that at least four occupants of the trailing vehicle stepped from that vehicle for the purpose of engaging the Ford's occupants, which they clearly did.

"As you would expect," she said, "there is ample evidence on the ground that the Ford's occupants were placed in the second vehicle and taken away. Or, possibly, placed in a third vehicle. I say 'third vehicle,' because there may have been a third car, one that trailed the Ford for much of its journey, possibly picking it up as soon as it departed Langley. The coordination of the ramming vehicle with the Ford's arrival at that stop sign suggests to me that a third vehicle was trailing the Ford on I-495, and radioed the ramming vehicle when the Ford moved onto the exit ramp. The Ford's occupants may have been placed in that third vehicle, which may have stopped on the pavement of the exit ramp itself, thereby leaving no trace of its presence in the dirt onto which the other three vehicles moved during the collision and its aftermath.

"Again, let me emphasize," she said, "there is no blood anywhere in the area of the crash, including along the tracks made by the runner."

Belton then thanked the crime scene unit's head for her report, and asked her to stay for the discussion. She nodded, and Belton resumed, addressing himself first to the lieutenant colonel … the base logistics officer.

"We do understand, sir," said Belton, "that this is a civilian matter, an' not a military problem. But since th' wrecked Ford is an' Andrews Air Base vehicle, an' since Luke Manguson an' Rebecca Clark had been booked by yer unit here t' fly t' England by RAF transport at 0400 this mornin', we wanna be sure yer okay with our usin' yer log here, plus th' evidence we just heard from th' crime scene unit, t' get movin' on what we're sure is an international capture-an'-hold by either Soviet KGB agents, or by a civilian hit squad hired by Soviet Embassy personnel, KGB or other. We jus' wanna be sure you've been given a good picture of all this before we start gettin' D.C. an' Maryland an' maybe Virginia law enforcement workin' on all this."

The officer nodded. "Understood, Mr. Belton. And much appreciated.

"And I must say that any individuals or organizations that have committed violence toward Luke Manguson and his family have got themselves a tiger by the tail. Whatever we can do to assist you —including use of our choppers or our specialized vehicles —just let me know. We'll arrange whatever you need."

Belton nodded. "Will do, sir. Th' very first thing we need t' do is t' talk t' th' clerk that took that phone call just before midnight last night, when Luke phoned here t' make arrangements fer himself an' his sister t' return th' Ford an' t' book space on the 0400 RAF transport.

"It seems pretty clear t' me that th' clerk had t' be th' one t' supply th' dirtbags that crashed th' Ford an' captured Luke an' Rebecca, sir, with info about their departure. How else would th' scumbags know anything about their plans?

"Hmm? Ya know what I mean? Hmm?"

The officer smiled. "Yes, Mr. Belton, I do, and I'd already formed that very thought, on my way over here. That clerk works the 1600 to midnight shift for us, four nights a week. His day job is as a dispatcher for a package delivery firm. I've written his contact information on this card for you. This side of the card shows his day-job address and phone, and, on the back of the card, you see his home address and phone.

"He will report to work here in fewer than four hours, if you want to wait."

"Sir," replied Belton, "th' miserable garbage bags who did this have had Luke an' Rebecca fer more than eight hours now, because we didn't know anything had happened t' 'em until Father McGriff, here, got t' th' church, mid-mornin', and got th' news from yer office here that th' Ford hadn't been returned an' that Luke an' Rebecca didn't get on board that RAF flight. We can only hope that Almighty God is protectin' 'em every minute, 'cause we sure haven't been.

"We gotta go talk t' this guy right now, sir."

"Mr. Belton," said the lieutenant colonel quickly, "I'd like very much to go with you, if you don't object. I'd like to look that clerk in the eye and I'd like to hear what he has to say about all this. I'd like *very* much to hear what he has to say."

The location of the clerk's day job as a dispatcher was only four miles from the Andrews AFB main gate. Belton, seeing the Maryland address for the package delivery firm, phoned one of his higher-up Maryland State Patrol contacts — one of the same officers who had been involved in the previous afternoon's rescue of Marie and McGriff from the KGB safe house —and asked for immediate assistance.

Receiving assurance of exactly that, Belton dismissed, with thanks, the D.C. police officer who had been detailed by Captain Johnstone to provide transportation.

In just 20 minutes, Belton, the Andrews logistics officer, and a very large Maryland state trooper emerged from the trooper's cruiser and entered the package delivery firm's office. The trooper, with the other two trailing, breezed past the front-desk receptionist, saying, "Afternoon, Betty … need to see Clarence."

Betty said nothing in return, but her eyes grew wide at the sight of the ramrod-straight lieutenant colonel in his splendid Air Force uniform, and at the small, hobbled, but somehow forceful man who clumped determinedly behind them. Entering the dispatcher's cramped, cluttered space, the patrolman began speaking immediately and in a voice that was loud and utterly no-nonsense in tone.

"Clarence," he said as he strode to the small desk and loomed over the instantly unnerved man, "I'll give you a choice.

"You can either tell these gentlemen *everything* they need to hear from you, or I will run you in for any of a dozen foul-ups I've kept in my back pocket, just waiting for something bigger to come along. Talk to them right now, or expect to spend the next 60 days in jail, and then longer, once we pull everything we've got on you outta the files.

"Understand?"

This last was nearly shouted, and was not actually a question.

Fifteen minutes later, the threesome was back in the highway patrol cruiser, headed back to Andrews. And 10 minutes after that, after thanking the trooper profusely, Belton and the logistics officer sat down at the transportation office conference table and reported to Adelman, Marie, and McGriff on the outcomes of their brief trip to visit with the transportation clerk at his day job.

"First," said Belton, "th' clerk is a regular informant for Tatyana Kuznetsova at th' Soviet Embassy. He's pretty regularly paid, he says, either by th' embassy or by Artur Volkov outta Volkov's own pocket. Last evenin', about 9:30 p.m., he says, Ms. Kuznetsova phoned 'im and promised 'im $1,000 if he phoned her immediately with any news of movements of CIA aircraft, Israeli Embassy aircraft, or Royal Air Force aircraft … any news of arrangements that would involve any of us.

"An' he had our names, folks, spelled out fer him by Ms. Kuznetsova: Luke, Rebecca, Jaakov, Jack, Marie, an' me. She gave 'im our first an' last names an' he wrote 'em down in this little notebook he carries with 'im everywhere, not in the transportation log here at Andrews. He handed over th' notebook t' th' patrolman, an' here are our names, right here."

Belton held the small notebook up for his associates to see.

"An' next t' Luke an' Rebecca's names, y' can see that, less than three hours after Ms. Kuznetsova had given th' clerk th' alert at 9:30, Luke called 'im just before midnight an' booked himself an' his sister on th' 0400 RAF flight.

"An' then, in this same notebook," continued Belton, speaking rapidly, "he shows himself phonin' Ms. Kuznetsova from a pay phone, just after midnight — just after Luke had called 'im —at some number that's not her embassy number… it's a different area code … it's a Maryland area code … an' reportin' t' her about Luke's travel arrangements … Luke's arrangements fer returnin' th' Ford and gettin' on th' flight."

An "aha" expression crossed the faces of his listeners.

"So that's how," said McGriff, "the assailants knew what time to crash Luke's Ford. Tatyana Kuznetsova took things from there, Mr. Belton?"

"Well …" replied Belton … "get *this* … th' clerk was authorized by Ms. Kuznetsova, in this midnight call, t' get in touch with somethin' he called th' Russian snatch-and-remove unit. She told 'im t' get in touch with th' head of that unit an' tell 'im t' stand by fer action. An' she told 'im t' talk t' th' head of that unit —a guy named Eremenko —in terms of a six-figure payout if he succeeded with th' snatch-an'-hold, an' t' count on ten percent of that figure fer th' clerk himself, over an' above th' one thousand she'd already promised 'im in th' earlier conversation."

Adelman's eyebrows lifted.

"This is a *civilian* unit, then, this snatch-and-remove team? Not a KGB snatch team?" he asked, clearly surprised.

"Right," said Belton, "a civilian snatch unit … geared up t' earn at least $100,000 t' do what we know they ended up doin' a few hours later."

The group fell silent, processing the information, before McGriff spoke.

"Did you get anything more from this man, Mr. Belton?" he asked.

"You bet we did," said Belton, "because th' clerk was terrified by our trooper, who looked like he might break th' clerk in little pieces if he didn't talk t' us, but even more because th' trooper kept sayin' he had a lotta stuff … low-grade criminal stuff he'd been keepin' in his pocket … an' he was ready t' use it all unless …

"So th' trooper," continued Belton, eager to finish, "pushed 'im t' give us everything he knew about this snatch unit, an' he came out with that name I already mentioned … Eremenko … an' said that th' phone number he'd used t' call Eremenko was just a storefront in th' city, a storefront staffed by Russian kids, if y' can imagine.

"So, th' clerk says that last night he called th' number —a D.C. number, not Maryland or Virginia —from th' pay phone, an' some Russian teen picks up, says th' clerk … an' th' clerk tells th' kid that he needs this Eremenko guy t' phone Ms. Kuznetsova right away at her home number … not her embassy number … an' then he … th' clerk … backs out of it.

"An' that's it," Belton concluded.

Another silence fell on the room while the participants turned these revelations over in their minds. McGriff spoke next.

"Did the clerk give you the address of that storefront, Mr. Belton?" he said.

"Yeah … got it right here," he replied.

"Good," said McGriff, then he continued. "We'll need Captain Johnstone and several of his units' contacts … and I think that some of my own contacts at church may be of use, as well. I'm also thinking of getting in touch with my colleague at St. John the Baptist Russian Orthodox Cathedral, located not far from our own church. He has become a good friend, and I know he'll be eager to help if he can.

"After all, we're talking about the city … sometimes hundreds of people dwelling in each block … we need to reach out to every possible source as fast as possible."

He looked at his watch and shook his head.

"I can't believe it," said McGriff.

"They were taken *10 hours* ago.

"Ten hours."

CHAPTER SEVENTEEN

THE ANDREWS AFB LIEUTENANT COLONEL ARRANGED FOR A car and driver to transport Belton, Adelman, Marie, and McGriff, at meeting's end, to Precinct Captain Horace Johnstone's office in the city. Belton summarized for his long-ago mentee the past two hours' revelations.

Johnstone mulled Belton's report briefly, then responded. "Yeah," he said, "I know this Eremenko guy. He's a first-class hoodlum, and he's got a small mob of second-class hoodlums working under him. And, disgustingly, he's got a whole bunch of adolescent kids who help him expand his communications network. They serve as his eyes and ears throughout that part of the city.

"Basically, though, Eremenko and his thugs … not the kids … beat people up for money. It's mostly the old protection racket: you give us money every week and we won't rough up you and your family. We won't burn down your house. We're generous guys. We're on your side. We want you to prosper and be healthy.

"These guys are good at it," Johnstone concluded, "and Eremenko makes sure he personally stays under the radar. I'm not sure we've ever even been able to charge him with anything. Of course, the biggest part of *that* is that people are afraid to report him or testify against him."

"He 'serves' the Russian ethnic community only?" asked Marie.

"Pretty much," said Johnstone. "He's certainly *willing* to 'serve' —good word choice, Mrs. Campbell —other communities and other ethnic groups," continued the captain, "but so far he mostly restricts his operations to the Russians who live in the areas around the two Russian Orthodox churches we have in the city: St. John the Baptist and St. Nicholas.

"And, by the way," added Johnstone, "like so many mob guys, it seems to me, he and his henchmen view themselves as God-fearing Christian people. Not sure how they convince themselves that brutality and intimidation fit with Christianity, but …"

His voice tailed off.

After a moment, McGriff stirred impatiently.

"Captain," said McGriff, "I feel a sense of real desperation, and so do we all in this room right now.

"Soon it will have been 12 hours since Rebecca and her brother were taken, and all we have is the name of this Eremenko person, along with the phone number and address of his contact site: a storefront staffed by some Russian kids … kids who answer the phone and sometimes get in touch with Eremenko.

"You and Mr. Belton are the experts here, captain … the veteran law enforcement professionals … but it just seems to me that we need dozens of police out in the city, right now, canvassing everybody they can find that might possibly help locate Eremenko … or, better still, some information about last night's snatch operation."

Johnstone nodded his agreement, stood, and strode toward the door. "I'll be back in five minutes, folks," he said over his shoulder.

McGriff looked at Belton, who nodded and said, "I'm guessin' he's gonna do just what ya said, and I'm guessin' that within 15 minutes he'll have couple a' dozen officers out there in those Russian neighborhoods.

"Th' thing is, though," Belton continued, "this is a needle-haystack sorta thing, ya know … where *10 times* that many officers aren't likely t' turn up anything. I think we gotta do somethin' more targeted than what Captain Johnstone can legally do.

"Know what I mean? Hmm?"

Marie turned to McGriff.

"You said you have a good friend at one of those Russian Orthodox churches, Jack? Can we go see him now? Would that be a good place to start?"

Johnstone burst into the office before McGriff could reply.

"We're going to fan out in those church neighborhoods right now. I've got about 30 officers geared up to start their canvassing, looking for Eremenko himself, or for any information about him and his people.

"Separately," he continued, "I've got two cruisers headed for that storefront … Eremenko's answering service. They'll see what they can get from those kids."

"Are you optimistic, captain?" asked McGriff after a moment.

"No," he said, "I'm not … but it's what we have right now.

"I am pretty sure that the Russian kids in the storefront will be there … they have two or three pool tables set up, so they stay occupied at all hours … but their usual ploy is to pretend they can't understand English. They just mumble in Russian and shrug their shoulders. And, when you think about it, why wouldn't they?

"Why would they put themselves at risk, providing actual information about Eremenko, when all they have to do is feign ignorance?"

"Have ya been able t' set up informants in th' Russian communities?" asked Belton, "or is th' whole thing just a big stone wall?"

Johnstone shook his head.

"Not a single success there, Sid. And not from lack of trying," he replied.

"Well, Captain Johnstone," said Belton, "lemme ask ya t' radio those two units you've ordered t' th' storefront.

"Tell 'em t' wait fer us. Let me an' Jaakov go in there instead. We're not in uniform, an' we got a little more leeway t' do what we gotta do.

"Know what I mean? Hmm?"

At Belton's phrase, "we got more leeway," McGriff's abdomen tightened. He was afraid he had an idea of what that was likely to mean.

It was mid-afternoon when a police cruiser dropped Belton and Adelman a block from the storefront that served as Dimitri Eremenko's contact location. Both were armed, their under-shoulder holsters relatively inconspicuous, although a trained eye could have detected at a glance that they were carrying weapons.

Arriving at the storefront, they did not pause. Adelman pulled open the entry door, held it wide for Belton, and followed him across the threshold. He then moved five fast steps to one side of his colleague, his eyes never leaving the array of teen eyes that shifted to the visitors as soon as the door began to swing open.

There were perhaps a dozen young men inside the dirty, cluttered space, most of them clustered around two pool tables, naked overhead bulbs providing the only artificial light in the 30-foot-wide-by-50-foot-deep space. Mirroring Adelman's movement, the young men spread out, their faces either hostile or expressionless.

Both visitors picked out the leader in seconds, detecting in the body language of the boys a barely perceptible deference toward one of the smaller individuals, he the only one who stood completely motionless, his arms at his side, his face impassive, no anxiety reflected in his countenance or in his stance.

After the passage of perhaps 10 seconds, the leader turned his head slightly and nodded to a tall, athletic associate who stood near the wall to the visitors' right. This spokesperson advanced several steps toward Belton.

"What do you want?" he said tersely.

"We need t' have a conversation with Dimitri Eremenko," Belton replied, "an' we know y' got his phone number."

The spokesman shrugged.

"Why you think we know this Eremenko?" said the tall adolescent.

Suddenly Adelman drew his 9mm Glock, pointed it at the head of the diminutive leader, and strode directly toward him, covering the distance between himself and the boy in six long strides. Meanwhile, Belton, his cane in his left hand, drew his .45 in a swift movement without taking his eyes off the array of adolescents in front of him.

What Belton observed was exactly what he expected. These were not seasoned, professional fighters. These were not experienced gunmen able to detect the fact that the safety mechanisms on both firearms were still in the "on" position, or that neither intruder had placed his finger on the trigger of his weapon.

These were surprised and suddenly frightened kids, utterly unprepared to contend with a former Mossad agent's assured advance across the room and his confident, practiced wielding of the Glock.

They shrank back in all directions, retreating toward the nearest wall.

They shrank, that is, except for the leader, whose eyes grew wide, but who did not move from his stance as the weapon neared his face. Nor did he flinch when Adelman moved the muzzle of the Glock under the young man's chin and pressed upward, forcing his head back.

"Call Eremenko," said Adelman simply, looking down into the boy's face, "and tell him that Ms. Kuznetsova wishes to know his current location. Call him now."

As he spoke the words, Adelman placed his free hand on the young man's shoulder and spun him around toward the one piece of furniture in the room, a battered wooden desk with a plain, black telephone sitting on one edge. As he spun the boy around, Adelman moved behind him and shifted the position of the firearm so that its muzzle was now pressed against the side of the leader's head.

During Adelman's maneuver, Belton waved his .45 to indicate that the several boys near the desk should move away as the lanky detective and his charge approached. They shrank further back, glancing at each other as they did, unsure how to appear the rugged mobsters they aspired to be.

Adelman, his back to several of the boys now, but covered by Belton's .45, said softly but commandingly in his captive's ear.

"Pick up the phone. Call Eremenko. Tell him that Ms. Kuznetsova wishes to know his current location. *Call now.*"

Seeing the boy hesitate, Adelman called upon his rudimentary Russian.

"Pozvoni seychas!"

The boy began dialing.

Looking over the bony adolescent shoulder, Adelman noted carefully the 7-digit number dialed by a youthful hand that was suddenly trembling. Together they listened to the successful connection and to the repeated tone of a telephone ringing somewhere in the D.C. area. At length, the system's voicemail was activated, and a male voice said something on the recording in Russian, something that Adelman was able to translate as, "Speak after the tone."

Adelman whispered near the boy's ear, speaking fast, "Ms. Kuznetsova wishes to know your current location. Call this number with your report."

They heard the tone. The boy spoke in Russian. Adelman translated the message as approximately the one he had dictated.

The boy replaced the receiver and Adelman holstered the firearm and moved around the desk toward the front of the store, while Belton kept the .45 trained on the group. Adelman pushed open the door, Belton slowly backed out, and the two men turned and began to retrace their steps toward the waiting police cruiser.

"Whaddya say t' th' kid in Russian?" asked Belton, looking up suspiciously at his long-time partner.

"Well," Adelman responded, "I *might* have said 'call now.'"

Belton looked up again, still more skeptically. "What else *might* ya have said, Jaakov?"

"Well ... I don't know ... but I'm pretty sure the words were Russian."

"So ya mighta said, 'Order me a ham sammwich.'"

Adelman smiled. "Probably not."

They continued along the sidewalk toward the police cruiser, and Belton quickly grew serious.

"Whaddya think of all that back there?" he asked.

"I think we were right," answered Adelman, "to focus the message on Eremenko's current location and to cite Ms. Kuznetsova as the requesting party. Nothing whatever is going to happen in that regard, of course, but, as we hoped, I was able to get the phone number by looking over the kid's shoulder as he dialed. I think the message you and I chose was the most plausible one to demand of the young man.

"We got the Eremenko number. That's all we could hope for.

"And I think," continued Adelman, "that we were also right that that kid, even though he was the least scared boy in the room, was much too surprised and confused by the Glock in his face to dial any number other than the one he actually uses for Eremenko. I think we probably have the man's actual business phone number, and, if we can get the network and the search warrant process going fast enough, we may be able to surprise Eremenko himself … and, God willing … to discover where Rebecca and Luke are being held … assuming they are still among the living."

Belton shuddered visibly, his teeth clinched in a simmering anger.

As soon as they were in the police vehicle, Belton asked the patrolwoman in the front passenger seat to contact Captain Johnstone on her police radio. She did, got Johnstone almost immediately, and told him that Sidney Belton needed to speak to him. She passed the radio handset back to Belton.

He spoke rapidly into the handset.

"Captain," he said, "I need t' ask ya t' take whatever steps y' need t' take t' get an address from a D.C. phone number we got right here … an' then t' get a search warrant fer that same address just as soon as ya can."

He read the number once, then repeated it.

"An' captain," he added, "speed matters here, ya know. Speed matters a lot."

Using the number given him by Belton, Johnstone moved swiftly through the processes of obtaining the Eremenko address and then requesting and receiving a search warrant for that address from a judge with whom the captain worked regularly. The captain then sent an officer racing to pick up the warrant, while he radioed one of the two-car units already canvassing the city, ordering the four-officer team to head for the address fully prepared for action as soon as the search warrant was in hand.

Meanwhile, McGriff and Marie, not yet aware of the two detectives' armed confrontation with the young men at the storefront, took a taxi to St. John the Baptist Russian Orthodox Cathedral to visit Priest Viktor Konev, an associate pastor there and a man who had developed a close friendship with McGriff.

They were taken without delay into Konev's office. And, after introducing Marie and Konev to each other, McGriff plunged in without additional formalities.

"Viktor," he said, urgency in his voice, "the Soviet KGB … or, rather, a Russian hit team almost certainly hired by Father Artur Volkov, whom, unfortunately, you and I both know … has kidnapped two people, and, we fear, will torture and possibly kill them both. We desperately need your help in trying to get information that might help us recover them alive. The snatch occurred last night … well, early this morning … shortly before 3 a.m., just as the two, Rebecca Clark and her twin brother, Royal Navy Lieutenant Luke Manguson, were nearing Andrews Air Force Base to board a 4 a.m. RAF flight back home to England."

At the mention of Rebecca's name, the priest's eyes grew wide.

"*The* Rebecca Clark?" he said, wonderment in his voice.

"Yes," replied McGriff, "the very person you and I have discussed before, in the context of her extraordinary gifts, and of her remarkable interventions over the years in a variety of threats to the faith."

McGriff and Marie then outlined the emergency for the priest, emphasizing both the nature of the publication plot and the violence of which the adversary was so clearly capable. Given past conversations between McGriff and Konev about Rebekka Yahalomin, Konev quickly grasped the ramifications of the snatch-and-remove action of the previous night. Although Konev had never had personal contact with Rebecca or others in the group, his horror was genuine and deeply felt.

When McGriff, with Marie's assistance at several points, made clear that Volkov's assistant, Tatyana Kuznetsova, had reached Dimitri Eremenko via a storefront contact arrangement that was staffed by Russian teens, and cited the street address of the storefront, Konev moaned softly and actually dropped his face into his hands.

After a moment, he looked up and shook his head in disappointment.

"I know those young men, Jack," he said, "and I thought we had gotten them moving in a good direction.

"But if they are actually serving as Dimitri Eremenko's go-between in criminal activity, we have certainly failed.

"What can I do?"

"Can you help us," replied McGriff, "to get through to Eremenko?

"Or, if that's not a plausible way to proceed, Viktor, can you tell us how we can try to find where Rebecca and her brother have been taken, before something terrible is done to them … if something terrible has not already been done?"

The priest was silent for several moments, his brow furrowed in thought.

"Let's start at that storefront, Jack," he said.

"Let's go over there now. A taxi can get us there in five minutes. We had made such good inroads with those young men; I'd like to hear firsthand … from them … what has happened to make them decide to work with a shadowy figure like Eremenko.

"They'll talk to me, Jack. I'm confident."

In just minutes, their taxi stopped at the teen hangout, and Konev, Marie, and McGriff stepped onto the sidewalk at Eremenko's storefront operation. Konev said to his companions, "Let me go in alone at the start. I want to sit down with the leadership committee —three of the boys, elected by the others —and see what they'll tell me, before I bring in two people they don't yet know.

"But I do want you to come in, once I've laid some groundwork. I think they need to hear you describe Rebecca and her brother, especially Rebecca's athletic history as an internationally ranked tennis player in her youth, and Luke's military exploits. These are the kinds of things that can make these young men sympathetic to the idea of helping us to find and rescue them.

"After all," he added, "they don't actually know Dimitri Eremenko. He's just a name and a source of money for them.

"These kids still have ideals. I think we must lead them to see how admirable and worthy of respect the two captives are, and how Mr. Eremenko is not."

Marie shook her head skeptically.

"I hope you're right," she said, "but I keep thinking that our getting help from these young people assumes that they actually *have* information.

"I fear that they may not."

In what seemed to Marie and McGriff to be fewer than 60 seconds, Konev returned, downcast. He stood for a moment, looking down at the sidewalk.

"They tell me," he said, "that they received a visit less than 30 minutes ago from two men who threatened them and demanded that they contact Eremenko. The boys' leader says he dialed Eremenko's number with a pistol to his head … literally.

"He says he was ordered by one of the intruders to respond to Eremenko's voice mail by saying that 'Ms. Kuznetsova wishes to know your current location. Call this number with your report.' He says those were the exact words he was ordered to speak.

"He says he then spoke those words, in Russian, to the recording, and the two men left the building.

"He described one of the men as short, using a walking cane. He described the other as tall and long-limbed. An angular face.

"Those boys are frightened, Jack. They know that Dimitri Eremenko is a dangerous man, and yet it was two *others* who just threatened them with weapons.

"Under those circumstances," said Konev, "I couldn't ask them for anything.

"You understand? I will need to start rebuilding trust with those young people, starting from scratch. There is no possible way I can push them to reveal anything about the emergency involving Mrs. Clark and her brother … even if they actually know something useful, which, as Mrs. Campbell just noted, is open to question."

The three stood crestfallen on the sidewalk, not speaking further.

Finally, McGriff said, "Viktor, I've no doubt that those men are with us … detectives Belton and Adelman … they got this address earlier today, from the Andrews Base transportation clerk.

"It did not occur to me that they would come here right away, or that, even if they did, they would actually threaten these boys with firearms."

McGriff made a small noise … a sort of moan.

"Oh, stupid!" he said to himself.

He turned to Marie. "Stupid. Stupid. Stupid. Of *course* I should have known, Marie. When Mr. Belton said he and Jaakov would, as civilians, have 'a little more leeway to do what they needed to do,' I should have known *exactly* what he meant.

"*Stupid!*"

She placed her hand on his arm. "Jack," she said, "they're trying to save Rebecca and Luke just like we are. They're accustomed to a certain way of operating. I'll bet those weapons were not even loaded."

"But those boys …" began McGriff in response.

The priest interrupted. "Do you mean two men from your own group did this, Jack?" said Konev. "That's unconscionable. Some of these boys are still *children."*

"Viktor," replied McGriff, "I'm so sorry.

"I take responsibility. I should have known what Mr. Belton meant when he said that about 'having more leeway.' I just didn't work it out fully in my mind. It's all my mistake. I'm so very sorry."

Konev looked hard at his friend for a long moment, then nodded, thoughtful.

"You know," he said, "perhaps I can help these young people to see that this is exactly the world they are headed into … that this kind of thing will happen increasingly as their lives go forward … unless they extricate themselves now. Next time, the man holding a gun to their heads may pull the trigger.

"Don't worry yourself about it, Jack. You didn't intend what happened, and in the long run this may turn out to be therapeutic."

The threesome had begun to walk back toward the cathedral as they talked. They walked another two blocks in silence before Marie touched the priest on his arm and asked, "Where are those boys' mothers, and where are their girlfriends?"

Konev looked surprised, and at first smiled, but quickly saw that her question was completely serious. He checked his watch as they stopped at an intersection.

"Well, Mrs. Campbell, we have a mother-daughter Bible study," he said, "that is scheduled to start in … oh … 45 minutes. Probably a dozen girls and their moms … these girls are eighth and ninth graders … same as many of the boys back at the storefront.

"The girls will have been in English-language writing classes most of the day. One of the area public schools has been offering these classes for several summers now. They've become popular with teens in our congregation … although probably just as much for social reasons as for academic reasons."

"Perfect," said Marie.

Once back at the cathedral, McGriff used the priest's office phone to get in touch with Johnstone. The captain informed him that he had used the phone company's address-finding service, available to law enforcement, and his own collegial connections with a D.C. judge, to obtain a search warrant. His officers, search warrant in hand, had just completed their raid on Eremenko's presumed business address.

They had found nothing. The address was simply a second empty storefront, this one unoccupied, possibly evacuated because of the recorded voice mail message Adelman had forced upon the leader.

Ten minutes after McGriff had received that disappointing news from the captain, Marie and the priest came into the same office, accompanied by three teen girls and their mothers. The three girls had been selected by Konev for the interview because he knew that each considered herself the girlfriend of one of the boys at the nearby storefront. With the women and girls seated, Konev began the session, standing, prepared to leave as soon as he had done an introduction of Marie and of the emergency she faced.

"Thank you for giving Mrs. Campbell a few moments of your time before our study session starts, ladies and daughters," he said, smiling at his "ladies and daughters" reference. The mothers returned the smile. Konev was well liked by the families whom he served as priest and pastor.

"Last night," he began, "or, actually, very early this morning, Mrs. Rebecca Clark and her brother, a Royal Navy lieutenant, both living in England, were violently taken from their vehicle near Andrews Air Force Base in Maryland. We don't know who was involved in the crime, but Mrs. Campbell needs very much to know if you girls … or you moms … have overheard anything today during your summer-school writing classes that might help her understand how to go about looking for them.

"The police are looking everywhere they can think to look," he continued, "but Mrs. Campbell and I are hoping you might have heard something that would help. I'm going to go down the hall and set up the room for our session, but I am asking that you tell Mrs. Campbell anything you may have heard … *anything* you may have heard … that might help us. You don't need to tell her your names, and, of course, she doesn't know any of you … and so you can just tell her what you've heard without mentioning whom you heard it from.

"And ladies … just know that I personally trust Mrs. Campbell completely. I want you to trust Mrs. Campbell just as I do."

Smiling his gratitude to the women and girls, Konev turned and left the office, closing the door. In the empty hallway, he leaned back against the door and murmured Jack McGriff's companion prayer to himself, the prayer that McGriff had offered him years before and which he had quickly adopted and taught to his own parishioners: *Father, be present, be present.*

As he prayed, Marie, sitting in Konev's chair in his quiet, carpeted office, looked into the faces of the mothers and their young daughters.

"Thank you so much for doing this," she said quietly.

She then simply looked down and sat with her hands in her lap, praying that God might lead one of those present to say what she knew … anything at all that might have floated through the corridors of the school that day.

After several minutes of uncomfortable silence, one of the mothers looked up at Marie and said softly, "Mrs. Campbell, I'm sorry. We need to go to our session now. Priest Konev starts on time."

Marie nodded. "It's all right," she said. "Thank you for sitting with me. I'm grateful."

Without a word, all six got up from their chairs and filed out of Konev's office, the last mother closing the door quietly behind her, but pausing to make eye contact with Marie before shutting the door fully. Marie remained seated, continuing her prayer, knowing that there was nothing else she could realistically do.

Minutes later, as she stood, picked up her purse and started for the office door, she heard a soft rapping … actually, more of a quiet scratching … on the other side. She opened the door.

The mother, who, as she had exited minutes before, had made eye contact with Marie, entered quickly, closing the door behind her. She took a deep breath, steeling herself to speak.

"I must speak, Mrs. Campbell," she said. "I excused myself from our class to go to the ladies' room."

Marie nodded and indicated one of the chairs. "Please," she said.

"No," said the woman, "I must speak quickly and return to our session. When I picked up my daughter from writing class, she told me a rumor was going around that the leader of the group of boys that hang around that storefront, not far from here, was a passenger last night in a car that followed another car that was smashed and knocked off the roadway. She told me this happened near the Air Force base.

"According to the rumor," continued the woman, "a woman who'd been in the smashed vehicle was placed in the car the boy was riding in. The woman's wrists and ankles had been taped together. They drove her to a house near the Potomac.

"She didn't say anything else about it, and some of what I just said could be wrong, but it's what I understood my daughter to say.

"That's all I know … I must run."

And she was gone.

As the afternoon sun began to drop toward the hills to the west of Washington, a long line of law enforcement vehicles —from Maryland, Virginia, and D.C. — moved south along the Potomac's left bank toward the KGB safe house where Marie Campbell and Jack McGriff had been briefly held just over 24 hours earlier. As the vehicles approached the KGB stronghold, they separated and slowed, by prearrangement, in order for the officers to converge on the structure, on foot, from three directions.

Belton, Adelman, Marie, and McGriff sat tensely in a police transport cruiser positioned near the center rescue group. They watched from there as the rescue teams, weapons at the ready, disappeared into the woods to move to widely separated points, finally moving from those points to within 50 yards of the house.

They listened over police radio while the officers talked to each other, preparing a coordinated assault. Once in position, with minimum delay, the units rushed the house in unison without shots being fired either by police or by those assumed to be defending the fortress, whether KGB agents or the civilian snatch-and-remove team.

Finally, reports came in over the radio.

"Nobody here," said the first reporting unit.

"Looks like people have been here," said the second, "but it could be from yesterday's snatch of Mrs. Campbell and Father McGriff. There's a little blood on the kitchen floor, but we understand there was a knife wound yesterday. This is probably just that. Very little blood, actually."

After the "all clear" had been officially given, Belton and his three companions were driven to the front door of the house. They entered and began a walk-through of the premises. Marie and McGriff walked gingerly into the kitchen where they had been held captive just one day earlier. They saw the patch of blood on the floor, and told the senior officers that that was exactly where Mrs. Clark's knife had drawn blood.

The couple, accompanied by two of the senior officers, then retraced the previous day's scrambling, stumbling run from the back door of the house to the jetty. All signs of human traffic appeared to have been made during their own escape.

Marie and McGriff returned glumly to the house, and found a dozen of the officers waiting for them in the kitchen, along with Belton and Adelman.

"Mrs. Campbell?" said one, as the crowded kitchen adjusted itself to accommodate the couple and their accompanying officers, "you spoke to the mother whose daughter reported the rumor from the school.

"What are your thoughts?"

"I do think that this house … this location … fits the teenager's story, as she reported it to her mother this afternoon," she said quietly, "but I just don't see anything to indicate that something happened here last night.

"Everything Jack and I see looks like yesterday's activity to us."

The group was quiet, disappointment consuming the room.

The most senior of the officers present shook his head.

"We don't really have anything to go on, do we?" he asked, "or am I missing something that we should be thinking about or looking for?

"Seems to me," he continued, "that either the kid got the rumor confused somehow, or the rumor was false to begin with. Got to be one or the other.

"We don't have anything to work with, do we, Mrs. Campbell? Detectives?"

Marie responded after a long moment. "The mother's words were, 'a house near the Potomac,' and I've assumed that this KGB house would be the spot, but maybe not."

The officer shook his head. "There are hundreds … actually, thousands … of houses near the Potomac," he said, "and if it's not this place, it really could be almost anywhere along the whole length of the river. A hundred miles. Either side of the water."

He looked again at the detectives, inquiring with his eyes.

Belton and Adelman glanced at each other and shook their heads.

"I'd say," said Belton, "we got nothin', folks.

"I'd say we got nothin' at all."

CHAPTER EIGHTEEN

REBECCA CLARK AWOKE NEAR MIDNIGHT FROM AN EXHAUSTION-driven 45-minute nap. She took a moment to recall where she was … and under what set of circumstances. Suddenly remembering, she sat straight up on the small, hard bench seat on which she had dozed, and looked around the darkened, cramped space.

In the faint moonlight that penetrated the curtained windows, she could see the shape of her brother, nearly within her reach, sleeping on a matching bench mounted on the wall opposite. She closed her eyes and listened, straining to hear any sound other than the steady, motorized hum that had helped lull them both to sleep.

No other sound registered.

Her thoughts now on her last conversation with Luke before they both drifted into slumber, she stood unsteadily, her head actually grazing the low ceiling, and shrugged off the lightweight blanket she had pulled around her shoulders before lying down on the bench. Tossing the blanket aside, she sat down cautiously on the bench, leaned over, and slowly untied and then removed each of her tennis shoes.

It was time.

Now barefoot, she stood again and reached into one of the small pockets in the slacks she had worn since getting dressed in the middle of the previous night, as she and her brother had dressed in preparation for the drive to the Air Force Base. She drew from the pocket one of the strong rubber bands she carried with her at all times, and swiftly pulled her long, thick hair into a tight ponytail.

Her hair now bound for action, she removed her slacks, folded them, and placed them neatly on the bench she had occupied throughout the ordeal.

Then she smiled at the gesture. *Why did I fold those?* she wondered.

Because that's what I do, she answered.

Wearing now only underwear and her light-blue *I Love New York* tee-shirt, she turned around carefully, knelt on the bench, and, pushing the flimsy curtain aside, began to slide the cheap, uncooperative, clear-plastic window laterally along its metal track, moving the window one grudging inch at a time. She was anxious, not so much that the tiny, grating noises made by the window's halting movements might awaken Luke, but that they might be detected by those who had so violently taken her and her brother nearly 20 hours before.

She pushed away from her mind the crushing disappointment that had flooded her heart as the hours of their captivity had passed, having known throughout that one of those hours included the moment at which she had expected to be reunited with her husband and children at the Lodge. And she once more fought off thoughts of the fear that doubtless tore at her husband, Matt, and at Luke's wife, Kory, forcing herself time and again to concentrate on the formulation of an escape plan.

Now, impatiently, Rebecca continued to work the stubbornly resistant window, soon achieving its maximum open width. The resulting aperture, roughly square, was slightly less than 12 inches wide by 10 inches high, providing a diagonal of 15 to 16 inches. That *might* be enough, she and her brother had agreed, to allow her to force her rangy, 6-foot, athletic frame through the opening, though clearly insufficient to permit Luke's massive shoulders and chest to pass. Thus, she reminded herself, the wisdom of their decision that only she would make the escape attempt that night.

Next, continuing to move slowly, fluidly, and, she hoped, silently, she reversed her position, now turning her back to the window. Standing, she reached down far enough to place both hands flat on the grimy floor, moved her weight onto her hands, and, in that head-down position, began to extend each of her long, sinewy legs, one at a time, upward toward the less-than-12-inch-by-10-inch opening she had created. Forcing herself to move slowly, she pushed each bare foot through the opening, her shins scraping painfully against the metal track.

Then, in a powerful, athletic maneuver, Rebecca pushed her upper body up from the floor, extending her arms fully, thereby executing a combination push-up and hand-stand in order to force her legs completely through the open window, a movement that she continued without pause until her hips reached the opening.

And there, progress stopped, just as she and Luke had expected.

She lifted each hand from the floor, one at a time, and placed them flat on the bench. Now, gathering herself once more, pressing with her hands against the bench, she forced her hips backward, rotating, squirming, and twisting them to take advantage of the diagonal's slightly more generous width, until she was able to squeeze her hips through the opening, drawing blood as the bare skin over each pelvic bone tore slightly against the metal track. As her hips cleared, she fought to slow her movement through the window as the weight of her legs and hips, now free, sought to pull her upper body fully out the window.

Although her hands were still flat on the bench, it was her taut stomach that was now taking the full brunt of her weight, her abdomen resting on the narrow metal track that had already shredded the skin over her pelvis. She tensed her hard abdominal muscles against the pain, paused briefly to breathe, and gathered herself for the final stage of the maneuver.

When she was ready, she shifted her hands swiftly from the bench to the windowsill, each wrist now tight against her rib cage, and then arched her back to force her shoulders and head to a position well above her hands. The resulting near-vertical position used gravity to advantage, and forced a sliding, downward and backward movement through the window, while both her abdomen and her chest screamed their protests as they scraped viciously across the angry metal track.

As she slipped slowly down and out of the window, she squeezed her shoulders together, each upper arm feeling its own pain as it raked through the opening. Finally, as her head followed her shoulders through the window and her arms gradually extended fully above her head, she hung down the outside of the structure, fingers clawing at the windowsill, her full weight now transferred to her powerful hands.

Now hanging suspended outside the makeshift prison she had occupied for nearly 24 hours, she whispered to herself Jack McGriff's companion prayer and filled her lungs with the fresh night air as she prepared to release her grip. She pushed gently against the vertical wall with her feet and legs, succeeding in moving her abdomen and chest several inches away from the wall.

Finally, she opened her hands.

Clad only in underwear and tee-shirt, her black tresses bound in the tight pony tail, the skin over her shins, pelvis, abdomen, chest, and upper arms raw and bleeding, Rebecca Clark dropped down the side of the speeding 92-foot Hatteras motor yacht and disappeared into the Atlantic Ocean.

As midnight approached in a District of Columbia police precinct office, the afternoon-evening shift drew to an end, and two-person teams began to file into the precinct's ready room, exhaustion and frustration written on their faces. They slumped into their chairs, some with fast food in their hands, others with coffee cups.

The room was silent except for occasional murmuring between partners.

Captain Horace Johnstone, who had been on duty since early the previous morning, addressed his troops.

"Everyone," he said, "thank you for what you've tried to do today and tonight. You have done everything I asked, and more. I'm grateful.

"As most of you know, we've had the occasional nibble, starting mid-afternoon with detectives Belton and Adelman extracting Dimitri Eremenko's business-office phone number from those kids who staff one of his remote offices. But our teams followed up at *that* address and found the office abandoned.

"Then Mrs. Campbell, here, was able to coax a rumor out of one of the mothers of a girl who apparently is the girlfriend of a boy in that same group."

Suddenly realizing that Marie was known to only a few of his precinct officers, the captain gestured in her direction, nodding his thanks to her. But seeing several puzzled, inquisitive glances being exchanged among his officers, he tried to explain.

"Mrs. Campbell," he said, searching for the right words, "goes with … ah … is the girlfriend of … I mean … she is …"

Johnstone was interrupted in mid-fumble by McGriff, who stood abruptly and said loudly to the officers, many of whom he knew from his work in the city, "Marie is my *girlfriend!* We're an *item!*"

He looked at one of his close officer friends, a fun-loving bachelor. "Eat your heart out, Mac," said McGriff, "she's way out of your class."

The resulting hilarity served as a badly needed tonic. The room relaxed and, after the general laughter began to die down, two of the policewomen began a steady applause, and were quickly joined by all three dozen officers present.

Finally, Johnstone resumed his summary. "Anyway," he continued, "Mrs. Campbell extracted an interesting rumor from one of the kids' mothers, and so we got organized, along with some of the Virginia and Maryland people we've worked with before, and conducted a crash assault on a KGB safe house on the

Potomac, not far from Andrews. Same place where Father McGriff and Mrs. Campbell were held yesterday afternoon, before they were rescued, but there was no sign that the place had been used today.

"The kid's rumor said that the two captives —Mrs. Clark and her brother — were taken to a house near the Potomac, but it didn't turn out to be *that* house, as far as we could tell, and so we haven't known whether or not to disregard that rumor as some kid's accidental or purposeful misdirection effort. And that's why we've continued our canvassing of the city, right on up until now.

"In the morning, with a fresh shift," continued the captain, "I intend to extend our canvassing of the city until noon, and then we'll have to close down the operation and turn to our regular set of priorities. So, when you come back on duty tomorrow afternoon, I don't expect us to continue with the efforts you've put in today and tonight, other than to be on the alert during regular rounds for anything you might hear or see that could bear on last night's snatch operation out near Andrews.

"Again, thank you, everyone. Let's call it a night."

Several officers began to stir from their chairs, but one of the shift leaders, a sergeant seated near the back of the room, stood and said loudly, "Captain, did you say that the kid's rumor was that Mrs. Clark and Lieutenant Manguson had been taken to a house near the Potomac?"

Johnstone nodded. "Right," he said.

"Well," responded the sergeant, "what's been done about *that* possibility … the possibility that the rumor is right … just not specific to that particular location?"

"We notified all those little police departments up and down the river," replied the captain, "going down all the way to the Chesapeake Bay, sergeant, but there are thousands of homes near the Potomac and on both sides of the river, and spread out over all that territory … it just wasn't feasible to request that those little outfits send officers knocking on doors all over that part of two states."

The room was silent. Some of the officers resumed their seats, thoughtful.

"Captain," said one of the policewomen who had begun the applause for Marie and McGriff earlier, standing to address Johnstone from her seat near the back of the room, "what if they have put those two people on a boat of some kind?"

Silence.

"What if," she continued, "they took them to a house near the Potomac so they could load them onto a boat … a boat large enough to hide them below decks, in a cabin … a boat that would be large enough to take them all the way to the Chesapeake … and beyond?"

More silence.

Finally, her partner spoke, looking up at her from his seat.

"That's nuts," he said in an obviously friendly way, smiling as he said it. "Why would they do that?" he continued.

"All they'd need to do," he said, "is lock those two in a basement … or in a garage … or even a toolshed. Why would they do something as cumbersome as getting them onto some kind of boat? You need sleep … go home."

The policewoman smiled and smacked her partner playfully on the shoulder.

Amid the general good-natured chuckling, the policewoman persisted.

"Captain," she said, "we're talking here about Russians, right?

"We're talking about people from the Soviet Embassy, and we're talking about KGB agents, and we're talking about a Russian hit team, and we're talking about Soviet businessmen here to negotiate some kind of trade agreement … we're talking about businessmen with lots of Soviet money in their pockets … businessmen with lots of access to really expensive things, like very large boats … with plenty of money to rent a yacht from one of the city marinas for a few days … along with a crew that would handle the boat for them, right?"

The captain nodded, suddenly intrigued by her line of thought. "Yes," he agreed, "yes, we are."

"What's the nearest Soviet satellite nation?" she asked, something in her tone indicating that she had convinced herself that she was onto something.

Silence.

Her partner looked up at her from his chair. "You're telling us you think Mrs. Clark and Lieutenant Manguson have been kidnapped, placed on a yacht, and are on their way to *Fidel Castro?* You think they're on their way to *Cuba?*"

She looked down at her partner and smiled. "Yeah," she said quietly. "It makes complete sense," she added, "just not to a nitwit like you."

Her persistently incredulous partner looked from her face to the captain's, as Johnstone continued to stand, thoughtful, at the front of the ready room. Then her partner looked up at her again, grinning broadly, and shook his head.

"You gotta be *kiddin'* me."

Rebecca dropped feet first down the side of the yacht, breaking the surface of the water cleanly, hardly making a splash. She did nothing to slow her underwater descent, wanting to drop well below the yacht's churning propeller. Her capacious lungs allowed her to remain under the surface for nearly a full minute.

She at last allowed herself to rise slowly to the surface, conscious that the noise of the vessel's powerful engine and spinning propeller had faded completely out of earshot. She broke the surface carefully and turned her face in the direction of the rapidly retreating boat. Satisfied that it was neither slowing nor changing direction, she turned her shoulders in the remembered direction of the distant lights she had seen from the cabin window before she had begun her elaborately scripted escape.

The stinging pain of the salt water against her cuts and abrasions was already lessening and was, in any case, the least of her concerns. Whatever those lights might indicate, she knew she needed to swim to them, find law enforcement quickly, and get in touch with the D.C. police. Either the U.S. Coast Guard or the U.S. Navy would be needed to intercept the big yacht, and she and Luke had agreed early on that its likely destination was the island of Cuba.

As soon as they heard the language —Russian —being spoken by their captors, and as soon as Luke gave considered thought to the size, seaworthiness, and fuel capacity of the 92-foot yacht, he had told her that Cuba was their destination. He was knowledgeable both of the waterways and of the geography of the American east coast, having flown into the U.S. Navy Base at Norfolk many times on RAF flights from England, both as a military and as a civilian consultant.

Once he had considered the distances involved in traversing the Potomac River, the Chesapeake Bay, the Atlantic coast from Norfolk to Miami, and the Caribbean from Miami to Havana, he had no doubt. He had explained to her that the ideal time for her to attempt to escape and swim to shore would be near midnight, because prior to that time the yacht would be plying the most desolate stretches of the lower Potomac and Chesapeake. Reaching shore in those regions could leave her miles from help.

Now, in the water, having dropped from the modest elevation of one of the vessel's starboard cabin windows to no elevation at all, she could no longer see the lights. But she launched herself in the remembered direction of the shoreline, her powerful flutter kick and her long-reach crawl stroke quickly beginning to eat up the distance to whatever beach might await her.

Always in superb physical condition, Rebecca's thrice-weekly runs and twice-weekly distance swims prepared her perfectly for this unexpected exigency. But the distance turned out to be much further than she had hoped.

Unable to maintain the fast, demanding freestyle stroke indefinitely, she changed after 20 minutes to the more economical side stroke, simultaneously changing her leg action to the scissors kick, and first using a right-side stroke, then turning to the left. Periodically Rebecca would halt her forward progress long enough to propel herself high enough in the water to see the distant lights, timing the maneuver to coincide with the peak of the regularly recurring swells. Thus, at several-minute intervals, she repeatedly confirmed the shoreward direction of her swim.

Fifty-five minutes into her watery journey, Rebecca began to hear the distant sound of surf. Overjoyed, she resumed the enthusiastic crawl stroke with which she had begun, and sped rapidly toward the shore, soon helped by what seemed to her an incoming tide. Finally, having ridden the waves into the shallows, she stood and splashed through knee-deep water toward the unknown beach.

She stopped, breathing deeply, on the sand. Suddenly conscious of her near-nakedness, she crossed her arms over her chest and peered through the faint moonlight. With the aid of the dim lighting cast by a row of street lamps lining a seawall, she was able to see, 30 yards ahead, the shapeless form of a discarded beach towel, obviously soaking wet and no doubt sand-encrusted, but better by far than nothing.

She walked to it swiftly, her legs gradually regaining their non-aquatic competence. Reaching the soggy towel, she gingerly lifted it by its corners and shook it out as best she could. She then wrapped the sandy, soaking towel tightly around her shoulders, shivering at the wet coldness of the thin fabric and the brisk ocean breeze that cut through it with ease and knifed into her back.

She found that she was actually colder with the towel around her than without, but her clear priority at the moment was to cover herself in anticipation of finding someone to help her reach a law enforcement office as quickly as possible. She walked up the sandy incline, the slope holding back the encroaching tide, until she found a ladder built into the concrete seawall.

She scaled the ladder quickly, despite having just one hand free from towel-securing responsibilities. She then crossed the wide, desolate boardwalk, whereupon she entered a narrow, darkened alleyway that led her eventually to a hotel-lined avenue running parallel to the beach behind her.

Assuming, walking the streets an hour after midnight with no proper clothing and no identification, that she would be taken for a homeless person, Rebecca stood barefoot and shivering on the cold sidewalk, looking up and down the street for any sign of either police or building-security personnel. Seeing neither, she began to walk briskly in the direction of what seemed to her to be the more heavily populated area, and had passed only three hotels when she saw what she hoped: a security vehicle just turning into the portico-covered front entranceway of a multi-story hotel.

She continued toward the vehicle as it came to a stop under the portico, and she watched as a burly, 60-something security officer, possibly retired from a local police force, she thought, rose from the driver's seat and stood beside his car. She saw that the officer had, after a moment, noticed her, and that he had immediately stopped to look more closely at her. His hand was still on the open car door, his face impassive.

She halted 10 feet from him and prepared to speak, but hesitated when she realized he was examining her exposed lower legs, her shins raw from the damage they had sustained during her escape from the yacht. The security guard spoke first.

"Are you hurt, ma'am, and can I help you?" he said, a kindness in his voice that she had not expected.

That kindness … a sympathetic voice from a stranger from whom she expected suspicion or even hostility … brought a lump to Rebecca's throat and tears to her eyes. The sudden presence of such emotion within her seemed somehow to drain her of all remaining strength, and, surprised at the physical weakness that was coming over her, she found herself sinking slowly to her knees, the fact of being saved from torture, death, and then, having escaped those two prospects, of evading another kind of death —drowning in the Atlantic Ocean —rushing upon her with full force.

She was helpless to halt the crescendo of emotion and found herself crying, and crying hard, the sound of her own gasping sobs building quickly to barely controlled weeping, as she knelt huddled on the pavement. The entire experience was so foreign to Rebecca that she could not recognize herself, this exhausted, bleeding, near-naked shadow of herself crouching on her knees on cold pavement. She only knew that she was unable to help herself, her body wracked with convulsive gasps.

After the passage of what seemed to her a very long time, but which was, in fact, no more than 15 seconds, she felt the security officer's hand on her shoulder. Looking up at him through a haze of tears, she saw the kindly gentleman bending low over her, concern written on every line of his weathered face.

"Ma'am," he said softly, "tell me what I can do to help you."

The D.C. policewoman who had articulated the snatch-to-Cuba hypothesis stayed after her shift ended at midnight to do what she could to assist the captain, as did her skeptical partner. He had gradually become convinced that her idea was not nonsense, and soon realized he wanted to be part of whatever solution might be developed.

Despite their public byplay, or perhaps because of it, the twosome formed one of the top partner-teams on the D.C. force. The woman welcomed her partner's help.

By 12:30 a.m., with Johnstone's weighty assistance, they had identified the James Creek Marina on the Anacostia River, a mile south of the U.S. Capitol building, as the most likely source for rental of a vessel of the requisite size, speed, and range, and had awakened the marina's listed owner at his home. The captain had then asked him —*urged* him in the strongest terms —to meet him and his two officers at the marina in 10 minutes. The owner arrived, impressively, at the same moment they did, dressed in shorts, tee-shirt, and bedroom slippers.

They explained that they needed to identify any large yacht that had been leased the previous evening or night. Looking at the marina's log, they saw that there had been but one, and that it had been rented for 10 days in the name of Artur Volkov of the Soviet Embassy, along with an operating crew of three. The vessel was a 92-foot Hatteras Cabin Cruiser, deep-water capable, with a listed range of 850 miles.

Back in the precinct ready room at 1:15 a.m., Johnstone and his two officers, newly energized despite the interminable length of their day, reported back to Belton, Adelman, Marie, and McGriff, that the 92-foot *Potomac Queen* had been leased by Volkov himself, along with a crew of three, for 10 days. Turning to a 6-by-6-foot wall chart of the east coast of the United States, they saw that the yacht's reported 850-mile range would require one fuel stop, if indeed its destination were the Soviet satellite nation of Cuba.

Charleston, South Carolina, with its excellent harbor and its multifaceted boating enterprises, presented itself as the most obvious refueling location. As they discussed their next phone call —whether to the Charleston city police or to the Charleston Harbor Patrol —Johnstone's young desk clerk knocked quietly at the ready-room door, then stuck his head into the room and addressed the captain nervously.

"Excuse me, Captain Johnstone," said the clerk, "there's a police sergeant on the line, calling from Virginia Beach, Virginia … says he's got a woman standing in front of him wrapped in a beach towel … says she identifies herself as Rebecca Clark, but says she's got no identification and no clothes … says she's got a long scar across the right side of her face ... says she's insisting that he call us to ask us to get in touch with Detective Belton or Father McGriff … says the woman claims it's an emergency … says he's sorry to break in like this, but the woman was brought in by a security guard that several of their officers know well, and the sergeant is convinced that she's for real, sir."

The message jolted every person in the room to her or his feet.

"Put him through!" shouted Johnstone to the clerk.

The clerk disappeared and in seconds the captain's desk phone buzzed. He put the phone on its speaker setting, and announced himself: "Captain Horace Johnstone here, D.C. Police. Sergeant, I need you to verify that the woman is Rebecca Clark."

Johnstone looked around the room for suggestions.

Marie said quickly, "Her children's names."

"Please ask her the names of her children, sergeant."

In the background, all in attendance heard Rebecca call out, "Joanna and Samuel, captain … is Mr. Belton or Father McGriff there with you?"

Belton, conscious always of his conversational quirks and limitations, nodded to McGriff to handle the call. McGriff strode quickly to the captain's desk.

"Rebecca!" he said, "we're all here in the room. Are you alright?"

"I escaped from my prison vessel, Father," she replied, "shortly before midnight, and swam for about an hour to the nearest shore, which has turned out to be Virginia Beach, Virginia. My brother is much too broad of shoulder and chest to get through the opening that I squeezed through, and he is not the distance swimmer I am, so we agreed early on that only I would make the attempt.

"But, Father McGriff," she continued, speaking rapidly in her exquisite British dialect, "please get in touch immediately with your military contacts … officials who can, in turn, get in *authoritative* touch with the U.S. Coast Guard or the U.S. Navy. That vessel must be intercepted before it reaches Soviet-friendly Cuba. Once it is there, in Havana, we will have no way to get Luke away from them. I fear for my brother's life, Father."

She caught her breath and paused, struggling with the recurring surges of emotion that had continued to sweep over her.

"And that yacht," she continued after several moments, "is filled with the same KGB agents who murdered the two Mossad agents, Father, plus Artur Volkov and Tatyana Kuznetsova, plus a boat's crew of three. The Russian hit squad that smashed our vehicle and captured the two of us turned us over to Artur Volkov and the others somewhere well south of Washington. Those KGB agents are armed to the teeth and have no intention of stopping for anything or anyone.

"They spared us torture and death only because Mr. Volkov obviously wanted to be able to torture and execute us at his leisure, surrounded by his Soviet allies in Cuba. And once he realizes that I have escaped —which could be right now —he will be enraged. I can hardly bear to think what he and his henchmen will do to my brother if they are able to reach Cuba."

"Rebecca," replied McGriff quickly, "we had already managed to identify the vessel and to make the guess that it is Havana bound, but given its fuel capacity, reported to us by its marina's owner, we know it will need to refuel several hours from now. We were just ready to phone authorities in Charleston, South Carolina, to ask them to prepare an armed intervention when the yacht pulls in to refuel."

"No!" shouted Rebecca into the phone.

"No!" she repeated.

"They will *not* refuel! They have lined the decks with carry-on fuel containers. They have more than enough fuel to reach Cuba. The marina owner you've spoken to would have no way to know anything about that, Father. They will *not* be stopping.

"Father," she continued, "I've looked at the sergeant's wall chart here, showing the east coast, and, given the way the coastline falls away to the west as it descends toward Cuba, that vessel will not pass within 200 miles of Charleston, or of any other U.S. port. It must be *intercepted* at sea. And the interception must be done by a heavily armed vessel, and the vessel must be launched very soon, or it will be too late."

Silence.

The ready-room participants looked at each other, dumbfounded at the new picture that Rebecca had given them.

After a long moment, Johnstone said into the speakerphone, "Rebecca, I'm going to take you off speaker for a couple of minutes while we huddle about this news you've given us … that the vessel won't need refueling at all.

"Don't go anywhere, Rebecca. We've got to think about the fact that they're going to remain at sea, plus the fact that your brother is not a U.S. citizen, and that he is being taken by the Soviets. We've got to think what authorities we can actually call on under these circumstances … with absolutely no Americans involved … and, of course, now, given what you've just told us, we've got to think how to get to them in mid-ocean.

"I'll be right back with you, Rebecca."

"Wait!" said Adelman suddenly.

"Wait," he repeated, striding toward the captain's desk. "Let me speak to her."

The captain again switched on the speaker feature of his phone.

"Rebecca … Jaakov here.

"I'm going to wake up the senior member of the CIA liaison unit we have been working with … the same people all of us, including you, Rebecca, met with at their facility at Langley … and I'm going to use the alarm phrase we've never had to use until now: 'Rebekka Yahalomin: Emergency One.'

"That will tell him," Adelman continued, "before I even begin to explain, that he'll need to get the other two team members up and moving, and that they will need to engage the appropriate military people right now. Specifically, I will tell him that we need a U.S. or Royal Navy destroyer to sortie out of Naval Station Mayport —that's the U.S. Naval Base at Jacksonville, Florida — within the next several hours, and to put to sea to intercept a Soviet KGB kidnap vessel that is holding a former Royal Navy combat *legend* —Mrs. Clark's brother —and to use whatever force is necessary to stop the vessel and get Lieutenant Luke Manguson off that boat and onto the decks of one of our destroyers."

Adelman continued with more detail, but his listeners by now had already understood that he had a clear plan in his mind, the broad outlines of which had been developed in advance, as a contingency, certainly with the Rebekka Yahalomin CIA liaison unit and, presumably, with other allied intelligence units and select components of the U.S. and U.K. military. When he finished, he paused.

"Rebecca," he said, "it's going to be okay."

Adelman waited for a response. Hearing none, he persisted. "Do you believe me, Rebecca?" he asked pointedly.

"Yes, Jaakov," she said, her voice still husky with emotion. "I'm sure I don't yet understand all those details … but, yes, I do."

Captain Johnstone interrupted. "Rebecca," he said, "we're going to sign off so that Jaakov can get busy."

Then he addressed the Virginia Beach sergeant. "Sergeant, let me formally request that you take care of Mrs. Clark tonight. Get her something to eat and drink right now. Get her some clothing right now. Get her a place to rest right now, there in the precinct quarters.

"And sergeant," Johnstone added meaningfully, "taking *excellent* care of Mrs. Clark is the most important thing you are going to do tonight.

"Do it well."

CHAPTER NINETEEN

WHILE ADELMAN INITIATED THE CHAIN OF REQUESTS INTENDED to lead to the use of U.S. or Royal Navy warships, Marie, McGriff, and Belton contacted the duty officer at Andrews Air Force Base and asked him to awaken the lieutenant colonel who had helped them identify and interrogate the base transportation clerk. In minutes, that officer, head of base logistics, was on the phone with them. They found that he needed no reminder of his promise to provide them with whatever he had at his disposal.

So it was that, at 0400 that morning, the twin-engine propeller plane christened the "carrier pigeon," in recognition of its daily flights carrying assorted mail packets back and forth among military bases, climbed into the sky with a flight crew of three and with Marie, McGriff, and Belton occupying three of its nine passenger seats. In addition to the passengers themselves and their overnight bags, the plane carried a standard duffel bag containing an array of women's clothes and toiletries for Rebecca, all of them selected by Marie during a private sweep of the base exchange store a half-hour earlier, her shopping excursion overseen by the lieutenant colonel himself and willingly paid for from his generous discretionary budget.

The slow-moving aircraft touched down at Oceana Naval Air Base in Norfolk, a city adjacent to Virginia Beach, a few minutes before 0530. The Virginia Beach police sergeant with whom they had spoken earlier was there waiting for them in one of his police cruisers, and he drove them directly back to his precinct office.

They found Rebecca sleeping in a makeshift, but quiet and comfortable, dressing area used by the women officers on the force. Softly placing the duffel with Rebecca's clothing and toiletries on the floor near her bunk, Marie and her two companions gratefully accepted the sergeant's offer of coffee and pastries from the pantry, along with use of his small lounge to read and doze until Rebecca should awaken on her own, or until they received news of Luke's fate, whichever came first.

The news came first.

Just before 7 a.m., the sergeant, minutes before he was to go off duty, received a call from Captain Johnstone in D.C. He listened briefly, then interrupted the captain, asking if Johnstone would prefer to give his account directly to Rebecca herself and to the other three visitors. Hearing the affirmative response, the sergeant raced to awaken Rebecca and to retrieve the others.

Returning in minutes with Rebecca, Marie, McGriff, and Belton in tow, the sergeant turned on the speaker feature of the desk phone and asked Johnstone to begin his report once more.

Sounding tired, but happy, the captain summarized events.

"Jaakov nailed it, folks," said Johnstone. "As it turned out, the Rebekka Yahalomin CIA liaison unit zipped through its military connections so fast that, within half-hour of Jaakov's first phone call to them, the Navy had authorized the base commandant at Naval Station Mayport in Florida to intercept Volkov at sea, using whatever force the commandant chose to use.

"It seems," continued Johnstone, "that the ingredients in the situation were perfect from the military standpoint: unlawful Soviet activity, including a double murder, plus two different kidnappings, all on U.S. soil; a civilian vessel being used as a prison ship to take a Royal Navy veteran and combat hero to a Soviet satellite nation for interrogation and likely torture and probable murder; and a long track record of working with the kidnapped Royal Navy veteran, his sister, and their colleagues.

"Now," he said, "*get this* … the Mayport commandant had several exercises going on already, including a combined U.S., Royal Canadian, and Royal Navy anti-submarine night-warfare training exercise located … if you can believe this … in an area about 150 miles east of Wilmington, North Carolina. And that placed those ships firmly astride the straight-line navigation route from Virginia Beach to Cuba."

"What?!" came the Virginia Beach chorus. "*What?!*"

"I know, I know," responded Johnstone. "Incredible … but there you are."

After a moment to let his listeners take in the astounding fact of the warships' perfect positioning to intercept Volkov, the captain continued with his account.

"The Mayport commandant," said Johnstone, "personally radioed the destroyer squadron commander leading that night-training exercise, and authorized him to grant permission to the one Royal Navy destroyer in the exercise to separate from the U.S. and Canadian ships and to cruise north, slowly, until daylight, along the projected Virginia Beach-Cuba route. The squadron commander duly gave that permission, and then recommended to the Royal Navy destroyer captain, as he began to move his ship away from the rest of the squadron, that he launch his ship's helicopter at first light on a search pattern most likely to pick up Volkov's yacht.

"He did exactly that. The Mayport commandant told me that the helo sighted Volkov's vessel almost as soon as it had gained several hundred feet of altitude. The pilot swooped down close enough to verify the vessel's identity, and then vectored the Royal Navy destroyer on a direct-intercept course."

Murmurs of excited anticipation came to Johnstone's ears over the speakerphone, then an anxious silence while his listeners awaited the climax. They knew the intercept would not be routine.

"Sounds as if," said Johnstone, "judging from the Mayport commandant's report, Volkov didn't give up easily. The destroyer crossed the yacht's bow and fired one round of 5-inch artillery a few feet over Volkov's head, plus a few bursts of .50-caliber machine gun fire into the water a few feet off the vessel's bow.

"The yacht finally cut power and drifted to a stop —wisely, I'd say —but it still took the Royal Marine boarding contingent approaching in their motorized raft with guns up, covered by an array of .50-caliber machine guns from the decks of the destroyer, before the 'dirtbags,' as Mr. Belton would say, laid down their arms and brought Lieutenant Manguson out on deck.

"He looked a little worn out," added Johnstone, "according to the reports relayed by the commandant, but not injured … not wounded … and he was quickly taken onto the boarding team's power raft, then over to the destroyer, and finally up and onto its decks. Breakfast and a good bunk … and Luke's ready to go."

There was a small, indistinct noise, a soft moaning sound, audible even over the speakerphone in D.C., made by Rebecca as she dropped to the hardwood floor in her Virginia Beach PD sweatshirt and sweatpants, kneeling in a silent prayer of gratitude. Marie leaned close to the sergeant's phone and said softly to Johnstone, "Sir, if you'd wait just a moment for Rebecca to complete her prayer. …"

Johnstone had already paused, assuming correctly the cause of the small sound.

After several moments, Rebecca opened her eyes and stood.

"Thank you, Marie," she said. "Thank you, captain," she added.

"Certainly, Mrs. Clark," answered Johnstone, and, after taking a moment to reconnect mentally to his own story line, he continued. "The Mayport commandant said that, after receiving the report of the successful recovery of Lieutenant Manguson, he gave direct permission for the Royal Navy captain to continue to operate independently of the destroyer squadron, and recommended that the captain head north at best speed and to close on Virginia Beach. Once they're near enough, they'll fly Luke to Naval Air Base Oceana in the destroyer's chopper.

"That's the same airfield where you three landed a couple of hours ago. The 'carrier pigeon' and its crew will wait for you three, plus Rebecca and Luke," Johnstone concluded, "and then fly the five of you back up to Andrews this afternoon."

Small cheers came over the line, and then Belton's rumbling voice. "Is Jaakov there with ya?" he asked.

"Yes," replied Johnstone, "and he's coming to the phone."

"Jaakov," said Belton, "this is th' best thing you've ever done … bar none … th' absolute best thing you've done in yer whole, rotten life. I gotta say, Jaakov … ya made me proud t' know ya last night.

"Know what I mean? Hmm?"

As Adelman neared Johnstone's desk, he responded to his long-time detective partner by saying, "I want to know which one of you prayed that those destroyers would already be at sea, engaged in night-warfare exercises, and precisely in the path of Volkov and his crew. Which one of you prayed *that* prayer?

"Come on, I know one of you did that."

Joyous laughter came through the speakerphone, and then Adelman and Johnstone, standing together at their phone, heard Marie's soft voice in response, saying, "Well, Jaakov, I certainly prayed a prayer that was something like that one, but I'm guessing none of us were prescient enough even to *think* of such a specific prayer. We were surely all praying …" here she looked quickly at McGriff, Belton, and Rebecca, who were all nodding happily, "but our prayers were just focused on Luke's being rescued somehow, and rescued without being hurt.

"Right?" she asked, looking again at her companions.

McGriff and Belton nodded again, but Rebecca shook her head.

"Well, Marie," said Rebecca, "I must admit that my prayers, after Jaakov explained his plan, and before I finally fell asleep, were focused on Jaakov himself and on all the others in his plan … focused on *Jaakov* … that he would be able to launch that incredibly audacious plan, and that all the other people that would need to hear, understand, and then execute the plan … including the U.S.

and Royal Navy officers in Florida and at sea in the Atlantic … and the Royal Marines who formed the boarding team … my prayers were for *all* of them … that they would be led to do their parts, and to do their parts bravely and well.

"I was praying for *you,* Jaakov, and for all the others you would call on."

Before Horace Johnstone signed off on the call with the Virginia Beach contingent, he fielded one more question, this one from McGriff.

"Captain," said McGriff, "what's happening with Artur Volkov and his people, and with the *Potomac Queen?* Did the commandant say anything about that? I'm just wondering if the Royal Navy took Volkov and his people on board as prisoners? Wondering if they maybe decided to take the yacht under tow, possibly all the way back to Mayport or Norfolk? Or something else?"

Johnstone thought for a moment, recalling his conversation with the Mayport base commandant. "I think most of that is unclear right now," replied Johnstone. "Volkov's status as an official with the Soviet Embassy makes him immune from almost anything a U.S. district attorney could charge him with, and the fact that the KGB agents killed two Israeli agents … not U.S. citizens … means that prosecuting them for that crime is a complicated issue, too.

"The commandant told me," continued Johnstone, "that he wanted only to retrieve Luke Manguson and to return him to U.S. soil. His instructions to the destroyer squadron commander and to the individual ship captains were to leave Volkov and his yacht alone, once Luke had been retrieved safely.

"I know that sounds wrong," concluded Johnstone, "but the pertinent international laws … and the protected status of embassy people around the world … form a mixture that yields a strange amalgam of regulations."

"Captain," interjected Adelman, standing next to Johnstone, "my experience suggests that the most likely outcome is that Volkov will simply turn that yacht around and take it back to the marina, right here in Washington, and that he and Ms. Kuznetsova will be recalled to Moscow. When they get there, I'd guess they'll be treated as heroes, possibly, or as *persona non grata,* just as possibly, and the decision on that will be 100 percent political … most likely a decision made at very high Soviet levels.

"Either way, I don't imagine those two people —Volkov and Ms. Kuznetsova —will ever again set foot in the U.S. Or in England, for that matter. Or in Israel, either.

"They're going to be unwelcome in those three countries, as a result of what has happened in the last few days … but that doesn't mean that anything punitive is going to be done to either of them by their own people. Maybe … maybe not."

"And the KGB agents who murdered the Mossad agents, Jaakov?" asked McGriff from Virginia Beach.

"Same thing," answered Adelman.

"Maybe something, back in Moscow. Probably nothing."

"So, they will get away with murder?" asked Marie.

"I imagine so, Marie," said Adelman, "unless Mossad decides to hunt them down as individuals, something that will be tricky, since no one really knows which KGB agents pulled the trigger that day.

"In any case, those of us who have worked for the intelligence agencies of the world," Adelman added, "know that life and death for all of us agents come pretty cheap. In a way, we're not citizens of any place at all, and we're not protected by anyone."

A long silence was finally broken by the D.C. captain.

"Well, everybody," said Johnstone, "I'd like to say that we had the best set of outcomes realistically possible for our own array of threats. Kazim Deng got rescued. Ivan Ivanovich and his family are on their way to their new life somewhere in the U.S., or soon will be. Artur Volkov's Jefferson Bible project got completely wiped out by a combination of Mrs. Clark's visions and Deng's and Ivanovich's heroics.

"And I got reports today from my FBI contacts that the Russian Mafia's illegal accumulation of hundreds of millions of dollars was exposed, just as planned, their leaders jailed, just as planned, and their access to all that money eliminated."

"And, thanks to Jaakov," added Marie, "we're going to have Luke back with us in a few hours."

"But I gotta say," Belton interjected, "that none of us woulda had any idea what had happened t' Luke if it hadn't a' been fer Rebecca's own toughness, ya know. She busted herself outta that scumbag's prison boat an' swam across th' whole Atlantic Ocean t' save herself an' then t' start th' ball rollin' t' save her brother. Volkov's yacht was never gonna come anywhere close t' Charleston, and without Rebecca's report we never woulda found Luke in time. He'd be in a Havana prison cell right now."

Johnstone and Adelman then heard the Englishwoman's voice quietly addressing her old friend, as the two of them stood near each other, close to the sergeant's speakerphone.

"I didn't actually swim the *whole* Atlantic Ocean, my dearest Mr. Sidney Belton," Rebecca said sweetly, "just enough of it to find a nice little strip of sand, a kindly security officer, and a considerate police sergeant."

And then they heard Marie's voice, addressing Rebecca.

"But we know, Rebecca, that you prayed those destroyers into position to rescue your brother. We *know* you did that."

Rebecca's delighted laughter was the last sound Johnstone heard before he wearily signed off and drove himself home and to bed.

The twin-prop "carrier pigeon" arrived at Andrews Air Force Base shortly before 5 p.m., and unloaded its five passengers onto the tarmac. Belton, Marie, McGriff, Rebecca and Luke descended the plane's down-folding three-step ladder to find Adelman and Kazim Deng standing together, waiting for them. Behind them was Deng's taxi, which had ferried Adelman from the D.C. police precinct to Andrews.

Despite the brevity of their separation from each other, the reunion was joyous, focused equally on Adelman for his wizardry in orchestrating Luke's rescue from the Atlantic, and on Deng, once more, for his brazen copying of the hard drive and the resulting destruction of the Ataka plot. After the hugs of happiness, the newcomers were informed that two air transports had been arranged for them.

First, an RAF flight to England was slated to depart Andrews in roughly one hour, with places reserved on board for Rebecca and Luke. Second, the Israeli Embassy had made its Learjet available to fly Belton, Adelman, Marie, and McGriff to Teterboro Airport in New Jersey, a 45-minute taxi ride away from the detectives' office in Lower Manhattan. After discussion, the foursome agreed they would prefer to spend the night in Washington, both to recover their strength and to collect their belongings from the CIA safe house. Accordingly, the Israeli pilots, waiting nearby, were asked to set up a 7 a.m. departure for the following day.

That settled, good-byes were again made to Rebecca and Luke, just as they had been once before in what seemed a very long time ago, but which was, in fact, fewer than 48 hours previous. As the four Manhattan-bound travelers headed for Deng's taxi, Rebecca called out after them, "Mr. Belton, can you give Kazim and me 10 minutes to talk before you leave? We have just a touch of unfinished business."

Belton, speaking for the group, replied, "Ya can have all th' time ya need, ma'am. We got no place t' get to in a hurry."

He glanced around at his colleagues. "Right, people?"

"Right," came the answering chorus.

Rebecca, wearing dark slacks, a light-colored, sleeveless blouse, and white tennis shoes —all selected from the duffel prepared for her by Marie, with help from the lieutenant colonel —gestured for Deng to walk beside her. She and he moved slowly away from the group across the expanse of tarmac, as she called over her shoulder to her brother, "Luke, I'll just be a few minutes. Go ahead to the transport, if you like, and take my things with you, please. We won't be long."

Then, matching each other's measured strides, their discussion began.

"You mentioned," said Rebecca, "when we were last together, that the two of us should speak sometime about visions. You said, I believe, that you have had some experiences you'd like to share with me. Do I have that right, Kazim?"

Deng, a compact, muscular 5 feet, 9 inches, looked up at Rebecca, easily 3 inches taller. He smiled and nodded. "I don't know if what has happened to me from time to time falls in the category of visions, Rebecca," he said, "but … well … they are certainly *something* out of the ordinary. Starting about the time I turned 20 years old, I began having … well … *visitations* … in the form of strong, clear images, usually overnight, during sleep. These were not mere dreams. These were … I think … messages … messages which always included a command of some kind."

They continued to walk, alone on the vast emptiness of the military taxiways. After several seconds of silence, Rebecca asked for more. "Can you give me an example, Kazim?" she said. "Give me an example," she continued, "of one of those commands, and tell me what sort of images made up the architecture of the visitation."

Deng replied immediately. "Two weeks ago," he said, "before any of the contacts I have had with you and the others, I had an overnight visitation that was focused on … well … *you,* Rebecca."

She stopped and looked at him closely. "On *me?*"

He nodded. "Yes," he said, "and this was before I had so much as *heard* of you, to say nothing of actually meeting you and talking to you."

She thought for a moment. "So, you did not know that it was I?"

"No," he replied, "but when I finally saw you in that meeting the other night at the CIA safe house, I had no doubt. That was you, in my dream-visitation."

They turned and began to walk again.

"And what command was contained in that dream, Kazim?"

"Eight words: *Help this woman. Defeat her enemies. Have courage.*"

"Hmm ... eight words," she replied, turning the phrases over in her mind, "forming three commands."

"Yes," he said, "and when, in the Soviet computer room, 'Rebecca Clark' was the focus —the *entire* focus —of Mr. Ivanovich's first interview with me, just hours after I had been taken to the embassy, it was easy to add two and two and get four: you and your enemies were the focus of that dream-visitation.

"And *your* enemies were *my* enemies."

She walked silently for several steps, then asked another question. "And how," she asked, "did the eight words come to you?

"Did I —my image in your dream —speak the words? Or something else?"

"Something else," he said. "The words just came to me," explained Deng, "as though planted in my brain. No obvious mechanism for the transmission.

"The words just came to me."

They turned around, without signal to each other, and began to walk back toward the others, both seeming to understand intuitively that the critical portion of Deng's message had just been delivered.

As they walked back, Rebecca nodded slowly to herself.

"Isn't it amazing, Kazim," she said, "how separately delivered divine messages can be interdependent, so that more than one person receives critical portions ... later found to have interplay ... later found to give a more complete picture than the separate, individual portions had given?"

They walked a few more steps before she spoke again. "This is not the first such instance, in my life, of this kind of thing happening," she added, thinking back to her first experiences with the messages, when her own dreams were connected to concurrent visions given to Martha Clark, the mother of Matt, the young man destined eventually to become Rebecca's husband.

Deng smiled. “Yes, Rebecca,” he said, “I think I suspected that, and that’s why I wanted you to hear a little of my own story before we go our separate ways.”

She stopped and gave him one of her inimitable bear hugs.

They stepped back from each other, but Deng hesitated.

“Yes?” she asked.

“Rebecca,” said Deng, after a moment, “just one more thing. Does this mean that you and I are … *mystics?*”

Rebecca laughed. “Oh, my goodness, no, Kazim,” she said. “Surely nothing so grand as that,” she added, “but then I have an impression, probably simplistic, that a mystic regularly communes with … well … I’m not sure how to complete that sentence. I started to say ‘communes with God,’ but I’m not sure that would always be the case.

“Regardless of how we should define a mystic, Kazim, I’m quite sure that I am merely a Christian wife and mother … a believer … one who grounds herself in a regular prayer life and who tries to be the best possible … *giver* … to the world.

“As we say, the ‘blueprint of the universe’.”

He smiled. “My life for yours.”

“Exactly,” she said. Then, after a pause, she asked, “But how did you know that phrase?”

“When your brother drove Mr. Ivanovich and me from the embassy to the CIA safe house, I asked him and Father McGriff many questions, Rebecca.

“They gave many answers.”

Rebecca reached down and hugged him yet again, then stood back. “Perhaps we shall meet again, Kazim,” she said.

“I hope so, Rebecca,” said Deng. “It would be my privilege”

Deng strode away quickly to rejoin the others.

Together, Deng and his four passengers waited to board the taxi until they saw Rebecca and Luke, now 200 yards away, starting up the ladder to the RAF transport. They waved their good-byes as the English pair stood and returned the farewell gesture, then disappeared into the cavernous aircraft.

A little more than 12 hours later, shortly before 7 a.m., and at nearly the same spot on the Andrews tarmac, Belton, Adelman, Marie, and McGriff were back, luggage in hand, preparing to board the Israeli Embassy's Learjet for the short flight to New Jersey. The aircraft's engines were warmed and its pilots already in communication with the air traffic controllers at Teterboro Airport.

Once airborne, the dominating, yet somehow soothing, sound of the powerful jet engines created a sense of privacy that Marie and McGriff welcomed. In the oddly secluded atmosphere, they began to talk earnestly about the future.

McGriff began. "Marie," he said, speaking just above a whisper, his mouth close to her ear, "I don't want to go back to our previous living arrangements. When we get back to Washington, I want us to stay in our CIA safe house rooms just long enough to find a pet-friendly apartment for the two of us … the three of us, counting Penelope, of course … and to make arrangements for the sale of our current homes … and then to move in together."

She turned her head to look at him, obviously puzzled. "So … you're asking me to marry you, Jack McGriff?"

McGriff, startled, found himself blushing, still a novelty in his experience. "Oh … did I leave out that part?" he said in honest embarrassment.

He looked down and shook his head in sad disappointment.

Marie, laughing, reached over and took his hand in hers.

"Well?" she said.

Taking her hands in both of his, he looked into her wide brown eyes. "Marie, I love you," he said. "Please marry me, Marie."

She laughed again. "Okay," she answered.

"Okay?" he repeated, incredulous.

"Okay," she said again.

He looked momentary dazed, then recovered sufficiently to ask, "That really wasn't appropriately romantic, was it? I mean, a person asking someone to marry him should create the most romantic possible setting, right? Like, you know, candlelight, symphonic music, just the right atmosphere."

"Oh, stop it," she said, still amused. "Jack, for a person who had no idea, just a few days ago, how to ask a girl on a date, I think you've traveled a long way."

Her face became serious. "Really, you know, the two important things are these. First, I *feel* loved whenever I'm around you, Jack McGriff. Always. Every time. Every minute.

"And second," she continued, "when I talked to Rebecca about this very thing, she endorsed the idea with no reservations at all. In fact, she was quite enthusiastic."

His eyes widened. "You talked to Rebecca about my asking you to marry me, Marie?"

"Of course."

"Well … what did she say?"

"Rebecca said a number of things, Jack," she answered, "and I liked them all. For example, she focused immediately on the fact that you are a believer, that you obviously like being in my company, and … let's see … her phrase was, I think … you are 'a courageous and versatile professional' and thus, an 'admirable man.'

"She also said, interestingly … and with emphasis … that you are an *adult.*"

McGriff sat back, stunned.

It had never occurred to him that the legendary Rebecca Clark had given him more than a passing thought. And yet, she had apparently thought about him seriously enough to speak profoundly evaluative words about him, and in the context of marriage to a woman whom Rebecca clearly liked and cared about. He had seen from the two women's first encounter, in the sixth-floor conference room in New York City, that the two of them were immediately close … close enough to be fast friends … friends who would share confidences.

The silence became lengthy, so much so that Marie decided to interrupt his train of thought, in part so that he would begin to realize that "thinking out loud" was an appropriate way to "be with" one's spouse.

"Jack," she said finally, "say what you're thinking. That's a better thing than leaving your … person … to guess."

"Oh … sorry, Marie," he said.

"I was, well, unprepared … and unequipped … for any of this," he continued. "I started talking about our living arrangements without asking the obvious first question. Then I was stunned to find that you and Rebecca had spoken about you and me in this way … since I had no idea that Rebecca had ever formed an opinion about me. Why should she? And yet, I find that she has strong views about me and, unless you are saving the worst for last, her views are favorable.

"Just a little out of my depth, Marie," he concluded.

She laughed joyously.

"Jack," she said, "I do *not* expect you to be 'in your depth' in this kind of conversation. You are accustomed to helping other people think through all kinds of issues and problems and opportunities in their lives, and you've spent half a career not giving much thought to your own.

"And that's why you need *me!*" she said facetiously, again laughing happily.

McGriff found himself beginning to relax, seeing that he did not seem to be in any great jeopardy, either with Marie or with Rebecca.

"Okay," he said finally, "what else did Rebecca say … about me … about us?"

"Let's see," said Marie, "she asked whether you and I had talked —first, about your employment by the CIA, and, second, about children."

"And?" he said.

"And I told her that, with the first question, you and I are equally uncomfortable with aspects of intelligence agency work, and that you would probably move in the direction of something else … something like setting up a branch of Sidney and Jaakov's detective agency in the Washington area. And I told her that, with the second question, we would accept whatever was brought to us in prayer.

"More specifically," she continued, "I told Rebecca that, if children were to come, that happy outcome would be the result of my marriage to a man who is a *believer*, a man who loves being with me, a man who is a 'courageous and versatile' professional and thus 'admirable' … a man who is, as she also said, an *adult*.

"In other words, Jack … *you.*"

He leaned over and kissed her softly on the lips. Then he sat back and, after a long moment, said, "There's still one thing I don't get at all."

"What?"

"How did you know I was going to do this?" he asked, bewildered. "How did you know I was going to start talking about living together, and, thanks to your response to that, talking about marriage … and children … and vocation?"

"Oh, *please,*" she said, "you asked me to marry you because I *wanted* you to ask me to marry you."

Silence.

"You mean," he said after several moments, still incredulous, "you … ah … *engineered* this clumsy marriage proposal of mine, Marie?"

She patted his knee and smiled. "Jack McGriff," she said, rolling her eyes playfully, "don't you know *anything?*"

The End

WALKER BUCKALEW completed his undergraduate studies at Duke University, where he was a midshipman in the university's NROTC program. Upon graduation, he was commissioned an officer in the U.S. Navy, and completed his active-duty commitment on board the USS Constellation, a Seventh Fleet attack aircraft carrier, with home port in San Diego and secondary ports in Pearl Harbor and Yokosuka, Japan.

Following his military service, Buckalew embarked upon a career in education. With graduate degrees from the University of Wyoming, he taught at St. Lawrence University (NY), the University of North Carolina Asheville, and Cumberland University (TN), where he became president and chief academic officer.

He is currently the senior writer for Independent School Management, a consulting firm serving private schools throughout the U.S., Canada, and abroad. He and his wife, Dr. Linda Mason Hall, live in Greer, SC.

Previous novels in Dr. Buckalew's Rebecca Series include:

- *The Face of the Enemy*
- *By Many or By Few*
- *Such Thy Mercies*
- *Choose You This Day*

www.ingramcontent.com/pod-product-compliance
Lightning Source LLC
Chambersburg PA
CBHW030425310726
48979CB00009B/1615/J
* 9 7 8 1 9 5 5 6 2 2 8 4 4 *